In a Time Never Known

Also by Kat Michels

Children's Books
Children Have Got to Be Carefully Taught
10 Cheeky Monkeys
Monsters in the Night

In a Time Never Known

A Novel

Kat Michels

In Heels Publishing

In a Time Never Known. Copyright © 2017 by Kat Michels. All rights reserved.

Cover design and photography by A. Sutton
Additional illustration by: Art and Picture Collection, The New York Public Library. "Lieutenant Bayard Wilkeson holding his battery (G, 4th United States artillery) to its work in an exposed position." New York Public Library Digital Collections. Accessed May 20, 2017.
http://digitalcollections.nypl/org/items/510d47e0-fa24-a3d9-e040-e00a18064a99

Manufactured in the United States of America

Library of Congress Control Number: 20177907357

ISBN 978-0-9989-2641-4
ISBN 978-0-9989-2643-8 (paperback)
ISBN 978-0-9989-2642-1 (ebook)

To Jolene, whose words of wisdom got me to start.

&

To Stacey, whose words of encouragement got me to finish.

Codebook

OPERATIVES	
NR : Northern Rose	Anna Bell
LR : Little Rose	Kady Bell
SK : Shop Keeper	Benjamin Grant
BD : Baker's Daughter	Elizabeth Van Lew
DR : Doctor	Donald Roberts
YD : Yankee Doodle	Jacob Hart
KA : King Arthur	Northern spy ring operative
ASSOCIATES/PEOPLE	
Mama Bird	Rebecca
Gardener	Thomas Henry
Watchdog	Soldier in Richmond working as double agent
Conductor	Guide on the Underground Railroad (UR)
Cargo	A slave travelling on the UR
Stockholder	A person who provides money or supplies for the UR
PLACES	
Thorns	Dismal Swamp
Bud 1 – 6	Entrances into the Dismal Swamp
Rose Garden	Kady's Richmond Residence
Smokehouse	Bell Plantation
Nest	Supply Yard in Richmond
THINGS	
Flowers	Shipment of goods
Exotic Flowers	Shipment of extreme value
Jesuit	Shipment of quinine
Harvest	Raid to confiscate supplies

As in every other period of crisis, the rules of sexual decorum were suspended due to emergency.
Gail Collins

March 1863
Virginia, Confederate States of America

1
A Slave's Revolt

Anna strode into the kitchen and approached the man at the door. She pointed to the packages sitting at his feet. "You may store those in the back pantry." One of the kitchen slaves made a move to escort the man. "No, no. I will show him. We wouldn't want the master's dinner to be late."

The slave looked at Anna appreciatively and with evident relief. The last late dinner resulted in every slave in the kitchen receiving five lashes, which for the master was hardly punishment at all. The only thing that spared them from more was the master's vanity, as there were guests expected for supper that evening and even the master could appreciate that a severe beating would result in an inferior meal.

"Right this way." Anna gestured for the man to follow her as she led the way out of the kitchen and down the hall to the walk-in pantry. She felt his presence behind her and imagined the rough texture of the blond stubble on his cheek scraping her hand as she touched his face. Her pulse quickened with every step she took. What was Benjamin doing here? The number of men visiting the plantation had certainly increased since the outbreak of war, but not as visitors to the kitchen. His presence would cause talk. Not to mention, she had just seen him two weeks earlier, and for everyone's safety, two spies were not to be seen alone together more than once a month. That was not a hardship with the other members of her spy ring. Her relationships with them were strictly business, but Benjamin had always been more than business. Anna counted down the days until his next arrival. Benjamin had awakened a part of her that had been shut down since the first days of her marriage, a part of her that she had repressed in order to survive.

Anna's betrothal to Andrew Bell, almost twenty years ago, had been arranged by her father. Their union appeared in newspapers up and down the coast; or more precisely, the merger between the great Bell Tobacco Company in Virginia and the mighty Waldoff Shipping in New York littered the pages. Their nuptials were merely a footnote. Their vast age difference—she was barely sixteen and her bridegroom almost forty—had been left out completely. Anna was the bow that tied the whole deal together, and that was all anyone cared about. Anna's mother had died during childbirth, so without her to intervene, Anna had no choice.

She cried the entire journey south and planned to continue through the ceremony, but her father threatened her with a beating if she embarrassed him in front of his colleagues. So Anna pulled herself together and played her part: the demure daughter through the ceremony and the obedient wife through the festivities that followed. Only after the guests had left and they were alone, did she allow her façade to crack. She knew what inevitably had to come, what has to come at the end of every wedding day before you are truly man and wife, and she was horrified. Anna knew nothing of this man. The thought of being at his mercy made her want to run away and never look back.

Without a word, her new husband grasped her firmly by the arm and led her to her bedroom, then presented her with her wedding gift: Mary, Anna's new personal slave. It sickened Anna that her husband thought a person was an appropriate gift, and it sickened her even more that she was powerless to do anything but accept. So accept she did, and thanked him for his generosity. He acknowledged her thanks with a grunt and left the room.

She did not know what to do. Mary suggested that she prepare herself for bed, so Anna allowed her new slave to help her into her nightgown, then sat on the edge of the bed, and waited. She knew only in vague generalities what was going to happen, but she knew to expect pain because her nurse-maid had cautioned her not to cry out lest she take away from her husband's enjoyment. That was where her knowledge ended. She had to sit and wait in ignorance. She waited for what seemed an eternity, her nerves fraying with every chime of the clock.

He never came.

Finally, on the verge of collapse, she called out quietly for Mary. It fell to Mary to inform her that her new husband had left for the night. Anna expected to feel relief at this news, but her reaction was utterly different. Here she was, a wife on her wedding night, and her husband did not want to come to her. The fleeting hope that a happy marriage might be possible vanished. She would have to endure the embarrassment and rejection of being snubbed. He did not want her, not even in the carnal sense. This truly was a business merger for him and she was the unfortunate aftereffect.

The tears flowed hard and hot down her cheeks. She cried in

anger that her father cared so little for her that he was willing to throw her aside for a better price on tobacco. She cried in humiliation that everyone would know her as nothing more than a living representation of a profitable merger. And she cried for herself, for the rejection and hurt that cut so deeply she could hardly breathe. He did not want her. No one wanted her. She would never feel a gentle hand on her cheek or see adoration shining through moist eyes when all words had been lost. She would never feel love because she was nothing more than a means to an end, a possession.

Mary enveloped her in her arms and rocked her until she fell asleep. In the morning when she awoke, Mary was still there and held her again when the tears resumed. That evening, Andrew finally came. He was drunk and smelled as if he hadn't stopped drinking since the day before. He climbed on top of her without even bothering to dismiss Mary or take off his boots. He fumbled for a moment trying to raise the hem of her nightgown, before frustration won out and he grabbed the neckline, tearing the gown open right down the middle. This sudden violence caught Anna off guard and before she realized what she was doing, she struck out at him, trying to defend herself. Her first blow landed square across his face replacing his bleary-eyed, drunken look with an unsettling smile.

Grabbing her wrists, he pinned them above her head while using his knee to forcibly separate her legs. Anna was still struggling when he thrust inside of her with all his might. His moan of obvious pleasure was drowned out by Anna's screams of pain. She felt as though her insides were ripping apart with every violent exertion he made. She tried to focus on something, anything else. The numbness spreading through her hands from her wrists being held so tightly, the incongruity of his cold metal belt buckle pressed into her thigh, the averted face of Mary, helpless to do anything but wait. Anna eventually went numb, either from the repeated concussions or simply her brain recognizing the need to be somewhere else. Once finished, he collapsed on her briefly, then stood, using her ruined gown to wipe the blood and seed from his now flaccid cock. Sloppily, he pulled his pants back up and left the room, calling for, and receiving, more whiskey. Evidently his comrades were waiting outside the door. Mary enfolded Anna in her arms once more, but Anna was dry eyed. There were no tears left.

Anna learned to accept the solitude of life on the plantation. She actually preferred the solitude to the company of her husband or his friends. The South was a whole different world from New York, a world she did not understand and had no inclination to try to understand. Eventually, she became pregnant and, much to her dismay, gave birth to a girl. The last thing Anna wanted was to bring a girl into this world of coquettish Southern belles, to flirt and flounce and stand prettily on a pedestal. What she despised even more was the way her husband doted on their daughter. Kady could do no wrong and wanted for nothing, no matter how ridiculous the demand. The only benefit for Anna was that her husband now left her almost entirely alone. He had their daughter to dote upon and plenty of slaves to take care of his baser needs. Anna was called upon for social occasions and that was the sum total of their acquaintance. Without Mary, Anna would not have had anyone to talk to or truly confide in, but even that relationship was tainted. No matter how close they became, the fact that Anna owned Mary would always come between them. This was Anna's life for fifteen years. Then she met Benjamin Grant.

As one Southern state after another seceded from the nation and a civil war was imminent, her husband was named a general for the Confederate Army – not that he was ever expected to don a uniform and fight. A man who owned as many slaves as he did was exempt. He hadn't even been assigned a regiment or any men. He was wealthy, had many connections, and the Confederate leadership was not composed of stupid men. A trumped-up title and the pretense of listening to Andrew's suggestions earned them much needed funding. Overnight, Anna became a general's wife, which meant there were many dinners to plan and attend. As such, the whole house needed redecorating, which meant frequent journeys to Richmond.

It was on one of her trips, this time to pick out new draperies, that she met Benjamin, the shopkeeper. He was charismatic, gentle, and sensed immediately the disquiet that Anna tried so desperately to hide. It wasn't long before Anna insisted she travel to Richmond more and more often on the pretense of needing to personally oversee all aspects of the renovations. Andrew paid little notice; as the months passed, Benjamin paid more and more. He helped protract her task of choosing first the materials then the hardware for her new draperies. Never in the history of remodeling had it taken so long to get the draperies right. Then they moved on to reupholstering the furniture.

When at long last Benjamin quietly locked the door to the shop and pulled Anna into the back, her face flushed and her heart raced, whether from fear or excitement she did not know. Before she could decide, Benjamin kissed her. It was like no feeling she had ever had, like no feeling she knew was even possible. A warmth spread throughout her body that she felt down to her toes. He kissed her again and again, until the warmth centralized itself into her lower abdomen and she veritably ached for him. His hands held her firmly, one on her lower back, and the other stroking rhythmically on the side of her bodice, nearly driving her to distraction. She wanted so badly to be free of her many layers, to feel his flesh on hers, to ease her aching as only this man could, right here and right now.

Then he stopped. As he pulled away from her, she saw that he was breathing as heavily as she. He looked down, slightly shaking his head, then looked up to her with the kindest, most loving eyes and gently placed his hand against her cheek. She felt so small next to him, his hand could have easily engulfed her entire face. He ever so carefully stroked her cheek with his thumb until she had to close her eyes to keep the tears at bay.

This was everything she had ever wanted, everything she had convinced herself only existed in her imagination, yet here he was, living and breathing right in front of her. He wanted her. He wanted her so badly he was willing to risk everything to have her. She would match his risk, for she wanted him as well and was willing to give everything she had if it meant being with him.

Benjamin suggested that he bring samples to the plantation, but Anna knew her husband would eventually hear of such an arrangement and not approve. Unless, of course, it was his idea to begin with. So Anna made a point of lamenting the terribly long journey to Richmond one evening at supper. Andrew was far from interested until Anna confessed her fear that the slaves were getting lazy in her absence. This got his attention, and before the dessert was served, he had left the table to prepare a letter demanding that this merchant accommodate his wife at the plantation. Upon receiving the message, Benjamin scheduled his first visit to coincide with one of Andrew's frequent absences. Even so, Benjamin and Anna took every precaution to be discreet, though Anna knew the slaves would never dare tell their master for fear he would literally shoot the messenger.

The first time they made love, Anna cried. Benjamin moved slowly and tenderly. He kissed her deeply and whispered that he loved her over and over until shudders ran up and down her body and tears overflowed her eyes in an unimaginable bliss. That day, Anna learned that sex could be pleasurable instead of painful. Afterward, he held her for as long as he dared before dressing and taking his leave. Anna stayed in bed for the rest of the day, claiming fatigue from the decorating. In truth, she was loath to leave the bed and his scent. She closed her eyes and relived every moment, afraid if she continued with her life as normal, the beauty would fade, and it would be as if it had never happened.

To keep up appearances, Anna still journeyed into the city on occasion. On one of these occasions, Anna happened upon Benjamin secreted away in the back of his shop with another woman. Anna had assumed that she was the only woman he brought to the back of his shop for privacy. Flames of jealousy engulfed her. Benjamin at least had the decency to look chagrined when he saw her standing there.

"Anna," he exclaimed. She turned to leave. "Anna, wait. It's not what you think."

She whirled back to face him. "Not what I think? How could it be anything else? The look of guilt on both of your faces tells me exactly what it is you were doing sequestered back here in your shop!"

"Anna, it's not that. I swear! I work for her."

"You work for her? Doing what? Seducing the wives of wealthy men – to what? Get them to spend more money? Buy more draperies?"

"No, she has nothing to do with the shop."

"Benjamin is part of my spy ring." The other woman had finally spoken. Anna was speechless for a moment, then let out a laugh verging on hysteria.

"Spy ring? So you expect me to believe that you are a spy? That you are in a spy meeting in the back room of your shop, and you blurt it out to the first person who walks in on you? How stupid and gullible and naïve do you think I am? You can have your little trollop, Benjamin, and all of the other trollops that I am sure you have waiting patiently for their turn. Let them believe your lies."

Fighting back tears, Anna stormed toward the front door, but Benjamin forcibly grabbed her and dragged her back into the rear of the shop. Anna fought against him furiously. One abusive man in her life was enough, she would not quietly allow another man to batter her. Despite her blows, Benjamin did nothing but try to restrain and calm her. It wasn't until she realized that his soft Southern twang had disappeared that she quieted and looked at him warily. Once he was sure she wouldn't bolt for the door again, he released her and stepped back.

"What happened to your voice?" Anna asked.

Benjamin visibly relaxed and let his New England accent come out stronger than normal to emphasize his point. "This is not my shop and I am not from the South. I am a lieutenant with the Second Maine

9

Infantry. When my uncle fell ill, he wrote to his sister, my mother, to ask for help running his shop. As I was already involved somewhat with intelligence work, I went to my superiors to tell them of the opportunity to place a spy in Richmond. Before my mother even had time to write a letter back to my uncle, I was on a train heading south. When I arrived, I discovered that everyone assumed I was from the South, so I let them believe their assumption and adopted my Southern drawl. It was easy after listening to my mother's for my entire life."

Benjamin finished his speech by switching back to his Southern accent, then sheepishly grinned at Anna, hoping his cleverness was enough to soften her demeanor. It wasn't. Anna crossed her arms and kept her distance. Before he could continue, the woman stepped in.

"That is when I approached him."

Anna took a moment to actually look at the woman and was surprised to realize that she knew her. Not personally, but she knew of her and had seen her before. Andrew was a longtime customer of John Van Lew's hardware business, and unless Anna was mistaken, she was now standing in front of John's daughter.

"You are Elizabeth V –"

Elizabeth cut Anna off before she could finish. "Call me Baker's Daughter. And Benjamin is Shopkeeper. We are both spies."

Anna was completely perplexed, her anger now gone. "Why are you telling me this? You don't seem like very good spies if you go around telling everyone."

Elizabeth laughed. "That is true, which is why I don't tell everyone. I am only telling you because I have been trying to convince this stubborn man to recruit you."

"No!" Benjamin interjected. "It is too dangerous." He glared at Elizabeth as he moved in between the two women, then turned to Anna. "Anna, it is too dangerous. If your husband found out, he would kill you."

"Then we make sure her husband doesn't find out, just like we make sure that nobody finds out about any of the rest of us. We are all in danger. That does not make her special."

Benjamin whirled on Elizabeth. "She is special to me, and I will not see her put in harm's way!"

"Don't you think that is her decision to make?"

Elizabeth and Benjamin picked up their argument as if Anna was not in the room. Anna's head spun. Everything she knew was being turned upside down. The man she loved was a Northerner, and he was working for the Union. She was both baffled and convinced that she had known this all along. She would always be a Yankee, so of course she would only be able to give her heart away to one. Somehow, she had gone from bitterly betrayed to even more deeply in love than ever before in a matter of minutes. Perhaps she was going insane, but there in front of her, large as life, were Benjamin and this woman arguing about whether Anna should be a spy.

The absurdity of it all made Anna laugh. The thought thrilled her. Carrying on an affair behind her husband's back was one thing; damaging his precious South using information she provided was certainly another. If he ever found out, it would enrage him and he would likely kill her as Benjamin feared. Thus, her only regret was that she would not be able to see Andrew's face when he discovered her betrayal. She could live with that regret.

11

"Do I get my own special name?" Unlike her earlier laugh that had not attracted either of Elizabeth's or Benjamin's attention, her speaking drew them both up short.

"What?" Benjamin snapped at Anna, still caught up in the heat of the argument, then blushed in contrition. Anna paid him no mind.

"If I agree to become a spy, do I get my own name like Baker's Daughter or Shopkeeper?"

Elizabeth jumped to respond. "Of course! I have already given that some thought. You would be Northern Rose."

"I like it." Anna smiled and glanced at Benjamin without allowing herself to linger on his hurt expression and thus dissuade her from accepting. "What do I do?"

Elizabeth's face beamed with success. Benjamin's was a picture of defeat. "Anna, please don't. My love, I cannot bear to stand by while you put yourself in danger."

Anna took a step toward Benjamin and caressed his cheek before leaning in to kiss him ever so softly. He half-heartedly kissed her back, instead closing his eyes and bending his head forward so that their foreheads were touching.

Anna cupped his face in both of her hands. "My darling, the war is raging through the countryside. I am in danger every day that I spend in Virginia. At least this way I can be of some use." Benjamin started to reply but Anna cut him off. "No. You do not get to make this decision for me. If you are allowed to put yourself at risk, then so am I."

She kissed him once more before turning to Elizabeth. "What kind of information do you want?"

Elizabeth looked to Benjamin, who shrugged and nodded his

head, before she replied to Anna, "Anything you can get your hands on."

Anna smiled and proceeded to tell them everything that her husband was currently involved in and any details she had heard. Benjamin had already known of some of the things, but most were new. Elizabeth was thrilled and committed everything that Anna said to memory. As their conversation had already kept the shop closed long enough to arouse suspicion, Elizabeth suggested that they all part ways and told Anna to expect a present of new shoes to arrive within the week. Benjamin would explain how they worked when he next visited.

So Anna entered into a dance of duplicity. The element of danger that her rendezvous with Benjamin held took on a new edge. It wasn't until a member of their ring was caught and hung for treason that the monthly rule was instituted. The new rule stated that spies could only be seen in each other's company – not counting large social gatherings – once per month so that it would be hard for an outsider to recognize any on-going affiliation. Because of this, Anna and Benjamin saw each other less, and Anna met more and more spies. She even recruited some of her own. Her own spy ring soon surpassed Benjamin's because she had the advantage of attending and hosting society functions where she could interact with multiple spies, several times within the same month, with no one the wiser.

Anna discovered a heretofore unknown pleasure in these societal obligations. Unfortunately, her husband also noticed her new enthusiasm and, assuming she was finally embracing the Southern way of life, had begun to pay more attention to her. She suffered these attentions as best she could and was subsequently pleased to discover that with a little gentle nudging, she could get him to disclose more than she had ever been able to find by snooping through his desk. Anna failed to mention to Benjamin that this was how she was getting her best information, and Benjamin never asked. There was an unspoken agreement between the two of them that in matters of spying, how and where the information was obtained did not matter. All that mattered was the brief moments of time that they got to spend together.

On this particular afternoon, Anna had been more than a little surprised, but pleased, to discover that the delivery that required her attention was borne by none other than Benjamin himself. He had explained to the slaves that he was doing one of the other merchants a favor by delivering the dry goods and, therefore, required the approval of the lady of the house. Anna opened the door to the pantry and gestured for Benjamin to enter, then she looked around. No one was in sight. Regardless, her husband was home today, so they had to be careful.

"No, no. Not there. Let me show you." She reprimanded him louder than was necessary. Anna felt a need to justify why she was in the pantry with this man in case any of her husband's men were close enough to hear. Before she had even gotten the door closed completely behind her, Benjamin pulled her into his arms and kissed her so deeply she went weak in the knees. Not that it mattered; his grip on her was such that there was no fear of falling. She clung to him and returned his kisses. The unexpectedness of their encounter fueled their fires so they burned white hot, much faster than normal.

The need was desperate, and having nowhere to go, Anna began

14

to pull up her skirts. Benjamin caught on immediately and insinuated himself under her many layers and practically ripped the underclothes off her body to reach his final goal. Grasping her buttocks he lifted her up against the shelves of the pantry wall. She instinctively wrapped her legs around his waist, and he plunged into her again and again. Anna bit the knuckle on one hand to keep her moans at bay while she used her other to hold back a row of jars containing jellied fruits that were perilously close to being shaken to the ground. Her upturned skirt, creating a physical barrier between their torsos, did not diminish their pleasure in the least. Their fervor was quickly spent, as are all things that start so hot, and Benjamin lowered her to the ground, where it took her legs a moment to regain enough strength to hold her weight.

For several long moments, they breathed heavily and soaked in each other's company. Anna was able to regain speech first.

"What are you doing here? Twice in one month, it's too dangerous."

He leaned in and kissed her, thanking her for her concern.

"I had to see you." He looked down, readying himself for what came next. "Because I don't know that I will be able to see you for some time. Or ever."

Anna's heart stopped and she had to remind herself how to speak. "What do you mean?" She dreaded the answer. Waiting a month was hard enough; she couldn't imagine how to go from day to day not knowing when, or if, she would ever see him again, feel him, taste his mouth on hers.

"Since my uncle is back on his feet and can run his shop again, I've been recalled to my regiment. They say I've done enough here.

Your spy ring has grown to such a degree that my participation is no longer needed." He smiled at her ruefully. "I'm to take the information I have, meet up with General Meade for a debriefing, and then report back to the Second Maine Infantry."

Before she could stop herself, her cheeks were wet with tears. It was worse than she could have suspected. Not only was he going away, he was going away to fight. She might not ever see him again. There were no words. He had become her every joy, her only reason for living, and he was being taken away. Seeing that she couldn't speak, Benjamin continued.

"I knew it was dangerous, but I had to say goodbye in person. I'm sorry, my love. I have to go." He looked at her and the sorrow in his eyes matched hers. "I need you to promise me something." Anna nodded her head numbly. "Promise me you will stay safe. Pass whatever information you can, but don't put yourself in harm's way."

Anna's tears renewed their vigor, but she choked them back enough to speak. "Only if you promise to stay out of harm's way as well."

Benjamin promised. They both knew it to be a lie.

"I have to go now," he said

Anna nodded her head and looked down in grief.

Benjamin lifted her chin until her eyes met his. "I love you."

"I love you, too."

Benjamin kissed her softly, then passionately, then, before either of them could get carried away, he turned and left.

"Be safe, my Shopkeeper," Anna whispered to the closed pantry door and stood staring for several seconds before she crumpled to the floor and sobbed. She did not care if anyone heard her, she did not care about anything anymore. Curling up on the floor, she cried herself into an exhausted sleep.

When Anna finally awoke, she had no idea how much time had passed. Painfully, she pulled herself up from the floor and took a leaden step toward the door. Her world awaited her on the other side, but she was not interested in a world that did not include Benjamin. She wanted to stay within the safety of the pantry walls but knew it was just short of a miracle that nobody had found her already, so she took a breath, opened the door, and reemerged into the bustle of the house.

The bustle she was accustomed to wasn't there. She couldn't have slept that long; they should be cleaning up from dinner, or at the least preparing the supper. There were to be guests tonight; how was everything so quiet? Her immediate concerns outweighed her heartache for a moment and her normal purposeful stride returned as she walked down the hall and into the kitchen. As she entered, all of the slaves stopped and stared at her for a moment, before one of them finally blurted, "Oh, we tried to find you, we did! There wasn't nothin' we could do, honest."

"What happened? What are you talking about?"

"The massa, he come down here. He come down here lookin' for you, 'cause he can't find you. So we says you down in the pantry."

Anna blanched. Did Andrew catch Benjamin? Seeing her face pale, the slave stopped in her narration.

"And what happened?" Anna pressed.

"He heads down that way. But, Mary…" She trailed off, not

wanting to finish.

"Yes, what did Mary do?"

"Mary tries to stop him. Says she seen you elsewhere, but he don't listen, so she spills the pot she's holdin' on him. She said it's a accident. She don't mean to, and it wasn't hot or nothin', but massa don't care for none a that."

Anna knew exactly how this story was going to end, the same way any story ended that involved a slave upsetting her husband: in a savage beating. Anna couldn't believe it. Mary was *her* slave. He wouldn't dare. He had never laid a hand on her. He wouldn't dare. Anna's fists were white-knuckled, and she realized she was clenching her teeth when she tried to talk.

"Did he...?" She couldn't even finish the sentence. She did not need to, they all nodded their heads, eyes averted.

Fury flowed through her veins as Anna ran from the kitchen and up the stairs into the house proper. She knew to look for him in the parlor. Ever since her daughter's sixth birthday, when she started piano lessons, Kady practiced in the morning then performed for her daddy in the afternoon. They had kept up this routine for twelve years, and today wasn't any different. Andrew was leaning against a bookshelf, listening attentively. Anna ran into the parlor and flew at him, screaming and spewing forth every bit of pent-up anger and frustration she had ever harbored because of the injustice of her life. Her fists violently beat against his chest.

"How could you? She is *my* slave! You are not allowed to touch her!"

Her rage surprised him at first and she got in a few good hits,

18

but it only took him a moment to regain himself. Deftly, as if shooing away nothing more than a fly, he pushed her away from him. She came at him again. Having had enough of her, he caught her by the wrist with one hand and slapped her so hard across the face with the other she would have fallen to the floor had he not been holding her up by the wrist. He stared at her coldly until her eyes stopped swimming.

"I may have given her to you, but like everything else on this plantation, you belong to me and, therefore, so does she. I will do as I see fit with my belongings."

It was as if his words ripped off the bandage she had wound so tightly around all of her old wounds. Against her will, her lip began to quiver, and she tried with all her might to make it stop. She refused to let him see her cry.

Seeing the defiance in her eyes, he smiled cruelly and hit her again, this time releasing her wrist so that she fell to the floor.

"Now apologize to Kady for interrupting her playing and leave," Andrew commanded.

Having never seen such emotion from her mother, Kady had stopped playing and was gaping at the scene in amazement.

Anna, holding her face, clenched her jaw to prevent any more of her fury from spilling out. Slowly she stood, her eyes trained on her daughter, daring her to smile at her mother's humiliation.

Kady looked away, ashamed.

"My apologies, please continue your playing."

Anna was already heading toward the door as she finished her sentence. Behind her, she could hear her daughter saying something in reply. Anna did not know what and did not care. Once out of sight, she

19

sobbed a single sob and felt the warmth radiating off her swelling cheek. She was hurt and she was upset, but she knew Mary was worse off and it was all her fault. She made it to the small closet of a room next to her own that served as Mary's sleeping chamber. Carefully, she opened the door so as not to startle Mary inside.

Anna gasped at what she saw. Not only was Mary's face swollen from being hit, her shirt had been removed revealing more red welts across her back than Anna could count. Some had broken the skin producing trails of blood that obscured some of the lesser marks. Obviously, whoever had been commanded to drag her up here had been instructed to leave her as is and not tend to her wounds. Mary started to say something and tried to hoist herself up from the bed.

"No, no, no. Stay there, do not move. Oh, Mary..." Anna could not continue. Somebody had at least brought up a basin of water and a cloth, which Anna gratefully took and, ringing out the cloth, gently dabbed at the blood on Mary's back.

"I am so sorry, Mary. This is all my fault. If I hadn't been in that pantry with Benjamin, you wouldn't have had to stop Andrew, and he never would have done this."

Overcome, Anna stopped her ministrations and sobbed into her hands. Everything was falling apart. She had lost everything she cared about, and the one person she had to rely on had been beaten so badly Anna couldn't even confide in her what had happened.

Mary was reaching out her hand to Anna.

"Oh, don't move, don't move. I'm sorry, I am so sorry. This is all my fault." Anna went to daub at Mary's back some more, but Mary shooed her hand away. Much to Anna's amazement, Mary was trying to sit up. "Mary, no. Lie still, let me take care of you. I caused all of this, let me at least take care of you."

"Don'," Mary replied. It was hard to understand her, but Anna was almost positive she had said, "Don't."

"What? Don't what? Don't use the cloth? Does it hurt? Oh my, I am so sorry, Mary." This time, Mary succeeded in sitting up, the grimace of pain on her face betraying the effort it cost her.

"Don't." Mary took the cloth from Anna and spit what looked like blood and a tooth into it, effectively clearing her mouth and making it easier for her to speak. "Don't you do that."

Anna was taken aback, hurt.

"Don't do what? I'm trying to fix what I caused."

"That. Don't you dare do that! Don't you dare take that beatin' away from me by feelin' guilty and blamin' yourself. Because I didn't do it for you!"

Anna was preparing to soothe Mary, to calm her down, when the shock of her statement hit her like a slap in the face. All thoughts flew from her mind, and all she could do was stare back at Mary in pained confusion.

Satisfied she wouldn't be interrupted, Mary continued.

"You walk around here too big for your britches because you freein' the Negroes. You sacrificin' for the Negroes. But I know better. I know better even if no one else does. You doin' this for you. To spite you's husband and get back at you's daddy. I might be a slave, but I ain't dumb, so don't you go pretendin' that you is spyin' for me, cause you ain't. And there ain't nothin' wrong with that.

"We all do things for our own reasons, and we all do things for our own selves. I chose that beatin' because it was all I had to give. There ain't a person in this whole war that ain't taken it personal. So don't you dare take that beatin' away from me! I did it so's my girl and my boy, wherever he may be, won't have to take no beat. I did it so's my grand babies won't have to take no beat. I did it so's I will never have to take no beat never again. You can says you sorry till the sun come up again, but you can't stop no whip hand. Only the back of a Negro can do that. So you let me do my part."

The look in her eyes dared Anna to say something, to contradict or punish her for her insolence. But all Anna could do was look down, ashamed because Mary was right. She hadn't once considered or thought about what this war meant to Mary and her people. She'd only ever thought of herself. Anna looked up to apologize, but the look in Mary's eyes silenced the words before they were ever conjured. For the first time in their relationship, Mary got the final word in a conversation, and there wasn't anything in the world that could have persuaded Anna to take that away from her.

An unspoken understanding passed between the two, and then with more dignity and grace than Anna had ever witnessed in one human being, Mary pulled her blouse on over her destroyed back and exited her room.

2
Tattletale

Kady barely managed to duck around the corner out of sight before Mary came out of her room. Thankfully, Kady had the presence of mind to hide in the opposite direction of the servants' stairwell, so she remained unseen. It took Mary a laboriously long time to descend the stairs, and Kady was not able to relax and fully appreciate all she had heard until the last footfall had faded away. The danger had passed, but she remained rooted to the spot, her mind racing. Her father had sent a servant to tell her mother that she would not be required at supper. Still overcome from the earlier scene, Kady had the impulse to see how her mother fared, so Kady sent the servant away so she could deliver the message herself. Kady had been about to open her mother's bedroom door when she heard the raised voices coming from Mary's closet. Sneaking over to that door, Kady listened intently. She knew she had to have heard correctly, because she wasn't half so clever to have come up with anything as exciting as what she had heard. Now the question became what to do with her newfound knowledge?

Her mother was a spy.

She rolled the words around in her head. Her mother was a spy. A spy. Her mother. She had to tell her father. Barely containing a squeal, Kady picked up her skirts and hurried down the stairs. How exciting! Maybe he would let her be a spy, too! They could have secret rendezvous, and it would all be very mysterious. Kady wasn't exactly sure what being a spy entailed, but it had to be better than sitting around all day. She still had her piano of course, and she could paint, but ever since her father forbade her to take drives out into the country in their new barouche, she had felt stifled. His fear of her being accosted on the road was completely unfounded. Her father was a general for the Confederacy, no one would bother her.

Kady's feet slowed to a walk as she connected her last thought with her new discovery. If her father was a general for the Confederacy, and it was her father who had beaten Mary for disturbing his search, then Mary likely did that to save Anna from being discovered doing spy business, which meant that she was likely a spy for the Union. Her mother was a spy for the Union, not the Confederacy! But how? Why? As soon as the question popped into Kady's mind she knew the answer. It didn't take a genius to realize that her parents did not like each other, and not just in the normal arranged-marriage-we-don't-like-each-other kind of way. Kady was fairly certain that her mother hated her father. So, of course, she was working against him. Kady felt foolish that she had ever thought otherwise, and surprisingly, she wasn't mad at her mother. Where she expected to find a feeling of betrayal, she instead found respect.

Realizing that she was still walking, Kady stopped just short of the door to her father's study. The sound of angry voices coming from within made her take a step back yet lean in so she could still hear. The last thing she wanted was for her skirt to give away her presence. Thankfully the two men—her father and someone else—were talking loudly enough for her to hear everything.

"I have given enough money, and I am not going to give you

24

more until I get a say or some recognition." That was her father speaking.

"President Davis values your input, you know he does. If you want more involvement than that, I reckon you should take charge of some men."

"I can't do that, I have my plantation to run."

"General Lee has a plantation to run. That hasn't stopped him."

"General Lee's not a businessman, he's a military man, always has been. It's not the same thing."

"General Bell—"

"No. No more sweet talking. If you want more money, I get more involvement."

The other man took an exasperated breath so loud, Kady could hear it all the way out in the hall.

"Why don't I suggest to President Davis that your plantation be used as a rendezvous point where officers in the field can take a respite and get your counsel when they're in the area?"

"That's a start."

"Then we'll look into doing a counsel of the officers here later in the year."

"Yes, that sounds good. I like that. Perhaps around the holidays—we'll make it a festive affair."

"Yes, beautiful idea. I am positive that the president will agree. In fact, why don't you give me some dates that will work for you, and I'll bring them back to Richmond with me."

"That's more like it!" Kady's father laughed good naturedly. "I knew we could find an arrangement that suits everyone's needs. Come,

25

let's take a scotch on the veranda, and we'll discuss this little shindig more thoroughly."

Kady heard footsteps coming toward the door and she lifted her skirts to run away. She just made it into the parlor when she heard the study door open, and she rushed to her piano and sat down, pretending to study the music on the stand. As her father and the gentleman passed the parlor they stopped and her father commented, "And there she is, the apple of my eye, my daughter, Kady."

Kady turned, smiling for the men and made to get up. Her father waved her back down. "No, child, stay there and study. We have more business to discuss. You plan some pleasant music for after supper."

"Yes, Daddy."

He smiled at her indulgently, and Kady turned back to her music until she heard the door to the veranda open and close. She slouched— as much as one can slouch in a corset—and sighed with relief. She no longer wanted to tell her father. No. She wanted to be a spy, and she had just proved to herself that she would be good at it. Straightening up, a thrill of excitement ran through her. She was going to be a spy!

3
Interesting Prospect

Anna felt at odds walking the streets of Richmond knowing that she would not be visiting Benjamin. He was most likely back with his regiment by now. She had had the impulse to walk by his uncle's shop but squelched that immediately. Seeing the shop without her Shopkeeper in it would only serve to make his absence more real. No, she had business to attend to, and now that she was finally alone she could accomplish her task.

It had never been a question of whether or not Kady would accompany her to Richmond. Kady always accompanied Anna, but they would part ways upon arriving. Kady would spend the day visiting with friends or shopping, and Anna would rush through her shopping so that she could spend the majority of her day with Benjamin. With no Benjamin, Anna wasn't sure what she would do all day. She knew that her routine needed to appear the same, lest she draw attention to her activities. Little did she know it would be Kady who varied.

When Anna asked which friends Kady would be visiting, Kady responded that all of her friends had fled the city. Anna knew this to be false. She named two girls who still remained, and Kady assured her that they were no longer friends of hers, for one reason or another, and that she would not be visiting them. Kady then announced that she had decided she wanted to spend the day shopping with her mother. Anna was stunned. Not only because they hadn't spent a day shopping together in more than ten years, but because there was no way that she would be able to deliver her letter with the latest artillery numbers to Baker's Daughter with Kady in tow. She would still be able to pick up Mary's new shoes and any correspondence waiting for her, as all of that would be cleverly hidden in the goods that she would buy. The problem was that her missive was in the hollowed-out heel of her boot. Anna had easy access to her boot as her skirts were much smaller than Kady's, but even so, Kady would notice that something was amiss if she saw her mother break off her heel and pull out a scrap of paper!

Anna found her salvation at the milliner's shop. Kady found half a dozen things that she had to have. Normally, all extravagant purchases were left at the shop until the approval of her father could be gained. Without fail Andrew Bell would grant his approval; no price was too high if it was something his daughter wanted. However, Anna had learned years earlier that she was not allowed to be so generous with her daughter. All gifts were to come from Andrew, so Anna had given up trying. Today was different though, and Anna acquiesced on the stipulation that Kady not tell her father about the new hat and that she still beg for one of the others when she got home. Kady squealed in delight and readily agreed. With the milliner's assurance that he could have it fitted in no more than an hour if the young lady was willing to stay, Anna was able to escape. She had the boy out front flag her a cab.

She didn't necessarily need a cab, as St. Anne's was not far from the milliner's, but Anna wasn't sure if she would be able to get to the church and into the correct pew right away and she didn't have much time. If anyone asked, Anna claimed she had begun to frequent this particular church after the war started. As it was called after her namesake, she said it granted her comfort. In reality, Anna and her other spies used this spot to exchange letters. If you knelt down to pray at the end of a certain pew, you would find a short floorboard (a patch from some earlier repair) that could be lifted up to reveal a small cubby hole. As long as no one was in that pew or the one adjacent, you could deposit or pick up letters with no one the wiser. It simply looked as if you were deep in prayer. The only drawback was that if someone was already in the pew, you had to wait until they left, and, for whatever reason, the devout in Richmond were fond of that particular spot.

As luck would have it, Anna was in and out in less than ten minutes. Having deposited her letter and collected one that was there, she was soon on her way back to the milliner's. Her curiosity was piqued by the letter, as she wasn't expecting one. However, she had learned long ago that trying to read anything before regaining the safety of her room at home was not worth the stress. Pushing the letter from her mind and enjoying the first solitude she'd had all day, Anna decided to take a meandering stroll in hopes that it would settle her nerves. Until the milliner's shop, she had begun to fear that she would be unable to deliver her message. Now that it was safely tucked away, she could relax. Relaxing meant that her mind turned to Benjamin. With her daughter fixed at her side, she hadn't dared to dwell on thoughts of him, but now that she was alone he filled her mind. She had not heard from or about him since his departure. Not that she expected word from him, but it saddened her all the same.

In fact, melancholy now filled her days since he had left. She needed something new in her life, something to distract her. Anna remembered there was a Confederate supply yard that one of her spies had been trying to infiltrate for several months, to no avail. If she had her bearings correct, it shouldn't be far from where she was now. With renewed purpose, she turned in the direction she thought the yard lay. Anna was almost correct about its location but eventually was forced to ask a passerby for precise directions as the condition of the buildings around her had started to grow shabbier and shabbier, and her hollow heel had started to work its way loose. Apparently she hadn't secured it back in place as well as she had thought.

Thankfully the directions she received were good, and Anna soon found herself standing in front of two giant wooden gates. It was immediately apparent why her spy had failed to gain any information: the supply yard was completely surrounded by a tall fence. Even a tall man would not have been able to see in, and from the looks of it, you had to be a Confederate soldier to gain admittance. Anna knew that she shouldn't loiter. What possible reason could she have for being there if asked? Even so, she couldn't help looking around to see if there was any avenue of entry that had been missed.

The fence was impenetrable, so unless she wanted to examine every board until she found a knot that could be worried out, looking there would be fruitless. Expanding her search, Anna's gaze fell on the buildings across the street. Unlike those on either side of the yard, these had two stories. At street level, there were signs advertising the skills of the craftsmen inside. It appeared that the second stories were strictly residential. If only one of them had a room to rent, all of her problems would be solved. This thought made her smile. She had never before wished to rent a room, much less one in an undesirable part of town.

"Excuse me, ma'am."

Anna practically jumped out of her skin when the man touched her arm. She was so engrossed in the buildings across the street that she hadn't realized that he had walked up or that he was talking to her.

"Please excuse me, I didn't mean to startle you, ma'am, but you don't look as if you're from around here, and I was thinkin' that you could probably use some help."

Anna pressed her hand to her chest trying to steady herself and calm her breathing. The young soldier, really more of a boy, was now holding onto her other arm and looking at her with a startled look. He probably thought she was going to faint, and for some reason that amused Anna, which helped her to regain her composure.

"Some help, yes, I could use some." Anna looked back across the street for inspiration, then back to the soldier. "I am supposed to meet my daughter at the milliner's, but I'm afraid that I have gotten myself lost."

The soldier smiled. "Why yes, you certainly did, ma'am. There ain't a mill'ner anywhere near these parts."

"Oh dear." Anna tried to make her face look as helpless as possible.

"Never you fear, ma'am. You stay right here, and I'll run over yonder to fetch you a cab."

"I would be ever so grateful. You are too kind."

"It's my pleasure."

The boy smiled widely, tipped his hat, and ran off down the road. Anna watched him go, thankful that he had believed her story, then made one more quick inventory of her surroundings. She wistfully looked back up to the second-story windows and saw a young woman

31

awkwardly situating a chair in front of the window directly across from the supply yard. The woman sat and pulled out what appeared to be a pencil and small book. From that vantage point, Anna was sure that the woman could clearly see everything in the yard.

The young soldier returned with a cab, and Anna redirected her attention to him as he gallantly helped her up and told the driver where to go. Anna gave him a coin and thanked him again. Thrilled, the boy tipped his hat and took off down the road, probably in search of some ale. As soon as he was gone, Anna turned to peer out the other side of the cab at the young woman in the window again. She had a perfect view. Anna turned back around and settled into the seat. Yes, she thought, she would have to send someone around to recruit that young lady. She would prove most valuable.

March 25, 1863
Package to be delivered next month. New messenger use first protocol.
NR

64-44-12-31-11 56-63 24-21-53-66
32-44-31-52-44-65-62 13-34 16-62
45-62-42-43-22-62-12-62-45
14-62-15-13 64-34-14-13-11 14-62-25
64-62-55-55-62-14-65-62-12 26-55-62
33-43-12-55-13 32-12-34-13-34-31-34-42
14-12

4
Additional Duties

A nna admired the pair of shoes on her dressing table as she waited for Mary to return with the hot water. Andrew was downstairs in the parlor listening to Kady play the piano, so now was the perfect time to talk to Mary. Anna had decided that it was time to make Mary part of her ring. She had taken a beating to keep Anna's activities concealed. If that didn't earn Mary a place, Anna didn't know what would. She had been struggling, trying to figure out a way to tell Mary, or even just to bring it up, when the idea of getting Mary the shoes hit her. It was perfect—an icebreaker and initiation gift rolled into one.

Mary entered noiselessly and filled the washbasin with the hot water. Anna stayed at her dressing table as Mary soaked a washcloth and rung it out before crossing the room to Anna's side. Anna turned to her, picked up the shoes, and announced the obvious.

"I got you a pair of shoes."

Mary's face twisted in confusion as she put her hands on her hips, wet cloth and all.

"Those is beat up worse than the ones I'm already wearin'."

Anna smiled. "Exactly! If I had gotten you brand new shoes, they would have drawn scrutiny, and the last thing we want is for someone to look them over and discover this."

Anna deftly twisted the shoe and the heel came off in her hand. Mary gasped in horror that Anna had just ruined the shoe, until Anna tilted the heel in her direction so she could see that the heel was hollow. As realization dawned, a smile grew rapidly across Mary's face.

"Is that so I can carry messages without nobody knowin' it?"

Anna nodded, handing the shoes to Mary and snatching away the washcloth, which she dropped on the floor. Mary didn't even notice, her attention fully on her new shoes.

"Do you have a pair of these?" Mary asked.

"I do. As long as you get the heel twisted on securely, they truly feel like a regular pair of shoes."

"And if you don't?"

"Well, then you better step carefully, otherwise you might wind up flat on your face."

Mary laughed nervously at that but didn't take her eyes away from the shoes. With no help from Anna she figured out how the heel reattached and after several tries was twisting the heel on and off with ease. Anna looked on appreciatively and realized that she was quite proud of how quickly Mary figured it out. Anna let her play with it until the wonder wore off enough for Mary to look up at her to find out what was next.

"Good, you've got that down. Next you'll need to sew little hidden pockets into your skirts, like the ones you added to mine. You won't always be wearing your shoes, or you might not be in a situation where you can easily access the heel, so you have to have a secondary location to stash a note."

"I already got those."

"You what?" Anna was surprised to hear this. Instead of responding, Mary clenched her teeth, fixed her eyes on the floor, and

34

dropped her arms to her sides. "What do you mean you already have hidden pockets sewn into your skirts?"

"I misspoke. I'll sew some in right away." Mary remained rigid.

"You just said that your skirts already have hidden pockets. What is wrong? Why are you lying to me?"

"Don't make me tell you why, ma'am."

Mary still hadn't looked up and confusion colored Anna's face until she noticed that, ever so slightly, Mary had begun to tremble in fear. Anna knew that it was going to take some time for Mary to fully recover from Andrew's beating. That being said, what in the world could Mary have done to make her fear a reprisal when Andrew wasn't even in the room? Anna felt her frustration rise. She was supposed to be making things right with Mary, not making them worse.

"Oh, for heaven's sake! I'm recruiting you to be a spy with me. Do you really think there's anything that you could say right now that would get you into trouble?"

"It's bad, ma'am."

"Have I ever raised a hand to you?"

"No, ma'am."

"Then tell me. I swear to you there will be no reprisals."

Mary took a deep breath then let it all come tumbling out at once.

"Before you ever came to the plantation, my mama taught me to sew in those little pockets, so that whenever I'm about the big house and sees something that won't be missed..." Mary trailed off.

"Yes."

"I can take it. Nothing big mind you, the pockets is small, but a candy here and there. A thimble. A piece of ribbon or a sugar cube. Every now and again a spare coin. I ain't never spent none of the money I took, and most of the other things I give away for birthdays or holidays. Or if someone just got a beatin'. It's amazing how holding onto something that was took from whitefolk can lift your spirits when you feelin' broken." Anna was silent, so Mary continued nervously. "I ain't never took nothin' a yours, Miss Anna, I swear. You been nothin' but good to me, and I ain't never took nothin' that you didn't give me." She paused. "I have taken a few things from Kady though."

At that, Anna laughed, but Mary remained wary and silent. The more Anna thought about it, the more her merriment grew, and as tears started to roll down her cheeks, she pulled Mary into an embrace and kept laughing until the rigidity left Mary's body. Mary even let out a small laugh of her own. Anna's mirth had become contagious. Finally Anna's merriment began to subside and she wiped her face with the back of her hand.

"Oh, I love you, you dear, sweet woman! You've been stealing from Andrew and from Kady." With that she let out a short bark of a laugh but stifled it before she got carried away again. "You, my dear, are going to be a wonderful spy. You've been practicing for years and didn't even know it."

This time both Mary and Anna laughed, the relief releasing what was left of the tension in Mary's body. Anna then showed her how to keep a note tucked up her sleeve and pull it out unseen. Since Mary was a slave it would have to be a travel pass or an order for the butcher, or something equally innocuous. That way, if anybody ever saw Mary slipping a note into one of her secret pockets and demanded that she hand it over, she would be able to secretly pull the piece of paper from her sleeve and produce it instead. Anna was delighted at how quickly Mary picked up the skill.

"You are a natural. I should have recruited you ages ago."

"Yes, ma'am, I reckon you should have." Mary smiled broadly at Anna, appreciating her own cheek, but Anna's face fell into a frown.

"Anna."

"What's that, ma'am?"

"No, no ma'am. When it's the two of us, call me Anna."

"That wouldn't be proper, ma'am."

"Who is to say what is proper and what is not proper? We have never known a time like this, and as such we must adopt actions that we never before would have thought possible. If I'm a spy for the Union, and you're a spy for the Union, then that puts us on equal ground. So if you're just Mary, then I'm just Anna."

"Just Anna." The name without the title "miss" before it came out awkward, but Mary smiled with satisfaction.

"Now, back to business. See if you can pull the note out of your sleeve and pass it to me as I walk by."

Anna grinned at her then hurried across the room so Mary could try the maneuver.

Apr 13, 1863
Longstreet scavengers ranging wider. Tell
informants to take care.
NR

44-32-12 24-66 24-21-53-66
42-34-14-65-55-13-12-62-62-13
55-31-44-22-62-14-65-62-12-55
12-44-14-65-43-14-65 25-43-45-62-12
13-62-42-42 43-14-33-34-12-64-44-14-13-55
13-34 13-44-52-62 31-44-12-62
14-12

5
The Valley of the Shadow of Death

"Yea though I walk through the valley of the shadow of..."
Martha stopped speaking to stifle a rising sob. She knew she
had to stay strong for her children, but she could not get past that word.
Another scream pierced the air and even the young Confederate soldier,
guarding the door with his gun at the ready, flinched at the sound. Biting
her lip, she swallowed past the lump of fear lodged in her throat, let her
eyes fall shut, and started again.

"Lord, though I walk through the valley of the shadow of death,
I shall fear no evil."

Emma hurried down the street. She was beginning to regret telling her
father that she did not want to take the carriage into town. The letter
tucked into her petticoats seemed heavier with every step she took.
Even though her family was Virginian through and through, seceding
from the nation had never set right with her father. It became a sore
subject among their neighbors along the Elizabeth River, and their
family received taunts and threats for being Union sympathizers. Her
father eventually fell silent and learned to keep his opinions to himself.
A new fire wasn't lit in her father's belly until Union troops captured the
Navy Yard in Norfolk. He went out at all hours of the night and slept in

39

small increments during the day. This morning he had looked so haggard Emma doubted if his head had made acquaintance with a pillow for several days.

Most disturbing, however, was when he was at home, he locked himself in his study and refused to speak with anyone. Until this morning, that is, when he had beckoned her into his study and had sworn her to secrecy. Although she did not understand why secrecy was so important—he didn't tell her anything. All he did was give her a letter and ask her to take it to the blacksmith when she went into town. Above all else, he had made her promise not to let anybody know or see she had the letter and to go about her business as usual. When she asked what it was about, he tried to take it back saying it was too dangerous a job for her, but she stuffed it into her petticoats before he could stop her. Much to her mother's consternation, the quickest way to get Emma to do anything was to tell her she could not. And so it was, with this scene replaying in her head, that Emma stepped into the general store. She had several shops to visit before arriving at the blacksmith's.

A muffled scream rent the air, stopping Martha's prayer once more, and then all was silent. Her resolve broke and she covered her face with her hands and started to sob. One of her sons broke free of his captor and, unhindered, knelt by his mother. Taking one of her hands from her face, he held it between his own and picked up the prayer where she had left off.

"Surely goodness and mercy shall follow me all the days of my life, and I will dwell in the house of the Lord forever." The innocence of his voice reverberated through the room contrasting sharply with the sounds of his father being tortured in the kitchen below. He knew something, and the Confederate lieutenant who had come knocking so innocently that morning wanted it—badly. The lieutenant had said nobody needed to get hurt. Martha doubted the truth of that assurance when he first uttered it and now knew it to be a bald-faced lie. For the past hour she had listened as her husband was being tortured. Apparently the information that he divulged had been insufficient.

At first Martha had believed her husband brave. She was unaware what information he could possibly possess that was so important but was proud he was willing to endure bodily harm to protect it. It was only after she had been dragged in front of him and forced to watch her eldest son be shot that she saw what men referred to as bravery was actually bull-headed stubbornness, and she told him so. She screamed it to the rafters and fought against her captors to be able to hold her dying son and afford him what little comfort she could. She was denied her pleas and had to watch from afar as her son bled to death, his last breath producing a gurgle of blood that was the macabre twin of the spit-up her infant son produced on a daily basis. Despite the tears streaming down her husband's face, he refused to satisfy the officer.

The lieutenant had begun to bark an order for the twin sons to be brought down when a man Martha had yet to even notice stepped forward and interjected.

"That won't be necessary. Take her back upstairs, she's of no further use." The lieutenant shot daggers at the man with his eyes—whom Martha noticed was wearing the uniform of an enlisted man, not an officer—and was about to upbraid him when the man continued, "Take her upstairs and tell her to pray for the immortal souls of her family, because *none* of them are of any use to us anymore."

As the weight of what the soldier said settled throughout the room, she screamed once more. Her husband began pleading with a fresh fervor and the lieutenant's vitriol turned to humor as a wicked smile distorted his face, and a laugh that chilled her blood escaped his lips.

"Well, good mornin', Miss Emma! What can I do for you? Another one of your father's horses throw a shoe?"

Emma smiled. Ever since she was a little girl, Blackie had always been able to make her feel at ease no matter what was troubling her. He was a burly sort of man, who never wore a shirt when he was working, and therefore, was always covered in black soot and sweat. Much to her mother's humiliation, the first time Emma had seen him as a child, she kept pointing and asking about the big white man who was all black, until he came over and introduced himself. He laughed off her mother's apologies and let Emma nickname him Blackie, which had humiliated her mother all over again. More importantly, it had created a bond between Emma and Blackie that held firm to this day.

"No, the horses are fine, thank you," Emma replied. She paused and looked around to make sure they were alone before continuing. "Father sent me with a message for you."

The big man's smile disappeared and was replaced by a frown that looked so unnatural on his face it brought her back to the seriousness of her task. He knew what her father's messages contained and did not approve of his choice in messengers.

Before she could reach into her petticoats to retrieve the missive, one of the field hands from her father's plantation came bursting into the blacksmith's, fighting for air. He had run hard the full mile and a half from the plantation into town. He took a couple of deep breaths before he was able to speak.

"Miss Emma," he cried, panting, "you gots to hide"—panting— "they be in the house, and" —big gulp of air— "the massa ain't long for this world."

The color drained from Emma's face. Blackie sprang into action grabbing a barrel for the slave to sit on and some water for him to drink. As the slave sucked down the water, Blackie began to interrogate him: Who was there? How many? What did they want?

As she listened to Blackie's questions and the vague answers from the slave, her terror grew. That was her family, her whole life back at the house. They were all home except for her. Her father had forbade all excursions off the grounds, with the exception of her weekly shopping trip. She couldn't stay here helplessly and let herself be hidden away; she had to do something. She sneaked out the back of the blacksmith's and, through sheer luck, found a horse already saddled. She realized her plan was ridiculous. Wearing a full skirt and petticoats, there was no way to mount, much less ride, a horse. She looked back into the blacksmith's, then out toward her family's homestead and clenched her jaw, steeling herself to her decision. She dug the letter out of her petticoats and tucked it safely into her décolleté, then in a most unladylike and unabashed fashion, set to undoing her hoop and other encumbering accoutrements.

A blush raced up her cheeks as she thought of the scandal that would result from a mound of women's undergarments being found behind the blacksmith's, but she pushed that thought aside as she mounted the horse—a daunting task. All she had left were her pantaloons and overskirt, the latter ridiculously large without the supporting understructure. After fumbling and falling into the side of the horse several times, she was forced to gather her skirt up in one arm in a most unseemly fashion to free her legs enough to mount. Mercifully, that same overabundance of material allowed her the maneuverability to sit astride the horse like a man, letting the voluminous skirt fall on both sides. Emma thanked the heavens her father had ignored the protests of her mother and allowed her to ride as a young girl—at least until her bloods came and her mother insisted riding would ruin her for her future husband. She was finally able to point the horse in the direction of home and dug her heels into the horse's sides.

Henry smiled to himself as he finished deciphering the letter in front of him. The old man had finally told the truth and it was because of him. He couldn't understand why people thought the only way to get information out of a person was to cause them pain. At least in his experience, a little fear was much better motivation than a lot of pain. He looked up at the bloodthirsty lieutenant waiting impatiently in front of him.

"The key is good," Henry confirmed. "According to this letter, they have rerouted their supply wagons because the informant, NR, tipped them off that we were planning a raid. The same raid that came up dry two weeks ago."

"Where does it say they rerouted them?"

"It says all new routes will be disclosed in future correspondence. It appears they follow the same guidelines as our coded messages in case they are intercepted: only one note of relevance per missive."

"Well, damn it all to hell! How am I supposed to go back and report we got the key for the letters, but all we were able to reveal was that our failed raid failed because they knew about it ahead of time?"

Henry clenched his jaw in irritation. Shortsighted officers like this one made him wish he had disobeyed his father at the beginning of the war. Then he could have bought himself an officer's commission. Instead he stayed out of the war until he was called up by the draft and forced to follow orders from men like this one.

Lieutenant General Longstreet had sent them out on a foraging mission. Originally, they were to skirt the edges of the Union's occupation of the Navy Yard in Norfolk to see what could be commandeered for the Confederacy. However, when Henry stumbled upon a piece of intelligence about a Union spy, they abandoned foraging and traveled further south down the Elizabeth River where they did indeed find a spy at the O'Neal plantation. Mr. O'Neal himself. Once again, Henry had done all the work, and Lieutenant Radcliffe would take all the credit. But only after Henry took the time to explain to him why their information was valuable.

"The victory is in the key itself, now we know that we have the correct table for deciphering. These letters are weeks old. We had already assumed their contents would be of little help. Besides—"

"Don't you talk down to me, boy! I'm not stupid! And don't you ever interrupt one of my interrogations again either! I am an officer and you will respect that!"

Henry ground his teeth. He did not know why it surprised him how quickly it had been forgotten that his interruption is what had won them the prize. For the hundredth time, Henry reminded himself that he had made his bed, for better or for worse, and now he had to lie in it.

"I apologize; there was no disrespect intended."

"Good." The lieutenant made a show of shuffling the papers back and forth; at one point, he even picked one up to read it despite it being in code.

"Permission to speak?" Henry asked.

"Granted."

"Word in town was that O'Neal had four sons. By my count, there are only three here. The one you killed and the twin boys being held in the nursery with O'Neal's daughters. Perhaps you did not actually kill his eldest son."

The lieutenant looked at him blankly.

"Perhaps the eldest son is out delivering messages for his father, which is why all we have here is old correspondence."

Slowly Henry's assertion sunk in, and the lieutenant got excited.

"Yes, yes!" The lieutenant pointed at a small man across the room. "You, Williams! There should be four sons! Take two men into town and find O'Neal's eldest son. He's there somewhere, and he's got what we're looking for. Go find him!"

Williams scampered off to obey orders.

The lieutenant looked back to Henry. "I knew that it was odd he let me kill that boy, but what father cares about his second-born son? Why didn't I think of that sooner? The eldest son is working with the father. Of course!" The lieutenant slapped his hand down on the table, congratulating himself for coming up with exactly what Henry had told him.

Henry turned his attention back to deciphering the letters to distract himself from his fervent wish to express his opinion of the lieutenant's intelligence.

Emma cut onto the road leading up to the plantation at a precipitous speed and almost bowled over the slave who jumped out from the trees. His appearance startled her horse, practically throwing Emma to the ground. Before she could regain her seat, the man grabbed her off the back of the horse and clamped his hand down over her mouth to silence the scream that had begun to issue forth. A second slave emerged from the side of the road and grabbed the horse's reins, calmed him, and led him quickly into the trees. The first slave followed him, dragging Emma along with him.

"Miss Emma, shhhh. Shhhh! We not gonna hurt you, but you needs to be quiet." She stopped struggling. Cautiously the slave removed his hand from her mouth.

She spoke in a breathless whisper. "Where is my family?"

"In the house with them men that came this mornin'."

"Show me."

The two slaves exchanged looks, afraid to disobey a command

even now, and turned to pick their way through the trees. The big house was in sight in no time and strangely there was little activity. There were several men outside watching the horses. Otherwise all was still. The second slave stopped with the horse out of view from the house, but the first slave led Emma to the edge of the copse before stopping and beckoning her to crouch down in the underbrush to wait.

She did so and immediately began to fuss with her skirt—not in her normal meticulous way, but in complete frustration. Her ride followed by the short walk through the woods had rendered her skirt completely ruined. There were brambles and burrs caught up in it everywhere, not to mention she had fought with it every step of the way until she had finally given up and let it drag behind her and tear on the branches. If they had to run, she would be completely hindered.

A gunshot echoed across the eternity that lay between Emma and her family, sending a flock of birds to the sky. Without thinking, she stood and began to run toward the house. Before she was three steps underway the slave grabbed her once more and tackled her to the ground. She started to struggle when the folly of her actions became apparent by the attention the soldiers outside with the horses were now directing toward them. They had heard her movement and were now debating whether it was worth investigating.

Even though she was now perfectly still, the slave's grip around Emma hadn't loosened, and her arms started to throb where his fingers dug into her tender flesh. Despite this, she did not protest. She had no idea how long they waited for something, anything, to happen. The soldiers finally lost interest and went back to their posts. She was about to struggle to get free when a second gunshot fractured the air. The slave's grip tightened in anticipation of Emma trying to run again, but she stayed down. She did not believe in the power of prayer like her mother did, but as the tears started to flow down her face, Emma prayed.

Disgusted, Henry followed the lieutenant out of the house and toward the horses. O'Neal had clearly told them everything, and the lieutenant knew that. So why he felt the need to shoot out both of the man's knees he couldn't fathom. Especially since the man was already so far gone that neither shot elicited much reaction. Even so, it provided the lieutenant with some sort of sick pleasure because he was now whistling happily as he pulled on his gloves in preparation to mount his horse. Before doing so he turned to Henry.

"Gather up all the Negroes and get them ready to march. We're taking them with us."

"Yes, sir."

"Then shoot the family and burn the house."

"But sir, we promised to let them live if O'Neal talked! They're children for God's sake."

Outraged, the lieutenant wheeled on Henry. "That is the last time you will ever contradict an order I give you! This is war, and you will obey my commands. If I want to make an example of traitors for all who may think to follow in their footsteps, then you will do it!" A twisted smile spread across his face. "In fact, you will do it personally." He raised his voice to address the remainder of the men. "Gather anything easy to carry that is of value and what Negroes come willingly.

49

Shoot those that do not. Henry here has volunteered to take care of the family. We ride out in five minutes." The lieutenant flashed Henry a hideous grin, mounted his horse, and left to oversee the foraging.

Henry hated that man to the core of his being. He turned and began what now seemed like a long walk back to the house. The looks on the men's faces he passed were equal parts horror and fear with the odd look of admiration and respect. They actually believed he had volunteered to dispatch a woman and her children. He would be afraid of himself, too. Entering the kitchen, Henry skirted past the semiconscious old man, who was still tied to the chair, and ascended the staircase one step at a time, each footfall a fateful premonition echoing throughout the house. When he reached the top, he took a deep breath, steadied himself, and entered the nursery where the family was gathered. One of the young boys was finishing a prayer while his mother and two sisters all sobbed quietly. He motioned with his head to the two men who were standing guard.

"Head out."

They did not have to be told twice and ran down the stairs and out of the house.

Henry did not want to think about this, and he did not want to have to hear them plead or cry any more than was necessary. He had his orders, and he had to follow them. Before Martha could turn around to look at him, he pulled his pistol and shot her and the young boy sitting next to her. It jammed, rendering the weapon useless. Dreading the thought of having to clear the jam and reload his weapon with the two girls and the remaining son screaming and crying in front of him, Henry dropped the gun and pulled out his knife, deftly slitting the throats of

50

the two daughters. He tried not to think of them as people. Instead of helping, that seemed to make it worse. The little boy had regained his senses enough to try to run away, but Henry caught him and snapped his neck with a small movement. It was no harder than finishing off a deer while out hunting back home. Slowly lowering the boy to the floor, Henry was sickened by the carnage before him; the work of his own hands. He swore the lieutenant would pay for this order.

Feeling as though his body was stuck in a vat of mud, he turned to pick up his gun and make his way out of the house when a small sound stopped him. Ever so softly, coming from the corner of the room, there was the gurgling sound of an infant, an infant who had inconceivably remained quiet throughout this ordeal and brought the count of sons to the previously discussed four. Henry doubled over and vomited, filth spattering his shoes.

Emma was by now openly weeping into the slave's chest. He had drawn her near as the screaming from the nursery started. Whether he had done this to comfort her or out of self-preservation to try to muffle the sound, she did not know because he remained ever vigilant to what was still unfolding outside of the cover of the trees. Finally, all was quiet with the exception of the one remaining horse that was tied to a post. It nickered its displeasure at the smoke tendrils creeping out of the upstairs windows. The smoke increased quickly and Emma involuntarily jerked when a window shattered, unable to withstand the heat and pressure anymore.

"Miss Emma, look. He's the only one left."

51

Emma turned to see a soldier, who was splattered in blood and coughing, emerge from the house, carrying the bassinet from the nursery. He ran over to the stand of trees to their left, trying not to jostle the bassinet too much. He set it gently in the shade and collapsed next to it, wheezing and looking around to see if anybody was present. Emma yearned to go check the bassinet, but held still, fearing what the man would do if he saw her. His breath regained, he took one last look at the baby, saw he was secure, and crossed to his horse. Clearly agitated, the horse needed no encouragement to break into a run as soon as the man mounted.

Emma waited until he had rounded the corner in the drive and was out of sight before leaping to her feet. This time, instead of stopping her, the slave quickly outdistanced her and ran into the burning house. Emma ran to the bassinet and found lying, poorly swaddled in a blanket, her youngest brother. She could not understand why the man had chosen to rescue the baby. Perhaps he had tried to save the rest of her family as well, but failed. She pictured him waiting in the burning house for the rest of his company to leave, so he could sneak the one soul he had been able to save out to safety. Emma had no idea how she would ever be able to repay this man for his kindness.

She quickly inspected the boy to ensure he was indeed unharmed. Before she could pick him up and hold him close, the slave staggered out of the house, dragging her father. She left the baby in the shade and hurried over to where the slave was laying her father gently in the grass away from the burning house. He was barely alive. Emma's tears flowed even more freely as she knelt down and took her father's hand in hers.

He looked up at her through unfocused eyes.

"Father," she was able to choke out before her emotions overtook her.

Immediately the bleary haze left her father's gaze and his eyes bored into hers.

"Emma?"

"Yes, Father, I'm here. I'm right here." She had thought that might give him some hope. He shook his head ever so slightly.

"Wild." He coughed up some blood and groaned before he was able to continue. "Tell Wild they have the key." He coughed and spluttered some more. "Tell him, promise."

Emma was taken aback. After everything that had happened, her father's dying words to her was a message for somebody she had never even heard of.

"But Father, who is—"

He cut her off before she could finish her thought. "General Wild," he sputtered and tried to pat her left arm. "One, one…"

"He has one arm?"

"Yes! Find him, quickly. The field, go." The energy it took him to bark out the order winded him terribly and he began coughing harshly.

Horrified, Emma stood. She was being sent away to leave her dying father and infant brother in the hands of slaves while she went to find a general who was probably out on a battlefield where she had no business going. She began to back away slowly, hesitant to leave, but the insistence in her father's eyes made her turn and head back toward the trees. The second slave had emerged from his cover, tied the horse to a nearby tree and was tending to the baby. She walked up to them and grabbed the horse's reins.

"You are to watch him and keep him safe until I get back."

The slave looked up at her incredulously but finally nodded in response.

She mounted the horse, an easier task the second time around but no less cumbersome, and urged it down the lane.

Emma knew the skirmishes that had been dragging on for the past week were another mile away from town. By the time she arrived on the outskirts, her inner thighs burned, chafed raw from riding. Mercifully she discovered she was on the correct side of the field and that Brigadier General Wild's tent was nearby. Clumsily she dismounted, garnering strange looks from all within eyeshot and limped over. When she reached the tent flap, a lower ranking officer immediately began to shoo her away. Frustrated, she called out.

"General Wild!"

All of the men stopped what they were doing and looked up at her.

"Brigadier General Wild, I have a message from my father, who is dead along with my entire family."

It took every ounce of self-control in her body to keep her tears at bay. Whether it was what she said, or the presence of a bedraggled young woman standing outside his tent, she did not know, but the General broke away from his men and came to her.

In a hushed voice he asked, "Are you Daniel O'Neal's

daughter?"

She nodded her head, fearing she would be unable to speak without crying.

"What is his message?" His seeming lack of empathy flared a righteousness in her that she did not know existed.

She spat back at him, "He died at the hands of the Confederate soldiers who were torturing him, and his last words were to instruct me to tell you that they have the key."

The general's eyes momentarily widened before he turned and ran back into the tent. A flurry of activity broke out and she was forgotten.

A bitter bile flowed through her veins as she realized how inconsequential she was to all of these men. How little they cared for her father, for her family, for her. Their only concern was this war and this key whose price was apparently greater than the lives of her family. Hot tears began to stream down her face as she stormed away. She did not know where she was going; she only knew she couldn't be by that tent and those men anymore. She tore through a small thicket of trees not caring that branches were raking their sharp fingers across her cheeks and arms and through the soft fabrics of what was left of her dress. When she emerged on the other side, she stopped dead in her tracks, paralyzed by the vista. Down in the valley below her, men were clashed in war. Gunshots rang through the air, but what took her breath away was that she couldn't distinguish who was who. Who was friend and who was foe? They were a wild stewing pot of flashing blades, exploding gunpowder, smoke, screams, and blood. More blood than she had ever imagined could exist in one place.

She felt as though she were standing on some great precipice, looking out on what was now her uncertain yet inevitable future. She wanted to run, to cry, to hide, but somehow she knew she was a part of this now, and nothing she could do would allow her to escape that fate. She was inextricably linked to this horror that had so insidiously crept into her life until it had consumed her entirely. She had nothing left except the last words her father had ever written. She looked down and pulled the missive out of the front of her dress and opened it. It was unreadable— a page of numbers that formed words, saying nothing at all. Nothing without the key to decipher them. Acrimony fueled a rage inside of her as she refolded the paper and replaced it in the front of her dress. She knew her father wanted her to do what was right. The only problem was that she did not know what was right. Looking back over the battle, she realized she did not even understand what they were all fighting for, and she certainly did not understand where she fit into that landscape.

6
Monster Unleashed

Henry pushed his horse as hard as he dared before reining her in, slowing to a stop and dismounting. Upon leaving the plantation, he could think of nothing except putting as much distance as possible between himself and the carnage he had wrought. He knew his company was on the march to meet up with Longstreet, but Henry had no desire to catch up to them yet, so he headed in the opposite direction. With his feet on solid ground, he stumbled a few steps before falling to his knees and retching into the weeds at the side of the road. He heaved until there was nothing left, yet his body still continued through the motions for a time, reaping no fruits for its labor.

When his stomach finally quieted and he was left with his haggard breathing, Henry realized he was crying. He had never killed in cold blood before and order or not, that is what he had done. He had been in skirmishes, had fired into the enemy and seen a man fall from it. He had grappled in close quarters knowing that it was him or the other man. Kill in order to survive. Still, the goal had never been outright death. They were given loftier goals: hold the bridge, take the hill, push the enemy back; goals that made the falling of men an unfortunate byproduct but not the intended mission, which made the messy affair more palatable. In striving for the good of the whole, the sin of the individual was forgotten and forgiven.

This was different. He had walked into a child's nursery, a place of sanctuary and respite, and spilled the blood of the innocents who played there. What he had done, what he had been ordered to do, was not for the good of the whole. That thought kindled a fire of hatred deep within Henry. He had been ordered to slaughter babes. He had been ordered to become a monster, but surely that monster had been lurking, waiting to surface, or he would not have so readily been able to carry out such an atrocious deed. Lieutenant Radcliffe had somehow been able to see Henry's true nature and had unleashed it. Whether Henry liked it or not, that door was now open, flung wide.

Henry was certain of two things. If he was to be a monster, he would be a monster of his own making. He would use this day to leverage himself into a position where men like Radcliffe would be unable to touch him, unable to command him to do their sadistic bidding. And second, Radcliffe would one day feel the wrath of the monster he had so callously unveiled.

Henry's tears had subsided by now and their trails on his face were indistinguishable from the sweat of an oddly warm spring afternoon. Slowly, he pushed himself to his feet and looked around for his horse. The mare had wandered farther up the road and, now recovered from their run, was nibbling the green grass in the shade of a tree. At his approach, she snorted nervously, afraid of another frantic decampment, so Henry gently took her reins and stroked her nose to reassure her that their next voyage would be undertaken with more dignity. Once she had relaxed under his hand, he gave her one last pat and mounted.

By now his company had a sizable head start, and if he did not make up ground quickly, his absence would be noted before he could catch them. Heading back the way he had come, now at a slower pace, he realized the countryside was nearly identical to that of his childhood. It then occurred to him that Norfolk was in the southeastern tip of Virginia, and they had ridden south from there. That placed him near the Carolina border and next to the Dismal Swamp, which his father's plantation in North Carolina abutted. His passing glances across the landscape turned into keen searches until he found a faint marker etched into a tree.

For years, hunters had traversed these woods and swamps and, in so doing, established a series of trails to follow the game that could only be found by those who knew what to look for. With the canals in the hands of the Union, this was the only way left to cross the swamp. This was Henry's salvation. Traveling at almost a crawl, Henry inched his way down the road until he finally saw a fresh mark indicating a trail was currently in use. He guided his horse off the road and onto the path. He wasn't entirely sure of his location, but once into the network of trails, he would be able to find his way quickly and easily make up the time he had lost.

Henry was able to reach the encampment as twilight fell and, much to his pleasure, he had beaten the rear of his company, albeit arriving from the opposite side of camp. First things first, he headed straight to his tent so he could wash his face and change his shirt, which was soiled and more than a little stiff with dried blood. He found that the men moved out of his way more adroitly than usual. Maybe his deeds had already run the grapevine, or maybe there was nothing out of the ordinary and his imagination was simply creating the picture he expected to see. Regardless, he was unable to make it to his tent before a young boy came running up with orders that Henry was to report to the lieutenant general's tent, double quick. Loath as he was to forego his ablutions, he dared not make Longstreet wait. So Henry handed off the reins of his mare and headed toward the center of the encampment.

Upon arrival, he announced himself to the lieutenant who was controlling admittance to Longstreet.

"Sergeant Henry reporting to see the lieutenant general."

The lieutenant remained engrossed in his papers. "What's your last name soldier?"

Henry fought back his annoyance. "It's Henry. Sergeant Thomas Henry."

At this, the lieutenant looked up. "You've got yourself two first names there haven't you? I bet that gets a might confusin'."

"Yes, sir, so I've been told, sir. That's why everyone calls me Henry and ignores the Thomas."

"Mighty sensible of you, Henry. The lieutenant general is finishin' up with someone right now. Wait here and you'll be next."

"Thank you, sir."

Henry saluted the man and stood aside to wait. He did not have long and was more than a little pleased to see Lieutenant Radcliffe exit the tent in a foul mood and storm off in the opposite direction. Whatever discussions had preceded Henry's arrival had clearly not gone in the lieutenant's favor and that lightened Henry's spirits measurably. He approached the entrance to the tent and, upon hearing a summons to enter, ducked and strode inside.

"Well, I can see by lookin' at you, there's no need to ask whether you carried out that imbecile Radcliffe's orders."

Henry was taken aback. He had never heard an officer disparage another in the presence of an enlisted man. More than that, it was obvious the general did not approve of Radcliffe's order to kill the family. Henry's mouth went dry, and he could hear the loud thump of his heart slamming against his ear drums. Longstreet had been unsure, maybe had even hoped, that Henry had disobeyed the order he had been given. What else could explain the look of resignation that fell across his face when Henry had entered the tent? The realization that Henry could have ignored the order and gotten away with it struck him like a blow and, had he had anything left in his stomach, he would have started retching all over again. There had been a choice after all.

The general started talking again, but try as he might, Henry could not make himself focus on what was being said. It was taking all of his effort to remain standing and hide the roiling turmoil that was seething in his brain. He could have chosen differently. He could have defied Radcliffe's orders. With yet another lurch to his stomach, Henry realized he had known all along. After all, hadn't he saved the infant? Hadn't he defied his orders in the leniency he had shown the babe? If he had the free will to defy the order in that regard, did not that mean that he had the free will to defy it in its entirety? With that awareness, even buried deep down, did not that mean that he had chosen to kill that family? It was this question that gripped him.

Searching for anything to anchor himself to the present and to get his mind away from the horrible, accusing thoughts that were flooding his brain, Henry desperately concentrated on his commander until his words started to break through. Mercifully, the general had not yet required Henry's participation in the conversation and appeared to be oblivious to the inner conflict raging behind Henry's stolid face.

"What I can't figure out is, if you stayed behind, how in the hell did you beat some of the men back? Those on foot escorting the slaves are still over a mile out to the north, and then I get a report that you've arrived at camp from the south. Now you're going to explain to me how in the blue blazes you managed to do that!"

Henry tried desperately to diminish the parched feel to his mouth. Failing, he spoke through the cotton that lined his cheeks and tongue.

"Sir, I took a hunting path."

"You mean through this swamp?" He poked his finger down onto the map spread out on the table in front of him, depicting a massive swamp that stood between their location and where Henry had come from. "This swamp that has no discernible safe trails and has been eatin' my men alive for weeks?"

"Yes, sir."

"These trails here?" Longstreet pointed to lines drawn through the swamp.

"No, sir, those are the canals. You don't have any of the trails marked."

"I'll be damned. When I was told the men had seen canals, I didn't believe it. Who puts a canal in a swamp? Can we use them?"

"Not easily, sir." Henry looked at the map more closely and pointed to a blank spot. "Lake Drummond is right here. After the Revolution, crews went into the swamp to build canals from one end to the other through the lake. The swamp got the better of them though, and they gave up before they finished. The canals can be used for stretches, but not all the way through. The hunting and deer trails are the only way to go from one side to another."

Longstreet nodded at the map. "Show me."

Henry swallowed hard, wishing he could give any other answer. "I can't."

Frustration flashed across the general's eyes. "Why not?"

"As your men have assuredly discovered, there are patches of this swamp that constantly fluctuate. Those patches grow and spill into different areas depending on the amount of rainfall. Therefore, the paths change, so you have to make sure you only follow the most recent marks on the trees that hunters leave. With all the hunters at war, there weren't any fresh marks. I managed to pick my way through because I know how to read the swamp as well as the marks. I could vaguely map out my path, or show soldiers the marks I made, but chances are it would only be good until the next rainfall."

Longstreet straightened himself and examined Henry as he continued to pour over the map, "How is it you come to know so much about this swamp?"

Henry moved the map on the desk so he could unroll it further, revealing the far southwestern edge. After a moment, he pointed to a spot bordering the swamp.

"My family owns this tract of land down in North Carolina. I grew up in the Dismal Swamp."

A smile spread across Longstreet's face. "That is the best news I have heard all day."

7
Sides Chosen

By the time Emma made it back to the plantation, her home was irrevocably lost to the fire. She had expected that; what she had not expected was to find her father and baby brother missing. The stress broke her, and panicking, Emma began to scream her father's and Peter's names and rush about trying to find them, going everywhere and nowhere at the same time. The two remaining slaves came out from their hiding place in the trees and approached her warily. Upon seeing them, Emma rushed to the slave in the lead and grabbed his shirt front.

"Where is my father? Where is Peter? What have you done with them?"

The slave in the rear rushed forward holding the bassinet.

"Here, here. The boy is here."

He put the bassinet on the ground and Emma collapsed to her knees and clutched the baby to her chest relaxing somewhat. She looked up at the slaves.

"Where is my father?"

The first slave replied, "A man came and poked around. Called for you. When he didn't find no one alive, he put the massa on his horse and rode off."

"Blackie?" The slaves stared at her blankly. "How would you know—never mind."

Emma rocked her brother and for a long moment stared into the still-burning flames, letting the pulsing heat wash through her numbness. She eventually realized the unrelenting gaze from the slaves was not going to cease until she said something to them. She had no idea what to do with them. She also realized she had no desire to have them around. From what she knew, slaves were completely reliant on their owners to tell them what to do. She had no need for that kind of burden right now. Dealing with Peter and figuring out what to do was enough. So she did the only thing she could think of.

"Go. You're free; I have no need of you. Find some other master, do whatever you need to do, only leave here."

Both slaves looked at her in disbelief for a brief moment before turning and melting back into the woods.

Emma returned her gaze to the inferno and let the dancing waves of destruction mesmerize her for a time. When the heat finally became too much, she turned away with no idea where to go. She looked for her horse, but being afraid of the fire, it had run off, probably back home to the blacksmith's. Blackie. It had to have been Blackie who came looking for her and took her father's body. He would help. Placing her brother in the bassinet and lifting it, she was about to curse herself for not properly tying up the horse, when it occurred to her that there was no way to mount a horse while still in her overskirt *and* holding a baby. Instead, she cursed the encumbrances of being a woman and began the long walk into town.

By the time Emma arrived on the outskirts of town, it was only sheer force of will that kept her putting one foot in front of the other. Her

65

inner thighs had begun to bleed from her ill-equipped rides on the horse; her feet were covered in blisters from walking into town twice in one day; and her arms felt as though they might fall off completely from carrying her brother. She had abandoned the bassinet, unable to take the added weight, and had simply been holding Peter to her chest by wrapping her arms around him and grasping her elbows. He was wailing, but she did not have the wherewithal to do anything about it. She had given up trying to fight her skirt and was stepping on it, trying her best not to trip and fall.

Mercifully, Blackie saw her crest the hill into town and came running to her aid. He lifted her, Peter and all, into his strong arms and carried her back to his rooms above the forge. From there his wife took the baby and instructed him to place Emma in a bed. Peter finally stopped crying and looked about with weepy, wide eyes, until Blackie's wife presented him with a cloth soaked in what Emma assumed was milk or sugar water. Peter sucked on it greedily, and only after the cloth had been rewetted several times for him was Peter content.

Blackie gave Emma a concerned look, whispered something to his wife, and then returned to the forge. His wife confirmed Emma's theory. It had been Blackie at the plantation, and afraid that he had somehow passed Emma on her way back into town, he threw Daniel's body across his horse, and retraced his steps. Still not finding her, Blackie detoured to the makeshift Army hospital—they were more than capable of handling a dead body—before returning home. He had hoped to find Emma there, but she was nowhere to be seen. When his missing horse arrived at the stable without her, Blackie had assumed the worst but had still kept a hopeful eye out for her all the same.

Emma listened, but showed no signs of comprehending, as Blackie's wife set about cleaning her up as best she could. She removed Emma's dress and placed the tattered remains on a pile of clothes that Emma vaguely recognized as her petticoats. Someone had obviously found them behind the forge. Then the woman heated up some water and set about cleaning the wounds on Emma's legs and feet, and once those were properly bandaged, cleaning the soot and dirt off the rest of Emma's exposed skin.

Emma allowed her to work and offered no resistance. She could not even find it within herself to be self-conscious or embarrassed at being exposed in front of someone she hardly knew. When Blackie's wife was finally finished, she covered Emma with a blanket and turned her attention back to Peter. He cooed and gurgled while Emma drifted off to a fitful sleep.

Emma awoke late the next day, rested but numb. The apartments were empty. Blackie's wife must have taken Peter with her, allowing Emma to sleep longer. Moving proved to be more of a challenge than she had expected; her whole body ached from the day before. Slowly she got up to look around for something she could wear, as she was practically naked under the bedclothes. She wrapped a sheet around herself, but before she could begin her exploration, she realized that she had not woken by chance. There was an intense argument downstairs that was almost loud enough to discern from her bed. She crept over to the door and cracked it open the tiniest bit. That was enough for her to hear clearly. Blackie was arguing with another man, one whose voice Emma did not recognize.

"It is suspected that she was workin' as a messenger for her father. You do not want to get caught up in that, do you? Last I checked, espionage is treason."

"I will say it again. I have not seen the girl."

"Liar! She was seen here yesterday morning."

"Yes, she came in, as I have said. Then she sneaked out the back and stole one of my damn horses! Why would I harbor someone who has stolen from me?"

"But you have her brother. Your wife was seen with the baby this morning."

"I found him when I rode out to the plantation to retrieve my horse. The house was on fire and Daniel was dead. The boy was the only one alive. What was I supposed to do? I don't care if they were workin' for the Union, I was not going to leave the boy to die. I'll warrant that you would have done the same."

There was a tense pause and Emma waited until the conversation resumed before she closed the door. She stood frozen and scared, looking down at her hand on the door handle. They were looking for her. She did not know who they were, but she did not want to be found. She could not stay here. Her visit the day before was already causing Blackie trouble. Peter was a baby. He could stay. He would be safe. He would be safe as long as he was not with her. Her heart clenched at the thought of leaving him behind, but she had to protect him, and her only hope of that was to abandon him. For everyone's sake, she needed to leave and get far, far away.

Emma crept silently over to her clothes. There was no way she could wear them. Whoever was looking for her undoubtedly had a description of her dress. Everyone in town had seen her in it yesterday morning. Not to mention, it was completely ruined. Dropping her dress on the floor, she scanned the small room until her eyes landed on a wardrobe. Inside, folded in a pile at the bottom, she found a man's breeches and shirt, which were much too small to have belonged to Blackie. It was then she remembered that they had a son; a son who had enlisted two years earlier when war first broke out, never to be heard from again. The thought made her feel a twinge of guilt as she pulled the shirt over her head and then eased on the breeches. His shoes were much too big for her, but with her blisters there was no way she was going to put hers back on, so she wadded up her stockings, shoved them in the toe of each shoe, and then pulled the laces as tight as they would go. Looking in the mirror, she thought she cut quite a dashing figure. Even with her sixteen years, she still had not developed the curves or bust that even her younger friends had—something she had previously lamented, not been grateful for. Taking a closer look in the mirror, she saw the feminine attributes that she did possess could easily be concealed by pulling her hair back and adding a coat. Both of which she was able to accomplish with further investigations into the wardrobe.

Her transformation completed, Emma stole downstairs hoping to slip out the back. Blackie was there waiting for her. It was as if he had known her intentions. Her appearance startled him, and he gazed at her as if he were seeing a ghost. Emma looked at him sympathetically.

"I apologize; were these your son's clothes? I had nothing else to wear."

Clearing a lump from his throat, Blackie replied, "That's all right, you're welcome to them. But you should not be out of bed."

Before he could continue, Emma cut him off. "I can't stay here; I'm endangering both you and your wife. I overheard your conversation with that man." She blushed at the admission.

"Forget him, we will keep you hidden. It will be all right."

"No, please. Someone would eventually find out. It's not safe."

"Emma, it is a risk that we are willin' to take. My wife and I spoke this mornin'—"

"Blackie, no, you don't understand. My family is gone, my whole family except Peter. So now, my only job in this world is to keep him safe, and the only way to do that is if he is nowhere near me. Tell me I am wrong. Tell me of a better way to guarantee his safety."

"This will blow over."

"I am not willing to risk you being wrong. I am not willing to gamble with his life. He's a baby." She paused for his rebuttal.

He did not say anything, though the look on his face said that he was not convinced.

"You know that if you stop me now, I will leave tonight when you are asleep, or tomorrow when you are working and distracted. With or without your blessing, I am leaving."

Resigned, Blackie rubbed at the back of his neck. "Where will you go?"

"I don't know. It is probably best if you do not know anyway. It is best if you forget I was ever here. They think I'm a spy."

Blackie nodded. "I have a little bit of money saved that I can give you, and you will take a horse." Emma started to protest, but it was Blackie's turn to cut her off. "No, you will take the money, the horse, and some food. I may not be able to stop you from leavin', but I'll be

70

damned if I will allow you to leave empty-handed."

"Thank you." Emma smiled up at him, and reluctantly he smiled back. "Promise me that you will take care of Peter."

"As if he were our own."

Emma fell into his arms and hugged him tight.

It was not until Emma was well out of town that she realized she had forgotten to say goodbye to Peter. Perhaps it was better this way. A few months from now, he would not even remember her and she did not need a fresh memory of his face to remind her of all that she had lost. She had enough images to haunt her: the battle in the valley, her father's tortured face, and her home in flames. Mostly it was the image of the soldier covered in blood gently placing her brother's bassinet in the shade that kept coming back to her. She could not make sense of his actions. Had he tried to save the rest of her family? Is that where the blood had come from? Why had he made sure no one was around to see him save the boy? She chewed over this action and its possible motivations as she rode with no particular destination in mind.

She stopped only when she had to. Mercifully, because of an extra blanket Blackie had provided to help cushion her damaged legs, she was able to ride for longer stretches than she had originally anticipated. When she did stop, she camped in the woods, dining on dried or salted foodstuffs that Blackie had given her and sleeping in starts, curled up behind whatever copse afforded the best concealment from the road. Her goal was to avoid people as much as possible, especially anyone in uniform, and she had been largely successful at accomplishing that goal. If she had not been so tired, she would have been proud of herself for transitioning into this new way of life so easily. It was as if she had been born to live on the run, existing in the shadows.

After a night filled with rain, however, the glamor of her new existence disappeared. So the next morning, when a merchant mentioned that troops were expected in town before nightfall, she heeded the warning. Despite her initial gut reaction to hide in the woods as far away from any soldiers as she could get, an ominous rumble in the sky convinced her that putting a roof over her head was an excellent idea. Emma decided to find the nearest room for rent and hunker down in there until the men and the storm were long gone.

She came upon a smallish inn first. They had rooms available and a stable in the back for her horse. The matronly woman behind the desk took her money eagerly. She offered, for a little bit more, to draw up a steaming bath in the washroom where "he" could relax while they washed "his" clothes. Looking down at herself, Emma noticed for the first time how filthy she was, so it only took a little more cajoling before she handed over the extra coins and took a gratifying breath, already imagining sliding into the hot water. Even more gratifying was when the woman called to her daughter to heat up water for "this young man."

The bath felt as good as Emma had imagined, however it proved to be much less relaxing than she had hoped. While the washroom was empty of any other inhabitants, the daughter kept popping in and out, first to gather Emma's clothes, then to see if anything was needed, then to offer a back scrub. While her back did need a good scrubbing, especially the places she could not reach, she was not about to ask the daughter to do it for fear of revealing her true gender. Eventually, Emma gave up on the bath and retreated to her room.

A week ago, if Emma had been asked to sleep in this bed, she would have made a fuss that it was lumpy and completely unsuitable. Today, she curled up and would have fallen into a deep sleep had the daughter not burst in to hang Emma's freshly washed clothing up to finish drying. The daughter lingered and only left when Emma expressly ordered her to do so and not to return unless she was called for. Emma had the distinct impression that the daughter normally provided a lot more for their young male clientele than merely a wash and dry service. When the door finally closed behind the daughter, and her footsteps on the stairs had faded away, Emma lay back and fell into a deep sleep.

When Emma awoke, it was dark and she was uncertain of exactly how long she had slept. The hunger gnawing at her stomach made her think she had slept through several days, but grabbing her shirt and feeling the remaining dampness, she realized that it was still the same day. She struggled into her clammy clothes, opened the door, and peered out into the hallway. There was no one around, but there was a ruckus coming from downstairs. Clearly, the soldiers had arrived and some of them had taken up lodgings here. Emma regretted dispatching the daughter so completely, as a meal in her room would be ideal right about now. She still had some dried food, but the thought of a warm meal emboldened her. Emma readied herself for what she might encounter and headed down. She wasn't half-way down the hall when she heard footsteps coming up the stairs and a voice she recognized, a voice she would recognize for the rest of her life: Brigadier General Wild. Quickly she ducked into the nearest room. As fate would have it,

73

it was Wild's room. Hearing him approach the door, she scanned the room for any possible exit. Not finding one, she spied the wardrobe and dove inside, getting the door almost completely closed before the men entered the room.

Emma held her breath and prayed the general had not returned to his room to fetch the jacket that was now brushing the top of her head as she sat wedged in the corner. Luckily, none of the men approached the wardrobe. Instead she heard them take seats, content to finish their conversation, unaware of her proximity. Breathing once more, Emma listened to the conversation.

"Do we know the extent of the damage caused?"

Emma did not recognize the first voice, but Wild replied, "Unknown at this point and we won't know for some time. We already have a new table, but until we have had time to disseminate it to all of our resources, they will continue to use the old one. Hell, most of them don't even know it's been compromised yet."

"Which means we're vulnerable."

"We're vulnerable. And worse yet, we have no idea if O'Neal gave them the newest key or an old one, or all of them for that matter."

"This is why we can't trust these small town folk. As well intentioned as they are, they do not hold up. We can't rely on them."

Emma bit into her knuckle to keep herself from crying, or screaming out in indignation, or bursting out of the wardrobe and kicking the general right in the shins. How could they say that? Her father had risked his life and had been tortured to death to keep their secret, and this was the thanks he got.

"What about that girl? Couldn't she tell us?"

"That damn girl ran off before we could interrogate her, and now no one can find her. How did she disappear like that? She's a girl for God's sake!"

Emma's anger abated somewhat from the pride that welled in her chest. They were looking for her, and she had outwitted them. She was sitting listening to their discourse and they were none the wiser. A small smile broke the stern set of her face. They would remain none the wiser and she would get whatever she could from them. These ungrateful bastards were going to pay for taking advantage of her family. A knock on the door startled her out of her thoughts.

"Enter!"

"Sir, sorry to bother you. There appears to be an issue downstairs. It seems one of the men made a pass at the innkeeper's daughter and him being not only a Yankee, but a Negro Yankee..." The man trailed off into silence, not wanting to finish the sentence. He didn't need to. The general was already up and halfway to the door.

"Blast them all to hell! This is the first warm bed I've seen in weeks!"

The general stormed out of the room, followed by his companions who slammed the door with a resounding slap behind them. Emma's smile had grown. If she had known the daughter was going to come in so handy, she would have been nicer to her earlier. Emma opened the wardrobe door, walked over to the desk, and started to shuffle through the papers to see if there was anything that looked to be of importance. For the most part, it looked like personal correspondence. Wild apparently wrote to his wife often, as well as some woman named Mrs. Stowe. Interesting. Buried underneath the pile of letters, she found a small scrap with letters and numbers on it in a grid that did not seem to correspond to anything. Upon closer inspection, her father's letter sprang into her mind. This had to be that table they had been talking about.

Emma sifted through the desk trying to find a blank sheet of paper, but there was none to be found. She held her breath for a second and then decided that Wild might not notice if one of his wife's letters went missing. Flipping it over she began to copy, as accurately as possible, each little symbol and number on the slip of paper. She was about half-way through when she heard the heavy tread of boots coming down the hall. She shoved the scrap back under the pile of letters, tried to make the desk look as it had before, and then crawled under the bed as the door opened and Wild fumed in. He began to pack up his belongings, including a broad sweep of his hand to gather all of the correspondence on the desk in one move. Emma breathed a sigh of relief; if he noticed the letter's absence, he would assume he dropped it in his haste while packing. As quickly as he had stormed in, he stormed back out yelling orders as he stomped down the stairs.

Emma stayed under the bed until she heard the commotion of horses and men outside in the courtyard die down, until all that was left was the baying of a hound dog whose sleep had been rudely disturbed. Carefully, she slid out from under the bed and snuck back to her own room. Once safely inside, she looked at what she had copied. She had only had time to get through about half of them, and the last couple were smudged a bit but were still discernible. Satisfied that even though it was not a complete table, someone would find it valuable. She tucked it away with the letter from her father and then climbed back into bed.

With the soldiers on the move, there was no reason why she could not enjoy the rest of the night sleeping in a bed. The thought of food crossed her mind briefly as she was drifting off, but she decided sleep was more appealing, and breakfast was not that far off.

8

An Absurd Proposition

For reasons that remained elusive to Anna, Kady continued to follow her throughout the house. What had started out as the occasional encounter became a less-than-discreet stalking, which had turned into a now dogged following of her every move. Anna did her best to ignore her daughter, and had even gone so far as to oversee the mucking out of the chicken coop to have an hour's respite of her company. What Anna had done to pique her interest, for the first time in the entirety of the girl's life, Anna did not know. Enough was enough. Kady might be content to follow Anna about like the worst spy in Christendom, but Anna was determined to lose her pursuer.

Stopping in the middle of the drawing room, Anna twirled on her heels in time to watch Kady career into her because she was not paying attention. Recovering from the shock of the impact, Anna held Kady out at arm's length.

"Good heavens, girl! What has gotten into your head that you must follow my every step from sun-up to sun-down? If you insist on acting like a lost little child, I shall have your father find you a new wet nurse, so I can go about my business without you tripping up my skirts."

Her words had the intended effect. Instinctively, as was her wont, Kady's lower lip started to jut out, quivering. Even with her eighteen years, Kady had never lost her childish pout, probably because unleashing it on her father got her whatever she desired.

"Well, out with it!" Anna had no idea what to expect from her daughter. The blunt, matter-of-fact response stopped the blood in her veins.

"I want to be a spy like you." Kady blushed slightly but kept her gaze steady on her mother. Anna's mind raced. How did Kady know she was a spy? And if Kady knew, had she told her father? Trying to stave off the rising panic, Anna reassured herself that there was no way Kady could possibly know. Perhaps she read about a spy in one of her father's newspapers and that put the idea into her head. Anna tried to brush her off.

"Stop being ridiculous and go practice your music." Dropping her hands from her daughter's arms, Anna turned and started once more across the room, holding her breath.

"I'm not being ridiculous; I want to be a spy like you. I heard you talking to Mary about it, the day she was beaten. I figure if a servant can be a spy, I can be a spy." Anna stopped, while Kady continued. "Life is so boring with the war going on. There are hardly any dances anymore, and letter writing is next to useless unless I can send a servant to deliver it. Not to mention, I haven't gotten any new music in months, I have to make up my own now. Spying sounds as if it would be a great diversion! So I want to be a spy. Teach me how."

Anna turned and, brushing past her daughter, walked to the open door, looked into the hall to make sure they hadn't been overheard, then closed it securely. Holy God, Kady knew. Anna felt nauseous and faint and as if she wanted to scream. The little twit actually knew. Why hadn't Anna been arrested yet? Why hadn't Andrew confronted her? How long did she have? Taking a deep breath, she turned and walked back to her daughter.

"Whom have you told?"

"Whom have I told what?"

Anna grabbed her arms roughly and Kady squeaked.

"Who else knows about the conversation you overheard?"

The sense of excitement had faded from Kady's face, replaced by fear from Anna's intensity.

"Whom have you told that I am a spy?"

"No, no one. I haven't told anyone."

"Not even your father?" Anna's grip tightened.

"Of course not! To be a spy you have to keep secrets, so I kept yours."

Anna loosened her grip on her daughter's arms, but her gaze didn't waver, waiting for the tiniest hint in Kady's eyes that she was lying.

"I swear, I didn't tell anybody. I didn't even tell Mary I knew, and she's in on the game. I also haven't told father about the hat you bought me. I figured you were testing me and it turns out that I am quite good at keeping secrets."

With a quaking sigh of relief, Anna walked over to a chair and sat down heavily, letting her face fall into her hands. She knew from the moment she had said yes to the hat that she would come to regret the decision. She just had no idea that it would manifest like this. At least Kady hadn't told anybody, yet. It was simply a matter of time before she did. She would either slip up and tell someone in her excitement, or get her feelings hurt and run to her daddy. That's what she always did.

Thank God she was bored, or Anna would be sitting in jail, not the drawing room.

How could Kady see this as a game? You do not become a spy because you are bored! Or maybe it could be a game. Maybe Anna could pretend to include her? Say she was a spy, but not actually involve her in anything. No, she would be as dangerous as a fake spy. Maybe if she hit her over the head hard enough she would forget the whole thing. It was possible. One of their slaves had fallen out of the hayloft of the barn, and when he finally woke up, the previous two months were completely gone from his memory. No, she couldn't hit Kady over the head. With Anna's luck she'd kill her, and then being a spy would be the least of her worries. She had to convince Kady that becoming a spy was a bad idea, and then somehow cajole her into keeping her mouth shut.

Anna rubbed her face and let out a quiet groan of exasperation. Taking this as a concession, Kady immediately brightened and practically skipped over to the chair next to her mother.

"Oooh, I get to be a spy! When do I start? What do I do? Is it dangerous?" The romantic relish she emphasized in her last question snapped Anna out of her contemplations.

"No, absolutely not. This is not a game to play. You are too young and far too silly—"

"But—"

"I said, no!" The words came out with a vehement finality that made Kady's face fall. Anna had to find a way to explain. Her eyes grew tender. "You want to know how dangerous? Mary got beaten to within an inch of her life. A member of my spy ring was discovered and then hung before the day was through. This is more dangerous than you can even fathom. I beg of you, forget this idea and go back to playing your piano and dreaming of the handsome man you want to marry. You cannot be a spy, I will not allow it."

"Then I'll tell Fa—" Kady stopped herself before she completed her age-old rebuttal. But it was too late. Anna knew how the threat ended and the tenderness in her eyes vanished, replaced by a burning fire.

"You'll tell your father, will you? That is precisely why you can't be a spy. You're still a little girl who runs crying to her father whenever she doesn't get her way." Bitterness had crept its way into Anna's voice. "You realize, don't you, that I'm working against your beloved daddy? If you join me, you'll be working against him, too, which means no more running to him when something goes wrong. No more basking in his attention and getting everything you have ever wanted, because when he finds out—and he will find out—he will not only turn against you, he will turn you out. No piano, no pretty dresses, no dowry, and especially no marriage. Your pampered life will be over. And if you go and tell him about me, after knowing for so long without saying anything, he'll think you're complicit anyway. Your only option is to keep quiet."

Kady looked hurt and was momentarily speechless. Anna felt a twinge of guilt at the threat, even if it was a hollow threat. She did not regret saying it, though; it was imperative that Kady remained silent. Kady finally regained her voice, but under Anna's withering gaze, all of her conviction was lost.

"Daddy would never turn me out."

"Are you willing to take that chance in order to have a little diversion during this 'boring' war?" Anna threw Kady's words back at her, and after a moment, Kady's gaze dropped. "That's what I thought. I don't want to hear you talk of this nonsense ever again."

Anna stood and exited the room, leaving Kady in her seat fitfully playing with the folds in her dress.

9
The Letter

Anna had never been so nervous in her entire life. It wasn't a big deal; Mary would be fine. She was simply dropping off a basket of tobacco at a neighboring farmhouse—something that she had done a hundred times. Yes, this time she was also picking up correspondence on her way back from a hiding place in a hollowed-out tree. But that was no reason to be concerned. After all, a slave walking up to a tree on the side of the road looked less suspicious than Anna walking up to a tree on the side of the road, and *she* had yet to arouse suspicion.

Or had she? Maybe that was what prompted Kady to start listening at doors. She had heard the slaves whispering. Nonsense, that was just bad luck, and Anna had taken care of that. She was certain that Kady would keep her mouth shut. There was no way the girl would ever risk displeasing her father. It was fine. She would stay quiet, Mary would return with no incident, and everything would go on as normal. Anna started pacing in front of the window in her bedroom. The window afforded her no view of the road Mary would be returning on, but Anna wanted to be somewhere private when Mary arrived so they could talk.

The door opened, and at the noise Anna let out a sharp scream of surprise, startling Mary who stopped in the doorway.

"If you don't quiet your nerves, you're going to faint," Mary warned.

Flustered, Anna rushed across the room, ushering Mary inside and closing the door firmly behind her. Mary walked in casually and began to straighten the bedclothes. Anna stared at her exasperated.

"Well?"

"That's where we get the water. You thirsty, I'll fetch a glass."

"What? No, I am not thirsty," Anna glared at Mary. "I want to know how your errand went."

"Jus' fine. It was a nice day for a walk." Mary moved on to straightening the already tidy dresser.

"Not too windy for you?"

"No, no. The breeze was nice." Mary turned to Anna and managed to keep a straight face but couldn't keep the sparkle of mischief out of her eyes.

"Good. Nothing untoward happened?"

"Oh no. I didn't run across a soul."

"Mary!"

At this, Mary smiled a wicked grin, and stooped to pull a letter out from her skirts. She had folded it to get it to fit.

"I did come across this here on my way back. I suspect it be for you."

Mary handed Anna the letter and walked out of the room, with Anna glaring at her the whole way. So this was Mary's way of telling Anna that she had made too much fuss over a simple letter retrieval. She couldn't help it. Anna didn't mind putting herself in danger, but she hated the thought of someone else getting into trouble. She would have to get used to that now.

Anna took a steadying breath and looked down at the letter in her hands. It was much larger than the normal missives she usually received. She sat and broke the seal.

July 1, 1863

My Dearest,

I have tried to write you so many times but have been thwarted in my attempts. I scarcely have time now. With the losses today weighing heavily in the air, there is a foreboding on the wind for what will come tomorrow. As such, I do not have time to code this, so will try to speak circumspectly. I rejoined my regiment in time to discover that it was being disbanded and men were being sent home.

My heart leapt that I would be back in your arms shortly. However, we soon found out that a large portion of us had signed three-year contracts instead of two. I signed a three-year contract and thus was transferred to the 20th Maine under Colonel Chamberlain. There has been much upset and rancor amongst the men, myself included! My only consolation is that Chamberlain appears to be a competent leader and the men in Company F, my new company, seem to be good lads, even if there are more than a few fresh fish.

I have never seen so many troops assembled in one place, as there are here. We lost the town of Gettysburg today, and while we have not received any orders as of yet, I'm sure we will try to take it back tomorrow, so I must finish this and get it sent off if I am to have any hopes of it reaching you. Keep your ear to the ground my love. Until I hold you again, my hands will forever feel empty. All of my love. SK

Aug 1, 1863

Did SK survive Gettysburg?
NR

24-31-63 34 34-32-45-61
23-25-23 43-46 43-31-56-36-25-36-66
63-66-55-55-11-43-51-31-56-63
54-56

10
Skeletons

At first, Henry was shocked when he was given his orders. He had unexpectedly received a field promotion to second lieutenant, along with his own men to lead. He had even been allowed to request that Williams, the only man Henry had met whom he truly trusted, be added to the roster. It was only after reviewing the specifics of his orders that it became abundantly clear why he had been promoted. There was a small contingent of slaves, assumed to be working for the Union Army that kept attacking Longstreet's foragers. Every time Confederate troops would try to engage them, they would simply disappear into the surrounding swamplands without a trace. Therefore, everyone assumed these slaves had escaped from neighboring plantations. The only way to catch them would be to send in someone who knew the area; someone who knew the area as only a little boy who had grown up in those swamps could know them. Someone like him.

So it was that Henry found himself once more riding his horse through the dense trees of North Carolina, not more than a stone's throw from the plantation where he had grown up. He had been given twenty-five men. Henry opted to take only four—those who still had their own horses but hadn't been transferred to the cavalry. He knew if they were to catch these slaves, it was not going to be superior numbers that would get the job done. He needed speed and maneuverability. At first, not even that helped. Henry and his men could never seem to get ahead of the slaves. They only saw the aftermath of where they had already hit and disappeared. Once into the swamp, there was no hope of tracking them. It was not until Longstreet and his men moved north that Henry and his men had a chance. With the foragers gone, there was only one supply route left in use. Henry began mapping out the ambush locations, which narrowed down where they would most likely strike next. Since they had yet to repeat a location, Henry figured there was only one viable option left.

As hoped, they made good time, arriving well before the supply line was supposed to go through. Henry pulled out his map and noted the different locations of each of the attacks to reassure himself that he was right. Yes. This is where they would attack, and Henry only had an hour or two to lay the appropriate trap. Despite the dense trees from which they had emerged, the vegetation was relatively sparse at this stretch of the road. There was only one tree big enough to provide any sort of cover and only then if you were willing to crouch down among its gnarled roots. On the other side of the road was a marsh that stretched for miles. It was the last place anyone would expect an attack. After a few minutes, one of his men rode up beside him with a map out.

"Henry?"

"Lieutenant." Despite the official announcement of his promotion, Henry knew the disregard often shown a brevet officer when out of earshot of commissioned officers.

"Second Lieutenant Henry, my apologies, sir, but are you sure this is the spot? Me and the boys were thinkin' this spot over here looks a bit better for a raid," the man said pointing to his own map. "You know, hills to hide behind. Trees. This over here is all marshy and open."

"I'm sure this is the spot," Henry retorted.

"All due respect, but—"

"Trust me." Henry grabbed the map and pointed at the men's spot. "Anybody who knows this area would never choose that hill because it is covered in poison ivy. Even if you were able to avoid the ivy, crazy old man Willard owns all of this land to the west of the road. He spends all day wandering across his property in the hopes of finding a trespasser to shoot, and that was before the war. Lord knows what kind of traps and weapons he has set up now. That right there is probably the safest stretch of road along the entire supply route." Henry dismounted and marched over to the side of the road. Pulling his knife, he circled the tree a bit, then began to dig under a gnarled root.

"Besides, if this isn't the spot, then what is this?" Making a clean slice with his knife he pulled the end of a rope free, and with a sharp jerk sent dirt flying up across the road as a trip line sprang free from its earthly confines. Startled, the horses began to panic and Henry immediately regretted his theatrics. Dropping the rope, he helped calm the horses.

"This is the first step of their plan: send all of the horses into a panic so they can attack during the ensuing chaos."

"How in the world did you know that was there?"

"Because it's what I would do." Truth be told, it's exactly what Henry had done as a boy, in this exact same spot, which also meant Henry knew who was leading these slaves.

"They'll come in using the ditch across the road so they're not seen, then hide in the marsh and here in the roots of the tree to wait for the supply wagons to come through." Henry began to rebury the rope, doing his best to make it look undisturbed.

"How are they gonna hide in the marsh?"

"You don't have to hide. As long as you hunker down and hold perfectly still, a man's eyes will pass right over you without registering you are there. It's the perfect location because no one would ever suspect men to be hiding there—too many snakes." The men stood staring at Henry, one a little squeamish from the mention of snakes.

"So, where do we hide so we can catch them once they're in position?"

"We don't. We catch them before they get into position. Follow me." With that, Henry remounted his horse and started down the road at a gallop; his men fell in line dutifully behind him.

When they were a couple of miles down the road, Henry turned onto a small rutted path, slowing down markedly so the horses could more easily keep their footing. Once the path had entered dense vegetation, Henry dismounted and tied his horse's reins to the nearest tree. His men followed suit, then stood anxiously, looking to him for orders.

"Dawson, you stay here. If I'm wrong, and they approach from this direction, I don't want them stealing our horses. If you see them, fire your weapon and we will double back. The rest of you, follow me. Stay close and keep quiet."

His men obeyed, without a word uttered. Apparently his uncanny knowledge of the area and how the attack was going to be carried out had earned him some respect. He set his pace as fast as the terrain allowed, and he soon heard two of his men breathing hard, struggling to keep up. Henry did not slow, though; they had two miles to cover, and he had no idea how early the slaves would arrive to await the convoy. They made good time, and when they were less than a quarter of a mile from the ambush location, Henry stopped so his men could catch their breaths. If the slaves were already in position, the soldiers would need to sneak up on them, and there was no way to do that with half the men gasping for air and clutching their sides. Clearly Henry should have chosen men not based on whether or not they had a horse, but on their athleticism.

"I'm going to move in closer to see if they have arrived yet. Williams, you come with me. You two stay here and, for God's sake, catch your breath! An old maid who's deaf in both ears would hear you coming."

Nodding their acknowledgment, the men collapsed to the ground, thankful for the respite. Henry disappeared into the trees, and Williams followed after. As they drew nearer to the ditch, they heard hushed talking and dropped to their bellies to listen. They couldn't understand what was being said, but Henry was able to make out four distinct voices. He held up four fingers to Williams, who nodded his agreement. Before Henry could decide upon a plan of action, the slaves split into two groups and headed in different directions. Two of them went away from the road, deeper into the woods. The other two, jumping into the ditch, made their way toward the road. It was in this pair that Henry recognized the light-skinned Negro, Nat. Henry ground his teeth, saddened that he was correct about who was leading this band, then gestured to Williams that they would follow the pair heading into the woods. Williams began to draw out his pistol. Henry shook his head.

"No shooting. We need to take them quietly and alive," Henry whispered.

Williams nodded his understanding and they started to pick their way after the two slaves. They did not have to go far before they found the two men preparing a sledge that was obviously to be used to haul away the supplies they were about to steal. They had gotten one of the runners stuck on a tree root, and thus they were both highly distracted with their backs to Henry and Williams. Henry signaled to Williams to take the one on the right, while he would take the one on the left. They sneaked out from the trees and behind the slaves without alerting them of their presence. Henry hit his man across the back of his head with the butt of his gun, knocking him unconscious with one blow, while Williams got the other one in a choke hold, wrestling him to the ground until he too was unconscious. Panting from his exertions, Williams looked at Henry.

"I thought you said no guns!"

Henry smiled. "I said no shooting, I didn't say anything about no guns."

Williams chuckled and shook his head.

"Should we tie them up?" Without waiting for a response, Williams grabbed a rope from a pile on the sledge and threw it to Henry before grabbing one for himself.

"Yes, and gag them, in case they wake up before we have the other two."

"Do you think there's only four of them causin' all this damage?"

"I don't see why not. They have the element of surprise on their hands, not to mention a deep knowledge of their surroundings so they

93

can disappear at will. With that trip line they set up, panicking the horses, I could have taken out all four of you this morning by myself. Superior brains will overcome superior numbers anytime."

"But they're Negroes!"

"Just because they are Negroes doesn't mean they are dumb. Why do you think they've lasted this long? Everyone has assumed they're a huge group of ignorant heathens overpowering our men. No one has given them credit for thinking and planning out these attacks strategically."

Williams was about to argue the point, when they heard someone approaching. They both fell back into the woods and were barely able to conceal themselves before one of the slaves from the other pair rounded the corner and, upon seeing his colleagues bound and gagged, ran toward them. Williams circled in behind him and cracked him on the head with the butt of his gun, knocking him to the ground. Williams smiled at Henry and pointed to the butt of his gun before stooping to tie the man up. Henry chuckled and grabbed the other two, dragging them into the underbrush by the path. When Williams was finished, he dragged the third over to his companions. Henry looked down approvingly.

"That leaves one."

"Should we go get the rest of the men?"

"Not yet, let them rest. After all, they'll be the ones hauling the sledge."

"Yes, sir." Williams smiled. "Number four then?"

"Yep."

Henry led off with Williams close on his heels. They made their way back down the path and, arriving at the ditch, jumped in and continued toward the road. The closer they got to it, the higher the water level became until they were up to their waists in murky, muddy water, which was actually a nice respite from the summer heat. The ditch eventually opened up into the marsh and they were right up against the bank to the road. Henry stopped and turned back to Williams.

"All right, he's probably going to be encamped across the way, hidden in the tree roots. I'm thinking this is as good a place as any for us to cross, but we have to stay down." Henry looked up the slippery bank. "The real trick is going to be getting up onto the road. See if you can find a good spot."

Henry started rummaging through the foliage along the bank trying to find an embedded root or some sort of foot hold they could use to climb up, when Williams started to slowly back away. He hissed, the panic in his voice rising precipitously.

"Sir, sir, behind you!"

Henry turned to see a water moccasin coming up on him fast. He was clearly in the snake's territory, and the snake was not happy about it. Backing away, Henry tried to get his knife pulled, but the snake was on him before he could get it out of his belt, striking at Henry with its white mouth gaping. He put up his arm to protect his body and the fangs sunk in below the elbow. Henry bellowed in pain. He finally got his knife free and sliced the snake in half; its thick muscular body falling into the water. He pried the fangs out of his forearm and flung the head out across the marsh.

The pain was immediate and intense, causing Henry to feel light-headed. Williams found a spot to scramble up to the road and from his vantage point above, reached down and dragged Henry up with him. Henry lay in the dirt clutching his arm. His mind was racing, but everything else around him seemed to be going slower than usual. Henry rolled over to give Williams instructions, only to see Williams busy trying to subdue Nat. Hearing the scream, and thinking it was one of his men, Nat had come to help. Before either man was able to get the upper hand, the supply convoy rounded the corner. Seeing the skirmish, several men leapt down from their wagons and now had their guns trained on all of them, unsure of what was happening.

Henry tried to stand up to explain the situation. He was so dizzy he fell back into the dirt. Williams, extricating himself from Nat with a final kick, stood up and explained who they were, and asked for medical attention for Henry. By now the convoy's commanding officer had joined them and volunteered to provide transportation. As they did not have a medic with them, they could do nothing more. Lost as to where they would go, Williams looked down at Henry, then quickly moved to his side to help him up.

"About five miles down the road there's a plantation to the right. Take me there," Henry instructed. "Williams, get the other men and the prisoners and follow."

Mercifully, the convoy's officer took charge and started barking orders to his men, two of whom grabbed Henry underneath the arms and half carried, half dragged him to one of the wagons. Once inside, it immediately started moving. An enlisted man ran up behind and jumped into the wagon with Henry.

"I hear you met a cotton mouth, nasty vermin those are. Not normally quick to bite, though. You musta found its nest, ya lucky bugger. Let's take a look." He helped Henry out of his coat, then abandoned all ceremony and whipped out his knife to cut off Henry's shirtsleeve. The area around the punctures was already bright red and significantly swollen, with the venom going about its business. The man took off his neckerchief and tied it tightly around Henry's bicep to slow the flow of venom. Retrieving his knife once more, he made a cut from one puncture wound to the other and began to suck out the venom. The man sucked on the wound and then spat the bloody mess out the back of the wagon for what seemed like an eternity. By the time the man stopped, Henry was clammy and cold all over, despite the hot day, and on the verge of losing consciousness. The man grabbed a bottle of whiskey from one of the crates in the wagon and swished it around his mouth several times to clear out the venom. Once he was satisfied that none remained, he took several deep swigs and then offered the bottle to Henry.

"No, no."

"Come on now, it'll do you good, and you're probably going to want a little before what I'm about to do." Henry looked at him wearily, then took the bottle. He took a small drink, and coughed at the burn of it going down. As soon as he had recovered, the man took the bottle back and poured a generous amount over the wound on Henry's arm, causing him to bellow in pain once more. The man then removed his neckerchief from Henry's bicep and wrapped it tightly around the wound. The last thing Henry remembered before passing out was the intense pounding waves of pain and the man grinning at him as he worked at finishing off the bottle of whiskey.

Henry flickered in and out of consciousness, spectral visions swimming in his mind. He's running through the fields as a young boy, taunting the younger slave boy, who lags behind, to catch up. The two boys play in a stream, catching toads and snakes.

Then as a wave of pain and nausea washed over him, a less pleasant memory: his father catches him playing with the boy, wrestling over who gets the favored toy first. Infuriated, his father grabs a nearby riding whip and starts to beat the young slave to teach him a lesson. Young Thomas tries to stop the attack, which only intensifies his father's anger and fuels more blows.

The boy's screams attract attention, and his mother rushes in to try to save him. She shields his body with hers and pleads, "Please, Massa, he's your son, don't whip your son. Please, whip me astead."

So his father does. He beats her so savagely, she is a puddle of black and red by the time he finishes. Then he grabs Thomas by the shirt collar and drags him into the house. Once in the house Thomas gets a beating, too, but, Thomas's mother is able to successfully intervene. Thomas's father raises his hand to her, then checks himself and lowers it, his fury redirecting to words.

"The boy is soft. Worthless, like you! Out playin' with Negroes. I'm sure you encouraged that."

"Who else is he supposed to play with? He is just a boy."

"Don't talk back to me, woman!" This time she does get hit. He turns back to Thomas, but his ire is spent and he stomps heavily out of the room. Thomas's mother tries to comfort him. He shrugs her off. Outside, the slaves are cleaning up. The young mulatto boy is badly injured, his mother, dead.

98

Thomas and his half-brother have learned. They now play deep in the swamp where no one can see them. They spend hours on the trails, deciphering the cryptic symbols carved on the trees, disappearing as if ghosts whenever they hear men approach. The young boy's skin is such a pale shade of black he could almost pass as white, if it weren't for the tell-tale scars of the frequent beatings he received.

A bump in the road jarred Henry to wakefulness. After taking the proffered swig of whiskey, he closed his eyes and slipped back under. Older now, Thomas dresses the part of a man but feels odd and out of place. He rides out to meet his father and his men for the inspection of the fields. As he gets closer, he hears yells and quickens his pace. Rounding the corner, he sees a small contingent of slaves has attacked his father and the men, unhorsing his father. The men have all but subdued the slaves, save one, who escaped into the woods. Thomas dismounts and chases after him. To Thomas's amazement, he catches him quickly; the slave has been injured.

"Nat, what in God's name do you think you're doing?" The slave stares at him long and hard, his left eye twitching slightly, an aftereffect from the blow of a riding crop long ago.

"If you have to ask, you don't understand."

"I understand that you're trying to get yourself killed!"

"Better than bein' a slave." Thomas's grasp loosens and Nat shrugs free, though he does not attempt to run. Thomas looks back toward where he left his father lying in the dirt, then back at Nat.

"Go." Nat looks at him but does not move. "I said go. Do it before I change my mind, and don't ever let me see you again." Nat nods his understanding, a look of gratitude in his eyes, and takes off through the trees. Thomas watches Nat limp off, staring into the trees long after he has disappeared, before turning back toward their father.

With a jolt, the wagon came to a stop, the lack of motion pushing Henry into wakefulness. The intensity of the pain in his arm had subdued somewhat, but he was still disoriented and it took him a minute to remember where he was. The commanding officer of the convoy had already dismounted and was speaking with the owner of the plantation. The irascible old man's tone carried far and wide. Henry made a move to exit the wagon, but the enlisted man pushed his shoulder back down to arrest his intention.

"I'd save your energy and stay where you are. That old coot doesn't seem likely to be sympathetic to your needs."

"Help me out of the wagon. He'll listen to me." The man lifted an eyebrow and cocked his head.

"Oh, you think you'll do better than the major, do ya?"

"That old coot is my father."

"Well, hells bells, why didn't you say so earlier? You coulda saved the major an earful!"

"No, he still would have gotten an earful. We're not exactly on the best of terms, but I've got something to entice him to help me."

The man scrambled out of the back of the wagon and assisted Henry down. Henry tried a step or two on his own, but a wave of dizziness overwhelmed him and he started to totter. Thankfully, the enlisted man had anticipated this and stuck close at hand. He grabbed Henry; and supported him as they walked forward toward the major and the old man who was still letting everyone within earshot know exactly how he felt about the order to turn his house into an impromptu medical hospital. When they were close enough for Henry to be heard without shouting, he addressed his father.

"We're not looking to set up a medical unit, only treatment for a snake bite." The old man redirected his glare at Henry, recognition flitting across his face, causing his glare to intensify further.

"Look what the cat dragged in. You can't even get yourself a proper war wound, can you? You go and find yourself a snake to do the job." Henry stiffened and, through sheer force of will, stood straighter.

"My men should be arriving shortly with four prisoners." He put a special emphasis on the word 'my,' hoping it might buy him some good grace that he was at least in charge of men. "Take us in, treat my wound, and I promise it will be worth your while. We've captured some renegade slaves, some of which belong to you."

His father sucked on his teeth for a moment before replying. "I don't suppose you plan on givin' them back to me, do ya?" Henry did not reply, mostly because it was taking all of his concentration to stay upright. Finally his father jerked his head toward the house. "There's a bedroom in the back by the kitchen. Put him in there."

Henry held his father's gaze and clenched his teeth, then choked out a thank-you before haltingly leading the way up into the house. On the veranda, an old female slave met them and silently helped direct them inside. Once they were out of earshot, the enlisted man whistled.

"You weren't kidding about not being on good terms. What could you have possibly done to make your daddy hate you that way?" The slave helped ease Henry on the bed and then set about pulling off his boots.

"I was born, that's what I did."

The enlisted man whistled again.

"I do not envy you or your men one bit stayin' here. And I thought that snakebite was the worst of your worries. Good luck to ya." With that, the man showed himself out and Henry collapsed back onto the bed, his head swimming. The slave returned with a basin full of water and a cloth.

"Now, Massa Thomas, we's gonna fix you up mighty good, you'll see." She set about cleaning up his wound, then the rest of him, including removing his wet breeches.

"Thank you, Sally." She stopped what she was doing and lovingly stroked his face. His father refused to acknowledge any of his slaves by name, but Henry had always found out what they were. Sally had always been one of his favorites; she'd taken over as best as she was allowed after Henry's mother passed away.

"You is a sight for sore eyes," Sally told him.

Henry smiled and closed his eyes to drift off.

"Now don't you start sleepin' yet. I still has some doctorin' to do that I needs you awake for."

Reluctantly, Henry opened his eyes and saw another slave enter the room carrying a steaming pot. He did not recognize this one. She was young and pretty; evidently his father hadn't gotten his hands on her yet. She put the pot down next to the bed, then hesitated, looking down at her feet. She stole glances at Henry, clearly curious about him. Sally had started to strain out the tobacco leaves that were steeping in the pot when she looked up, frustrated at the girl.

"Go on now. Make sure there's some food ready for Massa Thomas's men. They sure to be hungry." The girl bobbed a curtsy then turned to go, but Henry stopped her.

"Wait. Tell my men they are to retain custody of the prisoners. No matter what my father says, they are not to hand them over." Sally looked at him, a question in her eyes, and he replied in a hushed tone. "We captured Nat, and I don't want my father getting his hands on him." Terror flitted across Sally's eyes and she turned to the girl.

"You heard the massa. You run out to the road and you catch those menfolk before they gets here. You tell them the Massa Thomas's orders, you hear me? Go through the woods so no one sees you. The food can wait." The girl nodded her head then ran out the door. Satisfied, Sally turned back to Henry.

"Lord ha' mercy, you brought trouble along with you." Clucking, she unwrapped Henry's arm and set about packing it with a poultice of tobacco leaves. With the poultice in place, she checked the temperature of the liquid in the pot, then slowly started pouring the tobacco juice over the whole thing. The liquid was much hotter than Henry would have liked, and he gritted his teeth. Growing up, he'd seen Sally treat more snake-bites than he could count and she'd never lost a limb, so he wasn't about to question her method. She stopped ladling and with unnaturally strong fingers palpated up and down his arm. Satisfied, she held up a small wad of what looked like tobacco leaves wrapped around something.

"Here. Chew on this for a minute and then swallow it down."

He did as bidden, but nearly gagged at the taste. It was bitter, burnt, and astringent all at once. Sally helped him sit up and pounded on

103

his back as he coughed. Eventually, with much encouragement and some water, he swallowed it down and laid back onto the bed, his head swimming. Sally brushed the hair out of his face.

"Now you sleep. Sally's here now; you sleep." He closed his eyes as Sally started pouring the tobacco juice over his arm again. This time the heat was soothing and he drifted off to sleep.

While Henry's sleep was sound, it wasn't peaceful. Whatever Sally had made him eat had caused his visions to become lifelike and quite vivid. He finds himself standing in a bedroom, his mother breathing laboriously in the bed. Due to his father's fear of the tuberculosis spreading, no one is allowed in to see her, not even a preacher to read her the last rites. Young Thomas has snuck in anyway. He has to say goodbye. His mother's eyes smile when she sees him, but she holds up her hand to keep him at arm's length. Even when a wretched fit of coughing shakes her frame, she still keeps her arm out to forestall his comforting embrace. She takes a rattling breath and holds Thomas's gaze.

"Thomas, promise me. Promise me you will make your father proud and prove to him I wasn't a waste." Another bout of coughing racks her body. "That having to marry me when his brother died wasn't a waste. Promise me." Pleadingly, she looks at him, tears creeping down the fragile skin of her face.

"I promise, Mama. I promise." Thomas has no idea what she means, or how he can ever make good, but he knows in that moment he has to promise her what she asks. He can't let her go to the grave disappointed in him. With his promise made, she smiles and waves for him to leave. The boy obeys, leaving her to die alone.

With young Thomas now gone from the dream, Henry becomes a mere observer. He stays to watch what he has imagined happened so often since that day. As the door carefully clicks shut, his mother whispers, "I love you" so low it is barely audible. There is no more coughing, no more pain. She slips quietly away, happy in the knowledge her son will set things right for her.

Henry kneels by his mother's bed and expects tears to come. They never do. Instead, he ponders her last words. How was he supposed to set things right? What act could possibly accomplish that? From nowhere an anger begins to boil up inside of him. Why was this his job? Why did she burden him with such a task? What could he possibly do? Feeling more like a child than himself, Henry curls up on the floor by her bed and watches as one memory after another floats in and out of his consciousness, haunting his sleep.

When Henry finally awoke, the throbbing was only a hint of the pain he last remembered. He tested his arm, flexing it this way and that. He had odd, unpredictable twinges of pain but, as far as he could tell, full mobility and only a slight loss of strength. There was still a fairly substantial poultice in place, so he couldn't tell the extent of scarring. He figured he could tolerate a fair bit of disfigurement in exchange for full use of the arm. He was trying to get up when Sally came in and pushed him right back into bed. Apparently, she had been drugging him with her tobacco and herb concoction for several days. Now that he was awake, it would take a day or two before he would have his head and equilibrium back to normal.

Reluctantly, he stayed in bed and interrogated the prisoners from there, starting with Nat. Then he called his men to him and went over correspondence. A missive had arrived, ordering them into a backup position up in Virginia until reinforcements could be spared. They were to ride out as soon as he was able. The next day he received another dispatch and, much to Sally's displeasure, declared himself fit to ride. He called for his men to make ready and to assemble the prisoners. Sally gave him a worried look and several poultices for his arm to switch out over the next couple of days. She clucked repeatedly about her concern of rot since that fool soldier had cut his arm open instead of leaving well enough alone. Henry kissed her on the cheek, squeezed her hand in thanks and headed out to the horses.

His father, who had stayed clear of Henry for the entirety of his stay, was on the veranda overseeing the proceedings with a sour look. Henry saw that his horse and men were ready to depart before he turned back to his father and addressed him loudly enough for all present to hear.

"Sir, I was of a mind to return these men to you, as they are, I believe, your property. However, as they have perpetrated crimes against the Confederacy, they are traitors and the charge of treason outweighs that of a runaway slave."

At this announcement, his father made for the stairs to better get in Henry's face about the nature and treatment of his property. Henry held up a hand, indicating that he was not finished.

"And as traitors, the punishment is death." By now Henry had positioned himself in front of the slaves. He held Nat's gaze, and Nat gave the briefest of nods before Henry pulled his gun and shot him.

106

Henry's aim was true, and Nat was dead before his body could crumple to the ground. Turning away, Henry addressed his father again.

"Sir, if you would be so kind as to provide your men with pistols and shot to dispatch the rest of these traitors, we must be on our way." His father smiled and nodded at Henry approvingly, then barked for his overseer to fetch a weapon and shoot the remaining traitors. Without waiting for the men to return, Henry mounted his horse and spurred her down the lane. His men scrambled to follow after him. Henry could hear the hooves of their horses slowing as they caught up to him, just as three shots rang out. The deed was done.

Williams pulled up even with him.

"But sir, the order said—"

"The order said the slaves' owner was to deal with them as he saw fit, and you heard as clearly as I that he ordered those slaves be shot. Our orders have been carried out."

"Yes, sir, but only after you said they were to be shot."

Henry turned in his saddle and looked Williams squarely in the eyes. "If I had left those slaves to my father's devices he would have had them whipped to within an inch of their lives, let them heal, and then whipped them again. Then he would have had them crippled so they would never be able to run away again. Granting them death was a mercy they asked for, and I saw no reason not to comply."

"Oh." The implications of Henry's revelation washed over Williams' face. "I don't know what I was thinkin', sir. That man clearly ordered his slaves to be shot. I heard it with my own two ears."

Henry nodded and Williams fell back, glad to be moving on.

11
Promotion

Henry had hoped the rain would have let up by now, but it was actually coming down harder. It started shortly after leaving his father's and had been unrelenting for the past three days. It was as if the heavens disapproved of his actions and were sending the rains to keep him from his duty. They might succeed. The road became impassable several hours earlier, forcing Henry and his men to abandon it in favor of a trail under the shelter of the trees, which was passable but slow going. Henry was having a hard time discerning the trail. Dismounting, he led his horse by the reins so he could examine the markings on the trees up close. His senses were quickly overstimulated by the thunder, pounding rain, and sucking squelch of each step.

The terrain had adopted an incline, making the going even slower, but with the altitude gain, Henry was optimistic that they were nearing their destination. Their orders were to rendezvous with a small unit that was charged with holding a hill overlooking a railway exchange. It was said that, from the top of this hill, a man could observe the railways below for miles in either direction, and thus provide signals to oncoming trains of any danger ahead. Not to mention, once the promised cannon arrived, they would provide a certain amount of security from Yankee-raiding parties intent on destroying the switches. Until the engineers arrived, Henry and his men were to help the unit already in place gather building materials to build a permanent lookout.

As they neared the top, the trees began to thin, and occasionally, amid the squelching of the mud and crashes of thunder, Henry heard what he thought sounded like metal clashing and the screams of men. He raised his hand in a signal for his men to halt while he listened more closely. At first there was only the monotonous roar of the rain accentuated by the dripping of the trees in the more sheltered areas. Then, as his ears became accustomed, he heard it again, now more pronounced: the sound of a battle. No, a skirmish, as there was a decided lack of artillery. Concentrating on the sounds, he realized there was also a complete absence of firearms, which explained why he had not heard the fighting earlier.

Henry gave his orders. His men hobbled their horses and moved off the path to approach the top of the hill from the side in hopes of getting to survey the action before diving in. During the brief flashes of lightning, Henry started to see figures locked in combat through the sheeting rain. He saw one man break off and run down the path. A few more in Confederate gray followed. There had been no retreat called; these men were simply running. Abruptly a group broke away, crashing through the underbrush, not even bothering to find the path. Unluckily for them, they ran directly toward Henry and his men. Henry seized a soldier by the lapels and threw him back toward the battle.

"We have been ordered to hold this hill, and goddammit we are going to hold!" Henry screamed above the din of the weather.

A few of the men slowed their retreat to reconsider whether the cold fury coming at them was indeed worse than the chaotic battle behind them. All but one slowed to go back. That one soldier fell to his knees before Henry, sniveling disgracefully. Henry pulled his sidearm and drew a careful aim at the soldier's head.

"Return to your position or I will kill you myself." There was no malice in his voice, simply the cold, hard truth of conviction.

The soldier's response came on the tail of a sob. "But with this rain, our guns won't fire. The powder's too wet."

Deftly, Henry flipped his gun in the air, and catching it by the barrel, swung it down hard, coldcocking the soldier across the face. With a spray of teeth and blood the man crumpled, and Henry addressed the remaining, retreating men, whose unwavering attention he now possessed.

"If you can't shoot them, beat them with your guns. I don't care if you have to wrestle them to the ground and kill them with your bare hands, we will hold this hill!"

Before he finished his speech, a small contingency of Union soldiers began to breach the side of the plateau to join their comrades who had charged from the front. Henry smoothly flipped his gun back around and fired, causing the man leading the vanguard to fall and slip precariously back down the hill, taking one of his men with him. Henry was able to take out two more before his gun misfired, the powder drenched from the pouring rain.

Grabbing the barrel once more, the rain having tempered the heat of the hot metal, Henry let out a cry as he charged at the remaining two Union men. He bludgeoned them before they could react and redirected his charge toward the melee. Seeing the valor of this newly arrived lieutenant not only spurred the men to turn back to the battle and fight on, but rallied the troops to push ever harder to gain back the ground they had so recently lost.

Entrenched in the thick of it, Henry understood what had caused the men to retreat. The sheets of rain unleashed from the heavens not only rendered all firearms useless, it also harshly limited visibility and created a muddy quagmire of muck that was as much their enemy as their actual foes—not that they could distinguish who was foe and who was friend. Every man jack of them on the field was covered in filth from head to toe. He saw men struggling with one foot bare, the merciless mud having claimed one of their boots as its prize. For every man on his feet, there were two on the ground. Whether those men were injured, dead, or had simply fallen was impossible to discern. After slipping several times himself, Henry quickly determined that the surest way to stay upright was to step on the felled men, not the mud.

He was trying desperately to keep track of his own men, in order to avoid injuring or killing one of them. Realizing the futility, he instead tried to look each man in the face before bringing the butt of his gun down like a hammer. His arm throbbed and he soon lost any fluid motion. Grab. Look. Shove aside. Slip. Grab. Bludgeon. Wipe eyes. Too late. Pain. Grapple. Fall. Bludgeon. Scramble up. Spit blood. Bludgeon. Bludgeon. Bludgeon. Slip. Grab. Fall. No breath. Push man off. Can't breathe. Need to breathe.

Henry crawled to a nearby tree trying desperately to catch his breath. Much of the fighting was now taking place at the bottom of the hill. That is where gravity and slick mud had taken most of the men. Whether it was due to the overabundance of Mother Nature's intervention rendering all of their technological advances useless, or some other darker dealing, this combat was savage and unforgiving; more so than Henry had ever witnessed or felt. The fury unleashed in

111

his blood from being forced to grapple and kill with his bare hands had created a base, animalistic furor that answered to no one. He felt this surge of energy all around him. This was the sort of leaderless catastrophe that would only end when every man lay dead or dying on the field, having been churned in the mud as if butter.

Henry deftly sidestepped and flung an oncoming soldier into the tree he had been leaning against. His breath was back, mostly. He dodged the thrust of a knife, the sudden move throwing him off balance. Flailing, he grabbed the other man's arm, disarming him as they both went down. Claiming the knife for his own, Henry worked his way upright, feeling a sickening crunch under his foot as he stepped on the man's lower leg. More men crested the hill—always more men. He was about to give up hope, sure that every man present would still be fighting when they reached the gates of hell, when a flash of lightning illuminated an officer on a horse at the bottom of the hill, hopping about on the outskirts. He was fruitlessly yelling commands that were swallowed by the thunder.

Henry dropped his sidearm. By now it was cracked and useless, having connected with the heads of one too many men to remain whole. He gripped the knife hard and plunged down the hill taking as many men with him as he could on the slippery journey. Reaching the bottom, he wasted no time in getting to his feet. His clothes were now heavy and mud caked. He still had the knife, though, and put it to good use as he made his way toward the officer. When he was finally close enough to hear the commands bellowing forth, Henry found the origins of the chaos. The officer kept vacillating between ordering a retreat or a charge, and clearly his men had given up listening to him long ago.

Swallowing the regret he knew was sure to follow, Henry sliced across the horse's chest, causing it to stagger, screaming in pain. He hated to do it, for the horse was a beautiful specimen, but Henry could think of no other way to effectively unseat the officer. As the horse staggered, Henry moved around to the side and lunged at the officer, ripping him off the saddle. In the pursuant struggle, Henry's knife slipped from his hand and was lost to the muck. The officer managed to pull his own knife and began slashing wildly. Feeling a searing pain across his arm, Henry found himself on the defensive. Ignoring the blood and rain that streamed down his arm, Henry's entire focus shifted to the blade the officer wielded.

Henry frantically shot out a hand in an attempt to find his knife. Coming up with a rock instead, he smashed it into the side of the officer's head. Dazed, the officer recoiled slightly, providing Henry with the window of opportunity to fling the officer into the mud. Slipping himself, Henry struggled after the man, who was unsuccessfully attempting to regain his feet. Grabbing one of the officer's ankles, Henry pulled him face down into the mud. Finding a foothold, Henry launched forward onto the officer, grinding his face into a shallow muddy puddle. The officer struggled violently to free himself. Henry dug his knee harder into the officer's back and shoved his face further into the mire.

Slowly the officer's struggles became weaker and weaker until finally all was still. It took Henry a moment to realize that the tumultuous battle around him had also subsided significantly. Apparently the sight of an officer being pulled from his horse was enough to draw the attention of the men around them, which then rippled throughout the battlefield. Carefully, so as not to slip and fall face first, Henry raised himself to his feet, pausing only long enough to withdraw the saber still belted at the officer's side. Raising the sword of victory aloft, Henry bellowed, "Lay down your weapons, and your lives will be spared."

A crash of thunder accented his command, and what remained of the Union contingency dropped their weapons. Despite their exhaustion, the Confederate soldiers cheered. Even through the pouring rain and loud celebrations, Henry felt the odd sensation that the Union soldiers were more relieved than downtrodden by the outcome. Whether this relief was born from the cessation of fighting or because Henry had done them the favor of freeing them from an obviously lunatic officer, he did not know; nor did he care. Cradling his throbbing arm to his chest, Henry bent to retrieve the officer's sword belt, for he lacked one of his own.

This victory did not leave Henry exhilarated and ready for more. There was no trace of the invincibility one feels from surviving. Instead, all Henry could think of was a warm bath and shelter from the infernal weather.

Sept 8, 1863

Longstreet to reinforce Bragg.
Rappahannock vulnerable.
NR

43-66-16-55 32 34-32-45-61
26-14-54-63-43-55-56-66-66-55 55-14
56-66-25-54-15-14-56-12-66 51-56-24-63-63
56-24-16-16-24-52-24-54-54-14-12-46
36-31-26-54-66-56-24-51-26-66
54-56

12
Secrets Among Friends

Anna's initial trepidation at sending Mary out as a messenger was now completely gone. In fact, Anna wondered how much more could have been accomplished if she had only employed Mary earlier. Acting alone, Anna had to wait until she had a plausible reason, like a social engagement, to venture off the plantation. Mary, on the other hand, could be sent out on errands twice a day, every day, without anyone noticing, much less questioning her activities. It was common place for a mistress to send a trusted slave out on a five-mile round-trip to fetch something as simple as a spool of thread from a neighbor. Truth be told, they didn't even need to come up with a real errand. As long as Mary was carrying a basket and had a pass to leave the grounds, she came and went with little fanfare.

What had grown in the place of trepidation was impatience. Anna had never realized how much she relied on Mary for companionship until Mary was gone for hours at a time on a regular basis. Even when they weren't actively talking or doing something together, Anna simply enjoyed Mary's company. In addition to Mary's errand today, which was a real errand as well as an exchange of correspondence, Anna had broken her last embroidery needle, so she was bereft without Mary's company and had nothing to do. Tired of pacing her room, Anna went downstairs to sit on the veranda. There she would at least have some fresh air and a change of scenery.

No sooner had she sat down, then she felt someone lurking in the doorway behind her. She didn't need to look to know that it was Kady. The girl had not mentioned becoming a spy again, and her dogged following of Anna had decreased somewhat, but the girl could always be counted on to be nearby. She had also taken to repeatedly asking if there was anything she could do to help Anna—heavy emphasis on *anything*. The previous evening when she had asked, Mary handed her some darning, and Kady had screwed up her face in such disgust it had taken all of Anna's self-control to keep from laughing. To her credit, Kady sat down and darned the sock. Anna had to admire her persistence. She smiled. It was still annoying, but the girl was trying.

Anna was starting to guess how long Kady would linger out of sight before making herself known when Mary walked out onto the veranda. She looked parched and drawn from her journey, and while Anna desperately wanted to know what Mary had with her, she knew Mary needed some refreshment, and the laundress was within earshot. So Anna pulled out her best Southern mistress impersonation.

"There you are! I hope you got my new needles?"

"Yes'm." Mary nodded her head and handed over a small packet.

"Good! Now bring me some afternoon tea in my sitting room. I am wasting away from sitting out here in the sun." Anna stood and swept past Mary into the house, catching a glimpse of the laundress giving Mary a look of sympathy.

When Anna had first moved to Virginia, she had treated Mary like she had her nursemaid back in New York. Mary took care of all of Anna's needs, in addition to being her constant companion. She often asked

117

Mary to take tea with her or invited her on an afternoon walk. Mary would go along, she had no choice, but always did so reluctantly. Several months had passed before Mary had been able to work up the nerve to tell Anna, one night in her bed chamber, that they couldn't be friends.

"What on earth are you talking about, Mary? I can be friends with whomsoever I wish."

"No, ma'am, ya can't. Not here anyways."

"Well, why not?"

"The other slaves is startin' to talk and give me a hard time." Anna just looked at her confused, so Mary continued. "It's only natural for the mistress of the house to show favor for her lady's maid, that's natural. But you treatin' me like I's a white woman and that ain't right. I's a Negro, you got to treat me like I's a Negro. That's how it works here."

"I never wanted a slave! I never even wanted to come here!" Anna stomped her foot petulantly, then remembering she was now a wife, not a child, she straightened up somewhat. "It is just not fair."

Mary smiled ruefully. "That it ain't, but it's the way it is. So if you are going to survive here, you got to learn to play by their rules."

"So we can't be friends? I don't have anyone else to talk to here."

"We can't be friends out there." Mary gestured with her thumb to everything beyond the bedroom door. "When it is just us, in here, I can be whoever you want me to be."

Anna's face lit up. Despite the fact that Mary was only a few years older than her, Anna felt so young in comparison.

"So you will be my friend, as long as I am circumspect about it." Mary looked at her confused. "I mean, in private."

"If that is what you want."

118

"And will you teach me how I am supposed to behave out there?" Anna mimicked Mary's earlier gesture, eliciting a rare smile from Mary.

"Of course."

Thus began Anna's education in being a haughty Southern mistress. She was never able to fully embody the disdain for the slaves around her that she saw in other whites, especially not for Mary, but she learned to put on enough airs to get by. It was still widely whispered that Mary was pampered and living above her station. However, Anna remembered to make enough dismissive comments while in earshot of other slaves to keep them from completely ostracizing Mary. Anna had even made a game out of catching the eye rolls and looks of exasperation between the slaves whenever she made these comments. This didn't make her like the charade anymore, it simply made it more tolerable. It also made Mary's life easier, which was the real reason Anna did it.

When Anna reached her sitting room, she made sure that she was completely alone, then greedily tore open her little packet. Much to her chagrin, it contained needles. Thankfully Mary wasn't far behind, and as soon as she slid the door closed, Anna's impatience burst forth.

"These are just needles!"

"That's what you sent me out for!" Mary sat down gratefully and poured them both a cup of tea. When she picked up a plate and indicated that Anna should say what she wanted to eat, Anna shook her head.

"No, I'm not hungry. That is for you."

"Thank you." Mary began filling the plate.

"Where's the correspondence?"

"Wasn't none."

"None? Are you sure?"

"I even checked in with the doctor. He didn't have nothin' written down."

"Did he tell you anything?"

"He said he heard tell of a mission to copy some of General Lee's personal maps and notes at his camp. He didn't know more than that other than to suspect that whoever goes on this mission will likely need a place to hide for a spell. He was hoping that arrangements could be made here."

"Does he know when this is going to happen?"

"No. Could be next week, could be two months from now, could be never."

"That's helpful."

Mary nodded her head in assent, her mouth full.

"I guess we will have to come up with a plan quickly then," Anna decided.

Anna crossed to her desk to compose a message, leaving Mary to enjoy the tea.

Oct 13, 1863

Smokehouse ready as haven. Awaiting further instructions.
NR

14-12-55 34-61 34-32-45-61
43-64-14-46-66-52-14-31-43-66 56-66-24-23-11
24-43 52-24-36-66-54 24-33-24-25-55-25-54-63
15-31-56-55-52-66-56
25-54-43-55-56-31-12-55-25-14-54-43
54-56

13
Step One

Emma had wandered around aimlessly, eavesdropping and collecting little bits of information wherever she went. She had no idea why she was doing this, but it gave her something to do and took her mind off her situation. She was afraid to stay in one place for too long lest she be discovered by the Union officers who were out looking for her. She didn't even know if they were still looking for her, but she didn't want to take the chance. She had circled back around to check on her brother once. She had not made her presence known, just spied from a distance. Blackie had been true to his word; he and his wife were treating Peter like he was their own. He was rosy cheeked and happy. This lightened Emma's heart and convinced her that her choice to leave him had been the correct one. He was better off without her.

She knew if she were smart, she would head north and leave Virginia. It would be safer for everyone, especially herself if she headed toward Boston or New York and started over there. Try as she might to leave, she was inextricably tied to Virginia. There was still something she had to do. Her mind kept returning to that awful morning, to all of that loss and the one shining moment when that man had burst out of the door carrying her brother. She was convinced that he had tried to save her family. He had been too late to save them all, so he saved what he could. She didn't know why he had done it, but she was grateful and had built him up into some sort of hero in her mind. That one moment was the only good thing that she could hold onto from that dreadful day.

That is why she couldn't leave yet. Peter owed that man his life. As he was too young to offer thanks, it was up to Emma. She had to find him, she had to say thank you and then give him her father's letter as payment. Once she had accomplished that she would be free to leave Virginia forever. She just had to figure out who he was.

Nov 1, 1863
Rappahannock Station pontoon bridge key to
Lee. Early in command with La. Tigers. N
bank 2 redoubts. S bank artillery.
NR

36-16-51 56 56-52-43-65
31-26-11-11-26-32-26-36-36-16-12-41
44-33-26-33-23-16-36 11-16-36-33-16-16-36
35-31-23-24-64-61 41-61-15 33-16 21-61-61
61-26-31-21-15 23-36 12-16-66-66-26-36-24
54-23-33-32 21-26 33-23-64-61-31-44 36
35-26-36-41 45 31-61-24-16-55-35-33-44 44
35-26-36-41 26-31-33-23-21-21-61-31-15
36-31

14
Ripe for the Picking

Anna stood at the doorway of the slave's shack waiting for a verdict. "I have to take the leg." The doctor finished retying the tourniquet and then set about lashing Lieutenant Jacob Hart to the makeshift operating table.

"You can't," Anna decried.

"I wish I had a choice, but I don't. It's crushed too badly to fix and the rot has already started to spread."

"Can't this wait?" Anna glanced nervously back toward the big house.

"His only chance to survive is if I take the leg and I take it now."

"With no anesthetic?"

An edge entered the doctor's voice. "I didn't bring any chloroform, as I was not told to expect this level of trauma. He can't wait for me to fetch it. It's already a miracle he hasn't bled to death. If the blood loss doesn't kill him, the rot surely will."

Anna searched the sparse slaves' quarters until her eyes alighted on a few scraps of leather. She gathered the pieces, then slid them firmly between the lieutenant's teeth. In his pain-soaked stupor he barely acknowledged the addition.

The doctor looked up at Anna and shook his head. "I doubt that will do much good." Having determined the best place to cut, the doctor exited the hut to retrieve his bag and select which saw to use. Anna ran after him and he continued, "I'll have the leg off in five minutes, ten at the most if there are complications. With the first cut he'll come to his senses and scream as if there's no tomorrow. If he's smart, he won't fight it and will pass out. I'd go into the big house if I were you. It's not a sound you'll easily forget."

Exasperated Anna blocked the doctor's entrance back into the shack and lowered her voice. "You don't understand, he can't scream, even once. That house is full of Confederate officers," Anna pointed toward the big house before gesturing back to the shack. "And he is a Yankee lieutenant."

Horrified, the doctor froze. "But you said…"

"I said there was an officer in dire need of medical care; I never said which army that officer belonged to, which is why saving him will be pointless if the only way of doing it will alert all of them to his presence." The doctor glanced back toward the house. "I sent for you because I was told you were a supporter of the North."

"Where did you hear that?"

"From a reliable and trustworthy source, who never would have told me if they did not know your secret was safe with me."

"They are so close. If I'm discovered helping this man I'll be hanged as a traitor. Not even my oath as a doctor will save me from that!"

"You don't think I know that?! I'll be hanging right next to you in the gallows."

The doctor scoffed, "You're a woman. They would never hang you for trying to help a wounded man."

"That may be, but my husband would surely kill me himself.

126

He's one of the officers inside, and I don't think he'd take a fancy to finding out his wife has been passing information to the North. I am the Northern Rose." Recognition flashed across the face of the doctor. "Now you know my secret. I was supposed to rendezvous with that man so we could combine our intelligence. I have coded messages and he knows the new key. If you can't save him, all this has been for naught." Before the doctor could respond, the lieutenant began to thrash wildly on the table. A slave called from inside.

"Lord ha' mercy, the devil took his body!"

"It's not the devil, he's having a fit." The doctor pushed his way back into the shack. "Hold him down! Ma'am, I need to you to hold that leather in his mouth." The slave pinioned the lieutenant's arms to the table as best he could against the thrashing. As Anna moved to his head, the tourniquet gave way and blood started to gush anew from the gaping wound in his leg. Fighting back the urge to retch, Anna looked away from her now blood-smeared dress and firmly held the leather in the lieutenant's mouth. With a few final jerks, his body became still and his eyes lolled back in his head as the doctor secured the tourniquet once more. Afraid to look up and see the bloody carnage in front of her, but knowing she had no choice, Anna held her breath and found the doctor's gaze.

"Isn't there any way to—" A strangled cry stopped her mid-sentence. All eyes snapped to the open doorway to find Kady standing wide-eyed, tears beginning to well. Speechless, she staggered back several paces, then turned to run. Anna sprang after her; she knew where Kady was headed. Instinctively, she would head straight for her father and tell him everything. Anna overtook her not more than ten

127

paces from the shack. By now Kady was on the verge of a hysterical fit. Anna grabbed her by the shoulders and violently spun her around so they were face-to-face. A plan had formed in her head, a plan that couldn't possibly work because it forced them to rely on Kady. Kady, who despite her pleading to be a spy, had no idea what that meant. But Anna had no other options. Lieutenant Hart was dying and with him would go all of the information.

"Stop it! Stop it right now!"

"All that blood…that man—"

"That man is going to die if you don't pull yourself together." A sharp intake of breath signaled the beginning of hysterics that Anna did not have time to deal with. Before Kady could unleash the sob welling in her breast, Anna brought her hand down across Kady's face so hard it knocked her momentarily numb.

"Up until this moment you have been nothing more than a frilly little pet up on a pedestal. Well, here is your chance to be something more. If you want to be a spy, then you pull yourself together, get into that house, and make sure every officer in there is so diverted they wouldn't leave that parlor if the house was burning down around them!"

"How can—"

"I'm sure you'll figure something out! I usually can't pull you away from parties, you're so busy whoring yourself around from one gentleman to the next. This should be easy."

Indignation broke through Kady's hysterics, and her breathing leveled as she looked her mother in the eyes for the first time.

Sensing she had broken through, Anna cupped her daughter's face in her hands.

"Now go, and for the love of all that is holy do not fail or all of our lives are forfeit."

With that Anna turned and hurried back into the shack. A low moaning issued from the door when she opened it. The lieutenant was conscious again. The doctor looked up at her anxiously. Urging an edge of confidence into her voice that she did not feel, Anna answered the question burning in his eyes.

"It's okay. She's one of us. She's going to provide us with a distraction for the officers. Are you ready to begin?" The doctor hesitantly positioned himself by the lieutenant's leg and the slave sidled up next to him. He had obviously been given instructions on how to help while she was outside.

"What do you need me to do?"

"Ma'am, you don't want to be in here for this."

"This has nothing to do with what I do or do not want. Now where do you need me?"

Relenting, the doctor nodded his head toward the lieutenant's.

"Hold his head. If he has another fit, don't let him bite through his tongue. I have enough to do down here without having to sew that back on too."

With a look of grim determination, Anna positioned herself by Jacob's head and brushed the hair off his face. Nervously, she glanced toward the house and waited.

Kady made her way back to the house. She realized she had been subconsciously straightening her gown and flattening her bodice. She was infuriated by her mother's words. She did not whore herself around! It was not her fault if men found her charming. More importantly, what did that have to do with anything right now? How in the world was she supposed to be able to keep those men from doing anything? Did her mother intend that she flirt with them to distract them? That was ridiculous. She couldn't flirt with an entire room at the same time. And what were they going to do to that man? Who was he? A shudder ran down her spine at the memory of his blood-soaked uniform and mangled leg.

She entered through the back and stopped to check her reflection in the hallway mirror. Her tears had left no trace, but her cheek was red and tender where her mother had slapped her—that was going to be a problem. Turning her face to look at it more closely, she realized the added color actually looked quite fetching. Immediately she began to pinch her other cheek until the color matched. The added moisture in her eyes also increased the vibrancy of the blue and gave her a dewy-eyed innocent look that she was sure would be incredibly alluring if she added a slight pout to her lips. She made a mental note that she would have to make herself cry before her father's next dinner party, because it had done wonders for her appearance. The tinkling of a few keys on the piano in the side parlor broke through her primping and reminded her of the task at hand. They were in the parlor, with the piano. She knew exactly what to do.

With as much of a carefree flounce as she could muster, Kady made her grand entrance. At her arrival, the men in the room stood taller, straightening their coats. The look of approval she so craved flashed across every pair of eyes in the room as they took her in. Instead

130

of filling her with delight as it normally did, she felt a little dirty and didn't know why. Her father cut through the throng to make his way to her side as she bobbed a quick curtsy. Before he could speak, she addressed him loudly enough for all gathered to hear.

"Now, Daddy, where have your manners gone? All of these men with such a long winter ahead of them and the only entertainment you offer is idle chatter? I insist you let me play for you."

Concern crossed his face for a moment; she had interrupted an important conversation.

"Oh, come now. Supper will be ready shortly, and you can finish planning your little battles then. Let these poor men enjoy their drinks to some music. Don't make me beg." She leaned against his arm and pouted her lower lip.

Relenting, he gestured toward the piano, and she bobbed up onto her toes to kiss him on the cheek before skipping her way over to the piano, curtsying or nodding to the gentlemen with whom she had already become acquainted.

The general lamented, "Gentlemen, take a piece of advice from me. If you want a moment of peace in your life, don't have daughters. Wives can be controlled, but daughters seem to get away with whatever they please!"

The men laughed heartily at this, and those who apparently already had daughters nodded in agreement. Before sitting at the piano, Kady turned to give a quick smile to her father, acknowledging that she caught his gibe, when she noticed the stare of a young officer across the room. He was strikingly handsome. His nonchalant posture leaning against the service bureau showed he did not doubt for a second that he belonged in his present company, even though he was clearly the youngest man in the room. His confidence and piercing, approving gaze sent butterflies trilling through her stomach as she sat and turned to the keys. This was the sort of man she was most attracted to: tall, dark, mysterious, and clearly approved of by her father or he would not dare to stare so openly. These thoughts flooded her heart as she began playing the loudest, most energetic piece she knew.

Her fingers flew along the keys as the gentlemen behind her took up new, more lighthearted conversations. She relaxed into the familiarity, enjoying the feel of the keys beneath her fingers. Before the war, her father used to entertain on a regular basis, and she would always be called upon to play. By the time she was eight, she had mastered all her tutor knew to teach. So she started to teach herself. Her father saw to it she always had new sheet music; no expense was too extravagant for her. When water from a vase was accidentally spilled on the piano's keys, he simply bought her a new piano.

Kady knew no pleasure greater than playing while people behind her listened with rapturous attention. The music she was playing now would not elicit that kind of awe. She could sense her audience was appreciative nevertheless. She could still feel the gaze of the handsome officer on her back, could picture the smile on his lips, and his approval of her obvious talent, while in the distance she heard a faint scream of agony. Her back stiffened, and she flowed from one piece right into the next without pausing for applause.

No one else seemed to notice the screams. She played louder still, just in case. From her vantage point at the piano she could barely see the shack from the window. By her third piece the screams had subsided, and the men she was entertaining had returned their attention to each other. Out of the corner of her eye, she saw movement at the shack and looked over in time to see her mother stagger out and hand a bloody bundle to an awaiting field hand. As the hand turned to walk away, Kady realized what had been handed off; there was a boot sticking out from the corner of the sheet. Fighting back the urge to retch, she paused before beginning her next piece. Amid the distracted applause from the gentlemen she began something more subdued, a slow waltz, as tears began to stream silently down her face. She had gotten exactly what she had been begging for, and now that she had it, she wanted nothing to do with it.

Feb 8, 1864

Little Rose active.
NR

                     31-53-42 15 16-15-61-11
23-21-41-41-23-53 43-36-64-53
26-35-41-21-13-53
46-43

15
A Hero's Thanks

With winter fully upon them, Emma learned the value of small inns on the outskirts of towns. Not only did they provide a warm bath and moderately soft bed, there was also a wealth of information to be had if one knew where to look. Men were generally careless with their belongings once they were tucked away in the perceived safety of their rooms. All Emma had to do was wait for them to go downstairs for supper and she could gather whatever information she could find. She could also generally find a spare coin or two that would not be missed. If there wasn't anything worth taking, she would simply follow them downstairs, order some food of her own, and listen. Men loved to talk once they had some drink in them.

This information wasn't as blatant as the maps or messages she would find in the rooms; it was subtler and took some inference on her part. However, once pieced together, it was just as valuable. At first, Emma's problem had been figuring out what to do with the information she gathered. That was solved one evening while eating dinner in a taproom. She was the only customer until a Confederate officer came in and sat down. Watching him, she noted how assiduously he kept to himself, despite the barkeep's best efforts to engage him in conversation. Instead he busily shuffled through papers and made notes in a little book. Emma felt certain he was some sort of spy or messenger. Why else would he have all of that paper? This was perfect. She would give him all of the information she had gathered! Before she had properly made up her mind on how to approach him, he announced to the barkeep that he would return in a moment. Standing up, he gathered all of his papers, put them in his satchel, and strode purposefully out the door. Indecision gone, Emma tore through her own bag gathering every scrap of paper she had. Piling it neatly in a stack, she made for the stairs, nonchalantly dropping her stash on his seat as she passed.

It had worked! She made it upstairs without anyone seeing her do the drop, and the officer had returned to his seat only moments later. He was sure to have gotten the papers. This was all very exciting. Emma had handed off intelligence about the Union. She was truly a spy now. She gathered information and she passed it on. All she had to do was find a new Confederate messenger whenever she had more news.

Occasionally a pang of guilt would hit Emma that she was working for the Confederacy, when her father had spent his last months working so tirelessly for the Union. That guilt quickly passed when she remembered that in the end, the Union had done nothing to help her family. It was because of the Union they had all been killed. It was their information her father was protecting, yet they were absent when her mother and her brothers and sisters had needed protection. In fact, it was a Confederate soldier who saved her brother; it was his kindness that removed him from the burning house to safety. In contrast, the Union disparaged her father for his incompetence.

No, she had chosen her side correctly. The Confederacy needed the information she gathered, and she would give them all she had, except the letter from her father, which she kept safely tucked away and would give to the man who had saved her brother. It was trifling, she knew, but she couldn't think of any other way to thank him for his kindness. That letter was what they were looking for that day. She would give it to him so he could be the hero again. For now, she would hold onto it until she saw him again, whenever that might be.

Over a month had passed and Emma was sitting in the back corner of yet another inn, mostly in the dark since the sun had set. She had given up on learning anything useful for the evening and was gathering her belongings when a man came in and sat at the bar. He was followed closely by a second man who worriedly looked around before he sat next to the first. Thinking this could be promising, Emma settled back in. The first man was already on his second drink before his companion had worked up the courage to speak.

"Henry, you have to be smart about this."

"Captain."

"What?"

"It's Captain Henry, not Henry. Why can nobody remember that?" He slammed his glass down and, spilling a great quantity of the liquid, signaled for a refill. Emma caught her breath. It was him. This was the first time she had heard his name, but that was him. She would remember that profile until the day she died.

"My apologies, Captain Henry. None of us, your men, ever forgets that you are our captain. You're the best captain any of us ever had." This at least mollified Henry enough that his ire was no longer directed at the hapless man. "But Captain, you have to be smart about this. I know Lieutenant Radcliffe is—"

"A lieutenant." Henry finished his sentence for him. "A goddamn lieutenant and he has the gall to ignore my order in front of everybody. And to make it worse, no one corrects his insolence, even though he did it in front of two generals and another captain!"

This time Henry picked up his glass and threw it across the bar so it shattered against the wall. The innkeeper ducked out of the way and then scurried into the back. The second man stayed quiet for a moment to let Henry's blood cool before finally responding.

"Sleep on it. The man is an ass and will eventually get what's coming to him. If you still want to challenge the man to a duel in the morning, me or any of the men will be your second. We will stand with you if this is really what you want to do. Radcliffe's daddy has a lot of influence, though, and would make your life a living hell if you go and kill his son." As an afterthought he added, "Captain."

The man took a long, hard look at Henry and, not able to glean any response, slowly walked out. Emma knew this was her chance. She started to make for the bar before realizing that what she had to deliver wasn't the sort of thing you did in the open. So instead, she made her way to the stairs. She would wait for him to retire to his room and approach him there.

Henry propped his elbows up on the bar and, hanging his head, folded his hands over the back of his head. He was so frustrated he could spit. Since his promotion to captain, two of his missions had been utter failures. He had not had the respect of many of the other officers before then, and he held even less now. He could not decide if it was because he had gained his rank through field promotion or if they, as so many of the men had heard of his reputation, feared him because of his deeds and therefore reviled him. Either way he was an aberration and they all treated him as such. Heavily, he stood up, downed his drink, and made for the stairs.

Once in his room, he collapsed on the bed, only to hear his door creak open moments later. Jumping up from the bed, he grabbed his pistol from the nightstand and trained it on the door. The boy who had entered yelped and fell back against the door, latching it shut. There was something odd: the dress was of a boy, but the small scream was of a girl. With a more thorough inspection, Henry realized it wasn't a boy, but a young woman dressed as a boy. She had on buckskin britches, a blouse laced up at the neck, and a loose-fitting jacket. Looking at her, he thought she looked like a young girl playing dress-up in her older brother's clothes. Henry was in no mood to deal with her.

"Speak your business quickly, or you'll never speak again, girl."

Henry's emphasis on the word girl made her eyes widen. A little breathily, she replied, "I have something for you." Then she reached up to her neck and undid the laces. Henry raised an eyebrow. If his men had decided to buy him a romp to ease his bad mood, they had certainly picked a queer girl to send, but he lowered his pistol all the same. Queer he could live with, maybe this was what he needed. Instead of continuing to undress, the girl simply reached into her shirt and pulled out a folded and worn piece of paper, which she proffered.

"This is for you. I've been saving it for you."

Henry looked at her, confused, so she tentatively walked farther into the room to hand it to him. Replacing his pistol on the nightstand he took it from her and opened it up to look. It was a coded message.

138

Judging by the look of it, it was old and, therefore, probably worthless.

"What is this?" Henry was starting to lose his patience.

"It's a letter. Men came to my father's house, my father Daniel O'Neal, to find that. It wasn't there because I had it. So I've been saving it for you, since you saved my brother from the burning house."

Henry looked at her in disbelief.

"It's what you came for, and now you have it," she continued.

Despite the earnest look on her face, rage seared through Henry. This was Radcliffe's doing. He had sent her to mock him. He did not know how Radcliffe had learned about the infant, but this had to be his doing. Why the hell else would she be here other than to remind him of that evil deed? He had killed that entire family for nothing, and here this girl was standing in front of him mocking him with the prize they had been after. Henry crumpled the paper in his fist.

"Get out. Get out right now!"

The girl looked hurt but did not move.

"I said get out!"

The girl still did not move, so Henry grabbed her by the arm to bodily remove her.

"I don't understand. I brought it for you. I thought you would want it."

Henry stopped dead in his tracks and laughed.

"You thought I would want this? Why would I want this? It is almost a year old." Henry's blood boiled and he uncrumpled the paper and shoved it in her face. "You brought this to me because Radcliffe sent you, didn't he?" Henry slapped her. "Didn't he?"

Henry slapped her again and she started to cry. Henry was so

139

blind with rage he did not see. She tried to speak, only to get another blow, harder this time, that gave her a taste of blood, and the words disappeared from her mouth.

"He found out about the infant, so he's mocking me for not being able to finish the job." She cried out in pain at how hard Henry was squeezing her arm, and she tried to struggle free. Henry squeezed harder and hit her again. "For not being able to kill the whole family. He sent you to bring me this. This?" Henry slammed her against the wall, knocking her breath away.

"Do you expect me to believe you are stupid enough to come here and thank the man that killed your entire family?" She could only shake her head in confusion with tears streaming down her face. "Do you?"

Henry slammed his fist into the wall next to her head and she gasped. When she still failed to reply, Henry shook his head in disgust and shoved her so she slid down the wall into a heap on the floor. Henry paced in front of her, running his hand through his hair as he tried to decide what to do next.

From the floor, bewildered, she finally stammered out, "I didn't know. I thought you would want it."

Henry stopped mid stride and looked at her, as if she had just given him a brilliant idea.

"You want to know what I want?" He was to her in a single stride and grabbed her by the front of her shirt. He pulled her up from the floor then slammed her into the wall once more, pinning her. "I want to see Radcliffe's face when I throw his damaged little messenger in front of him."

Henry punched the wall next to her head again for emphasis, his knuckles leaving an imprint in the wallpaper. The girl, having managed to keep her breath when she hit the wall this time, began fighting wildly to get free. This just served to aggravate Henry further, so he grabbed a handful of her hair and pulled her toward the door. She intensified her attack, kicking him hard in the shin. The pain caused him to slacken his grip slightly, and she wrenched her hair free. Before she could escape, he caught her by an arm and pulled her back to him. She pushed against his chest, so he twisted the arm he held. It didn't seem to affect her. He grabbed her free wrist in order to pinion her arm, but she had grabbed the chain around his neck and it broke, sending a tiny cross flying through the air.

Henry froze. He had seen this before: a woman struggling for freedom. A man dominating her with strength and violence. A chain breaking, a cross flying. Only in this memory, Henry wasn't the man. He was a small boy cowering in the corner, clutching a broken arm and crying for his mother.

As if dropping something foul, Henry let go of the girl, who fell to the floor, unbalanced by her unexpected freedom. Breathing heavily, he backed up and watched her scramble away until she was against the dresser and could go no further.

Seeing her trembling there, so small and weak, Henry felt ill. He was indeed his father's son and the thought sickened him. She was the messenger. She did not deserve this; Radcliffe did. He stepped over her to retrieve his pistol from the nightstand and his mother's cross from where it had landed on the bed. He had to leave. He forced himself to take one last look at her, a memory of what she looked like to punish him for his deed, before walking out the door. She looked up at him through hurt and bewildered eyes and, barely audible, whispered, "Who is Radcliffe?"

Henry's mind raced to comprehend her question, to come to a conclusion, any conclusion, other than the obvious one. The harder he thought, the more his mind cleared, until he knew with certainty. His stomach dropped. She was an innocent. She had come to bring him the letter because in her misguided mind it was a prize. The self-disgust boiled up inside of Henry, fighting a pitched battle with the rage until it exploded, and he punched his fist through the wall by the door. The girl screamed.

"Goddammit!" Before he could inflict any more damage, Henry yanked the door open and stormed down the hall.

Emma was close to the bed, but she couldn't seem to find the strength to get up off the floor. The pain that ran through her was worse than any she had ever felt before. It was as if a deep chasm had opened in her chest and was now ripping through her from top to bottom, dividing her in half. Her skin was the only thing keeping the halves together against the pressure they exerted trying to break through and be free. She wanted to be free. Free of her body, free of this moment, free of this life. The tears streaming down her face were superfluous. They meant nothing, a child's token in an adult world. She had trusted that man, held him to a hero's status, and in reality he was the one who had murdered her family. She had idolized the man who had taken everything from her. How could she have been so blind to the truth?

142

The chasm ripped deeper, and the pain threatened to overtake her senses. The loss of her family, for whom she had never taken the time to mourn, came flooding through her—a rushing current, tearing at her wounds, keeping them fresh and bloody. A current that threatened to complete the job of tearing her in two, a current she could not control and that had no end in sight. She wanted the end. She hurt so much that eventually she could no longer think, could no longer feel, could no longer breathe. She lay still, holding the two halves of herself together, numb to the world and wishing for death.

16
Manufactured Kismet

From her upstairs window, Kady watched as her parents rode off in the barouche for the city. They were on their way to a dinner at the White House so would be spending the night in Richmond. Normally she would have thrown a fit and then spent the evening sulking since she wasn't invited. She had still thrown a fit—not one of her better fits mind you, but enough to keep up appearances. As it was, she had no intention of spending this evening sulking. After things had quieted down from that horrible day, her mother expressly forbade her from going to see the lieutenant out in the servants' quarters, presumably because she did not want Kady to draw undue attention to him by traipsing back and forth all the time.

At first, she had been perfectly content with this edict; the image of the boot sticking out of the sheet still haunted her dreams. Besides, she had the holidays to keep her occupied, and after that it was too cold to want to spend any time outdoors. However, as the days began to warm, she had started to rethink things. Her mother had said she could be a spy, which meant all of the dire consequences of getting caught by her father—disowned and thrown into the street penniless—could come true. While this eventuality made her shudder, she had realized one thing: that would only happen if he found out! As long as he did not find out, she was free to play spy with her mother. She could even learn to overlook the horrible boot incident, and if she were willing to overlook that, then perhaps she needed to meet this mysterious lieutenant.

Curiosity began to gnaw away at her. She had no idea if the lieutenant was handsome or plain—she had been so disquieted by all the blood the only time she had seen him, she hadn't even bothered to look at his face—but she had romanticized him in her mind to such a degree she was sure they would fall madly in love at first sight, even if he were to resemble an ogre more than a gentleman.

In her mind, he was brave and daring, grievously injured while barely escaping from behind enemy lines with crucial information that would surely turn the tides of the war. He would be a hero, the man who saved countless lives by putting an end to the ridiculousness that now swept the nation. He would be so lauded and loved, people would demand he travel from city to city so they could all thank him in person and glory in his presence. And there she would be, right by his side, helping him to revel in the glad tidings. It would be wonderful!

This fantasy was fully formed in her mind, so the timing of her parents' departure could not have been more perfect. She waited until the barouche rounded the corner and was out of sight before rushing down the stairs to the kitchen. Her mother had spread word that her servant Mary's daughter had fallen ill and had to be quarantined. That explained the food and doctor calls out to the shack. Since Mary had served her mother from the first day she arrived in the South, no one questioned Anna's concern and personal attention for the girl. For fear of contagion, all other visitors were banned. Trays of food were delivered and left at the door if brought by anyone other than Mary or Anna. Old trays were picked up when the new ones were delivered. The setup worked like a charm and provided Mary's capable daughter to be Lieutenant Hart's full-time nurse.

Tonight, however, Kady was going to bring out his tray and finally meet her future husband. She wasn't entirely sure how she was going to circumvent Mary, but she was sure she would come up with something when the time arose. The kitchen was sweltering, though it was not yet summer, and Kady's timing could not have been better. A girl was finishing putting together the tray to take out, and Mary was nowhere in sight. Kady's abrupt entrance startled everyone, and the cook dropped the pot full of water she was carrying to the stove, spilling it everywhere.

"Oh, dear! I certainly did not mean to startle anyone. Mother asked me to check in on Mary's daughter since she is out tonight. I have decided that I shall take her dinner out to her so you all may stay and finish your work here."

As soon as Kady finished speaking, she realized her mistake. The look of astonishment on every face before her confirmed her fear. She had announced her task far too cheerily. Normally any task set forth by her mother was met with procrastination, whining, and occasionally tears, until her mother would order a servant to do it for her.

"Don't look so astonished! Mother promised me some new lace as my prize for helping, and I've had my eye on some in town for quite some time now."

With her admission, a look of normality returned to the servants' faces. Apparently bribery was more feasible to believe than Kady doing something out of the goodness of her heart. She felt as if she should be insulted by that. It was true, though. She couldn't remember a single instance when she had done something for someone else where the action did not also greatly benefit her. She scanned her memory as far back as she could go, yet still came up blank. What she was doing now was selfless, though. And brave. She would help nurse the lieutenant back to health, and hopefully, since he had already been convalescing for several months, the nursing still required would be minimal. And once he was healthy again, they would put a stop to this war, fall madly in love, and get married—not necessarily in that order. It would be wonderful!

A sudden thought wrinkled her brow. Her helping the lieutenant wasn't selfless at all, because she would most definitely benefit from his recovery. She was stymied. Maybe her mother was right and she was completely selfish. Then again, was that necessarily a bad thing? After all, it had served her well thus far. She had no solution to her quandary and, quite frankly, was getting tired of thinking on it. She would leave it for some other dreary day when she had nothing else to think on but matters of character. The thought made her shudder, and she made a mental note to thank God later in her prayers for providing her a wounded soldier to dote upon.

The girl finished up the tray by placing a towel lightly over everything and looking warily at Kady. She hesitated, not sure if she was expected to carry it, or if Kady was up to the task herself. Truth be told, Kady had the same reservations. She'd never carried a tray in her life. Impatience won out over reason.

"Oh, for goodness' sake! I'll be fine. Hand it here."

Kady hadn't made it more than ten feet beyond the kitchen door before she realized the girl's concern was founded. Carrying a heavily laden tray was much harder than it looked! Everything kept sliding back and forth. For a moment, she thought she could balance the tray with one hand and use the other to put things back where they belonged. This idea nearly met with complete disaster. Luckily, she abandoned the endeavor seconds after it had begun, saving everything except for a slosh of soup that was now soaking through the napkin and coming dangerously close to dripping off the tray right onto her skirts. As much as she was loath for this to happen, she feared another attempt at a correction would find her wearing the entire tray instead of merely a drop. Thus, with that horrific eventuality firmly lodged in her head, she decided she could live with a drip or two.

After what felt like an eternity, she made it to the shack. Her arms were burning and had begun to shake from her exertions. She was thankful she was almost there. Then she realized that she had no way of opening the door, short of setting the tray down, which would be nearly impossible because of her hoop skirt. She almost dropped the tray on the spot, wanting to give up in frustration. Unexpectedly, Mary's daughter opened the door and rushed to Kady to take the tray from her, then hurried back inside. She must have seen Kady coming from the window, which was fortunate, because even if Kady hadn't dropped the tray from frustration, she was perilously close to doing so from fatigue.

With her burden relieved, Kady took a moment to adjust her appearance and compose herself before entering the shack. She was aware she needed to hurry, before anyone saw her without the tray, but a sudden swell of nerves washed over her, seeming to paralyze her legs. What if there was still blood everywhere? What if the lieutenant was haggard and gaunt and unseemly to look upon? That would ruin all of her plans, and she was so set on her plans working out perfectly. They had to! Then Kady remembered that if this was something she wanted enough, she would have it; that's what her father always told her, and so far he had been right. Why should this be any different?

Emboldened by this thought, Kady took a deep breath, tipped her hoop to accommodate the small door, and entered. Thankfully, the first of her fears was completely unfounded. The shack was perfectly clean, or as clean as a shack with dirt floors and only tattered muslin curtains covering glassless windows could be. There was no blood remaining, and that was what had worried Kady the most, so she was set at ease. However, she found the sparse and ramshackle furnishings quite appalling. In fact, calling them furnishings was a bit of a stretch. It took some imagination to realize the tacked-together bits of wood were a table and rickety chairs. There wasn't even a proper bed for the lieutenant. He was on what looked like a blanket covering a pallet of straw and was sitting propped up against the wall. Despite this meager bed, he actually appeared to be comfortable. He was gaunt as she had feared, but still handsome, and that handsomeness would only grow as he continued to heal.

Kady waved away the chair Mary's daughter offered her. Kady was quite certain if she tried to sit on it, it would break, throwing her to the ground. She would never risk that mortification. So instead, she made a production of adjusting her skirts and kneeling down next to the straw pallet so she was within an arm's reach of the lieutenant. The whole while he watched her skeptically. Once settled, she looked at him and smiled warmly.

"There, now isn't this nice?"

"If you call food fit for a Negro and getting covered in dirt nice, then yes I suppose it is *nice*. Especially now that the fleas are coming out."

Kady blanched; the thought of having fleas climbing on her made her skin crawl. She cursed herself for not thinking of that beforehand. The help were always carrying around fleas and having to have their heads shaved because of lice. She thanked her lucky stars she wasn't wearing one of her favorite gowns because everything she was wearing was going to be burned the second she got back to the house and could change into new clothes. Swallowing hard, she recomposed herself.

"Come now, why don't we talk of nice things instead of that. Here, this tray looks quite presentable." She motioned and the girl hurried over and set the tray awkwardly on the pallet, so Kady had to hold the corner to keep it from tipping over. She waved the girl away and repositioned it herself so it lay between the two of them. The lieutenant crossed his arms over his chest, looked at the tray briefly, and then looked away.

"See, here's some soup and some nice warm bread." Why did she keep saying nice? She sounded like a complete simpleton. "My name is Kady."

The lieutenant grabbed the bread and tore off a hunk.

"Something happen to the Negro who usually brings my food?" He did not look at Kady, keeping his focus on the bread.

It rankled her that she did not seem to hold any sort of appeal for him. She desperately wanted to be alone with him. She knew if only they were alone things would be different, but she couldn't ask the girl to step outside when everyone thought Kady was visiting her. She would have to accept that the girl would report the entirety of their discourse back to Mary or, worse yet, her mother. She would have to make do with what she had to work with. Ignoring his question completely, Kady strove on toward her goal.

"I believe in polite society a gentleman introduces himself after he is given a lady's name."

The lieutenant laughed. "You are assuming I'm a gentleman."

"Well, of course, you're a gentleman! You are an officer, aren't you? And besides, you have to be a gentleman. I am determined to fall in love with you, and I cannot fall in love with anybody but a gentleman!"

The lieutenant burst out laughing again, only this time much louder. He immediately clamped his hand over his mouth to squelch the noise.

Kady was flustered, and it took her a moment to realize the enormity of her blunder. She had said far more than she intended, and the rush of crimson racing up her décolleté and into her cheeks revealed her mortification. On the verge of tears, Kady started to pull herself up from the ground so she could flee back to the comfort of her room. The lieutenant grabbed her arm, arresting her movement. Kady struggled against him; she wanted nothing more to do with him. How could anyone ever fall in love with her after she had proven herself to be such a colossal ninny?

"Let me go!"

He tightened his grip.

Finally she stopped struggling and resigned herself to being ridiculed and mocked.

"Miss Kady." His voice was gentle now but she refused to look up. "Please look at me, Miss Kady."

She did not budge.

"I don't think I can reach your chin to lift your pretty face without rolling over onto my bad leg, but if that's what it takes, then that is what I shall do."

Against her will she smiled. He had called her pretty. As nonchalantly as she could manage, she wiped away the tears that had welled in her eyes and looked up at the lieutenant.

"I do apologize, Miss Kady. I'm afraid I've been in this war long enough to forget my manners. Will you ever forgive me?"

Kady did not trust her voice to come without a confluence of tears to follow, so she settled with nodding her head.

"Good. Then I do hope you will allow me the pleasure of introducing myself. I am Lieutenant Jacob Hart of the United States Regulars." He held out his hand for hers and, as if a girl at her first ball, she shyly lifted hers and placed it in his. He gently kissed her knuckles and looked back to her in time to see the blush renew itself in her cheeks.

"Now tell me. What could a pretty young girl like you want to do with me? I'm a stranger in these parts and a cripple to boot. Why don't you go after one of those young Confederate officers whose family has enough money to keep him out of the line of fire?"

"I don't want a Confederate officer. I'm a spy for the North." It sounded absurd coming out of her mouth, like something a little girl would say. Looking at the lieutenant more closely she saw the faint trace of wrinkles around his eyes and mouth. He was older than she had assumed he would be. Not only did she sound like a young girl, he must see her as one as well.

A smile stole across his face before he could stop it, but he refrained from laughing this time.

"I suppose I shouldn't be surprised. If your mama is a spy, then why shouldn't you be? You are Anna's daughter aren't you?"

"Yes. What does my mother have anything to do with it?" Why did he have to bring her mother into this? This had nothing to do with her mother; it had only to do with Jacob and her.

"I apologize again, I did not mean to upset you."

"I am not upset."

She was, but she had no idea why.

Jacob looked at her puzzled, unsure what to do next.

Kady could feel Jacob's gaze on her and knew she needed to say something, do something, but she was confounded. How is it she could navigate a party, exchanging flirtatious witticisms with a half-dozen men without putting a second thought to it, but five minutes with this man and she was a flushed, teary wreck? She did not know what to do with herself, and she did not know how to fix this encounter. The only thing she did know was that any self-respecting girl would flee this situation and forget it had ever happened. Strangely, she couldn't seem to tear herself away. Committing herself to the task at hand, she took a shuddering breath and looked the lieutenant in the face.

"I'm sorry, Lieutenant, it appears I am upset. For the life of me I cannot tell you why."

Jacob leaned toward her and gently wiped a tear from her cheek, leaving a smudge of dirt as evidence of where their skin had met.

153

"Please, call me Jacob, and no need to apologize. I can imagine the sight of me would be upsetting to someone like you."

"You are hard on yourself, Jacob. Why would you be upsetting to look upon?"

Jacob looked at her in disbelief and motioned to where a second leg should have been on the bed. "I'm a cripple."

This time it was Kady who laughed. "You are not a cripple, you are a hero, and I won't stand for you or anybody else saying any different."

Jacob's face softened as he looked into Kady's eyes.

She smiled at him. "Here, eat your soup before it gets cold and tell me all about what happened."

By the time Kady left the shack, night was well upon them, and she had long since missed her own supper. She did not care, though, and it was only the need to balance the tray that kept her from skipping back to the big house. Despite their rocky start, they had had the most wonderful conversation. Jacob's tale of how he was injured was thrilling, romantic, and heroic. She realized he had probably embellished a bit here and there for her sake. She loved him even more for that. Her reverie wasn't even broken by the sideways glances she got from the kitchen girls when she dropped the tray off, or the outright stare of disapproval from Mary. She simply requested a hot bath be drawn for her and a cold plate be brought up for her supper.

She ate her plate while the bath was heated and poured. Then her servants undressed her and helped her into the bath. Picking up her hand mirror to gaze at herself, she saw the smudge on her cheek where

Jacob had wiped away the tear. She smiled and gingerly touched it before turning to her attendants.

"I want all of those clothes scrubbed thoroughly, and if you can't get them completely clean, burn them." They looked at her in disbelief, but she had turned back to her hand mirror. "And this water isn't nearly hot enough for you to properly scrub me clean. So fetch fresh water and extra soap. Leave my face though; I like it exactly as it is."

The two servants looked at each other, stupefied, while hurrying to follow their orders.

17
Starting Over

After her encounter with Henry, Emma had wandered from town to town, letting her grief choose her direction. She was surprised at how quickly the pain from her injuries faded away, even if the bruises lingered much longer. The pain from her grief was another story. It was not until she found herself standing in front of the ruins of her old house, now overgrown with weeds, that she was shaken out of her lethargy. She needed a plan, or barring that, somewhere to call home. She contemplated riding into town, showing up at the blacksmith's shop, and announcing that she had changed her mind. Could he find her a place to stay? Could she stay with him and his wife and see her baby brother? The thought of seeing her brother again, her last living relative, made her heart clench painfully. No. It was no safer for her to be there now than it had been the day she left. For all she knew, there were people watching and waiting for her to return, ready to arrest Blackie and her the moment she showed her face. No, that was not an option.

She sighed. She still did not have a plan, but at least she had eliminated one. Rummaging through what was left of the house and the outbuildings, she searched for anything that might be of use or value. She found precious little and soon realized that she had not been the first person to do this. She did find a few items that held sentimental value, so her efforts were not completely wasted.

In honor of her sixteenth birthday, almost two years earlier, her sisters had made her a dream catcher with sixteen feathers on it. Their uncle, a trapper from Michigan who had been visiting them at the time, had taught her sisters how to make the hideous thing. Emma had hung it in the stable under the pretext of protecting the new foal, since she already had good dreams. At the time, she could barely stand to look at the savage thing. Now it was the most beautiful item she owned. Securing her new possessions on her horse, she mounted and headed north. She had no particular reason to head this direction, it just seemed to make more sense than going back the way she had come. It was a crisp, yet pleasant, late winter day, and she allowed her horse to set the pace.

She could start spying again, but for which side? Fury raged through her veins. This damn war. No matter what side you chose, they were all bastards. Bastards with their own plans who did not care upon whom they stomped in their pursuit. She took a deep breath to steady herself. She could not afford to get trapped back in those thoughts; they were too strong. She hated the South for killing her family and she hated the North for allowing it to happen. Mostly, though, she hated Captain Henry. She loathed him. Too often, she woke up in the middle of the night in a cold sweat, his face haunting her dreams. Emma pinched the bridge of her nose and took another deep breath. The bile in her stomach refused to settle.

She spit onto the side of the road. That seemed to help, as if she could remove the memories of him from her body, bit by bit. There must be something she could do; one swift act that could make everything right again. She had no idea what that would be or how she could do it. She didn't even know where to find him again.

That is when it occurred to her: she would spy for herself. She would figure out where he was and then…then…well, she would work that out later. This was a start! She would find where Henry was and then get even. Yes, she would take her revenge, and then make a new life for herself, far away from this war.

April 28, 1864

Hart fit to travel within the month. Handle
Yankee Doodle.
NR

33-14-24-32-34 65-41 43-41-62-42
21-33-24-22 12-32-22 22-13 22-24-33-44-54-34
46-32-22-21-32-23 22-21-54 53-13-23-22-21
21-33-23-36-34-54 15-33-23-64-54-54
36-13-13-36-34-54
23-24

18
Plan B

After the war had started, Kady's mother began to host afternoon gatherings of local ladies, and after attending one, Kady did her dead level best to avoid the rest. The ladies generally sat in a circle in the drawing room doing needlepoint and gossiping or playing games. While Kady was actually quite fond of needlepoint she was bored by petty gossiping. Why did anybody care if old widow Worthington muttered to herself during the church services or that Mrs. Turner's son was spotted with questionable company of a female variety? Kady certainly did not care, and she preferred her needlework to be done in silence. As for games, she was perfectly dreadful at them and on principle made it a point to avoid all things at which she was dreadful. After all, there were so many things at which she excelled, why waste her time looking ridiculous at those she didn't?

Much to her consternation, her mother had demanded she attend today because a few members of the party were her mother's informants, and if Kady were to be a spy, she needed to learn how information was passed. Kady was taken aback by this revelation. Her mother was planning to collect Southern secrets while her father was in the house? And this wasn't the first time! No wonder her mother had been so afraid when Kady found out. Not only was her mother a spy, her mother was the head of an intricate web. Her spies went out, gathered information, and then brought it back so she could compile it all and send it on to the proper places. Had Kady revealed her mother's secret, it could have toppled the entire ring. Her head was still spinning a bit by this news, but she tried to focus on the instructions her mother was giving her.

"Since the gathering of ladies will sometimes differ, each of the informants will take out a kerchief at some point and then tuck it loosely into the top of her left sleeve so a corner remains out. That way we can identify ourselves to each other discreetly."

"Do I need to—?"

"No. At this point I don't want to reveal you to the others." The response came a little too quickly and stung. Once more Kady felt the inadequacy she always felt around her mother. Anna did not believe Kady would succeed as a spy, and, therefore, her mother did not want to open herself up to the rebukes of her colleagues for letting Kady into the inner circle.

Unfazed, Anna continued, "I know there is intelligence coming in about troop movements. So once everyone is settled in, I will suggest we play a memory game. As the initiator, I will choose the game where we work our way through the alphabet, and I will suggest we do so using city names. I'll start with something like Albany and we'll go from there."

Kady was beginning to get nervous, and they hadn't even started yet. Not only was she horrible at memory games, she did not think she knew that many city names.

"Now pay attention, this is the important part. Let's say somebody has intelligence that troops will be moving through Charlotte.

161

When we get to 'C,' that woman will either suggest Charlotte be picked as the 'C' city or make some sort of comment about Charlotte. If somebody else has heard of a change of plans, they will refute the Charlotte comment and say the city that they heard."

Kady had gone from nervous to completely despondent. There was no way she was going to be able to remember the names in the game as well as all of the secondary cities for the troop movements.

"As an example if someone said to pick Charlotte because they love Charlotte at this time of year, I could refute them by saying, 'No, I rather prefer Raleigh in the summer.' Then we would have a laugh about how you can't say Raleigh for a 'C' city, and move on with the game. Now I have learned the troops were originally planning on moving through Charlotte, but for whatever reason have changed their plans and are now planning on heading through Raleigh. Does that make sense?"

Kady's face revealed the abject fear she felt, because her mother paused for a moment, her face softening, and touched Kady's arm.

"Don't worry. Today you are simply one of the ladies in the circle, there for a pleasant afternoon's diversion. Since you won't have a kerchief, there's no way for you to ruin anything. Just try to pick up what you can."

Thankfully, Kady did not have to hide the hurt look on her face for long because Mary entered to inform them the first of the guests had arrived. Anna started to leave, when she turned back to Kady.

"And for heaven's sake, try to act natural and not let on that there is something going on besides a ladies' circle."

Anna left the room, and Kady felt her face flush and tears begin to well up in her eyes. She had always suspected her mother did not care

162

for her deeply, but she had not been prepared for such open hostility. When her mother had found out about Kady's visit to the lieutenant, her rebuke had been venomous, and Anna had called her a stupid girl several times. Kady knew she wasn't in possession of a great intelligence, but she was smart enough to know that she shouldn't reveal there were spies present! A simpleton would know that, and yet her mother felt the need to point it out for her.

The sting of the comment began to subside as the flame of anger in her chest blew hotter. Somehow she would find a way to prove to her mother she was capable, that she was worthy of this great task. Her first step would have to be sitting through this afternoon and performing brilliantly, somehow. Maybe if she prepared herself by looking at a map to learn some names of cities she would do better. Yes, that was a perfect plan! Picking up her skirts, Kady practically ran down the stairs and burst into her father's study hoping he had left some of his maps out, or at the least easily accessible. However, upon entering she let out a squeak of surprise. There was a tall man leaning over the table examining one of the very maps she coveted. She recognized him immediately as the officer who had so openly enjoyed her piano playing that infamous day in the parlor. He was even more handsome than she remembered, and obviously startled as well. He was able to compose himself more quickly than Kady, and he offered her his apologies.

"I do apologize for startling you, my lady. That was not my intention."

Blushing, Kady instinctively fell into a curtsy.

"I fear the apology should be mine, sir. I have burst in upon your work, and I should leave you to continue." Despite her words she made no move to exit. The look in the officer's eyes bade her to stay.

"Please don't leave on my account, you were clearly looking for something when you entered, and you shouldn't leave without it." He took her hand and brushed her knuckles with his lips. "I am Captain Henry, and I am at your service."

Smiling warmly, Kady replied, "Pleased to meet you, Captain. I believe you are acquainted with my father?"

"Then you must be Miss Kady. I have never heard a man speak higher praise than he does of you. After the impromptu recital you provided, I fear his praise does not do you justice."

Blushing again, Kady quickly moved to change the subject. "I am actually in need of a map."

A smile broke across his face as Henry gestured toward the table. "Then you are in luck, because there are plenty of maps to be had. Does any particular map hold your interest?"

Moving toward the table, the map that lay on top piqued her interest. "How about this one? It's so pretty and intricate."

Henry laughed despite himself and replied, "I wasn't aiming for aesthetic beauty, but I'll take the compliment all the same."

Kady looked up at him in wonder. "Did you draw this?"

"Yes I did." Though he was trying to hide it, Kady sensed there was no small amount of pride in the captain that she liked his work.

"What does the map depict?" Henry smiled at her, then carefully turned the map so she could see it right side up.

"We, this plantation, are over here up the James River a bit. This area over here is a great swamp."

"Oh! That's the Dismal Swamp. It has such a horrid name I

remembered it from the first moment I ever heard of it."

Henry smiled appreciatively at her. "Very good. I bet you didn't know there are all of these paths and canals that run through it, and a lake, too."

"That's what you've drawn in here!"

"Precisely. Now truth be told, some of these paths disappear if it rains too hard, so I mainly focused on the canals, so men will know where to meet us when we carry," Henry hesitated, choosing his words carefully, "supplies and other such things safely through from the North Carolina side," he pointed to an entrance at the south, "to the Virginia side," he pointed to a spot to the north, "or vice versa. It's quicker and safer than it would be to carry those same supplies along the road." He traced his finger along the drawn road, all the while keeping his eyes trained on Kady's face.

She returned his look. "How clever you are. Show me more."

Clearly pleased, Henry turned his attention back to the map and explained the intricacies of the inner paths and the route up the James River that led them directly to the capital city of Richmond.

After her discussion with the captain, Kady retired to the upstairs sitting room to work on some needlepoint. She had no desire to interrupt her mother's gathering. It was early evening before Anna finally caught up with her. Stopping in front of Kady, with her hands on her hips, Anna fumed for a moment waiting for an explanation before finally speaking herself.

"Where have you been all afternoon? I knew it was pointless to think you could ever do this!"

Silently Kady handed her mother the needlepoint she was working on, walked over to the door, and after checking there was no one in the hall, closed the door and crossed back to her mother.

"Do you think this will make me happy? A hastily and ill-conceived rose bush?" Anna cried.

Without taking it away completely, Kady turned the needlepoint around in her mother's hand so it was sideways.

"On my way to your gathering, I had the good fortune of running into Captain Henry. He was promoted to captain because of valor in the line of duty as well as his knowledge of the Dismal Swamp. He was kind enough to explain to me the intricacies of the map he has drawn out depicting where supply lines and other things, which I'm guessing means correspondence, run." Kady paused long enough to enjoy the look of utter disbelief on her mother's face before drawing her mother's attention to the needlework and continuing.

"The ill-conceived rose bush represents the swamp. This winding branch here represents the road everyone takes to get around the swamp. Each red rose represents an entrance or exit. I did not bother to depict the routes within the swamp, because according to the captain, they change depending on the amount of rainfall. So I think it would probably be best for our men to set up ambushes at the red roses instead of wandering around lost inside."

"What do the pink roses inside the bush represent?"

"Oh, those are decoration. I thought it looked sad with nothing in the middle."

Without waiting for a reply, Kady turned and used every ounce of self-control she possessed to keep from skipping away, leaving her mother

166

standing in the middle of the room holding a hastily done needlepoint,

for once, completely speechless.

May 12, 1864
Rebs using Captain Henry to move supplies
through the Dismal Swamp. 6 access points,
but do not enter swamp. Map to follow in
form of rose bush.
NR

53-33-15 43-65 43-41-62-42
24-54-25-66 45-66-32-23-56
11-33-14-22-33-32-23 21-54-23-24-15 22-13
53-13-44-54 66-45-14-14-34-32-54-66
22-21-24-13-45-56-21 22-21-54
36-32-66-53-33-34 66-46-33-53-14 62
33-11-11-54-66-66 14-13-32-23-22-66 25-45-22
36-13 23-13-22 54-23-22-54-24 66-46-33-53-14
53-33-14 22-13 12-13-34-34-13-46 32-23
12-13-24-53 13-12 24-13-66-54 25-45-66-21
23-24

19
Teacher's Pet

"No, not that one, grab the old gingham dress in the back of the bureau." The servant pulled the dress out and then gave Kady a quizzical look.

"Why, miss, this dress ain't near big enough to go over your hoops, not nowhere near."

"Well, of course it isn't. I'm not going to be wearing them today."

The servant almost dropped the dress in shock and openly stared at Kady in disbelief. Since the day she had been given her first adult crinolines, she had never stepped foot out of her room wearing anything else. There was a joke among the house women that if the big house were burning down, they would have to draw lots to see who had to go up and help Kady into her dress so she could escape properly. Thankfully, Kady was expecting this response and had an explanation at the ready.

"Oh, don't you give me that look. Mama wants me to go out and look after Mary's daughter for a spell, and I'm not about to go ruining another one of my good dresses!"

Understanding washed over the servant's face. She clearly remembered the perplexing night she was instructed to burn her mistress's clothes. She brought the gingham dress over to Kady and slid it over her body. Walking over to the mirror, Kady examined herself as

she smoothed down the dress. It was odd to see such a straight
silhouette. She was so accustomed to having a bell shape that she hardly
recognized herself, and she did not like what she saw. She looked plain
and unadorned. She pouted silently for a moment, turning this way and
that, hoping her appearance would improve by changing the angle.
Maybe this was a bad idea. As much as she hated wearing one of her
beautiful dresses out to that filthy hovel again, she hated the idea of
Jacob seeing her like this even more. She was utterly torn.

Thankfully the decision was made for her when she heard her
father's voice outside upbraiding one of the livery boys for his shoddy
preparations of the barouche. Her parents were going out for something
or other but would be back for supper—which meant she only had a
couple of hours with Jacob, and she was not going to waste any of her
precious time changing clothes. She would have to go as is and make the
best of the situation.

Not waiting to see that her parents' barouche was on its way, she
hurried from her room and skipped down the stairs. It occurred to her
that while she did not like the look, it was much easier to navigate and
move about without her crinolines. She looked around cautiously when
she got to the back door. Nobody was paying any attention to her.
Nobody knew who she was! She was invisible in her own house simply
by putting on a shabby dress. Kady smiled and made her way out to
Jacob with a carefree bounce to her step. She was in such high spirits by
the time she got to the door, she forgot the niceties of knocking and
simply let herself in. Upon entering she was startled to discover Jacob
sitting in his underclothes. Immediately she turned away, blushing a deep
red.

"Oh, my goodness! I am so dreadfully sorry. I should have knocked. I should go. I'll leave." Kady turned back toward the door to let herself out but was so flustered she couldn't get the door to open before Jacob spoke.

"Miss Kady, don't go, please." Kady stopped fussing with the door but did not turn away from it. "I do wish I had something more to put on, to make you more at ease. I'm afraid Mary has taken all of my clothes for washing."

Kady still did not move.

"I would like you to stay. If you'd feel comfortable, that is. I haven't had anyone to talk to for days."

Kady stood without moving, thinking. She knew she had to leave. Propriety and decency demanded she leave this instant. There was a man, practically naked, sitting behind her who had no claim to her. They were not betrothed, or even promised. She had no business seeing him in this state of undress, much less spending time with him. Yet, she couldn't open the door. Her hand refused to move. She was in the same room as a naked Yankee soldier. How deliciously scandalous! Not that she could tell anyone about it. Or could she tell someone? Maybe she could let slip that she had heard there was a Yankee soldier on the loose besmirching the virtues of maids up and down the James River. That she knew of such a girl but had promised never to let slip who she was. Oh it would be scrumptious, all of those old women salivating to know what she knew. They might even try to bribe her into telling them. She would hold firm, for the sake of the poor girl's honor. She would be the only one who knew all the sordid details about the biggest scandal in the county. How fantastic. The next time she was forced to listen to all of the women gossiping, she could smile and look down her nose at them because they would be completely clueless she was at the heart of the biggest story of them all. A thrill ran down her spine. She had made up her mind. Turning, she looked right at Jacob with a forced air of nonchalance.

"Well, if you insist. I'd hate to think of you sitting here with no one to talk to simply because you have no clothes." Kady started toward the chair at the small table, but Jacob beckoned her to sit with him on the pallet. She blushed. Scandal was one thing, actually besmirching her virtue was quite another. She smiled sweetly at him and definitively took a seat at the table. They sat in an awkward silence. Kady could feel Jacob's eyes taking in her now svelte form. Without her skirts and padding to alter her figure she felt as naked as the lieutenant. He seemed to be appreciating what he saw too, which deepened her blush yet gave her a definite feeling of satisfaction.

She couldn't fault him for looking, though, because she found herself gazing unabashedly at his body: the thicket of curly hair on his chest; the defined muscles of his upper abdomen, and lower abdomen. Oh heavens! Why did the shape of those muscles along his hips make her feel so strange? A warmth had begun to spread throughout her body and the shack started to feel as if there were a fire burning. With some effort she tore her eyes away before they could drift any lower down his body. She had never seen a man undressed like this before. Well she'd seen slaves, but that was different. Or was it? To be honest, the deep ebony of the slaves was much more beautiful than Jacob's sickly white pallor. Jacob spoke, interrupting her thoughts.

"Perhaps you can help me with something."

171

"Of course!" Flustered, Kady practically leapt up from her seat, then blushed in embarrassment when she realized she didn't yet know what he needed help with, and therefore, she might not need to be standing up.

Jacob smiled at her. "I am supposed to be deciphering these messages your mother left me. However, I find it extremely difficult to write here in my bed and it becomes tedious. Perhaps you can help with the decoding?"

Kady smiled and nodded her head eagerly. "Oh, yes! That sounds marvelously fun. Where are they?"

"Right here." Jacob picked up a Bible from his side and opened it to reveal two pages of unfolded paper and several that were folded.

Kady carefully walked over and took the items almost reverently.

"How does it work?" she asked

Jacob indicated the top paper. "In the table is the entire alphabet as well as the numbers zero through nine. You fill in the key here on the left of the table and below the table." Jacob shuffled the bottom paper up. "Then you get a number from here—the first one is 24. The two corresponds with the numbers to the left, and the four corresponds with the numbers on the bottom."

"And where those two numbers intersect on the table, is the correct letter?"

"Exactly!"

"How do I know what key to use?"

"Ah, that right there is why your mama went to such great lengths to save my life. It looked as if I were going to be captured, so I memorized the key and destroyed the paper it was written on." Kady smiled at him and Jacob smiled back. "6-2-5-3-4-1 on the left and 3-2-5-6-1-4 underneath. It's of course different now, since so many months have passed, but that key saved the day, let me tell you."

Kady skipped back over to the table and sat down. "What is the new key?"

"1-2-4-6-5-3 on the left and 2-6-5-4-1-3 underneath. That open letter came from a spy outside of our ring. It has been sitting for a couple of weeks because none of our tables worked. Lucky for you, a new table came in this very morning."

	7	D	4	K	W	I
1	7	D	4	K	W	I
2	Y	0	V	P	2	S
4	R	J	E	9	Z	C
6	3	N	A	H	T	5
5	G	X	1	M	B	6
3	O	8	Q	U	F	L
	2	6	5	4	1	3

"I get to be the first to try it!"

"The very first."

Kady tried to hide her excitement and had Jacob repeat the

numbers to make sure she had written them correctly onto the table. She did and with a quick glance she saw that "46" equaled the letter "J," so she wrote it down. Jacob hadn't started on any of the missives, so she had a good amount of work in front of her; however, unlike Jacob's description of tedium, Kady quickly found that she loved the work. It was as if she had a great, complicated puzzle. Before she knew it, she had the date of the letter, "June 8, 1864." She turned to show her handy work to Jacob, only to find he had drifted off to sleep. That was probably all for the better; he was still healing and needed as much sleep as he could get. Kady turned back to her work and began to translate the letter. It was relatively slow work at first, but as each new word was revealed, a trill of excitement ran through her. After a while, she found she was translating with ease, only looking back at the table for letters not commonly used. Finished, and seeing Jacob still asleep, Kady sat back to read over her handy work by herself.

46-34-66-45 36 55-36-53-15
66-30-42-61-64-45-42-66 42-32-23-45
42-45-43-45-13-25-45-16
43-32-66-31-13-42-54-65-61-13-32-66
23-64-32-24-14-45-45-24-45-42 31-45-33-33
65-61 52-45-61-61-22-23-51-34-42-52
43-32-66-16-32-33-45-66-43-45-23
14-65

June 8, 1864

Northern Rose,
Received confirmation shopkeeper fell at
Gettysburg. Condolences.
KA

Sadly, the message itself was not all that exciting. Shopkeeper had fallen at Gettysburg. This news was awfully late. Kady knew next to nothing about battles, but even she knew the Battle of Gettysburg happened almost a year ago. Who was this shopkeeper? And why would his death be so important to her mother so long after the fact? Kady was so engrossed in these thoughts she didn't hear the person approaching the front of the shack. Luckily the noise had roused Jacob, and he was able to motion to her in time. She hastily shoved the correspondence and Bible at him and ran to the low window in the back. Shoving aside the shabby curtain, she didn't even take the time to panic about how she would climb through and simply flung herself through the window.

Landing roughly on the ground outside, she had to bite her cheek to keep from crying out in pain. She had smashed her elbow on the windowsill and scraped up both of her knees, not to mention the debris that was now clinging to her skirt and hands. She wiped her hands together to rid herself of the big pieces and then vigorously rubbed her hands on her skirt to remove the remaining dirt. She was sure she looked a frightful mess. Her hasty departure was necessary though, as she heard her mother's voice coming from inside the shack. Why wasn't she out with her father? Perhaps she didn't go, or something happened to the barouche and they'd had to come back. Either way it was damned inconvenient as now she would have to sneak back inside without either of her parents seeing her. She made a move to head back when her mother's voice froze her.

"Have you actually done any work, or am I correct in thinking that your request to become a courier for me was simply to prolong your stay here?"

"I've finished the first cipher for you. Here."

What did he mean he had finished the cipher? He hadn't done anything. She had done the cipher and he was taking credit! No, he wasn't taking credit, he was covering for her. Of course he had to tell her mother he had done the work himself, otherwise he would have to reveal that Kady had been coming to visit him. This quelled her anger somewhat. It still rankled her that she couldn't take credit for her work. Her mother's broken voice cut the silence from the shack.

"Are you certain this is correct?"

"Yes, I am. You knew this shopkeeper?" Evidently Jacob had at least read the message before passing it on.

With a bit more steadiness in her voice, Anna replied, "I used to work with him. I knew he was at the battle and never heard from him after. I have been trying to track him down since. If you will excuse me."

Kady heard the rustle of her mother leaving the shack. Kady leaned against the wall and after a moment realized she had been holding her breath. She let it out and took a deep gulp to replenish her lungs. She hadn't seen her mother's face, but from the sound of her voice alone, Kady knew she had been on the verge of tears. This shopkeeper, whoever that was, had been more than a passing acquaintance.

52-36-24-55 46-32 34-32-41-31
33-14-21-62-22-13-64-53
25-55-14-43-43-11-53-24-55-13 24-55-55-13
24-55-33 14-62-62-55-43-43 21-64 21-22-55
24-55-43-21 25-55-62-25-36-11-21 54-14-54-14
26-11-25-13
26-13

June 28, 1864

Watchdog reassigned. Need new access to
the Nest. Recruit Mama Bird.
BD

20
Secret Bliss

Kady began visiting Jacob more and more frequently. Since her mother had found out about the shopkeeper she had barely left her room, eliminating the need for Kady to hide her trips. The kitchen servants now expected her every evening. She even had an additional gingham dress made that she could wear without her hoops. Whenever Mary caught her on these trips, she would give Kady a disapproving look, but either she was not telling Anna, or Anna had given up caring. The latter thought troubled Kady, so she simply decided that Mary was keeping quiet. The kitchen servants had started to talk, though. Mary's glares had become so openly accusatory that rumors had started to circulate about Kady, Anna, and what exactly was going on in that shack. As much as it rankled her, Kady knew she had to do something about it before her father caught wind of the whisperings.

It had taken several days to think of something, and she didn't like what she had come up with. However, as she could think of nothing else, it would have to do. She hoped Mary was in the kitchen tonight, so she could carry out her plan before she lost her nerve. As luck would have it, Mary was preparing the tray as Kady entered, and the look that Mary graced Kady with was derisive to say the least. Planting her feet, Kady took a deep breath to brace herself, and summoning up the part of her that came from her father, she loudly addressed Mary.

"That look better not be meant for me, girl. You forget your place!"

The immediate look of shock on Mary's face was quickly replaced with a flush of anger.

Kady was taken aback for a minute. She didn't know somebody who was so black could turn red, but there was the proof right in front of her. Actually, it was more of a purple. Either way, Kady had no idea that could happen. Feeling the sideways stares of every other servant in the kitchen, Kady was recalled to her task.

"What was that? If you have something to say to me, girl, you say it." She could tell Mary was roiling, but surrounded by other servants and with Anna absent, her hands were tied.

Mary bowed her head, staring at her feet.

"No'm. Nothin' to say."

"Then I suggest you school those eyes of yours to be more civil, or if you cannot, maybe I will have to tell my daddy we have no need for a servant girl who's been sick for half the year and tell him to sell her off at his first convenience." Every servant in the kitchen froze, including Mary. Kady's father had often sold off children as punishment for insolent behavior. Because of that, the children were cared for communally in hopes of making it harder to tell which child belonged to which parent. Mary was the one exception. As Anna's personal servant, it was assumed there was a certain amount of immunity that Mary enjoyed from punishments meted out to the lesser servants. In one short moment, Kady had shattered the protective case around Mary.

"No'm, no need for nothin'. I's sorry for offense, didn't mean nothin' by nothin'."

The usually headstrong Mary was gone. Standing before Kady

179

was a cowed slave, a broken spirit who knew the heartache of watching a child walk away in shackles never to be seen again. Shortly before his marriage to Anna, Andrew had sold Mary's son in order to free her up for her new duties. Kady's heart broke. She had no idea her words would be so powerful, no idea Mary would actually believe her, believe her capable of separating daughter from mother. Kady wanted to rush to Mary, tell her she did not mean it, that it was all an act to get the other servants to stop gossiping. It was too late, though, the damage had been done.

"Good. Then I suggest you make yourself useful elsewhere. I will bring your daughter her tray."

Kady grabbed the tray and exited, leaving the kitchen in an uncomfortable silence. It wasn't until she was outside that she realized by taking the tray she had cemented her power over Mary in the servants' eyes. She had in essence flaunted how easy it was to keep Mary away from her daughter. Kady felt bile rising in her throat and tears welled in her eyes threatening to spill over. This is not what she had wanted, what she had intended. She wanted to stop the gossiping. She hadn't meant to hurt anyone. And the ease with which those threats had come out of her mouth frightened her. It had been second nature, as easy as throwing one of her fits to get her way. Before she knew it, she had arrived at the shack, set the tray on the table, and knelt to sit on Jacob's bed. His voice broke her out of her thoughts and she let out a short yelp of alarm, realizing his presence.

Jacob reached out and touched her cheek, trying to comfort her. "What's wrong? What happened?"

"Oh, it's nothing. It's silly. I'm silly. I said something I didn't mean and it all went sideways."

"Is everything all right?" Jacob looked in the direction of the big house, concerned. "Are you in trouble?"

Kady laughed. "I'm fine; I got exactly what I wanted." Relief washed over Jacob's features. "I'm upset at how I got what I wanted."

Jacob laughed, and stroking her cheek with his thumb, he leaned in and kissed her ever so gently on the mouth. Kady's eyes closed dreamily and relaxed as Jacob slowly kissed his way down her jawline to whisper in her ear.

"That's my sweet girl."

"I'm your girl?" The words were breathless and barely audible. Her insides were swimming as the altercation in the kitchen disappeared from her mind and exclamations whirred around instead. He had called her his girl! She was somebody's girl!

"Of course you are."

As though those words were enough to mark her as his property, he took her face in both of his hands and kissed her again. This kiss wasn't gentle. His tongue parted her lips and when she tasted his fervent yearning, she kissed him back and laced her arms around his neck pulling herself close to him. His hands had left her face and as they traced their way down her body, a slow warmth began to grow from deep down in her belly. When his hands reached her waist, he lifted her as if she weighed no more than a feather and laid her on the bed next to him. He did not climb on top of her, merely rolled onto the side of his good leg and continued to kiss her deeper and more passionately as his hand began a slow exploration up toward her breasts.

Kady's mind was racing. Jacob had kissed her before, however, they had always been sitting up or standing. This new dynamic, lying next to him, felt dangerous, wrong. She knew she shouldn't be doing this, but she wanted him. She wanted him in a way that was unseemly to say the least. When his hand reached her breast and started to caress the nipple that was standing prominently against the gingham dress, she let out a moan of pleasure.

Breaking away from kissing her, Jacob chuckled. "Oh, so you like that, do you?"

Much to her dismay, his hand left off its work and moved quickly down to her thigh to begin rucking up her dress.

Kady took in a sharp intake of breath and tensed. Jacob had reached bare skin and his thumb stroked her inner thigh while inching upward. Every ounce of common sense in Kady's brain told her he needed to stop. That she needed to get up and flee far, far away. But the warmth deep in her belly said otherwise and had grown and spread throughout her body. She could feel a warm dampness at the apex of her thighs, and despite her best intentions, she found her legs were slowly spreading apart to ease Jacob's way. He kissed her again, more sedately, and his hand ceased its progress upward, though the gentle strokes continued.

Jacob whispered to her, "Tell me you want me."

"Oh, Jacob, yes." Kady had surrendered to her desire. Propriety be damned.

"Tell me you need me."

"I need you, Jacob. Yes, I need you. I love you." Kady tried desperately to pull him back down to her mouth to kiss him, but he resisted.

"Marry me, Kady."

With that, Kady froze, a semblance of clarity cooling the heat she felt. She looked at Jacob incredulously but saw only Jacob's earnest face looking back.

"Marry you?" Her question was weak, yet hopeful. This is what she had wanted from the beginning, but so soon? That seemed a bit hasty, even to her. No, she needed to say no. He had not even been interested in her at the beginning. Sure he had warmed up and loved hearing her stories about the plantation, and all of the gifts that her father had given her, but marriage? The right thing to do would be to say no, but the man she wanted, wanted her, too! Her fantasy was coming true. With her indecision clearly stamped on her face, Jacob sat up with a serious look on his face. Kady did as well, so he could more comfortably look at her.

"The doctor said my leg is almost healed up, which means I will be leaving soon. The war effort needs me. I need to know that I will have you to come back to, you waiting for me back at home. Our home. I need to know that I am fighting for something I love." At those final words, all of Kady's hesitation melted away. They were going to have a home together because he loved her.

"Yes, yes, of course." Kady thought her heart would burst. Taking his face in her hands, she kissed him again and again interspersing more yeses until she was forced to break off, out of breath, giggling with a wide smile on her face. "We'll have to find a preacher, and I'll have to get a new dress."

"Oh no! We can't risk that," Jacob declared.

Kady's smile immediately fell. "What? What do you mean?"

183

"Darling, we can't get married in public while the war is going on. I'm a Union officer. What would your father say?"

Kady had no reply and her mood was plummeting.

"We have to get married in private, my love. We'll do it right here, right now. It will be our secret. Until the war is over."

"How can we get married right now? There's no preacher."

"You can jump the broom!" The excited voice from the back of the shack startled them both. As their eyes fell on Mary's daughter, she shrunk back. "I'm sorry, I'm not here. I'm sorry."

Kady had completely forgotten Mary's daughter was in the shack. She must have been sitting in the shadows and gotten excited at the thought of Kady getting married. Kady couldn't blame her, it was exciting.

"Don't apologize, you're right. We can jump the broom. Do we have a broom?" Kady was getting excited again. She beamed at Jacob, who reached behind her and untied the ribbon in her hair.

"And we will be handfast. We promise ourselves to each other, use this ribbon to tie our hands together, and jump over the broom." Jacob grabbed the broom from Mary's daughter who had ventured close to the pallet only to be motioned away again with the flick of Jacob's hand. "And, as long as we consummate the union, we're married." Kady blushed at the thought of continuing what they had started. Her body grew hot at the thought and looking into Jacob's eyes, she forgot about propriety, her father, even the big lavish wedding she had dreamed of as a girl. Laughing, she kissed him again.

"Yes, I will marry you. I will marry you right now!"

Moving the rickety chair, she placed the broom on the floor, correcting its placement so it lay at the right angle. Then she went to Jacob to help him up, although he had already gotten up with the aid of a crutch. Jacob maneuvered himself so he was standing in front of the broom, and once he was settled, Kady positioned herself opposite him. She smiled up into his face, as he took one of her hands in his and placed the ribbon over the top.

"Girl, come over here and tie this ribbon."

Mary's daughter moved with eagerness to obey Jacob's command, wrapped the ribbon around their hands twice, and then tied the ends. Finished, she disappeared back into the shadows of the shack. Jacob looked solemnly down into Kady's face.

"I, Jacob Ulysses Hart, take thee to be my wife."

Kady stifled a nervous giggle, then said in return, "I, Kady Susannah Bell, take thee to be my husband."

They both looked at each other for several moments.

"Is that all? What's next?" Kady looked to Jacob for guidance.

"I guess this is where we jump over the broom."

They both laughed and Kady tried to position herself so Jacob could lean on her instead of the crutch, which proved to be quite hard since their hands were tied together. In the end, the knot came undone, so they each held an end to ensure the fastening held until they were "legally" married. Their jump was awkward and precarious as Jacob still was not accustomed to his new center of gravity, but they made it over the broom and stayed upright. Once their laughter had subsided, Kady bit her lower lip and looked up at her new husband.

"So am I now officially Mrs. Hart?"

A mischievous smile lit Jacob's eyes.

"Not quite yet." Pulling her hard against him, he kissed her deeply and they picked up where they had left off.

When Kady awoke, it was midmorning. She opened her eyes cautiously, trying not to move her body, betraying that she was awake. The consummation of her marriage was nothing like she had imagined it would be. As soon as Jacob had climbed on top of her, it became abundantly clear his leg was not healed enough for this particular activity. He cried out in pain the second he tried to use what was left of his leg to bear any weight, and immediately shifted his weight to the other side of his body, effectively crushing Kady's hip, causing *her* to cry out in pain. At that point, Jacob rolled off her swearing under his breath. She had tried to console him, to tell him it wasn't important, they were still married even if they had to wait until his leg had healed some more. Jacob was adamant. The marriage had to be consummated, it was only right.

Rolling Kady away from him and onto her side, Jacob pulled her close, her buttocks fitting into the curve of his lap. After several moments of grunting and fumbling, she felt Jacob's hand and something hard and warm between her thighs. When his fingers parted her and she felt an exploratory probing, she gasped and tensed not knowing what he was doing. Exploration completed, Jacob's hands moved to her hips pulling her firmly down onto him as his own hips bucked, penetrating her with the full length of his shaft. Kady cried out in pain, and turned her face into her pillow to stifle the noise. Finding a rhythm, that was achieved more by him moving Kady than movements of his own, he worked with gusto, moaning his evident pleasure in her ear. Far from pleasure, Kady clung to the pillow crying, her insides screaming with pain. When he finished, she felt him stiffen, followed by a warm gush inside of her that spread to her legs when he withdrew himself.

Jacob nuzzled his face into her hair and kissed her neck briefly, then was asleep and snoring behind her before five minutes had passed. Despite the hot summer night, his arms were still around her, forcing her to try to clean herself up a bit while still spooned in his embrace. She throbbed with pain and now fully understood why brides bled on their wedding night. How anybody in their right mind thought something so big and hard was supposed to fit into what was obviously a small space was beyond her. Eventually giving up her attempt to clean herself, she tried to sleep, but sleep would not come. Instead, she stared at the wall for several hours, eventually cupping and holding herself in the hopes some pressure might ease the ache.

Sleep eventually came and the pain subsided during the night. Now that it was morning, she was left with a dull ache. Despite this, she was afraid Jacob would want to exercise his marital rites once more, so she pretended to be asleep. She knew she would eventually have to tell him she was awake, but first she was going to come up with a good excuse for why she would have to go back to the big house immediately.

No excuse was necessary, however. The door of the shack burst open and her mother practically fell over the threshold in her hurry. Kady sat bolt upright, grabbing for anything she could find to cover herself. Jacob, on the other hand, was unfazed. If she didn't know any better, she would have said he looked a little smug. Kady's mind was a blank. She had no idea what to say or do.

Anna broke the silence. "Good Lord in heaven. It's true."

187

21
Short Engagement

After depositing Kady in her room for a hasty toilette and a change of clothes, Anna retreated to the only room where she was sure to be undisturbed. She closed the door of her husband's study behind her, walked purposefully to his desk, and took the bottle of whiskey out of his bottom drawer. Removing the stopper she took a deep swallow, not bothering with a glass. The liquor burned her throat and its fumes wafted up through her sinuses. Before she could choke from the harshness, she took another swallow, gulping it down then gasping for fresh air. She didn't normally drink, but she needed something to quiet the rising panic so she wouldn't break out into hysterical laughter when she rejoined her husband in the parlor.

A young officer had come calling earlier that morning requesting to speak with her husband. Anna didn't think anything of it, until her husband summoned her into the parlor and instructed her to bring Kady down dressed appropriately to meet her fiancé. Anna's mouth had dropped open in shock. She was able to recover quickly and excused herself to fetch Kady. Anna arrived at Kady's empty room only moments before Mary came rushing in. Breathlessly Mary explained that when she went out to the shack to retrieve the morning tray, she had encountered her daughter who had announced excitedly that Miss Kady and the Yankee officer had jumped the broom the night before.

From the state Anna had found them in, she had no doubt it

was true. That conniving louse of a man had seduced her daughter. True, it probably wasn't hard, but she knew that of all of Kady's asinine ideas, this was not one of them. She took one last swallow of whiskey and stoppered it before returning it clumsily to the drawer. Now she felt light-headed. Had the entire world gone mad while she had grieved for Benjamin? Andrew was ready to sell off their daughter to the first man who came calling, not knowing that Kady had already sold herself off! A burst of laughter escaped her lips, and she grabbed the bottle out of the drawer again and took another swig. They were done for. Andrew was going to find out about her spying, and there was nothing she could do about it.

Kady had tried to explain as Anna dragged her back into the house to be dressed properly, but Anna didn't want to hear any explanation and told her daughter as much. She had practically thrown Kady into her room to the awaiting slaves who had skirts and a gown ready. Anna hadn't told her why she was being dressed and then escorted to the parlor. If she was old enough to elope, well, then she was old enough to face down her father as he introduced her to her bridegroom.

Panic started to tighten Anna's chest again. She had to do something. Was she actually crazy enough to think her daughter would be able to handle this situation without ruining everything? Anna rubbed her face vigorously trying to clear her head. It didn't help. Truth be told, she wouldn't have been able to solve this problem even before she drank the whiskey. There was nothing to be done except stand back and wait for everything to come crashing down around her. Resigned, she turned toward the door, took a deep breath, and left to escort Kady to their mutual downfall.

Neither of them spoke as they made their way down the stairs. Either the slaves had told Kady what was happening, or Kady had rightly assumed she wouldn't be getting any answers from Anna. There was a slight awkwardness to Kady's gait that made Anna cringe. For as much as the girl exasperated her, Anna had hoped she would have at least had the chance to prepare Kady for her wedding night, in the hopes it wouldn't be quite as awful as her own had been. She hoped for her daughter's sake it hadn't been that bad. At least on some level the lieutenant must have some feelings for her, beyond what he would gain from such an alliance, or Kady wouldn't have fallen for him. Even she was not that dumb. A pang of guilt struck Anna. Not only had she not prepared her daughter for her wedding night, she also hadn't prepared her in the least for what was about to happen. As loath as Anna was to acknowledge it, she was being petty. She was a mother and, as a mother, she had certain responsibilities. Anna slowed her steps and reached out to touch Kady's arm to stop her so they could talk, but Kady brushed her off and entered the parlor.

"Good morning, Daddy!" Kady glided across the room to her father's side and kissed him on the cheek. Then turning toward their guest, her face warmed. "Why, Captain Henry, how good it is to see you."

She dropped into a curtsy and the captain crossed to her so he could kiss her hand in welcome. Anna was stunned. The performance Kady was putting on was masterful. If she hadn't known better herself, she would have assumed Kady had spent the morning combing out her hair or practicing her watercolors, not in her ill-conceived marriage bed.

Andrew wasted no preamble, instead informing Kady that he had found her a husband, and since the captain could be called away at any moment, they were to have a short engagement. The marriage ceremony would take place here in the big house in one month, and then the newlyweds would travel to Richmond, to the house the captain had procured before asking for Kady's hand. Time seemed to stand still as everyone looked to Kady for her reaction. Anna held her breath waiting for Kady to fall apart, to say she couldn't, to break down crying or throw a fit. Instead, Kady gushed her thanks and threw her arms around her father's neck, praising him for always taking such good care of her, before coquettishly approaching the captain. Anna felt as if her head was about to explode. It was as if she were watching a play being acted out in front of her. She had to say something.

"Andrew, is it wise to be so hasty? Let us wait until after the war for the ceremony." Leaving Kady and the captain to talk privately, the general strode across the room and roughly grabbed Anna's arm.

"No one asked for your opinion or your presence. You may go." Loosening his grip, he crossed back to the young couple and proposed a toast. Anna looked urgently toward her daughter, but Kady averted her eyes so their gazes didn't meet. Feeling completely helpless and bewildered, Anna excused herself and left the room.

22
Out of Our Hands

After the deed was done, the general got up from Anna's bed and left the room. She had no idea if he was planning to retire to his own room or if he was on his way to find one of the young slaves to satisfy himself further. Either way, Anna did not care. She had stopped caring years before when she realized that Andrew used these little encounters to prove a point. Tonight he had reminded her that she had no say in any of his dealings and, if she were smart, she would remember that in the future.

Anna got up from the bed, walked to her mirror, and was grieved by what she saw. Over the years, she had grown numb to the assault done to her person by her husband. She had even learned to ignore the hateful things he whispered into her ear while violently thrusting inside of her. She did not even cry anymore, which she suspected perturbed the general, which, in turn, gave her a swell of satisfaction. But did he always have to rip her clothes?

She fingered the tear at the collar of her favorite nightgown. Mary had worked in secret on the embroidery for months and presented it to her for her thirtieth birthday. Tears started to flow down her face. She knew it was silly to cry over a torn gown. She also knew that it was not the gown she was crying for. This was the first time that a man had come to her bed since Benjamin, and her heart broke anew with the knowledge that Andrew was all she had to look forward to. She would never burrow her face into her lover's chest or feel his warm body wrapped in her legs ever again. She felt the crippling sorrow rising up in her once more. For almost a year she had feared he was gone but could not allow herself to believe it. She had held onto the tiniest fragment of hope that Benjamin had survived, even though so many others at Gettysburg had perished. That letter with the news of his death had severed her hope and unleashed her grief, a grief that had left her an empty shell, unable to rise from her bed. She wanted to return to her grief now, to forget that the world existed. No. She did not have the luxury of doing that again.

She closed her eyes and forced herself to focus on Kady. How did this happen? Did Kady love Jacob, or was he merely convenient? Could she grow to love Captain Henry? Should one marriage be annulled or the other one stopped? Did she even have the ability to do either? There was a quiet knock on the door, and Mary entered before Anna had time to compose herself. Mary had brought tea; she always did on nights such as this. She would bring tea and the two of them would sit for a spell while Mary worked on stitching or embroidery. When the hour was very late, Mary would comb out Anna's hair, and then they would both climb into her bed, and Anna would fall asleep wrapped in Mary's arms as she softly hummed bits of songs. These nights were both the worst and best of Anna's life.

Tonight was different, though, and Mary sensed this. She put down the tray and joined Anna at the mirror. Anna was still fingering her collar.

Anna whispered, "He ripped your beautiful gown, I'm sorry."

Unable to stop herself, Mary smiled. "Now don't you be silly.

Mary gonna fix that up real quick. Here," Mary went to the wardrobe and pulled out a new nightgown, "you put this on astead. Sit down with your tea an' I'll fix that right up."

Obediently Anna changed. Instead of sitting, she looked in the mirror once more and wiped the moisture from her face. She could not change the past, but here was hope that she could alter the future. Mary watched her warily as she began mending the torn gown. Anna made for the door.

"I have to do something." She opened the door and Mary started to get up to take her leave, when Anna turned back to her and said, "Stay." The pleading in her eyes belied the confidence in her voice. Though she said it as an order, she meant it as a request. Mary sat back down and smoothed the night dress across her lap.

"I'll have this done 'fore you get back." Gratitude washed over Anna's face and she left.

Anna stole down the hall, her confidence growing with each step. She could not let this happen. Somehow, she had to convince that girl that she could not marry the captain. Upon reaching Kady's door, she listened for a moment. Assured all was silent, she ducked into the room.

Kady was sitting in front of her mirror combing through her hair with her fingers and humming to herself. She hadn't noticed Anna. Anna watched her for a moment and her frustration with her daughter seemed to dissipate slightly. She was so young, so innocent. She had no idea what she was getting herself into. A warm ache filled Anna's chest. She wanted to cross the room and take Kady into her arms, protect her from all that surrounded them. The sensation was foreign, something

194

she had not felt since Kady was a baby. The general had decided Kady needed a proper Southern upbringing and, as Anna was not familiar with their ways, took Kady away from her and entrusted her to the hands of a well-bred wet nurse, then tutors. Anna had short visits that after a time became too painful, so she stopped. No one objected. Anna shook off the notion of comforting her daughter. The only thing worse than quashing the motherly impulse would be Kady's rejection of it. The warm feeling disappeared, replaced with the familiar cold, hard knot. Anna cleared her throat and startled Kady, who spun around as Anna spoke.

"You seemed awfully pleased with your father this morning."

"Is there a reason I shouldn't be?"

Anna clenched her teeth as Kady's cold gaze met hers. There it was, that entitlement she couldn't stand.

"I don't think you understand the predicament you are in right now."

"I understand perfectly." Kady's voice was clipped and low.

Anna laughed. "You understand perfectly? How could you possibly understand? Or do you not remember throwing your arms around your father's neck and thanking him for finding you such a wonderful husband not thirty minutes after I had pulled you from your wedding bed? Have you forgotten your little backwoods indiscretion so quickly?"

"What was I supposed to do, Mother? Protest? Say I did not want to get married?"

"Yes! What were you thinking?"

Kady stood and crossed to her mother, fists clenched in fury.

"I was thinking that regardless of how I actually felt, I needed to give father the reaction he expected lest he suspect something. If you think I should have told him outright that I couldn't possibly entertain the notion of marrying the captain because I'm already secretly married to a Union officer to whom my mother, the spy, introduced me, then I will go correct my error right now!" Anna grabbed her arm as Kady tried to push past.

"Don't be so melodramatic! You should have told him you weren't ready. Or pleaded that the wedding be postponed until after the war. Instead, you fell all over yourself thanking him and agreeing to such a fast wedding. What can that possibly gain?"

Kady ripped her arm free of her mother's grip.

"I gain information; all of his movements, all of his plans. If I'm to be wed to this man, it might as well happen sooner rather than later so I can get as much out of him as possible."

Anna was stunned. She had no idea her daughter was capable of such cold calculations. Maybe she wasn't as naive as she seemed.

"Kady, doing this will put you in unnecessary danger. You do not need to do this. You've already proven you can get valuable information from him."

"One map, that is all. As the captain's wife, I will have access to everything. I can read through his correspondence while he sleeps."

Anna took a step back. "You realize what you're saying, don't you?"

"I'm saying this could be a valuable arrangement."

"You are committing yourself to actions that are no better than a common whore in a country inn. How can you be so nonchalant?

How can you so easily sell yourself to this man?"

"Because I don't have a choice! Who can stop this? You?" Kady laughed, the coldness gone from her voice, replaced with bitterness. "As if father would listen to a thing you have to say. I think he proved that clearly enough downstairs. You have the bruise right there, if you don't remember." Kady pointed to the hand-shaped bruise on Anna's arm where the general had grabbed her.

Anna protectively covered the bruise with her hand.

"So you will be this man's whore without a fight?"

"At least I will have a purpose to my whoring. That's more than you got when Granddaddy sold you."

Indignation flashed across Anna's eyes. How did Kady even know about that? She searched for something, anything, to say in response. Her mind was blank. It was blank because Kady was right. Hurt replaced the indignation. Before tears could overtake her, Anna stormed out and down the hall to her own room.

Kady watched her go and stood motionless until the reverberations of her mother's slamming door had faded. Then she stole across the room and swung her own door shut, hearing it latch into place. Closing her eyes, she turned and rested her back against the door, letting her anger release into the hard timber behind her. Slowly, imperceptibly at first, the tension eased in her shoulders, and she slid down the door until she was sitting on the floor. As the tears started flowing down her cheeks, she folded her legs into her chest and cried into her knees.

She did not want to marry this man. She had chosen Jacob to be her husband, but everything had happened so fast she wasn't even sure that she wanted to be married to him, either. Why had she allowed herself to be swept away like that? One moment she did not have a care in the world. She was playing at being a spy and reveling in her risqué rendezvous. It was a game, an irresponsible game, she was playing. How had things gone so horribly wrong, so quickly? All she wanted was to run to her father and have him fix everything. That was the one thing she couldn't do; she could never go to him again. She had to fix this for herself. She had to do exactly what she had told her mother she was going to do: marry Captain Henry and be a spy. For the first time in her life, she was alone, with no one to protect her.

52-36-15-66 34-41 34-32-41-31
11-43 54-14-54-14 26-11-25-13
33-14-21-62-22-11-24-53 21-22-55 24-55-43-21
26-13

July 16, 1864
Is Mama Bird watching the Nest?
BD

23
Light the Candle

The summer sun beat down on Richmond. The day would have been intolerable without the breeze off the river. That breeze made this Rebecca's favorite spot to write. She gazed off into the distance, eyes failing to focus, as her concentration was inward. She did not know how to finish her poem and needed to get it right on the first try. She glanced down at the small book in her lap and the misshapen collection of joints that clumsily gripped her pencil. Not only was writing a painstaking enterprise, but writing implements were a scarce commodity, and she hated to waste them on the wrong words. With an intake of breath, she made a decision and began to write out the final lines. Finished, she set her pencil on the bench by her side, stretched her sore hand as best she could, and began to read.

My country she is crying, but there is no one left to hear.

Her sons are waging war against the brothers they hold dear.

Her fathers stand to argue that what they believe is right.

Her mothers make the bandages to wrap wounds good and tight.

Her daughters are forgotten, like the passing of the day:

Waiting, simply waiting for there is nothing more to say.

My country she is crying, deep rivers of blood red tears.

My country she is crying, but there is no one left to hear.

"That is beautiful. Did you write that?"

Rebecca gave a strangled yelp. She had been so engrossed in her work she hadn't realized she was reading out loud, or that a girl had sat down beside her.

"I apologize, I didn't intend to startle you. That poem is so beautiful; I have to know who wrote it. Did you?"

Rebecca looked around nervously. There was no one to save her from the conversation. She nodded yes, then started to close her book. The girl stopped her.

"Oh, no. Please don't put it away. I would love to read it. May I?"

Rebecca looked up into the girl's face and saw that she was in earnest. There was no hint of malice anywhere. Cautiously she relinquished control of the book and watched as the girl took it and began to read. Though her face was beautiful, it was her eyes that captured Rebecca's attention. They seemed to ignite with passion as she read and reread the poem. Rebecca had never seen that kind of unadulterated appreciation, especially not for something she had done. She was accustomed to pity and frustration; appreciation was new to her. Her sister constantly chided her for wasting paper, even when Rebecca used scraps. All her sister ever saw was Rebecca's crippled body, helpless and useless.

Her brother-in-law would take pity on her sometimes, bringing home a fresh sheet of paper and smuggling it to her. It was their secret, and she loved him for his kindness. For her twenty-fifth birthday, he had presented her with her very own book of clean paper and two pencils. She would have cried out of gratitude had her sister not begun to berate her husband for wasting money. True, the cost of paper had come down, but an entire book was an extravagance. Why did a cripple, who contributed nothing to the household, need something so grand? In the end, her sister had demanded a good number of the pages be ripped out and put to practical use, so Rebecca had instead cried out of loss. Regardless, she treasured the book and was determined to put only the best of words in it; therefore, it was still almost entirely blank.

The girl carefully closed the book and handed it back to Rebecca, who clutched it protectively to her chest.

"You are a beautiful poet."

Rebecca blushed and the girl laughed softly. "Has no one ever told you that before?"

Rebecca shook her head.

"You don't talk much, do you?"

Rebecca smiled despite herself and shook her head once more. She could not remember the last time anyone outside of her family had ever taken notice of her, much less talked to her. It was nice. This girl was nice.

"Rebecca." Her voice came out barely louder than a whisper, and the girl leaned in to hear better.

"Pardon?"

"My name is Rebecca." She instilled a bit more conviction behind her words, though her voice still quavered.

"It is lovely to meet you, Rebecca!" The girl broke out into a wide smile. "My name is Kady."

"It's nice to meet you, Kady."

"Do you come out here to write often?"

"Whenever I can slip away. I write at home, mostly. During the day only, or my sister scolds me for wasting the candles."

"Oh, you live with your sister?"

"Yes. On account of my hand and leg. She says I can't take care of myself."

"What's wrong with your leg?"

Kady peered suspiciously at Rebecca's long skirt.

Rebecca blushed with embarrassment that Kady was so openly asking about her deformity. She had been taught that she was to keep her legs hidden and never speak of them. However, beneath her embarrassment, lurked a queer feeling that Rebecca could not place. She had never felt it before, but she desperately wanted to confide in this girl who admired her poetry and treated her as if she were a normal person. Holding her breath, and ensuring they were still alone, Rebecca brushed her skirt aside ever so slightly to reveal a spindly, underdeveloped calf with a clubfoot. At Kady's gasp, Rebecca smoothed her skirt back into place, feeling foolish. Why had she done that? Now Kady would run away disgusted and rightfully so. She was still there, though, gaze still intent on Rebecca's skirt.

Kady's eyebrows had knit together in concentration, then smoothed out as she looked up at Rebecca with a twinkle of recognition in her eyes.

"You had morning paralysis as a girl, didn't you? That's what it's called, isn't it? One of our servants got it and she had to be shut in for months. When she finally came out, her leg looked like that. Her hands are fine, though, so she does all of the sewing. It is a pity yours are not, you being a poet and all. Have you ever tried writing with your other

202

hand? It seems to be fine."

Rebecca was stunned. All of the usual reactions were absent. This girl, who clearly came from a wealthy family, was not disturbed or upset, despite having gotten a good look at her leg. Before she could stop herself, Rebecca blurted out, "Why don't you care that I am a cripple?"

"Why should I care that you are a cripple? You have a pretty face, you write beautiful poetry, and, quite frankly, I have escaped from a boring luncheon and want someone to talk to."

Unable to help herself, Rebecca let out a rueful laugh.

"My mother used to say there wasn't anythin' pretty about me; my sister got it all."

Kady leaned in to Rebecca and whispered conspiratorially, "I think your mother should meet my mother, they would get along famously."

This time they both giggled, and that giggle grew into laughter until Rebecca felt tears welling up in her eyes and her ribs ached from pushing against the stays in her corset.

Kady and Rebecca had whiled away the entire afternoon by the time Kady's mother found them and scolded Kady for running off. At this, Kady glanced back at Rebecca and rolled her eyes, forcing them both to stifle their giggles. Rebecca didn't think she had ever had a more pleasant afternoon, nor had she ever smiled so much. That smile was still on her face as she laboriously made her way home. Kady had wanted to know all about her and had listened with rapt attention to her stories. The only time she had interrupted was when she found out

Rebecca's room was on the second floor. Kady had been appalled and insisted that making a cripple climb up and down stairs all day was ridiculous. Rebecca reassured her the room had been her choice. She liked to watch the comings and goings down below, and she had a beautiful view of the moon on cloudless nights that she would not give up for the world.

Kady was skeptical and wanted to know what was so interesting to justify climbing the stairs.

Rebecca wondered if this was what having a friend was like—a person who cared for your well-being and someone you could trust with your secrets. She thought maybe it was. So Rebecca told Kady of her secret pleasure in watching the army supply yard that was located across the street. She told her how some of the hands worked in such a way that it seemed like a dance as they loaded and unloaded the goods; and she told her about how she liked to hear the racket of the wagon wheels on the road and guess from the sound whether the wagon was full or empty, coming or going.

When Kady asked if she ever wrote at her window by candle light, Rebecca had laughed. That definitely qualified as a waste of a good candle. She used either the light of the moon, or sat and simply enjoyed the evening when it was too dark to see. Kady insisted this was a waste of good talent, not a waste of candles. She said she would send some candles for her, and paper, too, if she was in need.

At first, Rebecca had said no, that was not necessary; her sister would not approve. She had adamantly refused, but Kady was stubborn and eventually got her way. Rebecca had insisted, though, that Kady come up with some way she could repay her for her kindness.

Kady's first request was odd. Whenever a wagon was being loaded to take supplies out, she asked Rebecca to place her lit candle so the flame was visible through her window. If the wagon's escort was larger than normal, or there was something unusual about it, she was to add a second candle. The more Rebecca thought about this, the odder it felt. Kady clearly had ulterior motives, but Rebecca had been so afraid that Kady would never speak with her again if she said no, she agreed without any questions asked. In fact, she had pretended that this was a perfectly normal request, and Kady had reassured her that her supply of candles would never run low. That luxury alone made it worthwhile.

The second request was not so easy. Kady had insisted she take a copy of the poem, as she was determined to get it published. Rebecca argued it wasn't any good, and it was a silly proposition. Besides, why did Kady care so much?

Kady simply responded that it sounded like a fun diversion, and they were friends now and friends did nice things for one another.

Though she was touched by the sentiment, even this was not enough to get Rebecca to relinquish the poem. It was only when Kady said that she would she keep Rebecca supplied with clean paper and try her best to get some payment for the poem that Rebecca finally relented. The thought of being able to make her own money, to contribute to her family, lightened her heavy step. Without any further thought, Rebecca had ripped the page from her precious book and handed it over.

July 25, 1864

Contact with Mama Bird made. Will
introduce Nest on next contact.
LR

52-36-15-66 46-51 34-32-41-31
62-64-24-21-14-62-21 33-11-21-22 54-14-54-14
26-11-25-13 54-14-13-55 33-11-15-15
11-24-21-25-64-13-36-62-55 24-55-43-21 64-24
24-55-23-21 62-64-24-21-14-62-21
15-25

24

Into the Swamp

It wasn't until summer that Emma heard more of Captain Henry. She was out preparing her horse to leave when two men rode up and dismounted behind her. As she only ever dressed in her buckskins, she didn't draw their focus and they paid her no mind. Her movements became slower, and she instinctively began to listen for any part of the men's conversation that might be of use to her. Thankfully, neither man was paying her the least mind, or they would have thought it queer that she had been securing her horse's bridle for over five minutes.

For the most part their conversation was unhelpful. They had picked up correspondence, so they must be messengers. They also mentioned goods. She didn't know if they were referring to personal supplies or something potentially of more value, as they didn't say specifically what they had. However, Emma suspected something more valuable, as they were both removing their saddlebags. Perhaps they were couriers. Then Emma heard a name that made her heart skip. The two men were reassuring themselves that as long as they were quick about it, they could have an ale and get back to camp without Captain Henry ever knowing.

Emma didn't dare move until she heard the door of the tavern close. These were Captain Henry's men! Should she go inside and try to listen in on their conversation, or should she try to follow them to their camp? She was frozen in indecision. Following them would be of most value, as they could lead her directly to Henry. The problem was figuring out how to follow them without being seen? She wasn't a tracker. She wasn't even that good on a horse! She knew she had to try though. She would not get another opportunity like this.

Decision made, Emma mounted her horse. She had the time it took to drink an ale to figure out a good way to follow them. They had come from the north, so logic said that when they left they would head south. Emma headed south, scouting out the landscape, hoping to see a good place to hide. She figured they would be on this road for quite some time, as there wasn't anything of note until Norfolk. So if she could hide until they passed her, maybe she'd be able to stay out of sight, and not lose them, by following the dust their horses kicked up.

By luck she found a little clearing next to a bend in the road. Instead of hiding, she would throw out her bedroll and pretend that she had picked this spot to camp for the night. She was in swamp country, which made her skin crawl, even though this clearing was relatively dry. She stifled her unease because if she positioned herself correctly, she would be able to see the men as they approached the bend in the road and then follow their progress as they rode away from her. It was perfect. She would hide in plain sight!

Emma steered her horse off the road and set up a meager camp. She wanted to have enough out to convince anyone passing that she was staying for the night, but not so much that she couldn't pack it up at a moment's notice. To that end, she took her bedroll down, but instead of flattening it out, left it rolled to use as a seat. She took out a few cooking things, but decided that she would pretend to be lighting the fire when anyone passed, so she wouldn't have a live fire to contend with before leaving. This was as far as she got in her preparations when she heard someone coming up the road. Instinctively, Emma wanted to freeze and not look to see who was coming in case she drew their attention. Then she reminded herself that she would appear stranger by not looking. It was human nature to look, so as nonchalantly as possible, Emma paused what she was doing and glanced over her shoulder at the approaching riders.

It was Henry's men, and they didn't even act like they had seen her—or so she thought, until they rounded the bend and then slowed down to a walk. Emma held her breath, which was unnecessary since their attention was on the opposite side of the road. Carefully, both men picked their way down the slope off the road and disappeared into the swamp. Emma couldn't believe her eyes. They had just ridden into the swamp. There was no road there; she would have seen it. Were they crazy? Emma ran out of the clearing and across the road to investigate where the men had gone. To her amazement there was clearly a path. How had she missed that? Turning back toward her horse it became obvious. Of course she had missed it. Why would she have seen a little path, when there was a gorgeous clearing on the opposite side of the road?

Running back to her horse, Emma threw her belongings back together and hastily tied them to her saddle. Grabbing the reins, she led the way across the road and down the slope after the men. She knew it would be faster if she mounted and rode, but she didn't trust herself on this uneven terrain. Once into the swamp, it was really less of a path and more of a deer trail. Because of that, she knew the men wouldn't be traveling fast, so she hoped she'd be able to keep up. Thankfully they were talking rather animatedly, so she followed their voices whenever she lost sight of them.

At the second fork in the trail, Emma began to worry that she wouldn't be able to find her way back out. Especially since, with the canopy of trees overhead, it had gotten dark, fast. Reaching into her saddlebag, she pulled out one of the linen strips that she used during her monthly courses and tore off a piece. She tied it on a branch to indicate which way was out before continuing. While she always thoroughly washed her strips, she was certain that it would still have the scent of blood on it and might attract some kind of animal. She shuddered, considered going back for it, then decided to leave it. She might encounter an animal, but at least she would know the way out. Emma understood why Henry camped in the swamp. Nobody in their right mind would follow them in here.

After what felt like hours of picking her way through the undergrowth, Emma finally heard another voice mingled with the two men she was following. They must have reached their camp. Emma tied the reins to a tree and continued on without her horse. The trail started up a hill and she was afraid that if she stayed on the trail, she would be completely visible when she reached the top. But she was more afraid of what she might encounter off the trail, so she crouched down and continued up the trail on all fours to make herself smaller.

When she reached the top, she saw them, and ducked behind a tree. One of the men was adding the goods from their saddlebags to a pile on the ground, while the other man hobbled their horses. A third man, sitting at a fire about twenty yards away, hollered at them to bring over some food for supper. Their tasks finished, they picked some food out of the pile and headed over to the fire. Emma waited until they were all seated and busy preparing food before she ventured out from behind her tree. She kept low to the ground and didn't take her eyes off the men as she crept over to the pile of supplies.

She reached the pile and froze to make sure they hadn't heard anything. They were oblivious to her presence, so she scanned the pile to ascertain what was there. When her eyes alighted on some quinine, a smile spread across her face. That stuff was as good as gold. She could sell it to either army and make a fortune, as malaria ran rampant through all of the troops. As an added bonus, Captain Henry might get into trouble, too. Taking her jacket off, she piled all of the quinine into the center of it and tied it up in a bundle. What else could she take? There was a massive bag of flour, but when she tried to lift it, she knew there was no way she would be able to carry it quietly, so she abandoned that and decided on two smaller bags of salt.

Gathering her items, Emma checked back on the men at the fire, and seeing them all engrossed in each other's company, she tiptoed back to the trail and down to her horse. She cursed that her saddlebags were so full. She had room for the quinine and salt, but not much else. Maybe she could repack the bags, or roll something up in her bedroll to transport it? Before she could make up her mind, there was a scream in the distance followed by a gun shot, followed by another scream. To her horror, Emma realized that the last scream had come from her own lips. While it hadn't been loud, it surely had alerted the men at the campfire to her presence.

Emma flung herself onto her horse and turned to head out of the swamp. Her heart pounded as she prayed that the men would assume her scream belonged to whomever had let loose the first, and that the markers she left on the trail would be sufficient to get her safely back to the road without incident.

25

Justice Served

Henry swore under his breath and stopped for what felt like the hundredth time to try to get his bearings straight. He had received orders that he was to retain command of three of his men. They were to form a supply depot, composed entirely of supplies they raided from the Union. The work suited him perfectly, and he and his men quickly fell into a practiced rhythm. Henry had dismissed the suggestion of setting up in a farmhouse outside of Richmond and had instead found an ideal location in the middle of the Dismal Swamp. Its best attribute was that unless you knew exactly what to look for, it was impossible to find. That also happened to be one of its chief drawbacks. In the dark, it was easy to get turned around and wander about aimlessly for hours. As they always returned from raids in pairs or separately, to keep from drawing notice, every man had gotten lost at least once and, upon finally stumbling into camp, been teased soundly—except Henry, who always managed to be the first one back. It had gotten to the point that the men had wagers going, betting on how long it would take before he got lost. Now, brushing at the bark of a tree to feel the freshness of its mark, Henry wondered who was about to win the bet.

He was considering whether it might be time to break the cardinal rule and light a torch, but looking up he could see the moon starting to peak through the drifting clouds. He silently urged them to move faster. He turned his attention back to the tree, which he could already make out a little more clearly, when he heard what sounded like a woman's scream coming from some distance off to his right. The noise was too muffled to have been a panther, so after a moment's indecision, Henry tethered his horse, pulled his gun, and carefully started to pick his way toward the noise. He knew escaped slaves often sought refuge in the swamp. There were even camps set up where they could safely rest for a few days. Safe, of course, being relative, as the Negroes considered snakes, panthers, and bears more welcome bedfellows than the white men hunting them. Henry couldn't say he disagreed with them. Still, for one of them to scream was unusual and warranted investigation.

Before long, the moon's light was fully unleashed allowing Henry to sneak as noiselessly as was possible in a swamp. He started to hear low grunts filtering through the underbrush, and the occasional sob. He knew these sounds, but they did not register—not here, so foreign against the backdrop of the wilderness. Crouching low to the ground he inched his way forward until he could plainly see what his ears had already told him. There in a small clearing a man with his britches down around his ankles was raping a slave woman, his white ass, incongruous against the dark night, pumping up and down. With a final shudder, he finished and collapsed onto the woman who by now had stopped audibly crying. The man picked himself up, and brushing himself off, pulled his britches back into place, then reached for his coat that was being held, to Henry's horror, by a little slave girl. She could not have been more than ten. The man patted her on the head, then, lifting her chin so she looked him in the eye, spoke. "Too bad for you I'm exhausted from riding all day, or I would have taken care of you next."

Henry saw red. Before he knew what he was doing, he charged

into the clearing with his gun held at the ready. The woman and the girl both screamed as the man turned to face Henry. A sneering smile broke across the man's face, replacing shock, as he recognized Henry.

"You're not going to shoot me. You don't have the stones."

Henry pulled the trigger, and the bullet broke through Lieutenant Radcliffe's forehead before a look of shock had time to register on his face. Henry watched him fall. Dazed, Henry could feel the weight of the gun in his hand, smell the powder in the air, yet he could not believe it was Radcliffe lying at his feet. Henry thought he surely must be dreaming, amd he would wake up at any moment to find Williams making coffee. Then he realized the girl was still screaming. Turning his gaze to her, she shut her mouth and in terror fell to her mother's side for protection. No, this was not a dream. Slowly he lowered his gun and knelt down in front of the women.

"I'm not going to hurt you."

Despite this reassurance, neither of them looked comforted.

Henry cleared his throat hoping it would make his voice less rattled. "Do you know that man?" With this he got a definitive head shake, no. "Do you know what he was doing here?"

The woman stole a glance at Radcliffe's body, then back at Henry warily.

"I'm not going to hurt you," Henry repeated. "You're okay now."

"He said…." She was clearly still shaken. "He said he had a message, but got lost…." The woman trailed off.

"And he happened upon you and your daughter?"

She nodded her head, eyes still wide and agitated.

Henry sat back on his heels to think for a moment. Had Radcliffe been sent into the swamp to find him? Henry had provided his commander a rough map showing their location. Everyone had agreed that the fewer people who knew its whereabouts, the better, so Henry hadn't expected anyone to venture into the swamp. Shuffling over to the body, Henry rummaged through Radcliffe's coat and pockets but came up empty. Looking around, he spotted Radcliffe's horse a few yards away. He strode over to the beast, a beautiful stallion who calmed at Henry's touch. Henry rifled through the saddlebags and came up with a small packet of letters, which he tucked safely into his coat pocket. He kept looking and came upon Radcliffe's rations. Removing them from the bag, he crossed back to the slaves.

Kneeling down, he extended his hand, offering the food. The woman looked wary, but she took the bundle.

"Do you know where you're going? Or where you're staying tonight?"

The woman nodded her head.

Henry had serious doubts that she was telling the truth, but decided if she wasn't going to offer herself up as a problem for him to deal with, he wasn't going to heap it upon himself. "All right then."

Glancing around and seeing they had no provisions to speak of, he crossed back to the horse. Henry untied Radcliffe's sleeping roll and brought it back to the slaves. With a businesslike manner he pointed off into the swamp.

"All right then, off you go."

The woman stared at him for a moment so Henry pointed again. "Off you go, unless you want me to round you up and take you back to your master."

There was no threat in his voice, yet both slaves were on their feet in an instant. Henry started to turn back to the body when the woman hesitantly spoke.

"Thank you. You a good man."

Now it was Henry's turn to stare for a moment, before he composed himself.

"No, I am not." Henry glanced back at Radcliffe. "A man like that deserves worse than a bullet in the head."

The woman looked at him, confused, but nodded her head in acquiescence before she turned and with her daughter by her side, headed into the darkness. Henry watched them go until he could no longer see them, then turned to the task at hand. He stripped Radcliffe's body of anything that would identify him or was of any value and stored the items in the saddlebags. He grabbed the reins of Radcliffe's horse, mounted up and, with a click of his tongue, turned the horse's head back in the direction from which he had come, leaving Radcliffe's body for the swamp to do with as it may.

Henry was able to find his way back to his own horse easily. He reached down from the stallion's back, untied his horse, and leading him along behind, soon found the path that had eluded him earlier. Henry figured his luck was probably due to heightened senses leftover from the rush of energy from the encounter. In the event it was God smiling down on him, he sent up a prayer of thanks. Then, as an afterthought, he added one for the two slaves who by now were, hopefully, huddled up somewhere sleeping.

It was late by the time Henry made it to camp. The campsite

was on a knoll to avoid all but the most severe flooding, and they used a nearby abandoned bear den, which they had dug out and enlarged to their purposes, to store their goods. Its entrance was obscured from view. As he had approached from the direction of the den, he tied up both horses there so they could more easily be unloaded, before crossing over to the small fire his men had burning. He was heartened to see each of his men had made it back safely. That feeling only lasted a moment, though, as one of his men spotted him and shouted hallo. Henry braced himself for the teasing. They were all surprisingly quiet, but with expectant faces as he finally took his seat. The tension was palpable. Williams broke the silence.

"Everythin' all right, Captain?"

"Yes." Henry looked around the circle suspiciously. They all looked as if they were fit to burst. The man sitting next to him, Little Jack, reached out a hand and touched his arm consolingly.

"We all know the swamp is scary, Captain, but there's no need to be firin' your pistol and carryin' on like a little girl!"

The tension broke and the men roared with laughter, falling over themselves and throwing out more jibes as their mirth allowed. So much for their concern over his well-being. Before long, he was laughing with them. The laughter subsided, only to be rekindled when Little Jack fell backward off his log and required the help of Henry and Adam to get himself righted.

Once all was settled again, Adam spoke. "So, what happened, Captain?"

Henry had known this question would be asked but was not sure how much he wanted to divulge.

"I came upon a situation, and I handled it."

A few eyebrows rose.

"I did get a mighty fine horse and a pair of boots as reward for my efforts, though." This was enough to distract the men from further inquiry. Henry tilted his head toward the den. "Go, and unload the supplies while you are over there."

The men scrambled off, chattering like excited boys on Christmas morning.

"Pay up! I won the bet!"

"You didn't win. Captain wasn't lost; he was dealin' with a situation."

"Yeah, a situation he found 'cause he was lost. Pay up!"

"Ow! Whad'ja hit me for?"

"For bein' an idiot."

"What does bein' an idiot have to do with anythin'?"

Their voices faded into the night, and Henry found himself not alone, as he had wanted. Williams remained sitting next to him. His head was down, looking into his cup of coffee waiting for Henry to speak. When it became clear Henry wasn't going to speak, Williams asked.

"Did you kill him?" Henry looked at him startled, and Williams smiled. "I figure the only thing that would cause you to show up with that look on your face is if you interrupted a man takin' advantage of a woman."

Henry's eyebrows shot up. How in the hell did Williams know that?

"I know you didn't make that woman scream, and contrary to your reputation, you are not the sort of man to stand by and watch harm done. So I ask again. Did you kill him?"

Henry nodded his head. "He had raped a woman and then threatened a girl."

"Sounds like justice to me."

"They were Negroes."

Williams froze for the briefest of moments, then looked at Henry. "I don't know that it would have occurred to me to come to the rescue of colored girls. Huh." Williams shook his head slightly as if trying to wrap his brain around the notion, then stood. "Well, you're a better man than me."

Henry let out a low indistinguishable noise. "No, I'm not."

"As you say, sir." Williams took a step toward the men and the horses. "I guess I should go help."

"It was Radcliffe." Henry felt as if a weight had been lifted from his chest.

Williams stopped and looked down at him. "Really?"

"He had messages for me," Henry patted his pocket. "I guess he decided a little recreation on the way was in order."

"Well, I'll be damned." Williams smiled and clapped Henry on the shoulder. "I wouldn't worry yourself too much, Captain. That bastard got better than he deserved."

"True."

Williams looked over toward the den. "We'll have to scruff up that horse a bit and sell him the first chance we get. He's too recognizable."

"I was thinking the same thing."

"I'll take care of it." Williams made to leave, then paused. "You didn't take the quinine out of Jack's pack before we split up earlier, did ya?"

"No. Is it missing?"

"When we heard the screams, I went over to check on our goods and the pile seemed too small. I almost wrote it off, then I looked closer and saw that there was only one bag of salt and no quinine. I could've sworn that me and Adam both had a bag of salt, but I could be rememberin' that wrong. There wasn't no quinine, though, and I know I saw you put some in Jack's pack."

"You think the men stole it?"

"I don't see who else it could've been. It don't make sense, though. Jack was with me till the swamp. Who's he gonna sell to in here? And why would Adam take the salt, when those big bags of flour will fetch more money? I can't make sense of it unless one of them stole from the pile here in camp and stashed it somewhere."

Henry nodded his head. "From now on you and I will load everything into the den as soon as we arrive. No one else goes in there. Let's also come up with some camouflage to hide the entrance better."

"I will tell the men."

"No. If it is one of them, I don't want him to know that we are on to him. Keep it lighthearted tonight. I will come up with some reason for the decision and announce it tomorrow."

"Yes, sir." Clapping him on the shoulder once more, Williams headed off, raising his voice so the men could hear him. "You better not be arguin' over who gets those boots! As the captain's second in command, I get first pick!"

There was a roar of outrage from the men.

"Who said you was second in command?"

"I did, that's who!"

Henry chuckled to himself as his men continued in their good-natured squabbling. He couldn't imagine that one of these men was stealing, but like Williams, Henry had no other plausible explanation. He would deal with it tomorrow. He reached down and picked up a half-empty pan of beans from the fireside and started to eat.

26
Sentiments Dismissed

Henry sat stiffly at his makeshift desk. He could not remember the last time he had written a letter that did not pertain to the war. He had not had anybody to write to before; now all of that was about to change. General Bell had looked favorably on Henry's proposal and the wedding day was fast approaching. At first, the general's haste surprised Henry, although his reasoning was sound, so Henry agreed. These were uncertain times, and in uncertain times, fortune looked upon those who seized opportunities instead of letting them pass by. So Henry was to be wed. However, try as he might, he could not come up with the necessary words to write to his father. He pushed the unfinished letter aside. Instead, he felt the need to write to Kady. There were things that needed to be said, and he would not get the opportunity before the ceremony to say them in person. Centering the paper in front of himself, he dipped his pen and began.

> August 23, 1864
>
> My Dearest Kady,
> I hope you can forgive my familiarity, but as we are to be wed, I cannot help myself. I count the days until you will be my Kady forevermore. I find myself thinking of nothing else, and I find myself unworthy of such a great thing. This war

The weight of what he was to say caused him to pause.

August 23, 1864

My Dearest Kady,
I hope you can forgive my familiarity, but as we are to be wed, I cannot help myself. I count the days until you will be my Kady forevermore. I find myself thinking of nothing else, and I find myself unworthy of such a great thing. This war **causes men to do atrocious things. Things I cannot claim innocence from. I have done the unspeakable, and of that, I am not proud. I will not burden you with the telling, but please know that is not the man I want to be. Not the man I will be for you. From this day forward, my life will be devoted to you and your happiness and comfort. I will see that you want for nothing, and I will strive to be a good husband to you. Your kindness and virtue quell the monster I have within.**

Henry stopped and read over what he had written. How could he tell Kady such things? She was young and innocent. He couldn't tell her of his horrible deeds or this monster inside of him that constantly fought to break free, ruining all within its wake. He would arrive for his wedding day to find his bride had run off for fear, and he would not blame her. She should run, and stay as far away as possible. He was not a good person. His father was a horrible man and he had raised Henry to follow in his shadow; the curse fathers pass to their sons. He stared at the letter for a long moment, then crumpled it into a ball and threw it into the corner of the tent.

27
Sleeping with the Enemy

Emma dropped her pack onto the floor, kicked the chair away from the table and slumped down into it. By now she had lost track of how many taverns and inns she had frequented, and yet she still had not heard anything useful. Well, in truth, she had heard plenty of useful things, if she had been any part of this war, but nothing of any worth to her. After making it out of the swamp safely, she had camped for the night in the clearing across the road, too tired to go anywhere else. The next morning, after watching the swamp for several hours and seeing nothing, she ventured back in, this time with pencil and paper to record her route. In the daylight, she didn't dare go up the hill to look into the camp, even though all was quiet. She crouched behind a tree listening for a spell, then gave up and made her way back out of the swamp, gathering her markers and hopefully erasing any sign of her presence.

Since then she had ventured back into the swamp twice but hadn't seen Henry either time. She started to doubt that she had found his camp at all. The man had disappeared without a trace. Maybe he was dead. She was not sure if that thought lightened her spirits or depressed her further still.

A barmaid ambled over and Emma ordered food and, surrendering to her frustration and depression, an ale. She remained alone with her thoughts for some time before the maid returned with the food and drink. Emma ordered a second ale before she had even taken a drink from her first.

Upon hearing her order, a man a couple of tables over held up his own drink and saluted her. "I'll drink to that."

Wryly, Emma raised her own mug and took a deep drink. Thankfully, this particular brew was not strong and it went down smoothly, so she didn't cough. She had started drinking ale and, while she enjoyed the numbness it brought, she still had not become accustomed to the strong taste or harshness of the home brew often served in these backwoods taverns. This one was quite good, though, and when the maid deposited her second mug on the table, Emma noticed the man was still observing her, and she raised her mug again to him. "Why don't you join me? No sense in both of us eating alone."

The man snorted. "I do believe you will have to be the one joining me. You are a bit more ambulatory."

With the last statement, he gestured downward, and Emma realized the man was missing a leg. She flushed with foolishness. Leave it to her to ask a cripple to walk across the room to join her.

Regaining her composure, she responded, "Well, yes, I do believe you are right."

Cursing her impulsive invitation, she began to gather her things. After her embarrassing remark, all she wanted to do was blend into the shadows and pretend she wasn't there. Instead she had to go over and talk to the man. Draining the contents of her first mug, both for courage and the economy of having one less thing to carry, she hoisted her pack onto her shoulder, picked up her plate and the second mug, and crossed to the man's table. She kept her eyes averted as she situated herself but could feel the man studying her. She could also smell him.

He had already had more than two drinks and was drinking something much more substantial than ale. Maybe this wouldn't be too bad. He would probably pass out before she was done eating.

"What brings you to these parts?" He was still eyeing her in a way that unnerved her slightly, but his voice was friendly.

"I'm looking for a man."

"Your husband?"

Emma choked on her bite of food and coughed violently. The passing barmaid helpfully pounded her on the back, and after a few swallows of ale, she was able to clear her throat. Emma could see his wide grin through her watering eyes. He clearly took her reaction as an admission he was right. Emma coughed once more and took another drink. Clearing her throat, she tried to speak.

"I am not married. How did you know," she lowered her voice, "that I'm not a boy?"

He laughed.

Despite the smell coming off him, he seemed to be stone-cold sober.

"It wasn't hard."

Emma made a noise, affronted, and he chuckled.

"Don't get me wrong, you are doing a mighty fine job with that getup you've got on, but no self-respecting man, or boy, sits with his ankles crossed while eating his supper."

Emma's attention fell to the floor, where, sure enough, her feet were tucked neatly under her chair, crossed primly at the ankle. Hastily, she uncrossed her legs and planted both feet firmly on the ground.

The man laughed again and, to her mortal humiliation, slid his one remaining foot between her calves, knocking her knees apart, which caused her to clamp them together even harder. Returning his foot to the floor, the man laughed at her.

"If you're going to dress like a man, sit like a man. What are you doing, squeezing a penny between your thighs?"

Despite the ever-deepening flush on her face, she realized he was right. The room had begun to fill with men, and every one of them sat with a definite gap between their knees. Trying mightily to keep her breathing steady, she relaxed her legs and let her knees fall slightly apart. She felt even more scandalous than the day that she looked at herself in the mirror wearing buckskin breeches for the first time. Emma took another drink from her ale, hoping it might help her ride out the embarrassment. Praying her voice wouldn't shake, she asked, "Better?"

The man laughed again. "You are a queer bird, you know that? But I think I like ya. We'll work on it." He raised his glass to her.

Raising her own mug, she allowed them to clink together, before joining him in a companionable swig.

"Thank you." Emma wasn't sure why she had thanked the man. He had already humiliated her twice, but there was something about him. He had seen who she was immediately. However, instead of calling her out or causing her trouble, he had chosen to help her blend in better. Maybe he could be an ally, someone who was in on her secret. It occurred to her that she did not know his name, nor did he know hers.

"I'm sorry, I never introduced myself. My name is Emm, er Daniel."

The man cocked an eyebrow and grinned. "Nice to meet you, Emerdaniel. My name is Jacob."

229

She smiled warmly at him, and for the first time in she did not know how long, laughed.

Emma and Jacob spent the rest of the evening immersed in each other's company. Jacob spoke little of himself, and what he did tell her, Emma suspected was full of lies and half-truths. Though he hid it well, every now and then he would say a word with an odd accent that belied he was not from the South as he claimed. Not that she could fault him; she hadn't told him anything truthful about herself, either. Their conversation stuck primarily to what they had heard about the war and its participants. Emma felt no little amount of pride that she knew much more than he. He even told her he was impressed that she had been able to learn as much as she had. She wasn't sure if it was to do with the large quantities of ale she was drinking or merely the power she felt, knowing she could keep this man riveted by revealing or withholding information as she pleased, but she had a heady, weightless feeling which she found to be quite agreeable.

That feeling crashed when Jacob happened to mention the name Henry with no little amount of derision. Emma tried to find an anchor to calm her thoughts. Had she finally found a link to the captain, or was he merely talking about some other Henry? It was quite a popular name, so it was possible. She desperately wanted to know more and ask a hundred questions but did not want to seem too eager. Eventually impatience won out and she asked him outright if he was talking about Captain Henry, which shocked her somewhat. She had never been that forthright before. If Jacob had been taken aback, he did not let it show. He confirmed he was indeed referring to Captain Henry of the

Confederate Army. While neither of them had wanted to reveal the true reason behind their particular hatred of the man, it was agreed upon that he was, indeed, mutually hated.

Jacob told her of the captain's current presence in Richmond and of his activities shuttling supplies through the Dismal. It only took Emma a few moments to connect this revelation with a bit of intelligence she had picked up several days earlier. A bit so good, she had originally intended to sell it, but if it meant bringing down Captain Henry, that was payment enough. Emma told Jacob she had overheard there was a mess of gold bars that had been secretly given to President Davis and he was arranging to move it out of Richmond to a safe place beyond reach. When she heard this, she had been so focused on Henry, the man, and not what he was doing, that it hadn't occurred to her that his camp in the swamp would be the perfect hiding spot.

Jacob agreed with her. It had to be Henry's unit moving the gold into the Dismal Swamp. After all, how could you find a better hiding place than a swamp! They had both become giddy with excitement, exchanging every bit of information they knew to see if they could piece together anything more about the mission.

By the time the tavern proprietor kicked them out so he could go to bed, they had devised their own plan and had drunk to Henry's demise several times over.

Upon standing, Emma realized she was unable to walk without assistance. She giggled and, clutching a table for support, was trying to get the room to stop spinning when Jacob arrived at her side, gallantly offering to escort her. They made quite the pair as they stumbled out of the tavern. On his own, Jacob seemed quite sturdy on his foot, but as he only had the one and relied upon a crutch for walking, Emma was not entirely sure if Jacob's efforts were helping or hindering her situation.

Mercifully, the room she had rented for the night was across the road and they were able to make it into the building without any substantial mishaps. The stairs, on the other hand, proved to be a challenge neither of them was ready for. They fell backward twice before making it past the second step, and then Emma collapsed onto the stairs declaring she would simply sleep there for the night. Laughing at her ridiculousness, Jacob sat down on the stairs and started to make his way up by lifting himself up on his butt one stair at a time. He positioned himself above Emma, then reached down and, grasped her by the wrists, dragging her up the stairs so they were even. This movement elicited a scream from Emma that she immediately squelched for fear of waking the other inhabitants. She then dissolved into a fit of snorting laughter, every snort eliciting more laughter from them both.

Sweating and clutching their sides from the effort of trying to laugh quietly, they finally made it to the top of the stairs, then crawled a bit away from the edge before attempting to stand up. Once on their feet, they ricocheted off the walls of the hall until they finally made it to her room at the end. With some difficulty, she got the key inserted and the two of them practically fell into the room, dropping their bags and letting them lie where they fell. Once inside with the door shut, darkness enveloped them. The only illumination was a small shaft of moonlight coming in from a high window. They were both breathing heavily, the laughter replaced with a kind of kinetic energy. Emma felt Jacob's arm tighten around her waist, and before she knew it, he had turned her toward him so they were face-to-face. Despite the dark, she could see into his eyes and the longing that burned there. When he pulled her tight against him and kissed her, she kissed him back.

As his ardor grew and she felt his hands exploring her body, tugging at her clothes, some part in the back of her mind was screaming this was wrong, that she needed to run, to scream, to get away. But the fire racing through her body told another story. She wanted him even though she wasn't entirely sure what that meant. Following his lead, her hands began to fumble with his clothes as they struggled toward the bed. She fell back on to it and the room began to spin to such a degree that when Jacob climbed on top of her, she saw two of him. She had enough time to shake her head, reuniting the image, before he started kissing her again.

Emma must have passed out, because the next thing she knew Jacob was snoring softly in her ear. Emma slid out from between the sheets, which proved difficult as her britches were down below her knees. She was quite sore in a number of unspeakable places and there was a disconcerting stickiness between her legs. A bit unsteadily, she pulled her pants up and started to make her way to the ewer on the table across the room, when she kicked a bag on the floor at the end of the bed. It took her a moment to recognize the bag wasn't hers, and if it wasn't hers, then it had to be Jacob's. She knelt down and began to quietly rifle through the bag. She could still hear him snoring so she removed several envelopes. They were coded letters, which confirmed her suspicions that Jacob was a spy, or at least a messenger. She, of course, had no idea what they said. Several of them were in the same handwriting and were signed LR. One letter was different. It was written in sentences she could read, though some words had obviously been substituted so she couldn't make heads nor tails of what the actual message was supposed to be. This one was in the same handwriting as the letters marked LR, but it was signed Kady. Emma smiled; LR was clearly the code name of a woman named Kady.

A rustle of the bedclothes made Emma jerk her head up to look, the movement resulting in a wave of dizziness and an uncontrollable urge to retch. Dropping the letters, she reached for the chamber pot from under the bed and proceeded to vomit into it until she was certain she had nothing left in her body. She was still drunk. Pushing the pot back under the bed with a disgusted shove, she crawled over to the small table and shakily poured herself a glass of water from the ewer. She drank it carefully in small sips lest she become sick again. Her stomach remained uneasy, but the water stayed down. With a hiccup, she set her glass back on the table and crawled back to Jacob's bag. She was so tired. She knew she had to put the letters back. With this accomplished, she curled up on the floor, using her own bag as a pillow. The room was swimming again and she welcomed the approaching oblivion of sleep. However, somewhere in the back of her mind she kept repeating to herself, so she would not forget, LR is Kady. LR is Kady. LR is Kady.

Sept 26, 1864
Smokehouse has lost value. To be replaced
by Rose Garden.
NR

36-24-14-62 33-32 41-45-32-42
36-21-11-34-24-65-11-43-36-24 65-51-36
54-11-36-62 44-51-54-43-24 62-11 63-24
64-24-14-54-51-15-24-56 63-13 64-11-36-24
26-51-64-56-24-61
61-64

28
Sacrifice

By the time Kady and Henry arrived in Richmond after their wedding, Kady's nerves were in tatters. The carriage ride from their celebratory luncheon had been taxing. Due to troop movements, they had to stop several times on the road between her father's plantation and Richmond, and neither of them had been able to find easy conversation. Once in the city, they found the main thoroughfares blocked, which had forced them onto side streets and then an alley before finally arriving. Waving off the coachman, Henry turned to hand Kady down himself. Taking a deep breath, she started her descent only to trip on the front of her skirts and fall into Henry's arms. Easily catching her, he set her on her feet.

"Are you all right, my love?"

A flush of crimson raced up Kady's cheeks as she looked down.

"I am fine, thank you. I lost my footing."

She made a move toward the front door but Henry stopped her. He lifted her chin until she was looking into his eyes.

"There is no need to be nervous."

Kady blushed deeper still, not because he had pinpointed the cause of her fall but because he must think she was worried for what inevitably was to come after the wedding. In truth, she was worrying about Jacob. By the time Kady had worked up the nerve to tell him of her upcoming nuptials, he was gone. His leg had healed enough, so he had been spirited away in the middle of the night with a parcel of messages from her mother for delivery. Kady silently cursed herself. She would have to be careful not to let her thoughts stray while in Henry's presence, lest she give herself away. Doing the only thing she could think of, she smiled sweetly and stood on her tiptoes to kiss him. Content he had allayed her fears, Captain Henry offered her his arm. Arriving at the front door, he grasped her firmly by the waist and lifted her over the threshold. Kady giggled despite herself, and Henry looked down at her with a mock-stern expression.

"To keep the spirits from following you in."

Playing along, Kady stifled her mirth. "Very sensible."

Henry's face broke into a smile and he kissed her before taking her hand and ushering her into the house. He gave her a cursory tour of the downstairs rooms, acknowledging, but otherwise ignoring, any servant they passed. He also ignored the portraits hanging on the walls, portraits that clearly belonged to the former occupant. She bit her tongue. Kady knew the house had been seized from a wealthy widower who had been suspected and charged as an alien enemy. How Henry had come into possession of the house she didn't know. Under the circumstances, she thought it might be best to remain ignorant of the details, lest she know exactly what crime it was she was being accused of by the piercing portrait eyes. Besides, she rather liked her new house and did not want any sad stories to ruin the tour. Walking into the last room, Henry stopped and pointed to something on the other side.

"I bought that especially for you: a wedding present."

Kady was speechless. Across the room sat the most beautiful piano she had ever seen. There was even sheet music out as if someone had left off playing only moments before. Henry slid his hands around her waist and leaned down to whisper in her ear.

"From the first time I saw you sitting at your father's piano, headstrong and confident, an equal to the room of great men around you, I knew I must have you. And now I do."

That day came flooding back to Kady. That day had changed her life forever, in more ways than she would ever be able to comprehend.

"Do you like it, my darling?"

Returning to the present, she tore her eyes away from the instrument in the corner and turned to face him.

"It is the most beautiful thing I have ever seen. I love it. Thank you, Henry."

"Please, you are my wife now. Call me Thomas."

"Thank you, Thomas." The name felt awkward crossing her lips. He had always been Captain Henry or plain Henry. She would have to make a conscious effort to remember to call him by his first name.

"Come." At her utterance of his given name, he smiled, took her by the hand, and swept her out of the room. The tour was over. He led her to the grand staircase and escorted her up. Only once he had crossed the threshold into the bedchamber at the top of the stairs did he slow down. Turning around, he let go of her hand and took her in, reaching out to cup her cheek in his hand. Tenderly, cautiously, he kissed her.

Kady felt no spark, no excitement; none of the raging fireworks she felt the first time Jacob had taken her into his arms. This was different, restrained, more like a stroll in the park on a Sunday afternoon. Was he afraid he was going to break her? When he stopped, she could see a passion burning in his eyes for her. Afraid he would not see that same passion reciprocated, Kady turned her eyes to the door.

"Should I call in my girl so I can change for you?"

"No." In two easy strides, he crossed to the door and closed it, then turned back to her. A trill of apprehension ran through her as she realized she wasn't going to get a moment alone to compose herself before the inevitable act. She felt his eyes survey her person from top to bottom and back up again. "I want to undress you myself."

It had not been as horrible as Kady had imagined. As soon as they were safely behind closed doors, Captain Henry's stiff demeanor had melted away. To her utter amazement, he was a gentle and slow lover. He kissed her passionately and deeply. Never roughly. He actually loved her, and his devotion spilled out in the murmurs he whispered in her ear. She did not think she would ever tire of hearing nice things said about her in that husky voice, and unlike with Jacob, it hadn't hurt. It was still one of the strangest sensations she had ever felt, something foreign shoved up inside her, filling her up. When he was finished, he kissed her once more, encircled her in his arms, and held her. He was still whispering endearments as he fell asleep and began snoring softly into her hair.

In any other world, in any other circumstance, she would have been in heaven. Her father had found her the perfect husband: devastatingly handsome, successful, rich, and utterly devoted to her. Too bad she lived in this world—a world that found her lying in the arms of a man on the wrong side of the war; praying to God her mother would be able to find Jacob to tell him the news, and that after hearing, he would not act rashly. She couldn't think of that now. She had her own circumstances to worry about, which included a dawn that would bring with it prying eyes eager to catch a glimpse of her virginal blood staining the sheets—virginal blood that had already been spilled. Mercifully, her mother had thought of that and had decorated her hair with a comb sharp enough to prick her finger after her captain had sated his lust and retired to his own bedchamber.

Neither of them had anticipated Henry would instead choose to take his repast holding his newly appointed wife tight in his embrace. Worse still, he had taken down her hair. So all of the sundry hairpins and the coveted comb lay out of reach on the stand by the bed. Henry's deepened and rhythmic snores had signaled some time ago that he was fast asleep. She knew she had to chance it, to try to get the comb. If she did not take care of this now, she may never get the chance. Come morning he might insist on bathing together or something equally absurd, and spirit her away before she could do the deed. Worse yet, he might see the lack of blood himself. Holding her breath, she counted to three then carefully tried to roll out of his arms. Feeling her intended absence, he pulled her back in tighter and nuzzled his face deeper into her hair. If this was how he planned to spend every night, she would have to get used to sleep deprivation. How he expected her to sleep in a vice grip she had no idea. With a sigh, she tried to reach out with her arm, only to be thwarted again.

However, this time his hand brushed against her breast as he pulled her back, and in that brief moment she felt a faint surge of hardness grow and then fade against her. Closing her eyes and clenching her teeth, Kady realized how she could get him to loosen his grip on her. Her mother's words came flooding back to her, "You've chosen to make yourself no better than a common whore," as she gently took Henry's hand and guided it back to her breast. Once there it needed little coaxing before it started to massage and explore the wonders of her svelte feminine form. His tumescence grew faster than his wakefulness, with the aid of some discreet stroking, so by the time he found himself awake he was in full cry.

With his susurrations of love already spent, he made short work of rolling Kady onto her back and insinuating himself atop her. This act mirrored her night with Jacob much more closely and, with his initial thrust, she cried out. However, unlike Jacob, Henry froze at her cry, and confusion, then understanding, moved in succession across his face as he came fully awake. His eyes spoke volumes of regret and disgust as he rolled off her and sat on the edge of the bed, his head in his hands. He spoke softly, huskily.

"I'll leave you to get some sleep. My apologies."

With that, he got up and walked silently out of the room, not bothering to cover his naked form. She watched him go, fighting back the tears making their way down her face. At the click of the closing door, she was no longer able to hold back the torrent of tears and, so, rolled over to sob into her pillow. When she had no more tears to spill and had steadied her breathing, she reached over to the bed stand and clasped the comb in her hand. However, even with only the feeble moonlight as illumination, she could see from the sheets that the comb was not necessary. Henry had done his duty and consummated their marriage. She had done her duty and bled for it.

                                    Oct 16, 1864
Rose Garden is planted. Discontinue
smokehouse.
NR

                        11-15-62 41-32 41-45-32-42
64-11-36-24 26-51-64-56-24-61 52-36
14-54-51-61-62-24-56
56-52-36-15-11-61-62-52-61-43-24
36-21-11-34-24-65-11-43-36-24
61-64

29

Bad News Taken Badly

Anna paced the parlor, unable to quiet her nerves enough to sit. Once more, she cursed her daughter's name, then in the next breath prayed the girl would be able to keep her wits about her and thus keep their secret safe. Captain Henry seemed like a good man, but Anna sensed he was hiding something. For Kady's sake, Anna hoped that hidden something was not violent. No one deserved that, not even a spoiled little fool like Kady. The memories Anna fought back made her shudder, and she pulled her shawl tighter around her shoulders.

Despite the potential danger that lay in wait for Kady, Anna felt Kady was getting the better end of the bargain. She was ensconced in Richmond with her new husband, while Anna was left to track down and deliver the news to Jacob. This time Anna cursed Kady's impetuousness. The little coward hadn't worked up the courage to tell Jacob about her impending betrothal before he was whisked away in the night to carry messages North. The plan was to hide him in plain sight among a convoy of injured soldiers that had been given leave to return home. His missing leg was actually proving useful. It was not safe for Jacob to return to the South immediately, in case someone recognized him from the convoy, so Anna included a package that needed to be delivered all the way to New York. Everything else could be left at the Union line. This should have taken him a couple of weeks at the most, but a month had already passed with no sign of him.

243

Anna considered sending a message after him so she could be done with the distasteful task, but she knew this news could not go in a letter. This precaution was in no way out of respect for Jacob or in deference to his feelings; the bastard could rot in hell as far as she was concerned. However, if that letter was intercepted and somehow decoded, the results would be disastrous. If word got around that wives of Confederate officers were spying for the Union, the flow of information would dry up in an instant. General Lee's wife, Mary Anna, was amazingly tight-lipped. However, when she did let something slip, it was always invaluable. Even if an officer did not suspect his own wife, he would stop telling her anything important for fear her gossip would reach the ears of a wife who was a spy. Or he would forbid her to attend ladies' circles or luncheons, which were Anna's best resources. It was at such a luncheon earlier that day that she had received word to expect Jacob after nightfall.

Anna stopped in the middle of the room, agitation written across her features. She needed to find something to do or she would go mad waiting for Mary to bring word of Jacob's arrival. Her eyes fell on the piano and she crossed to it slowly, running her fingers along its side before seating herself before the keys. It was a beautiful instrument, but it was not hers. Hers had been destroyed years before when the girl had spilled water across the soundboard. After that, the notes had become sour and Andrew, instead of fixing it, had simply bought Kady a new one. Anna had never played it, disheartened by the loss of her childhood instrument and loath to play on something that was so obviously Kady's. Anna would listen to her daughter play, though, discreetly from across the hall or upstairs. The music always seemed to soothe her mind.

Anna reverently touched her fingers to the keys, not depressing any of them, just getting the feel of them. She tested the pedals, which moved easily. It was a magnificent instrument. Cautiously she began to play, unsure if she would remember how after all of these years. She closed her eyes, letting the notes flow through her, and her playing gained confidence. She didn't need to think, her fingers knew what to do, as if she had only taken a break of days instead of years. "Dido's Lament" filled the room. It was her favorite piece and the sound of it brought her back to easier, less complicated times. As she played the last note and languidly opened her eyes, she realized she was crying. It was such a beautiful piece.

Without thinking or consciously deciding what to play next, her fingers began to move once more. Anna lost herself in the music. After a while, her fingers began to ache. She didn't care; she kept playing. When she finally stopped, her knuckles were throbbing and her lower back was tight from sitting on the stool, but the calm bliss that engulfed her made it easy to ignore these minor discomforts. She lowered the cover over the keys and lovingly ran her hand along the wood. Turning, she saw Mary sitting in one of the high-back chairs. Somehow, her presence was not surprising. It was as if they had been transported back twenty years and Mary was right where she had always been, sewing and listening to the music.

"Jus' as beautiful as the first time I heard you play." Anna smiled at her, then with a movement of her head toward the slave's shacks, asked if Jacob had arrived.

Mary nodded.

"Why didn't you tell me?"

245

"If the good Lord sees fit to speak to you and send you comfort, who am I to interrupt?" Mary smiled conspiratorially and lowered her voice. "'Sides, he can wait."

Anna's smile warmed. "Yes, he can."

Anna was delayed further still when she discovered her husband was availing himself of one of the slaves downstairs and therefore blocking her exit. Loath to be seen by him, Anna waited patiently in the kitchen and Mary fixed some tea and a plate of bread and butter. The two of them had done this many times, so if any of the slaves saw them, no suspicion would be aroused. They finally heard the heavy clump of Andrew's boots on the stairs, and Mary checked to make sure the coast was clear before Anna donned Mary's cloak and stole out the kitchen door. She made it to the slave shack, and with a look behind her to ensure she was alone, ducked inside.

Startled, Jacob fell off the chair he had been sitting on and then awkwardly tried to scramble upright, first grabbing his crutch upside down, then abandoning it and using the chair to help hoist himself up. He had dozed off, or she would not have been able to startle him so thoroughly. Anna felt a reproach rising in her throat but swallowed it back down. From the look on his face, he was aware of how careless falling asleep had been. Despite her lingering anger toward him, seeing him sheepish and vulnerable softened her countenance. No matter how big of a louse he was, the news she brought would hurt him.

"Please sit down." Her tone belied the tenor of what she had come to say.

Jacob straightened himself, tucking his crutch, now right side up, firmly under his arm. "If it's all the same to you, ma'am, I'll stand. I

246

prefer to take bad news on my feet." He looked down, and with a slight blush rising on his cheeks, amended himself, "Well, foot now. I guess."

He looked at her from under weary, hooded lids. His voice was husky, whether from drink, emotion, or sheer exhaustion she could not tell, although he did not appear to be in his cups. His posture was surprisingly solid for a man with one leg. It must be emotion or exhaustion then. Anna wagered he knew something was seriously wrong—why else call him back? Anna had debated with herself whether it would be better to tell him slowly, or all at once. Standing in front of him with those tired eyes and feeling the weight of the day settling back onto her own shoulders, she decided bluntness was her best option.

"General Bell has married Kady to a Confederate officer."

Jacob was struck dumb. Anna could see the thoughts race across his face.

"You mean, she's been promised to a Confederate officer?"

"No. She was married by a minister." Anna put a little extra emphasis on the word minister. "Had you not dallied so long in New York, you would have known sooner."

"No, she would have told me. She couldn't have."

"She didn't have time to tell you. Her father works surprisingly fast when he gets his mind set on something."

"But she wouldn't have. She's married to me."

"She had no choice! Don't you see? She couldn't very well tell her father she was already married without putting all of our lives at risk. She had to act as if she was the same silly girl she's always been and go along with everything her father said." Hearing Kady's words come out of her own mouth with such conviction gave Anna pause. "She had no

247

choice."

"She's my wife, dammit!" The sudden ferocity of Jacob's statement caused her to step back involuntarily, and her forgotten anger at the man surged to the forefront.

"Not anymore she isn't, if she ever was to begin with. Trust me when I say the veracity of your so-called vows and motives are highly questionable."

"Questionable? She loves me and I had the decency to wed her before taking her to bed. I didn't have to do that."

"So you think that makes you a gentleman? Tricking a young girl into marrying you so you can sleep with her!"

"She is of marriageable age and fully capable of making her own decisions!"

"She is my little girl. You had no right to her then, and you have no right to her now!" The vehemence in her voice brought them both up short, and she realized she had been yelling. Lowering her voice, which actually served to sharpen the edge it contained, she continued, "I suggest you move on, and forget you ever met her. It is the best course of action for you both."

Without waiting for his response, Anna turned and left. The sound of a chair being thrown against the wall and splintering wood followed after her as she made her way back to the big house.

62-63-26 14-53 52-53-16-56
51-42-26-63-23-41-62-31 23-35-42-25-41
25-54-32-62-25-11 62-66 35-21-62-26-46-63
66-45-62-51-35-25-11 46-22 26-23-35
22-35-11-26 63-62-22-66-46-25-32
24-41

Oct 28, 1864

Watchdog heard rumors of exotic flowers in
the Nest. Confirm.
BD

Nov 8, 1864

YD confirmed. Exotic flowers are gold. Plan
harvest. DR has tools.
NR

22-62-55 53 52-53-16-56
64-41 63-62-22-66-46-25-32-35-41
35-21-62-26-46-63 66-45-62-51-35-25-11
42-25-35 31-62-45-41 65-45-42-22
23-42-25-55-35-11-26 41-25 23-42-11
26-62-62-45-11
22-25

22-62-55　52-14　52-53-16-56
22-35-11-26　62-54-26　62-66　25-35-42-63-23
22-35-35-41　26-62　51-42-46-26　66-62-25
22-35-51　23-42-25-55-35-11-26
45-62-63-42-26-46-62-22　62-25　66-46-22-41
22-35-51　42-65-65-25-62-42-63-23
41-25

Nov 12, 1864

Nest out of reach. Need to wait for new
harvest location or find new approach.
DR

Nov 17, 1864

Postpone harvest. Gardener moving Jesuit
through the Thorns. Bud 5.
LR

22-62-55　52-12　52-53-16-56
65-62-11-26-65-62-22-35　23-42-25-55-35-11-26
31-42-25-41-35-22-35-25　32-62-55-46-22-31
33-35-11-54-46-26　26-23-25-62-54-31-23
26-23-35
26-23-62-25-22-11　24-54-41　36
45-25

22-62-55 14-34 52-53-16-56
32-46-11-11-35-41 32-35-35-26-46-22-31
51-46-26-23 33-35-11-54-46-26
64-41

Nov 23, 1864

Missed meeting with Jesuit.
YD

41-35-63 52 52-53-16-56
51-42-26-63-23-41-62-31 23-35-42-25-41
35-21-62-26-46-63 66-45-62-51-35-25-11 26-62
32-62-55-35 26-62 26-23-35 26-23-62-25-22-11
24-41

Dec 1, 1864

Watchdog heard exotic flowers to move to
the Thorns.
BD

Dec 12, 1864

Gardener to move exotic flowers on Dec 20.
Mama Bird will sing. Harvest before the
Thorns.
LR

41-35-63 52-14 52-53-16-56
31-42-25-41-35-22-35-25 26-62 32-62-55-35
35-21-62-26-46-63 66-45-62-51-35-25-11 62-22
41-35-63 14-43 32-42-32-42 24-46-25-41
51-46-45-45 11-46-22-31 23-42-25-55-35-11-26
24-35-66-62-25-35 26-23-35 26-23-62-25-22-11
45-25

30

A Convergence

Rebecca set down her pencil, abandoning the pretext of working on her latest poem. Instead, she watched the milling throng down in the supply yard. Her mind had been distracted ever since Kady's note had arrived earlier that morning announcing she would drop by in the afternoon. While Rebecca found this odd, she welcomed the visit. Kady had visited three days earlier with fresh supplies and Rebecca's first payment. Somehow Kady had convinced a newspaper to not only print her poem, under a pen name, of course, but also pay for the poem and request more. The girl was a wonder, and Rebecca thanked God for her friendship every night in her prayers.

That being said, Kady also worried her. From the beginning, Rebecca had suspected Kady had an ulterior motive for befriending her. She had made that odd request with the candles, and after all, who wants to be friends with a cripple? However, hadn't Kady also visited several times without asking about the supply yard at all? In fact, Rebecca was the one who brought it up at their last meeting. While Kady was interested in the information, she was much more interested in Rebecca's most recent poem. Kady had clutched it to her breast after reading it, then spirited it away with promises for a higher payment since this poem was longer. A smile broke Rebecca's stern countenance and she reproached herself. Maybe it was possible, despite everything her sister told her, for someone to like her for herself. Maybe it was possible for someone to look past her misshapen body and see a person worthy of love and friendship. This thought warmed her heart and eased her troubled mind somewhat. She did, however, take particular note of the movements below, as there was an unusual amount of activity.

Rebecca found the morning melted away while she made one mental note after another of the supply yard's goings-on. She had never seen this much laborious preparation go into what looked like a single shipment. Therefore, the small knock on her doorframe startled her and she emitted a rather embarrassing squeak. As the door itself was already wide open, she had no time to compose herself. She turned abruptly in her chair and saw Kady standing there with a genuine, if not bemused, smile on her face.

"My apologies, I didn't mean to scare you. Your niece said you were still in your room and, as I have never gotten the opportunity to see your room, I couldn't resist coming up straight away."

Rebecca flushed at the attention and self-consciously looked about her meager room in the hopes that all was in order and presentable. It was, of course, as she did not have enough belongings to ever be out of order.

"It's charming. Exactly as you described it, Rebecca. And yes, you are quite right. That desk is more than serviceable; no need to replace it." Kady smiled warmly at her and Rebecca blushed again, before remembering her manners.

"Would you like to sit?" She gestured toward the bed, then realizing the impossibility of sitting on a bed in a hoop skirt, started to rise so Kady could have her chair.

"Oh, no, no. I am fine standing. Sadly, I can't stay long. I just had

254

to stop by to give you this." She produced a wrapped package from behind her back and presented it to Rebecca. Dumbfounded, she stared at it for a moment, so Kady plopped it down on the desk. "Open it!"

"A present for me? Why did you, I mean, that wasn't necessary."

Kady laughed. "Of course it wasn't necessary. It is Christmas and I wanted to. Now open it!"

Rebecca laughed, too. "It isn't Christmas yet!"

"Oh, close enough."

Caught up in the excitement, Kady untied the ribbon herself and opened the box, pointing inside to encourage Rebecca to retrieve the treasure. She did and found a small pewter figurine of a mouse industriously scribbling away at a scroll. Overwhelmed, she could do no more than let out a breath of admiration, which was clearly enough of a reaction for Kady who clasped her hands joyously.

"I knew you would love it! I saw it in the window of the tinker's shop and immediately thought of you. I decided it had to be yours. A mouse for my little mouse!" A bubbling laughter filled the room, and she plucked the figurine out of Rebecca's hands and started a slow tour of the room. "Now where to put you?" She paused at the window to see if he fit nicely on the sill, then picked him back up. "Where do you want to live, little mouse?"

Rebecca laughed at this and closed her notebook. "Here. He should live here on the desk."

"Well, of course he should! How else can he dip his pen when he runs out of ink?" Kady crossed back to the desk and ceremoniously placed him on the corner. "Perfect. Do you like him? Tell me you like him."

Rebecca clutched her hands and looked up into her beautiful face. "I love him. Thank you, Kady. A little friend from my friend."

A look of perfect pleasure spread across Kady's face and she bent to kiss Rebecca on the cheek.

"Now that you have a constant companion to keep you company, I won't feel half so dreadful about having to take my leave from you."

Rebecca stood stiffly. "You can't be leavin' already."

"I'm so sorry, Rebecca dear. I have other errands to run before nightfall. Henry doesn't like me out past dark. I promise I'll come back next week."

"I haven't told you about the wagons yet."

Kady froze, startled. In all honesty, Rebecca had startled herself, too. Where had this boldness come from? But she had started down that path, so she may as well continue.

"I know you are interested in the shipments comin' out of the supply yard, and while I don't need to know why you are interested, you'll definitely want to know what's been happenin' for the past two days. It is unusual. After all, isn't that why you befriended me in the first place?"

Rebecca held her breath, her heart in her throat, and waited for Kady's reply. When Kady wordlessly turned toward the door, Rebecca almost cried out for her to stop. She was sorry and didn't mean what she had said and only wanted Kady to stay her friend. However, Kady simply closed the door, turned, took a breath, and crossed the room back to Rebecca. Taking her hands, Kady indicated for Rebecca to sit, then knelt down in front of her.

256

"Rebecca, please believe me when I say you are my friend, and you would still be my friend even if that window were to be boarded up and we were never to speak of the supply yard again. But yes, you are correct. I am interested, and if you can tell me more than I was able to observe when I looked out the window, I would be grateful to hear."

Rebecca swallowed hard, trying to push her heart back down into her chest. Kady was her friend. Although, as Rebecca suspected, she was also a spy or something like that. She was also more observant than Rebecca had given her credit for, as Rebecca had not even realized that Kady had already inspected the supply yard for herself. Her mind made up, Rebecca leaned in close and spoke barely above a whisper.

"You know that game the street urchins play in the street to swindle money from people? The one with the three thimbles and the pea?"

Kady nodded her head.

"I think the soldiers are contrivin' to do the same thing. They've spent all mornin' paintin' and equippin' three wagons so they all look exactly the same. But one of them has a steel chest in the back, while the other two have bags of sand. I didn't see what they put into the chest, but I think it's our pea."

Kady's face looked troubled. She was still nodding her head ever so slightly. She was clearly dismayed by the news.

"That complicates things, doesn't it? I'm sorry."

"Why are you sorry? This most definitely complicates things, but now we know ahead of time, thanks to you. Now we can try to have people in place to follow all three wagons."

"Wouldn't it be easier if you knew which wagon to follow from

257

the beginnin'?"

"Of course it would, but how would we know that?"

Rebecca hesitated a moment, then threw caution to the wind and volunteered. "I can continue to watch them until they leave. They are used to seein' me, so that will not cause any suspicion. I'll keep track of which wagon has the chest and then leave a signal with the candles."

The look of dismay vanished from Kady's face. "Yes. No! Not with the candles. With all of the extra guards they have on duty, someone might notice. So what can you do?" Kady stood and with hands on her hips looked about the room for inspiration. She found it on the desk. "Your mouse!"

Rebecca looked at her blankly, not comprehending.

"As soon as it gets dark, you'll light two candles and space them evenly across your window sill. If the correct wagon heads west, place the mouse to the left of both candles. If the correct wagon goes north, place it between the two candles, and if it goes east, place it to the right of the candles."

"Won't that be hard to see?"

"Exactly! Only someone looking for it will be able to distinguish that it's there at all."

Rebecca smiled. "That is perfect."

Kady smiled back, embraced her, and then held her at arm's length with her hands still on Rebecca's shoulders. "Are you sure you want to do this? You don't have to; you will still be my friend."

The earnest look in Kady's eyes warmed Rebecca down to her toes. "I want to do this. I want to help."

"And you're sure you don't want to know anything more?"

Rebecca was touched by Kady's concern for her. "I know you are my friend. I don't need to know anythin' else."

Kady smiled, kissed her on the cheek, then practically skipped from the room.

Rebecca shook her head, amused. Kady had to be the most unlikely spy ever to grace a war. Looking down at her mangled hand, Rebecca laughed, the irony of that thought sinking in. No, *she* had to be the most unlikely spy. Who would ever suspect a cripple would be good for anything? Smiling, Rebecca placed two candlesticks on the windowsill, carefully spacing them out. Then with a glance down to the supply yard to ensure nothing had changed, she opened her notebook and picked up her pen. She would show them.

Kady tried to appear as nonchalant as possible when she left Rebecca's house, strolling casually down the street. However, as soon as she had turned the corner, she picked up her pace while chewing over her new conundrum. How in the world was she either going to find, or get a message to, Jacob? While she was exceedingly proud of herself and Rebecca for solving the dilemma of the three wagons, what was the point if no one else knew about the issue? Kady's spy ring had been planning for a month and now it might all fall apart. She racked her brain trying to remember if Jacob had given her any indication of where he would be this afternoon. He had to be in the city already. As dangerous as it would be for him, there is no way he and his men would risk missing the wagon if it left early. Therefore, he had to be somewhere nearby.

She was so absorbed in her contemplations she did not see the man rounding the corner into her path and she bowled right into him. As he was substantially bigger than she, she took the brunt of the impact and would have fallen over, had the man not reached out and caught her at the last minute. The man righted her onto her feet, and Kady, brushing her dress back into place, looked up to thank the man, only to let out a yelp of alarm, necessitating him to reach out and steady her once more. Captain Henry chuckled and caressed her crimson cheek.

"My darling, are you all right? What are you doing here? I called at the house. They said you weren't in and I feared I would not get the chance to see you, as I have to leave this afternoon."

Kady reached up and took his hand. Anything to help steady herself and get her mind to focus on the fact she was now standing in front of her husband. The wrong husband.

"How fortuitous to run into you then." She blushed further still, realizing that she had literally run into him. "I was delivering a present to an invalid friend to brighten her day. And you? Where are you headed?"

"As you weren't at home, I decided I would sup with my men." Henry's face brightened. "Join us. They would love to meet you."

Despite her urgent business, Kady smiled warmly at him and moving to Henry's side tucked her hand into the elbow he offered her. "I would love to. Such a treat."

Frustrated, Emma raised her mug for a drink only to realize for the dozenth time it was still empty. She should order another, as there was no sign of Jacob and she had been waiting for an hour. She was certain she was in the right tavern for their rendezvous. Maybe he was waiting for some of the Confederate soldiers to clear out. Most had by this point, but there were still three men who had settled in and looked as if they weren't leaving anytime soon. Resigned, Emma walked to the bar to order another a drink. While she was waiting, she heard the door open, and checking in the big mirror behind the bar to check for Jacob, she froze. A woman in a beautiful gown had entered, followed by none other than Captain Henry.

Emma paid for her ale, keeping her eyes fixed on Henry. He walked over to the group of men, who all stood to be introduced to the woman. Once she sat, they all took their seats again and ordered food.

Carefully, Emma made her way back to her table in the corner. She could clearly see the entire party, but she was not able to make out their conversation. She desperately wanted to move closer so she could hear, but fear of Henry recognizing her kept her seated where she was.

The rumbles coming from her stomach did not help matters, so she ordered some food of her own. She almost ordered something for Jacob, then decided he could fend for himself. By the time her food was delivered, she had only been able to pick up bits and pieces and none of it relevant to their mission today. She was able to glean the woman was Henry's wife. She seemed to dote on her husband and he more than returned the affection, which made the bile in Emma's stomach rise. Sopping up the gravy on her plate with a roll, she finished it off before she could lose her appetite. She took a gulp from her ale and began to wonder if the wife could be used when Emma exacted her revenge on Henry.

Before she could ruminate further on that possibility, Jacob sidled up and sat down opposite her. Two hours late. He moved with a surprising quietness for a man with one leg. He wasted no preamble.

"Did you see our boy Henry over there?"

Emma shot him a scathing look. "How could I miss him?"

Jacob smirked. "Have you overheard anything useful about the gold shipment?"

Emma shook her head. "No. He came in with that woman, whom I'm guessing is his wife, and it's been all stories of Henry from his men to embarrass him ever since."

"Yes, that's his wife, Kady." Jacob reached across and grabbing Emma's ale, drained it. "So glad to see them so happy."

The derision in Jacob's voice was obvious. Emma neither knew nor cared why it was there. She was focused on the name he had said. Kady. Kady. Why was that name familiar? Jacob had signaled to the barkeep that they needed more ale and, in doing so, caught the eye of the young woman with Henry. A flicker of recognition flashed across her eyes. It was gone in a second, and she returned her attention to the men at her table. Before Emma could ask, the barkeep came over with the ale. She took a drink.

"You have enough men to carry the gold, yes?" Emma asked.

"It won't be a problem. We will hijack the wagon on the road and steal the gold that way."

"On the road? Why not in the swamp where no one will see you?"

Jacob gave her an incredulous look. "How are we supposed to go into the swamp without getting lost?"

Emma returned his look. "With the map I brought for you." Emma slapped a piece of paper onto the table in between them. "You don't remember? I told you that I would bring you a map."

Jacob looked at her sheepishly, and it was an odd look on his face. She guessed that he wasn't the type that admitted he was wrong often. She took pity on him.

"At least I didn't forget; take it. Now you can do your ambush in the swamp."

"Perfect."

Jacob's eyes had a glint to them and she could tell he was thinking. However, she did not need to stick around watching him think. She wanted to get out of Richmond before it got dark, so she got up to take her leave. Jacob stopped her.

"Wait. Will you deliver a message for me?" Emma sighed heavily, which Jacob took as acquiescence. "I'll write down the address. Ask for Mary and give it to her."

Emma waited while he tore a piece from her map and scribbled on it. Henry's party began to rise and collect their things to leave. Emma noticed Kady's wrap was draped across the back of the chair. She patted it reassuringly. Yet when she walked out with Henry, she left it behind.

Kady raised her hand to shield her eyes from the setting sun. Night was fast approaching.

"My darling, I am afraid I am unable to escort you back home; we must report for duty."

"Don't you worry yourself. It's not far and I fancy a walk." The

263

wind was picking up and Kady shivered.

"You will freeze to death, let me hire you a cab. Where is your wrap?"

"Oh! I left it inside, how silly of me. Go with your men. I would hate for you to be late on my account. I'll go fetch it and all will be well."

Henry gave her a worried look and she laughed.

"I will be fine. Go! The sooner you leave, the sooner you will come back to me."

Henry relented and bent to kiss her. "Be well, my love. I shall return."

Kady smiled warmly at him and watched as he and his men walked away, waving when he turned back before rounding the corner. As soon as the last of them were gone from sight, Kady turned and hurried back into the tavern. Jacob was sitting with a young man, and Kady wasn't sure how she would be able to speak to Jacob privately. As Kady snatched her wrap from where she had left it, she saw, out of the corner of her eye, the young man stand up and leave. Kady took her time putting her wrap on to ensure the young man had left, then looked around to see that no one could easily overhear before crossing to Jacob.

Jacob indicated for her to sit in the vacated chair. She shook her head. Her stomach was a huge knot. This was the first time she had seen him since her marriage to Henry. Kady did not know for sure, but she was fairly certain that her mother was intentionally keeping them apart. Therefore, they had not had a chance to talk about it, and they were not going to have the chance now. So Kady plunged right into her news.

"You were right, the gold is here and it's leaving tonight. Henry and his men are the ones moving it, but there are three wagons, not one.

Each will have mounted men escorting it: one man driving it and two guards inside the wagons themselves. Each wagon will leave down a separate road into the city, before they all head for the Dismal Swamp. Once there, the two men in the back of each wagon will stand guard, while Henry and his men load the gold onto a sledge for their horses to drag to their camp. Once Henry and his men are into the swamp, the guards will get back into the wagons, and they'll continue on to Suffolk as if they still have the goods."

Jacob's brows had furrowed.

"I have arranged for there to be a signal for you, indicating which wagon has the gold. Mama Bird will have two candles burning in her window. If the gold is in the wagon heading west, she will place a small figurine to the left of the candles. Oh, it will be her left, so to your right. Okay, yes, if the figurine is to the right of the candles, go west. If to the left, go east, if between the two candles, follow the wagon going north. It was the best I could do." She paused for a moment, then added, "I'm sorry."

Her apology was not for the hastily made plans, and from the look in Jacob's eyes, he understood and she was at least somewhat comforted.

"It is a good plan. We will make it work." Jacob reached out and, taking her hand, squeezed it gently.

She squeezed back before pulling her hand away.

"I must go. If you do not have enough men to safely take the gold from the wagon, then let it go. The Doctor has a back-up plan." She gave him a small smile that he returned, then she left.

Kady pulled her wrap tightly around her shoulders and hurried down the street. She wanted so badly to stay and watch to make sure Rebecca placed the figurine and that Jacob and his men saw it, but she knew that was folly. What possible excuse could she have for loitering about next to the supply yard; and worse yet, what if she ran into Henry again? It was no good. Mary could go! Mary and her mother were in town on the pretense of shopping for the holidays. Kady could send Mary to investigate. No, that didn't work either. Henry would recognize Mary in an instant. The only option was to go home and trust that everyone would play their parts correctly.

A thought seized her heart. If everyone were indeed to play their parts correctly, then one or two of the men she had dined with might wind up dead. Henry might wind up dead. No. She would not think of that eventuality. Jacob's men were going to subdue the men in the convoy, not kill them. They wanted to leave the men alive so that word would get back to President Davis that the Yankees had taken the gold. They wanted Davis to know that not even something as secret as this shipment was safe. They wanted to rattle his trust in his own government. Jacob's men needed to leave Henry's men alive so they could be messengers. This eased her tension somewhat, but she quickened her pace all the same. She wanted the security of her home. Her mother and Mary would be there, probably getting ready for tea, which would be a comfort.

Kady wasn't sure which was stranger: the thought of Henry's death causing her grief or that she badly wanted to see her mother.

New intelligence – have map. Gardener will
be silenced.
YD

31
Message Relayed

Rebecca looked down at her finished poem. Despite the vigilance she had paid to her duty of watching the wagons, she had written quite a passable piece. Perhaps splitting her attention had allowed her words to flow more freely as her scrutiny was placed elsewhere. Smiling, she gazed out the window. The sun had begun its descent for the night and the sky was split in rapturous indecision—unsure whether to hold on to the bright charge of day for a few moments more, or succumb to inevitability and plunge into darkness. Into darkness ... there was something in that. Soldiers plunging into the darkness of the battle ... into the darkness of the war ....

She placed a new sheaf of paper on her desk, when out of the corner of her eye, she saw movement below. She froze, fighting against her instinct to turn her head in order to look closer. With the sun setting, there was a direct beam of light shining through her window. None looking up would find it odd to see her sitting at her desk, as it was her custom to use the good light; but they would definitely find it odd if they found her staring with her mouth agape down into the supply yard. Besides, she could plainly make out what was happening without looking directly.

They were covering the wagons, and she could see the middle wagon contained the steel chest. Once they were properly covered, two men climbed into the back of each wagon, another into the driver's seat, and two men on horseback flanked either side. Five men per wagon.

Not for the first time, she wondered what in the world was in the chest that was so important to warrant such a big production. As big productions went, this one was well organized. Despite the number of men and horses involved, they were opening the gates of the supply yard and the wagons were rolling in short order.

With a sudden surge of panic, Rebecca realized that as soon as the wagons passed through the gate, she would no longer be able to see what direction they took from her seated position. She would be unable to perform her one job. She surged to her feet and frantically groped for some reason for her to be standing at the window. She could light the candles! They weren't necessarily needed right this minute, but it was as good an excuse as any. Ignoring the cramp in her crippled leg (the darn thing did not approve of any sort of hasty movement), she tried to be as nonchalant as possible as she carefully lit the two candles and adjusted their positions. Her timing was perfect. The three wagons split off down the three different roads as she was finishing, allowing her to see the chest heading north. No longer in such a hurry, Rebecca sat back down, stretching out her leg gingerly. Once settled, she picked up her mouse and, with a loving little pat on its head, placed it between the candles. Her duty discharged, she turned back to her paper and began to write.

32
Conflicted Allegiance

Anna leapt up from the piano at the sound of the front door crashing open. She had been playing for Mary, it wasn't as if she had been doing any harm to the instrument, yet Anna distinctly felt as if she had been caught red-handed doing something unscrupulous. She felt a blush redden her cheeks and silently cursed herself for being a complete ninny. She could play her daughter's piano without permission if she wanted to. There was no need to feel guilty; she had not done anything wrong. She prepared to say that as Kady rushed into the room, but the look on the girl's face forestalled her, and before she knew it Kady had flung her arms around her waist and buried her face in Anna's neck. More than a little astonished, Anna stood for a moment, arms akimbo, before she realized her daughter was upset and had come to her for comfort. Gently wrapping her arms around Kady, Anna gave Mary a quizzical look. Mary returned it in kind, shaking her head and shrugging her shoulders in stupefaction.

Returning her attention to her daughter, Anna lifted a hand to stroke it down Kady's hair. She was terrified the touch would make Kady recoil, and as much as that would break Anna's heart, the impulse was too strong to ignore. Bracing herself for the worst, Anna's hand gently cupped the back of her daughter's head for the briefest of moments before running it down her hair. To her astonishment, Kady did not recoil, quite the opposite. All of the tension in her body seemed to vanish as she melted into her mother's embrace. That is when Anna realized she had been holding her breath. With a stuttering exhalation, Anna pulled Kady as tight into her as their gowns allowed and stroked her hair, whispering everything would be all right. Kady clung to her, not crying but, Anna suspected, simply needing comfort. From what, she did not know. The longer they held the embrace, the closer Anna came to tears. As much as she did not want to cry, she did not know if she would ever be able to let her daughter go.

The moment was broken when a slave entered carrying a tray with a late tea. Mary took it from the slave and busied herself setting it up and pouring while Anna and Kady separated from each other and composed themselves. As Anna sat down, Mary handed her a cup and saucer, then handed one to Kady and made to leave the room.

Kady reached out a hand, grabbing Mary's arm.

"Please stay. Have some tea with us."

For a second time, Anna looked at Mary speechless. A brief hint of utter disbelief flashed across Mary's face as well, as if she would have expected Kady to ask her to dance a jig before she would have asked her to join them for tea. Mary, however, had not survived this long by letting her emotions give her away. She quickly adopted a thankful look, and with a slight nod to Kady, sat down and served herself a biscuit, as there had only been two teacups on the tray.

Kady noticed the oversight.

"Oh dear, we need another cup for you. I'll go ask for one."

"No'm. I fine. I don't need more than a biscuit, thank you."

Kady, who had already half-risen, settled herself back into her seat.

Anna looked at Mary gratefully, loath to let Kady out of her sight, lest she return as her old self. The three of them sat in an awkward silence for several minutes, until Anna realized Kady was not going to divulge what had caused this odd behavior without some prodding. Setting her cup down, Anna cleared her throat.

"Kady, what's the matter?"

Kady took a deep breath. Unable to hold her composure, her words came rushing out. Speaking quickly she recounted the day's events in astonishing detail. She finally slowed down enough to take a sip of tea, as Anna and Mary both gasped at Kady's description of Jacob and Henry in the same tavern.

"Of course, once Thomas was on his way, I only just had time to tell Jacob of the new plan before running back outside. It was all so horribly awkward. Then I had to walk home by myself, and the whole way with this knot in the pit of my stomach that something dreadful was going to happen. I started to imagine Thomas and his men transporting the gold with no idea that they are going to be ambushed. Then I started worrying about Jacob, since he is going to be doing the ambushing and might not be able to handle five men per wagon. Then I realized I wasn't really worried about Jacob for some reason. So I went back to worrying about Thomas, and I kept telling myself I had to get home; you and Mary would be here and you would tell me everything was going to be all right. So tell me everything is going to be all right!"

The last came out in a barely controlled sob.

Kady had worked herself into such a frenzy, Anna was afraid she might faint if she did not get her breathing calmed down or her corset loosened. Anna reached out for Kady's hand and squeezed it

272

gently. Kady's squeeze in response was much stronger and the pleading in her eyes made Anna's chest go tight. Had Jacob not told Kady the new plan?

Anna replied carefully, "You did well, Kady; you took care of everything perfectly. You're going to be all right."

Kady blinked at her, puzzled for a moment. "Well, of course *I'm* going to be all right. I'm not the one transporting a shipment of gold with men hunting after me!" A note of hysteria had crept into her voice. "Tell me Thomas is going to be all right. Tell me Thomas's men are going to be all right. Tell me they are not going to wind up dead!"

In her frustration, Kady pulled her hands from her mother's grasp, which was good, as Anna would have dropped them when she raised her own hands to cover her mouth in horror. Of course Jacob hadn't told Kady. He had left that onerous job to her. Anna's face clearly showed her thoughts, and Kady fell silent, a look of desolation hardening her features despite a slight glimmer of hope still in her eyes.

"Kady, I am so sorry."

Kady's hand clutched her napkin to her breast as she took in a sharp inhalation.

"I got word that the plans have changed. Instead of subduing the convoy on the road to the swamp, Jacob's men plan to follow the convoy into the swamp to discover the whereabouts of their supply cache. Once there, they will capture the gold and all of the other supplies."

"And Thomas and his men?"

"Are to be killed."

The hardness spread to Kady's eyes and solidified as her hope

273

died away. "Why was that decided?"

"I don't know. It must have been Jacob's decision as no one else has had contact with him."

"It was Jacob's idea." Kady swallowed hard. "He didn't tell me when I saw him."

"I doubt—"

Kady cut her off with a wave of her hand and stood. Anna could not tell if she should offer consolation or not, with Kady's immutable expression. Anna wished there was something she could do, could say, to make everything better. She wished they could go back to when Kady first entered, could hold her and never let go, not let her ever hear this truth.

Kady wavered where she stood for a moment, then seemed to make a decision.

"If you will excuse me." She waved her hand vaguely in the direction of the rest of the house. "I had a room made up for you. They can show you where it is if they haven't already."

Avoiding both Anna's and Mary's eyes, Kady left the room. Anna watched her go, then turned to Mary.

"I shouldn't have told her."

"You had to. She had a right to know."

"She's too young for all of this." Anna set her cup on the saucer, harder than was necessary.

"She is older than you were when you was given to the general, and far's I can tell this ain't as bad as that. You survived."

Despite herself, Anna smiled weakly. Looking toward the direction Kady had left, Anna reached her hand out to Mary, who took it and patted it reassuringly.

With nowhere else to go, Kady walked upstairs to her bedroom. She closed the door and leaned her head against it, feeling the smooth grain on her forehead. She was not going to cry. This was war. People died in wars. Besides this could be a good thing; after all, she had one husband too many, and it had been her father who had set up her marriage to Thomas. Captain Henry, she corrected herself. First names were too personal. Her father had arranged her marriage to Captain Henry; she had no say in the matter. Whereas she had chosen Jacob, so it was only right that, if she were to wind up with one of them, it should be Jacob. Not Captain Henry. Therefore, this was a good thing. Jacob was simply tidying up the mess, taking care of her.

Frustrated, she hit her hand against the door and paced into the room. She was the worst spy that ever lived. She could not even lie convincingly to herself. This was not a good thing. How could this possibly be anything other than horrible? Jacob was not taking care of her, he was jealous. He was jealous and furious that she had married Thomas, and that green rage was going to condemn Thomas and all of his men. The worst part was that there wasn't anything she could do.

No! The worst part was that she had helped. She had unwittingly helped Jacob kill Thomas and his men. She turned, ready to fling herself onto her bed and beat her hands into the pillows until she was exhausted, when she froze. There, sitting prettily on her pillow, was a small bouquet of flowers atop a letter. In a trance, Kady strode to the bed and, pushing the flowers aside, grabbed the letter and ripped it open. She scanned the text without actually reading any of it, until her eyes rested on the name at the bottom. It was from Thomas. Of course, it was from Thomas. He told her that he had called for her here. When he had not found her, he took the time to write a note. Forcing herself to breathe deeply, Kady began to read.

December 20, 1864

My Dearest Kady,

I apologize for the brevity of my letter. I have only a few moments. I fear I will be unable to join you for the Christmas holiday. I have been tasked to oversee a shipment of the utmost importance, one that I pray may help turn the tide of this war. I hope you will understand and forgive me for placing my allegiance to my country above my duty to you. It pains me to think of you spending our first Christmas alone, so I have arranged for you to travel to your father's plantation in time for the holiday. I will look for you there upon my return. Until then, I shall spend my every waking hour devising a suitable recompense for my absence. Travel safely. Be well.

Yours in perpetuity,

Thomas Henry

Kady read the letter over several times before she crumpled to the floor, her skirts billowing around her, and began to sob.

33
Short-Lived Success

Henry smiled as the sound of his men celebrating reached his ears. Despite the late hour, everyone was still keyed up from their expedition, more so since everything had gone off without a hitch. Williams was finishing up a drunken rendition of a song he had made up about the swamp.

"I love the Dismal in the morning! I love the Dismal at three. I love the Dismal most any time of day. So why don't the Dismal love meeeeeeeee?" As he warbled out the last note, the singing stopped abruptly when Little Jack pushed him backwards into the bog.

"I thought I'd give you the chance to get to know the old girl a bit better!" The men roared with laughter while Williams dragged himself out of the water and Little Jack threw a blanket at him.

"I am much obliged to you." Williams swept a deep bow and then, upon straightening himself, shook as if a dog, spraying Jack with water before stealing Jack's bottle of whiskey and scooting to the other side of the fire.

Henry chuckled as he carried the last load of goods into the den. Despite the folly, he full well expected to find all three of his men thoroughly drunk and soaked through by the time he finished burying the gold. It was a good thing they had a large fire burning. Normal protocol stated that they keep the fire small and the noise to a minimum, and he would have chastised Williams for the loud singing and Jack for his childish prank, but they had all needed a success. Henry had volunteered to stash the gold even though it was Williams's turn to unload. Hearing his men celebrate was enough for him now, especially since he knew he would be joining them shortly. Deep in the den, with their revelry hardly discernible, Henry found he was able to make quick work of his task in the stillness and natural warmth. He was moving the last crate into place when a gunshot, followed shortly by another, made him jump. Henry instinctively reached for his pistol as he ran to the entrance of the den, but by the time he made it above ground, two more shots had cracked through the air.

Carefully, so as not to disturb the underbrush he had moved into place to mask the den's entrance, Henry strained to see what was happening in the camp. A small unit of Union soldiers was tearing the camp apart, while a one-legged man leaning on a crutch held a gun on the kneeling Williams. Henry could only guess the mounds on the ground were Adams and Jack, already dead. Henry fought back the urge to break free of the underbrush, to rush the soldiers in order to help Williams, but he knew that would get them both killed. So he ground his teeth and prayed that Williams, with his silver tongue, would be able to talk himself free. Henry's prayers were for naught, because before Williams could finish shaking his head, the soldier cocked his pistol and fired, sending a bullet exploding into Williams's skull.

Henry fell to his knees and pounded the earth in rage. As much as he wanted to scream, he kept his mouth shut. Williams had been with him since the beginning. He had become like a brother to Henry, and Henry had stood there and watched him die. Logically, Henry knew he had no choice, but logic be damned. Henry wanted to shout his curses to the heavens and take his revenge on those soldiers. Instead, he had to content himself with silently pounding his fists into the frosty earth. He could hear the one-legged man shouting orders to his men to keep searching; the gold and supplies had to be somewhere.

A certain degree of satisfaction welled in Henry's breast when, after almost an hour, they still had not come anywhere near the den. The one-legged man was becoming more irate by the minute. He wanted the gold found, and he wanted it found immediately. Another man made the unfortunate mistake of pointing out that had they not killed all of the men, they would be able to ask where the gold was located. This remark earned him a whack with a crutch and quite a colorful tongue-lashing. Henry had to admit, the man did have a good point. It was on the tail end of this tirade that Henry thought he heard his own name. Certain he was hearing things, he listened more intently. Sure enough, the man was hollering that they had not killed all of the men, because Captain Henry was not among the dead. He wanted the gold *and* Henry found.

The blood froze in Henry's veins. How did that man know his name, and how had they been able to find them? Henry swore under his breath. Somebody must have talked to the wrong person about the gold. Even so, how had they connected it to him? Among the other officers, there was an ongoing joke about Henry and his swamp: men go in and Henry comes out with their belongings. They kidded, but he had earned their respect. It was known he could get anything moved. His reputation provided the connection. Of course the gold would be entrusted to him. Oh, God! Maybe they had been following him the whole time in the hopes that he would eventually lead them to the gold. No, he would have lost them in the swamp. That was the beauty of the swamp! Except his men had been making enough racket to wake the dead. Even a child from a mile off would have been able to find their camp tonight. Overtaken with rage again, Henry pounded the earth. Why hadn't he made them be quiet? His men were dead and it was his doing. Racked with grief, Henry punched the earth a few more times before collapsing, sweaty and breathing hard. He faintly registered the noise from the camp as the Union soldiers fought over bedrolls and the best places to sleep for what was left of the night. Evidently, someone had convinced old One Leg that continuing to look in the dark was pointless. He wondered if that man had gotten whacked, too.

As the soldiers settled in, the night slowly became silent save for the natural noises of the swamp. Henry risked crawling out of the den to relieve himself and to see if he could assess exactly how many men were there. He was not entirely sure, maybe around eight. They had left one man up on sentry duty. He had his back to Henry, and from the angle of his head, Henry guessed he had nodded off. Even with that advantage, there were too many men to subdue by himself. He contemplated trying to leave, but he could not stomach the thought of abandoning his men. The least he could do was provide them with a good burial. He would not let the creatures of the swamp take them.

So Henry added to the shrubbery that was camouflaging the entrance of the den and tried to erase any signs of human presence in the immediate area. He worked carefully, keeping a wary eye on the camp at all times. A scream from a catamount roused the sentry and several of the men, who set about stoking up the dying fire, reassuring themselves it would not come close with so many people around. With this new activity in the camp, Henry decided that what he had done would have to be good enough, so he retreated back into the depths of the den where he retrieved a bottle of whiskey and sat down in the corner amid the supplies to drink himself to sleep.

It was midmorning before he awoke and carefully crawled his way up to the entrance of the den. The Union soldiers were searching once more, this time sweeping the areas around the camp. Henry sat and watched as the soldiers gingerly picked their way through the swamp, jumping out of the way at the slightest movement, apparently unaware that all of the snakes were hibernating. The one-legged man stayed in the camp. He made a game of holding still and waiting until a bird or other scavenger had alighted on one of the corpses and then throwing bits of whatever he could get his hands on to scare them away. When that got old, he simply threw the little bits and pieces at the bodies, celebrating whenever he got a bit to land on a hand or in an open mouth.

Henry's blood boiled. As much as he hated that man, as long as he was so grossly outnumbered, there was nothing he could do. When night fell once again, Henry retreated to the back of the den, ate some salt-pork and finished off the bottle of whiskey he had been sipping on all day. The next morning was much like the one before, except the soldiers were now passing within twenty yards of him, yet remained oblivious to his presence. By early afternoon, one of the soldiers started to sweep within feet of the den's entrance. Henry readied himself to attack in the hopes he would at least be able to take out several of the soldiers before he was killed himself.

However, his preparations were unnecessary as the nearest soldier remained oblivious to his presence and then eventually started to

281

move away from him. As the afternoon started to wane and the one-legged man woke from his nap, he declared that they were to move out because these were obviously not the men who had transported the gold, despite what their intelligence had promised. They must be decoys. Not to mention that he was cold, and the smell from the corpses was starting to turn his stomach. He wanted to be elsewhere by the time they were to eat their supper.

The men packed up anything worth taking and left. Henry watched them leave and, despite the feeling he had in his gut that they were truly gone, waited until after dark before emerging from the dank hole. Even then, he headed out in the opposite direction and made a wide circle back in case someone returned. Once back in the camp, Henry did not bother looking to see if there was anything worth salvaging. He had watched the soldiers either take or destroy anything of any value, so he knew there was nothing. As they had taken the horses, too, Henry would have to hike out of the swamp and then, with any luck, hitch a ride to the Bell Plantation. He really should head straight for Richmond, but he could explain that the stop was necessary to procure a new horse from his father-in-law. In reality, Henry wanted to see Kady. He had an aching need to hold her and feel her arms around him. It was almost as if he believed that her embrace could piece him back together. Henry shook his head to clear his thoughts. He couldn't think of that now, there were things to do. Taking the shovel firmly into his hands, Henry began to dig.

He would have liked to build coffins and dig three separate graves for his men, but he lacked the supplies, and the only place that he could dig deep enough to keep the bodies safe from animals was on top of the knoll. There was only enough room for one grave up there, so it would have to do. Henry was surprised at how deep he was able to get before he hit water. Standing up straight, he was in the ground up to his waist. It wasn't as deep as he would have liked, but under the circumstances it would suffice. He lined the bottom of the grave with a blanket then climbed out and fetched the bodies. He wanted to lower them gently into the grave, but having no rope, he eventually resigned himself to rolling them in. Once they were all in the grave, Henry draped a blanket over the bodies and stood before them. Unable to find the proper words to say, he sank to his knees, lowered his head and vowed that their deaths would not be in vain. As trite as it was, the vow eased some of the heaviness weighing down his shoulders. Slowly he stood up, took the shovel back into his blistered hands, and covered his men with dirt.

34
Stupid Girl

Emma sat wringing her hands. She was dying to know what had happened, and of course Jacob was late, again. Only this time, Jacob was over a day late. He was supposed to raid Henry and his men, then meet Emma outside of Richmond to pay her for the information she provided, before continuing on into the city. And hopefully give her news of Henry's devastation. She knew that Jacob's order from the head of his spy ring was to leave Henry alive. Order or not, Emma had serious doubts that Jacob would be able to control himself when face-to-face with the man. She wasn't sure which outcome she was hoping for. Emma stared at the door of the tavern willing it to open and Jacob to walk in. No such luck.

She could get food, but she wasn't hungry, so she sat spinning a coin on the table top. She didn't know how much longer she was going to wait. Not that she had anywhere to be; it just felt pathetic sitting there waiting for someone who clearly wasn't coming. She slapped the coin to the table and, picking it and her bag up, walked out the back of the tavern to use the outhouse. She debated leaving, but the lure of the gold convinced her to wait just a bit longer. Upon reentering the tavern, she saw that Jacob had arrived and was sitting in the corner with a glass of whiskey and sour look on his face. Emma walked up to his table and sat down.

"Where have you been?"

"Where have I been? I've been in a god-forsaken swamp trying to find this treasure trove of gold and goods that I was promised would be there!"

"So you made it into Henry's camp."

"And all I got for my trouble was saddle sore and eaten alive by bugs."

"What?"

"There was no cache of goods or bars of gold, anywhere. My men looked! The entire thing was a huge waste of my time thanks to you."

"Thanks to me; how is this my fault?"

"How is it anybody else's? Because of your map and promises of supplies, I followed them into the swamp instead of ambushing them on the road like I was supposed to, and I have nothing to show for it! You ruined everything."

"My information was good, it is not my fault that you couldn't fulfill your end."

"My end? There was nothing at my end, not even Captain Henry!" Jacob stuttered a few words before seizing onto a new tack. "You probably told him we were coming. You were helping him."

Emma's outrage rendered her speechless for a moment.

"Why, why would I help that man? I hate him! I was trying to help you!"

"Well don't. Don't help anymore, you are just a stupid girl."

"Why did you even show up here, if you feel that way? To tell me that I'm stupid?"

"Yes, because somebody had to tell you so that you don't go

285

around ruining anyone else's plans. Go home so your idiocy only affects your father."

With that, Jacob gulped down what was left of his drink and snatched his crutch up from the floor. As much as he could with one leg, he stormed out. Emma sat stunned for a minute before the anger returned. He was right, she was stupid. She had been stupid to trust anyone. Tears filled her eyes and threatened to overflow when she thought of how he had used her. Everything had been about him and what information he could get to help his own cause, and now that she held no value for him, he threw her away.

The night he had taken her to bed, she had just been another warm body to him. Furious, Emma pushed back from the table so violently her chair fell over behind her. She didn't even bother to pick it up before grabbing her bag and heading for the door. She needed to get out of there. She needed to move, somewhere, anywhere. Mostly she needed a new plan. One that she would carry out all on her own. One that got her revenge on both Henry and Jacob.

35
Truth Will Out

Kady had been restless ever since arriving at her father's plantation. Her mother and Mary tried to keep her occupied with correspondence. Inevitably, she would find herself out on the veranda pacing back and forth with a half-deciphered letter shoved into her bodice. From there she would be able to see anyone coming up the drive. She also was able to hear the distant movements of troops on the road and even the occasional skirmish that broke out. Union forces were still trying to capture the railway stations at Petersburg, and the South was desperately trying to keep them from succeeding. There was an unrest in the countryside she had not been privy to while in the city—except the days around Christmas, those were quiet and seemed to aggravate Kady's nerves even more. The sense of movement, of action, that returned as the New Year approached seemed to give her hope. Hope for what, she did not know. Maybe hope that someone would return to her with news. She was in the middle of a prayer when Mary came up to her and gently took her arm.

"You will want to go out to my shack for a spell." Kady looked at her, not understanding for a moment, before realization dawned on her. Jacob. Jacob was in the shack. What had she expected, that he would walk up to the front door? Of course not! She turned to go, but Mary tightened her grip. "After nightfall, so no one sees you. Unless you can think of a good reason to go there now."

Frustrated, Kady realized Mary was right. She could not go traipsing out to the servant shacks in the middle of the afternoon. She let out an exasperated sigh.

"What am I supposed to do until then, twiddle my thumbs?"

Mary laughed silently. "Come, play your piano and it will be sundown before you know it."

Kady agreed and followed Mary into the parlor.

Again, Mary was right. The next thing Kady knew, the sun had started to fall and the playing had relaxed her significantly. The summons came for a light supper, and foregoing changing her dress, Kady went straight to the dining room and hastily ate without tasting any of it. Her father, disconcerted, started to watch her and spoke.

"You seem out of sorts this evening. Are you ill?"

It took Kady a minute to realize he was speaking to her and blushed slightly as she looked at her father. "No, I am not ill. Simply distracted."

"You had hoped Captain Henry would have joined us by now."

"Yes, I thought he would be here by now."

"You women always worry too much. He will return when he is done with his duty. That is that."

"Yes, father." Kady gave a weak smile.

To her surprise, as her mother rarely spoke at meals, Anna suggested, "Perhaps some fresh air would—"

"That is what I was about to say. You always interrupt me, woman!" Her father glared at her mother, and Kady felt ashamed at his treatment of her mother. "Some fresh air will set your mind right. I will take you for a stroll after I've had my brandy."

288

"That is kind of you, Father, however, I don't know if my nerves can hold out that long. If you will excuse me, I think I'll take a stroll on my own." Her father made a move to get up and protest. "No, it's all right, stay. I will not go farther than the servant quarters. I will be plenty safe there and the little children always lighten my spirits."

Her father looked at her warily before nodding his head in acquiescence then turning to the awaiting servant to order that dessert be served.

While he was distracted, Kady turned to her mother and mouthed the words "thank you."

Anna gave her the barest of nods, and Kady made her escape from the room before her father changed his mind.

Once outside, Kady discovered the fresh air did help. It was cold, though, and she realized, too late, that she needed a shawl. She would have to do without, as she was not turning back. She tried her best to appear to be taking a stroll with no particular destination in mind, but failed miserably and arrived at the shack a little out of breath. She did not care. She flung open the door and rushed in.

Jacob was sitting in the dark eating from a tray. He scrambled up at her entrance, and she was in his arms in two steps.

To her chagrin, she started crying and Jacob held her tight. Eventually she was able to compose herself, and when she looked up into his face, Jacob kissed her hungrily. He tasted of liquor and roasted chicken, and from the desperate searching of his hands, Kady deduced he was intending to have her for dessert. She pushed back from him with some difficulty.

"What took you so long? I have been out of my mind waiting

289

for some word."

Jacob laughed ruefully. "I was expecting you to be in Richmond. Imagine my surprise when I show up there, only to find out I have to backtrack to find you here."

"Oh." Kady hadn't thought of that. It made perfect sense.

"And I have to leave tomorrow morning to make it back to Richmond in time for a rendezvous."

Kady stopped him as he bent to kiss her once more. "Why did you change the plan?" The question came out with more vehemence than she knew she had, but now that it was unleashed she realized that she was truly angry with him.

"What?" Jacob had been stunned into temporary paralysis, allowing Kady to take a step back.

"The original plan was to subdue Henry and his men, then take the gold. Why did you change the order to have them killed?"

"I didn't change the order." Jacob had responded immediately and there was an edge to his voice that made Kady question the truth of his assertion.

"My mother said the plan had been changed to follow the men into the swamp and kill them and it was your idea. Was she wrong?"

Jacob seemed tongue-tied at first. "My idea? Well ... yes, I did change the order so we would follow them in, but it was somebody else who decided to kill them."

"So you didn't kill them then?" Kady held her breath.

"My men did before I could stop them." Kady took a shuddering inhalation. "Not Captain Henry; I didn't let them kill him."

Kady took a few breaths to steady herself before speaking.

"Why did you spare him?"

"For you, of course." Again, the speed of his reply rang false. "You would be cut off from your source of information if he was dead, and that was the reason you married him, right? To keep your father from finding out you were a spy and to gain intelligence?"

The edge in Jacob's voice as he finished speaking was tinged with hurt and Kady felt guilty. Jacob loved her, and though she had not had a choice, she had betrayed that love. She fell into Jacob's arms once more, apologizing for ever doubting him, for ever thinking he would do anything that wasn't in her best interest.

Jacob kissed her again, and as his hands started moving across her body, he swore, "Christ! Did you have to wear all of this? I'll never get through it all."

Kady laughed. Before she could respond, the door of the shack opened and Mary walked in.

Startled, Kady yelped, "Mary! What is it?"

"I was sent to fetch you from your stroll back to the house." Neither Kady nor Jacob moved. "Quickly! Before your father comes a lookin'!"

Kady felt the blood leave her face and turned back to Jacob. "I have to go, I am sorry." She kissed him briefly, and before he could respond, rushed past Mary and out the door. Mary glared at Jacob.

"I would get gone, if I were you. She's goin' to her real husband," she said as she slammed the door behind her.

Kady rushed in through the kitchen door and found her mother waiting for her. "What's wrong? What has happened?"

291

"Captain Henry has arrived."

Relief at her mother's words washed through her. "Where is he? Is he okay?"

"He went upstairs to your room. I don't think he's injured, but he doesn't look right. Do you know what happened?"

Kady was already moving to leave. "Yes. No, I mean I am not sure. I have to go to him."

Moving as fast as she was able in her skirts, Kady made her way up the narrow servant's staircase, then into the main house, brushing past her father as she raced up the grand staircase to get to her room and Henry. She was breathing heavily when she burst into the room. The sight of Henry stopped her dead. He was bedraggled, with slumped shoulders, perched on the edge of the bed, unsuccessfully yanking off a boot. His self-assurance and bravado were gone. He looked broken, and Kady wanted nothing more than to wrap him in her arms and hold him until all of his pieces had fit back together. She crossed to him and gently placed her hand on his, which stopped his efforts. He looked up at her, as if realizing for the first time that she was in the room. She brushed the hair back from his dirty face and smiled at him.

"Let me."

He surrendered the weight of his leg to her, and with only a little difficulty, she pried off first one, then the other boot. Those taken care of, she removed his stockings. He seemed to be in a daze and let her undress him fully, not actively helping, only moving where her hands instructed him. Once undressed, he sat back on the bed.

Without a word, Kady started to undress herself. Henry pulled the laces of her corset free when she turned her back to him. Other than that, he simply watched. Finally, she stood in front of him, as naked as he was, and took his face in her hands. She bent to kiss him, and to her surprise, he kissed her back. Gently at first, then with a ferocity that took her breath away. If it was possible, her arousal grew faster than his and she opened her legs, climbing onto his lap to comfort him. His hands clung to her with a need to possess her fully, to find a release in her body.

He moaned as he entered her and she arched her back to seat him deeper inside of her. Preoccupied with keeping her firmly seated on his lap, he had broken off kissing her. Kady dug her fingers into his thick hair and pulled back until she had access to his lips once more. The thrill of being an active participant in this act made her giddy. It made him lose all pretext of gentleness. In one swift movement, he had her on her back. He buried his face in her neck and made love to her with a feral necessity. Unlike every time before, he said nothing. Only a moan or grunt of exertion passed his lips as he took her totally and completely. Kady had never known such emotion and passion could lie in the breast of a man. Every taut, sinewy muscle in his body was employed with every plunge into her he took and her fingers explored them all.

Her hands found their way down his body until she had a firm grasp of his buttocks urging him to thrust deeper and harder, which he did greedily. Unable to stop herself, moans started to emanate from deep inside her. His lips found hers and while the kiss was fevered, it was short lived. Waves of ecstasy had begun to roll up her body, and grasping his hair firmly in one hand, Kady pulled his mouth from hers so she could moan in pleasure and call out his name. This seemed to

293

inflame his desire to a critical apex and his thrusts quickened further still with a kind of desperation. With a cry that seemed mingled with equal parts agony and ecstasy, he reached his climax and released his seed into her.

Panting and exhausted, he lowered himself gently on top of her until his strength gave way, and she felt the full weight of his strong body. Still reeling herself from the pleasure he had wrought upon her, she protectively wrapped her arms around his neck and gently nestled his head to rest in her bosom.

After some time they both regained their breath, but he did not move and Kady gave no indication she wanted him to. Instead, she indulgently ran her fingers through his hair and pretended she did not know he was crying.

They fell asleep in each other's arms, until Henry awoke a few hours later. He untwined their limbs and when Kady rolled over to resettle herself, he pulled her into his chest and engulfed her in his strong arms. She practically disappeared in his embrace, and Henry fell asleep once more.

In the morning, Kady awoke before Henry. She was loath to move. She began to feel skeptical that the previous night had ever happened, or at least, not as she remembered it. She had not been aware such feelings in her body were even possible. However, the ache from overuse that pervaded the muscles in her lower abdomen was proof enough that she had not imagined anything.

A coy smile formed on her lips and a slight blush raced across her cheeks as she recalled the pleasure he had been able to give her. She wanted to feel that again, and sensing he was beginning to stir to wakefulness, Kady decided to expedite the process and take her pleasure into her own hands. Rolling over so her breasts conformed to his chiseled chest, she hitched her top leg over his hip, ran her fingers up into his hair, and began slowly, seductively to kiss his lips, his jawline, his neck. At first Kady thought her advances were not working, until his hands began a judicious exploration of her body. At a particularly sensual caress, Kady broke off kissing his neck and moaned loudly. Having already opened that door, she found that not only was she quite good at a salacious moan, but she rather enjoyed it as well.

Henry chuckled and taking this as his cue, swiftly maneuvered himself on top of her, finding his place wrapped in her long legs.

Henry's desperation from the night before was replaced with an eagerness and he set about making love to Kady with gusto. He had also found his tongue and the purlings of adoration he whispered into her ear made her whisper back. Before she knew what she was saying, she told him she loved him. Instead of this giving her a start, Kady embraced it and Henry with open arms as his passion stampeded through her, causing her to cry out in pleasure, this time with her husband's voice adding to her crescendo. Their energy quickly spent, Henry once more collapsed onto Kady where he dozed listening to the steady beat of her heart.

Kady would have gladly let him stay nestled into her forever. Except now that the sun was up and the passion of the night had passed, she was overwhelmed by a stench unlike any she had ever smelled. To her horror, it was coming not only from her husband's clothes, strewn across the floor, but from her husband as well. Good Lord! Did she smell like that now, too? Her skin began to crawl at the thought and she fought back a shudder. She carefully extricated herself, whispering in Thomas's ear to sleep some more. Kady pulled her nightgown on, hastily picked up his clothes from the floor, and, holding them at arm's length, left the room.

Finding a servant steps from her room, Kady thrust the foul garments at her with instructions that they were to be scrubbed until they no longer smelled as if someone had died in them. If that was not possible, they were to be burned. As the servant started to walk away, Kady allowed a shudder of revulsion that she had denied herself while in bed. Then, remembering, she ran after the servant and ordered enough water be brought up for a bath. Scalding water, with a lot of soap, and maybe some lavender for good measure.

Instead of returning to her bedroom, she went into her dressing room to await her bath. Sitting down in front of her mirror, the strain of the previous few days finally broke and she began to cry—not wracking sobs, just a steady stream of tears down her face. They were tears of relief and confusion. Relief that Jacob had spared Henry. Relief that Henry had come home to her, that she was the one he sought comfort in. Confusion because she found Jacob took up little of her mind. The part he did inhabit was in relation to Henry. She had told Henry she loved him, and though she said it in the throes of passion, Kady truly felt she had meant it. She loved Henry. So where did that leave Jacob? Could she love both men? If not, where did that leave her?

A servant entered to begin filling the copper tub. Kady wiped her hand across her face to clear away the tears. Several other servants followed in quick succession, and in short order she had a lovely, lavender-scented bath waiting for her. Before she could undress and get in, she heard Henry stirring in the bedroom. She opened the door adjoining the two rooms and saw him standing naked in the middle of the floor looking around bleary eyed for his clothes. Unable to help herself, she laughed and Henry spun in her direction, startled.

"Your clothes are being washed. They smelled dreadful. Come. There's a bath ready. You smell dreadful, too."

To her amusement, he blushed slightly and with a small smile walked to her, paused to kiss her gently, then continued to the bath. She knew she should let him bathe in peace, but she could not bring herself to leave. Instead, she closed the door and turned around in time to see Henry gingerly lowering himself into the water. He sucked in his breath as his backside met the steaming water, and he manfully settled himself in all the way.

Apparently the servants took her request for scalding water seriously. With a smile, she crossed to the tub, pushing the sleeves of her nightdress up. His skin was pink from the heat of the water and she could see the muscles in his back begin to relax, despite the fact he was still leaning forward in the tub instead of reclining back. Kady took the sponge, and, dipping it in the water, sponged his back so rivulets of water ran down.

He sighed and relaxed further, finally leaning back against the tub. She started to sponge his chest.

She had heard Jacob's account of what happened, but there was something niggling in the back of her mind that there was something off with his story. She wanted to know from Henry.

"What happened?" she asked quietly.

Henry stiffened under her hand, and Kady rolled her eyes at

herself. She had meant to bring it up slowly to see if he would tell her of his own accord. Instead, she had blurted it out. She fully expected to be told those matters were the business of men and to be ejected from the room so he could finish his bath alone.

Instead, he reached up and grasped her hand, sponge and all.

"My love, you do not want to hear such horrible things, but I fear I must tell someone or I shall break."

Without letting go of her hand, his story began to tumble out. He tried at first to remain emotionless in the telling. That soon became impossible.

Kady felt awkward hearing something so personal while standing behind him, though she had a feeling it was that distance that afforded Thomas the ability to tell her at all. So she did not try to move. She clutched him protectively as he recounted hearing the gunshots that killed his men. She was openly crying, from both grief and anger, as he spoke of shoveling the last bits of dirt onto the grave. Jacob had lied. He had not spared Henry; he simply had not been able to find him. She was furious, and was about to express this, when she realized Henry was still talking, blaming himself for everything that had happened.

Her anger pushed aside, Kady moved so she could look Henry in the face. His eyes were red and his face anguished. In one swift movement, she had her nightdress off and had joined Henry in his bath. She did not fit, but was able to get in enough to wrap her arms around him and hold him tight. Her position was awkward and uncomfortable. Her legs were draped over the side of the tub, forcing her to twist her upper body to embrace him. She ran one hand down his hair while fiercely holding him to her with the other, all the while telling him in no uncertain terms that what had happened was not his fault. There was nothing he could have done to save his men. She kept saying this over and over until finally he relented and, at her urging, repeated it back to her.

By this time, both of their tears had been spent and they clung to each other until the water had lost its heat and both of them had lost feeling in their legs from their positions. With Henry's help, Kady levered herself out of the tub, and despite the now lukewarm water, she insisted Henry finish his bath. Kady used the entire cake of soap on him, washing every part of him at least twice. He half-heartedly insisted he was able to bathe himself. Kady didn't pause in her ministrations, sure that he enjoyed her attentions despite his complaints. When she finally declared him properly clean and handed him the giant linen towel, he climbed out of the tub, wrapped her up with him, and held her close.

"I want you to return to the city after the New Year, it is too dangerous in the country. I was being sentimental when I sent you here."

"All right. What will you do?"

"I must leave right away for Richmond to report to my superiors."

Kady stiffened, remembering the location of Jacob's rendezvous. "No!"

Startled, Henry pulled away from her so he could see down into her face. "No? Kady, I have my duty."

"I know you do, and I know you have to report in, but don't head straight back to Richmond." She pulled herself tight into his chest. "I can't explain it. I have the most awful feeling that if you leave for Richmond right now, I shall never see you again. So please don't. Go

299

back to the Dismal for a spell. Move whatever supplies you already have to the troops in the South. I'm sure they need them now that Sherman has taken Savannah."

Henry froze and Kady with him. Why did she say that? Why in the world would she know about Sherman's march from Atlanta to Savannah? Especially since he had taken Savannah less than a week earlier.

Once more, Henry pushed her away from him far enough that he could see her face. "What did you say?"

Kady's mind raced and miraculously landed on a solution. "Daddy got news yesterday that someone named Sherman had captured Savannah. From his choler, I figured that wasn't a good thing; and from the look on your face now, I think I am right."

Henry's face relaxed. "You are correct, that is a very bad thing." He kissed her gently, and when she reopened her eyes after returning his kiss, she saw his face was much softer. "As you wish, I will not return to Richmond immediately."

"Thank you." The relief in Kady's voice was evident and Henry smiled. He kissed her softly once more.

"I still must leave right away, and I still want you to return to Richmond. Promise me you will return and stay there where it is safe."

"I promise." Kady stood on her tiptoes and kissed him, wrapping her arms around his neck. "Perhaps right away could mean this afternoon?"

Kady's eyes sparkled with mischief and she bit her lower lip. Grinning, Henry dropped his towel and lifted Kady so she could wrap her legs around his waist.

36
Co-Conspirators

Anna watched from the porch as her daughter said goodbye to Captain Henry. She felt as if she were intruding on their moment, even though they did not know she was there. Earlier that morning, when she came down for food, Kady hurriedly told Anna everything, then disappeared back upstairs to help Henry repack his saddlebags. They must have taken great care with that packing, because it took them several hours. Anna smirked, knowing full well how they had really spent their time. She pulled her shawl more securely around her. It was cold, but she had needed to get out of the house. Andrew had announced that they were all going to leave by the end of the week for Richmond. The slaves had the packing well in hand and she was simply in the way.

Shortly after sitting down, she saw a horse brought around for Henry. Andrew had given him one of the best in the stable. He couldn't have his new son-in-law riding an inferior mount; it would reflect poorly on the family. The horse was soon followed by Henry and Kady. Anna studied their interactions. Kady truly cared for him; it was not an act. Anna looked away as they kissed goodbye, to give them what privacy she could. She did not look back again until she heard Kady's step approaching.

Kady gestured to the chair across from Anna, and Anna nodded her head that Kady could join her. They sat in silence for a while, each wrapped up in her own thoughts. Without looking at her daughter,

Anna spoke.

"You love him, don't you?"

"Yes." There was a long pause, and Kady looked down at her hands in her lap. "I guess that not only makes me a whore, but a careless whore, doesn't it?"

Anna looked over at her, shocked by the statement. It was then that Anna remembered that she had been the one to call Kady a whore in the first place. Anna reached out a hand and laid it on Kady's arm.

"No, it makes you lucky."

Kady looked up at her mother, and Anna saw that she had tears welling in her eyes.

"It makes you very lucky. Love doesn't find everyone."

Kady grasped her mother's hand and squeezed. "Have you ever been in love?"

Anna smiled at her. "Yes, I have."

"With Daddy?"

The obvious shock in Kady's voice made Anna laugh, and she squeezed her daughter's hand back before settling back into her chair. "No, I have never been in love with your father."

"Was there ever a time he loved you?"

Anna tightened her shawl around herself. "No."

Anna could feel her daughter's eyes on her, waiting for more. She did not know what else there was to say on the matter.

"Will you tell me about the man you did love?"

Anna looked at her startled. There was such earnestness in Kady's face, that for the first time since his death, Anna wanted to talk about Benjamin. Despite the initial awkwardness of sharing something so intimate with her daughter, Anna told her everything. She told Kady about how they had first met and her fit of jealousy when she had found him in the back room with another woman. She told her how she cried the first time they made love, and how she cried after the last time. Then she cried afresh when she spoke of the letter telling her of Benjamin's death, both the grief for his loss and the relief at finally knowing for sure. Kady cried with her.

Kady told her she had actually been the one to decode that letter when it came, and, even from outside the shack, sitting in the dirt, she had known the man mentioned had meant something to Anna. Oddly enough, Anna found comfort in that. Even though she had not known it at the time, there was somebody else there, in her darkest hour, sharing in her pain. Desperately needing to talk about something other than Benjamin, Anna asked Kady about Jacob. How had they ever come to be married? Kady relayed the whole sordid affair, and they both found themselves laughing at how naive Kady had been. This moment of levity disappeared when Andrew stomped out onto the porch, and seeing Anna, crossed to them.

"There you are, woman. I should have known you would be out here wasting away the afternoon instead of getting our things packed up. Worthless as ever!"

Anna cringed inside, but her face had turned to stone, the way it always did when she was around her husband. She could not stop him from hurting her. That didn't mean that she had to let him know that she was hurt. Automatically, she began to rise to obey, when she felt Kady's hand on her arm.

"Oh Daddy, calm down. You know full well the servants can

pack everything up by themselves. They don't need to be supervised." Anna froze, looked first at her daughter, then up at her husband who appeared to be speechless. "Mama and I are having a lovely chat, so you go find someone else to bother. Shoo, shoo!"

Anna stopped breathing. She had never seen anyone speak that way to her husband, teasing or not. He had never been anything but kind and loving to their daughter; however, Kady had never defied him, either. Anna scrutinized his face, trying desperately to read his conflicted emotions. If he lashed out, she was almost positive she would be able to insinuate herself between the two. Better he hit her than Kady.

Andrew's mouth fell open as if he was going to say something then, unable to come up with anything, closed it with a clack. He started to turn to leave, then hesitated, having finally found something to say.

Anna started to jump up to block his way, when Kady spoke.

"Oh, yes! We would love some hot tea sent out. That is so kind of you to think of it, Daddy."

Dumbfounded, Anna froze once more, hands braced on the arms of her chair.

It took Andrew a moment to regain his composure before he replied, "Yes, of course. I was just about to say that. You should not be out here without something hot to drink. It is not good for you. I will have something sent out immediately."

Kady bounced up from her chair and kissed him on the cheek, then smiled up at him serenely. He kissed her on the forehead before turning to leave.

At the door, he looked back at them with a slightly dazed look on his face, as if he still was not entirely sure what had happened.

Once he was gone, Kady sat back down, and Anna realized she must have the same look on her face, since Kady broke out in a giggle.

Anna shook her head slightly, relaxing back into her chair, then looked back at her daughter, almost to assure herself that she was still there and she hadn't imagined the entire thing.

Kady smiled at her ruefully. "I am sorry Daddy treats you the way he does. From now on, he won't get away with it if I am around."

Kady reached out for Anna's hand and Anna took it. She had to look away, her eyes filling with tears. They sat in companionable silence until Mary came out with a tray of tea. Kady insisted Mary join them and they talk about something entirely silly to lighten the mood. Wiping her eyes, Anna smiled at her daughter and laughed.

37

Disposable

Rebecca looked down into the supply yard. She did not know what had happened with the wagons and the chest, but she knew something had gone horribly wrong. All of the men in the yard had grown agitated, and then she had received a letter from Kady saying she did not know when she would be able to visit again. Kady continued to send writing supplies, though, which was a good thing, because Rebecca's sister, Rachel, had confiscated everything the night the wagons had left. Not knowing how long she needed to burn the two candles, and afraid to extinguish them before the message was received, Rebecca had left them burning all night until they were down to tiny nubs. The extra light was such a luxury that Rebecca had become immersed in her writing and had not heard Rachel come up the stairs and enter the room until it was too late.

Seeing her sister's unconscionable waste, Rachel had flown into a fit of rage. Her tirade was the same as it always was: all Rebecca did was waste resources and she was good for nothing because she was a cripple.

For the first time in her life, Rebecca had actually been able to fight back. Those candles were hers to waste if she wanted, she told her sister. She had earned them with her writing and therefore could do with them as she pleased. Not to mention, she was good for something. Hadn't she given Rachel every penny she had earned so far? Hadn't she also promised there would be more to come? Besides, she was not wasting candles; people were relying on her to light them.

Rebecca regretted saying those words even before she finished speaking them. She had gone over that moment a hundred times since that night. How could she have been so careless? She may as well have said outright that she was up to no good. Rachel tore through Rebecca's room looking for anything incriminating. She was confident Rebecca was doing something that could get the entire family into trouble, and she was not going to allow that. Not under her roof. Not after all of these years of providing for Rebecca. Unable to find anything, Rachel stormed out and locked the bedroom door so Rebecca couldn't "run off to consort with" her accomplices.

Remembering Rachel's red face when she had said "run off," still made Rebecca laugh. Despite the seriousness of the situation, she had immediately pictured herself trying to run down the road. As much as she told herself it was wrong, the image struck her as funny. The humor did not last, though, and when it passed, she unstitched the top seam of her pillow and pulled out the letters from Kady. When she had first hid them there, she was not sure why she felt the need. Now she was glad for the impulse. She read each of them one last time, appreciating Kady's fine penmanship and savoring her kindness. Then she placed them one by one into her washbasin to burn them to ashes. Burning them one at a time took what felt like hours; Rebecca was afraid to do more, lest she accidentally burn the house down. Eventually they were a little pile of ashes, and she carefully upended the basin out her window and watched them scatter to the wind.

The next morning, Rebecca heard Rachel quietly unlock her door. Rebecca was surprised, she had assumed that she would be locked in until supper. Rachel didn't feel it was appropriate to use a switch on Rebecca when she misbehaved, so instead, Rachel had a lock installed on the outside of the door and would simply lock Rebecca in her room as punishment. In all honesty, Rebecca didn't mind. She'd rather be locked in her room then around Rachel when she was in a foul mood.

By the time Rebecca made her way downstairs, Rachel had left for the market. When she returned she did not say a word about the incident the evening before. She almost acted as if nothing had happened. She was even pleasant when the note and supplies arrived from Kady. It was unnerving, so even though there wasn't anything untoward in the note, Rebecca burned that one, too. As if the supply yard knew of the raised tension in their house, the daily activity slowed down significantly, allowing Rebecca to breathe and leave her candles out of the window for a spell. It was only after the New Year was ushered in that the supply yard started up into full operations once more.

Shortly after, a new note arrived. Thankfully, Rebecca had been out on the porch at the time, so Rachel was not even aware of its existence, as this note was definitely not an innocent missive. It was not from Kady, either, which was odd. The writer obviously knew about the arrangement, though, because it said to pay careful attention to the supply yard for the following week. One candle if all appeared to be normal, two candles if the number of guards in the evening increased. The letter did not say anything else, and she was glad for it; the less she knew the better.

The first two nights of her watch, she only had to light one candle. She was starting to think tonight would warrant two, as there were definitely more men around than usual. She was not sure, though, as they seemed to be milling about, not on guard. Did that count? As the afternoon came to a close, the yard started to empty. She figured the men were heading off for their evening meal. She should do the same shortly. First, she had to decide whether to light only one candle or follow her gut and light two. No, she would trust her eyes, not her gut. One candle only. Besides, she would check again after supper. She could always light another one then. She was placing the candle in the window when she heard her sister ring the dinner bell.

Rebecca called over her shoulder, "I will be down in a moment." When she glanced back down at the yard, she saw men starting to come out for the evening patrol, only there were a lot more men than usual. Her gut was right! It was a two-candle evening. Rebecca grabbed the second candle from her desk, and lighting it off the first placed it in the window. She made sure their spacing was even, and that they were securely on the sill so they would not tip over. Satisfied with their placement, Rebecca turned to go down for supper, stopping quickly to straighten her desk first. She hated coming back to a messy desk. This accomplished, she headed for the door once more only to see her sister standing in the doorway, arms crossed. Rebecca yelped and placed her hand over her heart.

"You startled me." She laughed nervously and straightened her posture. "I am on my way; you didn't need to come fetch me."

"Get your shawl and come downstairs."

Rebecca looked at her confused, "My shawl? Why do I need my shawl for supper?"

Rachel's face tightened. "You aren't comin' down for supper.

There are some men here to talk to you about those candles and whoever it is you are lightin' them for."

Rebecca felt all of the blood leave her face, and her knees felt weak. "Men? What men?"

"They are from the army. There have been rumors circulatin' that someone is signalin' when shipments come and go from that supply yard." Rachel pointed emphatically toward Rebecca's window. "They have been investigatin' ever since a convoy was ambushed resulting in three deaths. They questioned all of the guards and they all seemed to remember seein' candles in your window. Four days ago, they took James in. They questioned *my* husband all day." Rachel was fighting back hysteria as she spoke. "He lost an entire day's work and might have lost his work permanently if rumors had spread that he was a traitor. The only reason they let him go was because I went down there and told them about you and your little candles!"

"You did what?"

"I got them to release my husband! That is what I did. They were very interested to hear all about you and your mysterious packages, and the money you have given me."

"That was for my poetry!"

"You expect me to believe someone would pay for some words on a piece of paper?"

"Yes! Because it's the truth."

"Nonsense, they, whoever they are, are payin' you for information, and you were too dim-witted to see."

"I am not dim-witted!"

Frustration flickered across Rachel's face, and with a glance

310

downstairs, she crossed the room and grabbed Rebecca's arm. "Stop that. If you are guileless then they won't do nothin' to hurt you."

"Why should you care? You are the one who turned me in."

"You are my sister! I only turned you in because I knew you had no idea what you were doin' and therefore would not get into trouble. I turned you in because I had to get James back. How are we supposed to survive without him? How are we supposed to survive labeled as traitors? Everyone knows you are a cripple and therefore had no idea what you were doing."

Rebecca started to crumple under the weight of her sister's words. Surprisingly, Kady's words fought to the forefront of Rebecca's mind giving her strength. She was a brilliant poet and a trusted friend. She was more than her deformity. A look of defiance filled Rebecca's gaze, countering Rachel's frustration.

"I am more than some cripple, and I will not play dumb, because I am not dumb. You and James had nothing to do with this, and I will tell them that, but I will not act as if I am a useless simpleton because it makes things easier on you. I do not care how many times you say it, I am not, nor will I ever be, a useless simpleton!"

Rebecca ripped her arm out of Rachel's grasp and started toward the door. She pulled her shawl off the hook, then made to leave. Rachel grabbed Rebecca's arm again.

"Tell them that you know nothin'!" Some of Rachel's anger seemed to have shifted into fear.

"I am not going to lie to them, Rachel."

"Rebecca, tell them—"

"The truth. I am going to tell them the truth because I am not

311

ashamed of what I have done. If that is wrong then I will face the consequences, but I will not hide behind my deformity to ease your conscious. If you are ashamed of what you have done, that is not my problem to fix."

Rachel released Rebecca's arm. "Rebecca, please. I only did this because I love you."

Rebecca snorted. "No you didn't. You did this out of selfishness." Wrapping her shawl around her shoulders, Rebecca left to face the soldiers.

There were two of them and they mostly spoke to James with only the occasional comment directed at Rebecca. Rachel was standing with her back against the newel post at the bottom of the stairs, arms folded tightly across her chest, looking down. Rebecca realized she had not been listening to anything they said. When they gestured for her to leave, she did so without hesitation. They had brought a horse for her to ride, not realizing her infirmity meant that she had never learned to ride a horse. They decided she should ride in front of one of the men so she would not fall off.

It took some time to accomplish this, and Rebecca did her best to ignore the stares of the neighbors. None of them was brazen enough to come outside to look, though it seemed they had no scruples about peering around curtains. Finally they left, and only when they were about to turn a corner so the house would be completely out of sight, did Rebecca turn back to look. The candles still flickered in her window. That last message had been a trap and she had fallen for it. How could she have been so blind? Furthermore, why had she not known that

James had been taken in for questioning, and why did she not realize before now that her sister would always choose James over her? She would choose anything over her. Rebecca turned back to the ever-darkening street ahead and tried not to imagine what lay before her.

Jan 12, 1865
Mama Bird fell from perch. Aid needed when
found.
LR

52-45-35 15-23 15-12-26-56
55-45-55-45 33-46-31-44 66-51-41-41
66-31-65-55 61-51-31-62-32 45-46-44
35-51-51-44-51-44 14-32-51-35 66-65-13-35-44
41-31

52-45-35 15-56 15-12-26-56
14-45-36-62-32-44-65-54 65-35 41-65-65-21
65-13-36 62-45-41-41 65-35 44-65-62-36-65-31
66-65-31 31-51-61-65-31-36
33-44

Jan 15, 1865
Watchdog on lookout. Call on Doctor for
report.
BD

38
Dumb Luck

Emma entered the inn bone-tired and praying they would have a room available. She didn't even care how much as she had liberated a purse from a drunk two days earlier and was willing to hand over every last coin for a bed. Or a bench. Or even a table underneath which she could curl up—anything to get her out of the infernal wind for the night. Seeing all of the empty tables, with the exception of a lone man in the corner, her heart leapt. That boded well. The proprietor, however, was nowhere in sight, and she got no response when she called out. That did not bode well. She called out again, and this time got an answer, from the man at the table.

"There's no point in hollerin'; no one is there to hear you."

Emma whirled around to face the man.

"Pour yourself a beer and pull up a chair. He'll be back eventually."

Emma gritted her teeth. "Jacob."

He smiled in return. "Get me one while you're over there."

Emma dropped her pack on the nearest table and made her way around the bar. It took some searching before she found a clean mug for herself and one that looked suspect for Jacob. She spit in his for good measure then filled them with beer. As she made her way back around, she looked at her gear meditatively, then decided to leave it by the door just in case. She set down the two mugs, sliding one to Jacob, then kicked his foot off her chair and collapsed into it. Jacob laughed. Apparently her coldness to him was funny.

"I see you are getting better at being a man," he joked.

Swallowing a big gulp, she wiped the froth off her upper lip with the back of her hand. "Why? Because I've lost my manners?"

"No, because you don't give a damn anymore."

Emma eyed him as he downed half his beer in one go. There was something different about him, something resigned.

"I'm surprised you are so happy to see me. Wasn't I supposed to run home to annoy my father with my stupidity?"

Jacob scoffed, "Bygones." He finished off his beer and slammed the mug down on the table. "We all get bad information from time to time."

Jacob picked up his mug, remembered it was empty and slammed it down again. Emma flinched involuntarily. He may be willing to forget what happened, but she wasn't ready to let it go. She was trying to think of something to say. Jacob continued before she had the chance.

"She warned him. I don't know how, but she warned him. That is how he got away."

Emma was stunned. He had accused her of warning Henry, now Jacob apparently had another scapegoat for his failure. "Who warned him?"

"Kady."

"His wife? The woman at the bar that day?"

"*My* wife! She was my wife first goddammit!"

Jacob slammed his fist down on the table. Emma hardly noticed.

Her mind was racing. Jacob and Henry thought they were both married to the same woman. Henry's wife was a spy and Jacob was clearly in love with her. Ha! Emma could take them both down with one woman. This was perfect! Emma felt the elation bubbling up inside of her. Then it came back to her. That night in her room … after Jacob … looking through his bag … what was it she had tried to remember? Kady is LR. Kady is LR! She shouted it at Jacob.

"Kady is LR!"

Startled, Jacob broke free from his dour mood and stared at her as if she were crazy. Emma repeated, softer this time, "Kady is LR, right?"

"Yes and her mother is NR. Northern Rose and Little Rose. What about it?"

Emma let out a sigh and realized she had been holding her breath. She had inadvertently let slip that she had gone through Jacob's bag and read his letters. How else would she have known about LR? Thankfully, Jacob was too drunk to put that puzzle together.

"Oh, nothing. I hadn't realized that before, that's all." Emma needed to change the subject in order to give herself time to think. "We need more beer. I'll go get some."

Before he had time to say anything, she was up and heading across the room. Captain Henry's wife AND mother-in-law were spies. This was even better. Emma filled the mugs and restrained herself to keep from skipping back to the table. It only took a little coaxing to get Jacob to tell her the whole sordid story. It was almost as if he had been waiting for someone to tell it to, someone to confide in about the whole mess. Emma felt sorry for him but not enough to change her mind

317

about hurting him, after all, she did not think he actually loved the girl. He was definitely upset about something though. Who knows? Maybe there was something about Kady. Maybe she had actually been able to get two men to fall head over heels in love with her, because Henry was definitely in love. She had never seen a man dote on his wife the way he had done that day at the tavern. It was actually kind of sweet and horrible at the same time, knowing his love was not returned. It made her smile. Henry was going to get exactly what he deserved. And once Jacob realized that Kady's undoing was his fault, he would get what he deserved too.

Emma brushed the hair off Jacob's face and whispered in his ear, "Thank you." He had passed out and Emma folded his arms onto the table to rest his head, and to keep him from falling over. Then she rifled through his bag and stole the correspondence he had inside. Crossing the room, she picked up her pack. Emma did not care the proprietor had never returned, as she no longer needed a room. She was headed to the Dismal, the thought of the buffeting wind no longer on her mind.

39
Best Served Cold

Emma picked her way down the trail. Today was the day she would get her revenge on Captain Henry—assuming, of course, she would be able to find the encampment in the swamp. By now, she had the twists and turns of the trail correctly memorized, but her route had flooded and she couldn't find any way around the water to get back onto the path she knew. She wasn't going to give up that easily though, so she had spent the last hour trying to find a new route to the camp. So far she had managed to get herself thoroughly lost. Her frustration was about to get the better of her, when she heard a horse approaching from behind. She debated for a second whether to hide or get out of the way. The narrowness of the trail did not allow much leeway, so she turned to see who was coming and stood her ground.

The man who approached was not in a proper uniform, more a hodgepodge of pieces he had been able to scavenge together. To her dismay, Union blue was the predominant color. However, she was lucky enough to spy the highly polished belt buckle proudly displaying "CS." It did not matter how desperate the man was, no self-respecting Union solider would wear a Confederate States belt buckle. This man had to be Confederate.

Upon seeing her, the man slowed his horse and stopped a few feet away. He was clearly uneasy and his hand drifted back to the gun at his hip. Emma had anticipated that her presence would put anybody she encountered on edge, so she had stolen a skirt from a clothesline. A woman in the swamp would be unusual, but not necessarily a threat. The fact that this man was clearly unsure of how to approach her, meant that her wardrobe change had paid off. She decided to capitalize on his hesitancy and take control of the situation.

"Oh, thank goodness you showed up, I am so lost!"

He looked confused, but more at ease. She was a damsel in distress.

"Miss, I would be happy to help you, but what are you doing out here?"

"That is a good question, sir! I will never forgive my cousin for sending me on this harebrained errand. My cousin is Captain Henry's wife, and I have been sent to find him to get his input on some important household matters. I was given directions, and like the stupid girl I am, I thought I could remember them and did not write them down."

The solider eyed her suspiciously, and Emma held her breath.

"All due respect, miss, I'm havin' trouble believin' that you would be sent to ride out here into a swamp over household matters."

"You are?" she exclaimed. Her story was ridiculous. She knew this. It was not supposed to be believable. She needed him to think that he had outsmarted her.

"I am. I can spot a lie from a mile off, and that one that you just told is a doozy."

Emma deflated in her saddle and hid her face in her hands. "I knew this would happen. I knew I would be no good at this!"

"Oh, come now. Lyin' takes skill and practice. I think it speaks highly of you that you cannot lie."

Emma looked up from her hands.

"Why don't you tell me why you are really out here, and I will see if I can help you."

"I am not supposed to tell anyone."

The soldier looked around conspiratorially and whispered, "It will be our little secret, I promise."

Emma took a deep breath and tried to look as if she was making a hard decision. "Well, it must be our secret; you cannot tell anyone."

"I swear on my mama's grave, I ain't gonna tell a soul." He made the sign of the cross, then winked at her.

"I've been sent by General Humphreys to deliver a secret message to Captain Henry, and I was given explicit instructions that no one was to know my business."

"Well lucky for you I came along! I happen to be headed to Captain Henry's camp and forgettin' things that people tell me is one of my best skills."

Emma laughed and looked at him demurely. "It must be my lucky day."

The solider smiled. "Why don't you follow me and I'll see you safely there. Any cousin," at this the soldier winked at her, "of Captain Henry's is a friend of mine."

Emma spent the next twenty minutes keeping a steady stream of small talk flowing. The soldier was originally a private out of South Carolina but had gotten out of the main line of fire when he had been reassigned to Captain Henry's command. He joked it was because he could cook a snake as well as he could kill them, and as they were camped out in the swamp, that was a good skill to have. He, of course, had to wait for the snakes to stop hibernating before he could show off his skill. Still, the skill was there.

Emma laughed at his jokes and quickly realized she was indeed lucky he had come across her, because they soon left the main trail, and Emma was sure there was no way she would have found the camp on her own. She let the soldier dominate the conversation as she focused on remembering the route they were taking. She, after all, would be exiting the swamp alone if all went according to plan.

The solider interpreted Emma's quiet as unease from being in the swamp and decided to try to rattle her further by telling a ghost story. Apparently, all of Henry's men had been killed; the man did not know how but said the captain was still shaken up by the ordeal. He had been tight-lipped ever since getting his new men and did not talk to anyone, aside from giving orders. He also expected his men to remain similarly quiet when in camp.

At this part of the story, the man leaned over toward Emma and began to whisper, "The rest of the men and me think there was some sort of ambush and Henry's men were killed right here in this swamp. There be eerie sounds around these parts at night. Not your normal nighttime swamp sounds, which are bad enough, there be this faint moanin' that sounds as if it's comin' in on the wind. Only there ain't no wind."

Emma felt goose bumps ripple down her arms.

"And the captain has his tent set up not ten yards from this mound of earth. There ain't no other mounds of earth nowhere else, just that one. So all us thinking his first men are buried there, and the captain stays close to protect them. Or maybe he stays close to keep 'em in the grave. No one rightly knows which."

Emma shivered and the man laughed. "Don't you worry! We'll get your message delivered and get you back outta the swamp before the sun goes down. You'll be plenty safe."

Emma smiled. "Thank you."

Their conversation turned to lighter topics, and before she knew it, she was getting a rundown of all the different ways a snake could be cooked and which way was best for which type of snake. With this new conversation, Emma was able to pay only marginal attention. She realized that no matter how hard she tried, there was no way she would be able to memorize the route they were taking. The skirt she had stolen had little bits of ribbon woven into the eyelets of the ruffles, and she discovered that by tugging on them she could get them loose. As they were now riding single file, she was able to drop a piece of ribbon on the trail every so often. Even so, she tried to memorize the route in case a squirrel or bird decided to decorate their nest with the ribbon she was dropping.

By the time the camp came into view, Emma was almost out of ribbon and she was actually hungry for stewed snake. The man's easy banter had let her forget the goal of her mission for a spell. Now that the camp was in sight, it came back to her. The man dismounted before helping Emma down. He ducked into the captain's tent to announce she was waiting.

Emma waited impatiently by her horse.

The man finally emerged and indicated the captain would see

her. She took one last look at her horse. How easy it would be to climb back into the saddle, ride off, and forget all about revenge. But she knew she would never be able to live with herself if she abandoned her mission now. She had seen with her own eyes what happened to men who let the fear of success paralyze their ambitions. Those men littered the bars and taverns across the countryside. She would not join them. Captain Henry had a debt to pay and Emma had come to collect. Trailing her hand along her horse, she gave him a pat, held her head high, and entered the tent.

Henry was sitting at a small table across from the entrance. Due to the unusually warm January day and the informality of the camp, he was dressed only in his shirtsleeves and britches, the rest of his uniform hung by the bed. The front and back flaps of the tent were secured open to let in light and allow for airflow. There was still a sense of privacy, though, due to the thick foliage behind the tent. Henry looked at her skeptically and spoke first.

"I was told you had a message for me from General Humphreys. Would that be General Andrew Humphreys?"

"Yes, sir. The one who is a personal friend of President Davis."

"Right, that General Humphreys. You have a message for me, from him?"

Emma swallowed hard. Why was he so suspicious? Had Humphreys died or something?

"Yes, I have a message from General Andrew Humphreys."

"Unless that message is to say that he has turned coat and switched sides, I'm going to have to call you out as a liar. Despite his friendship with our President Davis, General Humphreys is with the

324

Union." Henry placed his pistol on the table with the barrel facing Emma. "I am going to have to insist that you tell me what you are really doing here, before I shoot you as a spy."

Damn! Those fools that she overheard had been talking about a Union general. How had she not picked up on that? She raised her hands to show that she did not mean him any harm. His gun did not unnerve her too much. She had seen men posture like this before. Despite him calling her a spy, Emma did not believe that Henry would actually shoot her. In fact, the appearance of the weapon provided some comfort, because now she knew the location of his gun. Better to have it in plain sight than have it pulled from some discreet location.

"Okay, you are right. General Humphreys, or anybody else for that matter, did not send me with a message. However, I think you would find it is in your best interest to hear me out, as I carry intelligence that directly involves you."

Henry stared at her intently for a moment and then chuckled, removing his hand from his gun, leaving it on the table. He folded his hands behind his head and stretched out his long legs.

"That must be quite the important message for you to come all the way out here by yourself. Enlighten me."

"I'm surprised you don't recognize me. Our paths have crossed before."

Henry looked her over once more, this time much more closely. No hint of recognition crossed his face. "I can't say I remember."

He did not recognize her and he was already growing tired of their conversation. A new hatred for this man surged through Emma. He had killed her family. Then he had beaten her and left her for dead

325

and he did not even remember! She was not sure which made her hate him more: that she had spent every day thinking of him, or that he had not thought of her once. She had to restrain herself to keep from flying across the tent to hit and claw at his body, to exact as much damage as possible. Knowing she could not succeed in inflicting much harm, she kept her feet firmly planted.

Emma replied through gritted teeth, "Surely you remember, sir." She practically spit the word "sir" at him. "You killed my family, but since I only saw you save my baby brother, I placed my faith in you. Then you took that faith, you threw it in my face, and you beat me."

Emma stopped speaking in order to keep her tears at bay. She had said enough and could see on his face that he now remembered. She did not understand his next emotion, and he immediately replaced it with a hard, wary look as he straightened himself in his chair. Then, on second thought, he stood. She had forgotten how tall he was. He was quite an imposing figure.

"I suppose you've come to exact your revenge. What is your plan? Kill me? I do not see that working out for you. We're in the middle of a swamp, in a camp of my men."

"No, I did not come here for blood. You destroyed everything that I held dear. I've come to do the same to you."

A sadness settled over Henry's face. "I was ordered to kill your family. I did not want to do it, and if I could take it back I would, but I cannot. There isn't anything you can do to take it back, either. Now go home before you get yourself killed. You aim too high, girl." Henry started to move to the opening of his tent. "I'll have one of my men escort you out of the swamp."

Frustrated, Emma grabbed the captain's gun off the table. Hearing her movement, Henry spun around and saw the gun trained directly at his nether region.

"I think you'll find that my aim is actually quite low."

Henry put his hands up in a show of reluctant acquiescence. "So this is your plan to destroy my family? You're going to shoot me so that I can never have children?"

"I already said I'm not here for blood." Emma's frustration was mounting. He was not taking her seriously even though she had his gun. If he did not take this seriously, he would not believe anything she said either. She had counted on him being stupefied or paralyzed with shock long enough for her to make her getaway. That was not going to happen. She needed something else to distract him long enough. A thought came to her. "Take your clothes off."

Henry looked at her incredulously and put his hands on his hips. "My clothes? Why should I do anything you say? You've already confessed you're not here to shoot me."

"I said I did not come here to shoot you, not that I am not willing to shoot you."

The captain still did not move, so Emma cocked the pistol and took aim. Begrudgingly he pulled off his shirt. He sat so he could pull his boots off. After several hard tugs, Emma lost her patience.

"Leave the boots on."

Henry looked at her hard for a moment. Then he stood, removed his belt, undid the buttons on the front flap of his britches, and let them puddle around the tops of his boots. Before he had time to ask, she gestured with the pistol that he was to continue with his undergarments, too. Finished, he straightened his back, crossed his arms in front of his chest and stared at her, naked from the knees up.

"Now what?"

"Now, I tell you what I came here for." The sight in front of her was making her blush. This was not going the way she wanted. "Sit."

"Very well." Henry sat, arms still crossed, and stared at Emma waiting for her to speak.

"The reason your missions keep failing is because a spy keeps sharing the details of all of your plans to the Union."

Henry laughed. "If that is your big revelation, you have wasted your time. I already know that."

Emma continued undaunted, as if he had not interrupted her. "A spy who goes by the initials 'L. R.' Those initials just happen to be the code name for your wife, Kady. And she sends along that information to her lover."

Finally, she was back on her plan. She paused to let what she had said sink in. Kady's betrayal would kill him a hundred times over and she got to see the first death up close. There was a certain poetic justice to the whole thing—assuming, of course, he believed her, but by his silence she guessed that he wasn't entirely sold. She needed to taunt him with something more specific.

"How else could those Union soldiers have known about the gold and ventured into this swamp to look for it? It was Kady's idea." Emma finished her sentence in a singsong voice.

"You lie! She would never—" Henry made to stand up. Emma gestured with the gun that he was to remain seated. It was still cocked so he obeyed. The seed of doubt was planted. He would go mad until he had sought out the truth of the matter for himself. It was perfect, and Emma couldn't help herself, she had to torture him further.

"I read a letter she wrote to her lover with my own two eyes. She holds him so dear, she promised she would always keep one of his love letters close to her heart." For emphasis, she gently patted her chest. Kady's letter had not actually said anything like that, but Emma thought it was a nice touch. "If you don't believe me, why don't you ask her yourself? In fact, if you rode home right now, you would probably find her with him."

A flood of emotions ran across the captain's face. His reaction was everything she had hoped it would be, and she reveled in his obvious pain. He seemed unable to form any words as his face flushed a deep crimson. Henry was clearly fighting with his emotions, wanting to rage but reining it in because of the gun. He could call for his men, but she could kill him before they ever got close. He was stuck, and Emma loved it. Her position was precarious at best, though. So when Henry leaned forward, running his hands roughly through his hair and over his face, Emma decided it was time she took her leave. She hit him on the head with the butt of the pistol as hard as she could. At first, she didn't think she'd hit him hard enough because he just sat there wavering. Then he crumpled to the ground.

Emma dropped his pistol next to him and hurried to her horse trying to look natural. She whipped the reins free from the branch and mounted, tearing her skirt in her haste. She did not care. As she turned her horse to exit the camp, she looked over her shoulder and saw the man that had helped her to the camp. He smiled and waved, oblivious as to what had just happened. Emma smiled back and returned the wave,

329

then turned to the trail and urged her horse into a gallop. Henry had not remembered her when she arrived, but he would certainly remember her now.

40

If You Give a Man a Biscuit

As they made their way past the cramped and filthy cells, Rebecca said a quiet prayer for the men inside. She shuddered to think what any amount of time spent in one of those cells felt like. Her own cell was more akin to a room at an inn than an actual jail cell. Having never had a female who was infirm as a prisoner, her jailers had been at a loss as to what to do with her. The jailor's wife came up with the solution. The men moved the furniture from one of the guest bedrooms in the jailor's house into one of the offices on the main floor of the jailhouse. The problem was, being an office instead of a cell, the door locked from the inside, not the outside. So Rebecca had given her parole that she would remain on the grounds. For good measure one of the guards would escort her past the cells every morning as a reminder of where she would end up if she broke her word and tried to escape.

This was unnecessary. Rebecca did not intend to escape, and even if she had wanted to, she did not know where she would go. Rebecca oscillated between bitter anger and abject depression over what her sister had done. Free from having to endure her sister's comments on a daily basis, Rebecca began to realize how much Rachel treated her as if she was an imposition, an unwanted duty thrust upon her, which had to be endured. Rebecca began to question whether her sister had ever loved her at all. This last thought was the one that seemed to haunt her in the dark of the night, as she lay curled up alone in her bed. Even if Rebecca could escape, she would have nowhere to go.

Therefore, she dutifully followed along every morning. After the first week, she got the sense that this exercise was as much for the guards' benefit as her own—to remind them that she was indeed still a prisoner, because outside of this ritual they treated her more like an honored guest. They checked in on her constantly to make sure she had everything she needed. After they discovered that she had a knack for making biscuits, she was given free range of the kitchen, and they began to lovingly call her "Miss Rebecca," instead of "the prisoner."

Despite the favor they showed her, they questioned her exhaustively. With the exception of withholding Kady's name, she eventually told them everything she knew. What she knew was little; she thanked her stars she had told Kady not to give her details. After a while the questioning stopped. It seemed clear to everyone that Rebecca had been involved in some sort of espionage. However, as she did not know details about anything, the army was at a loss as to how to punish her. She had been told on more than one occasion that if she were to say she did not understand what her actions meant, this could all be over and she could go home. However, she was adamant that she knew exactly what she was doing, so they remained in a stalemate. Truth be told, she didn't want to go home, especially not by admitting she was dim-witted like her sister believed her to be.

Once the questioning had ceased, she actually began to enjoy herself. At first she worried that the men would hate and mistrust her. She had, after all, provided information to the Union. However, as they could not officially connect her to any Union spies, and none of them had personally known any of the men from the swamp, the guards were content to give her a pass. Besides, the novelty of having her around seemed to outweigh her indiscretion. Her only regret was that she wasn't allowed paper. That was remedied one afternoon when she happened upon a marketing list left in the kitchen, the backside of which was blissfully blank. Unable to control herself, she sat down to write.

Unlike her usual poetry about the war, she found herself writing something much more lighthearted. In fact, it was downright satirical, poking fun at one of officials who often visited the jail. Of course, she was caught with her contraband and not allowed to explain herself. Her guard confiscated the paper and left. Rebecca berated herself. She could just imagine that guard handing her paper over to the very man she had been writing about. Had she just ruined everything? She fled to her room and fretted away the rest of the day waiting for her punishment. No one came except a small Negro girl with a tray of dinner. Rebecca couldn't bring herself to eat and eventually fell into a fitful sleep.

The next morning, she awoke early and sat on the edge of her bed. She was not entirely sure what she was waiting for, but she couldn't bring herself to leave the room. Shortly after nine o'clock there was a quick rap on her door.

"Miss Rebecca, it is Lieutenant Johnson. Are you decent? May I enter?"

"Ye ... yes. Please enter," Rebecca stammered and blushed. The lieutenant entered and stood in front of her. He had the incriminating evidence in his hand.

"I confiscated this from a group of prisoners this mornin' who were gathered around it, gigglin' like little school girls. From what I can gather, it passed through the hands of all of the enlisted men on duty last night then continued its journey through the incarcerated men. After reading it myself, I can see why it traveled so quickly. It is quite clever."

Rebecca was about to apologize, but his unexpected compliment rendered her speechless.

He continued, "I'm sure you can imagine, this piece could have caused you quite a bit of trouble had it fallen into the wrong hands." The lieutenant crossed the room to the fireplace as he spoke. "As it so happens, the page was accidentally destroyed before it could reach that far." He dropped the paper into the flames and waited for it to catch before turning back.

Rebecca finally found her voice. "Thank you, and I do apologize, Lieutenant. I certainly didn't mean to cause trouble. I promise that it will never happen again."

"Nonsense! I haven't had that good of a laugh in years. Just stick with Union officers from now on. Maybe General Sherman next?" The lieutenant gave her a mock-serious look and pulled a folded piece of paper and a pencil from his jacket and set it on her desk. "And perhaps take some of the flourishes out of your handwritin' so it's not so obvious that a woman wrote it."

Rebecca bit her lower lip to keep the grin on her face to a minimum. "Yes, sir. I'll do what I can."

"Good. Now I believe you are needed in the kitchen."

With a click of his heels, the lieutenant nodded at her and strode out of the room. Rebecca let her smile expand across her face and crossed to the desk. Reverently she picked up her treasures and held them to her chest for a moment before hiding them under her mattress and heading to the kitchen.

Rebecca became the first person the guards sought out when they arrived for duty, and they all made a point to bid her good night when they left. The new and unexpected popularity made her head spin. She had even made friends with Mammy, the cook. Much to Rebecca's embarrassment, it was over a week before she realized Mammy was a nickname, and the cook's real name was Josephine. Josephine explained to Rebecca that Mammy was a name given to black women by white folk who were too lazy to learn their real names.

Rebecca was fascinated, and even when she was not helping by making biscuits, she spent most of her free time in the kitchen. Truth be told, Rebecca had never spoken with a Negro before. She had seen them, of course, but as her family had no servants and she did not do any of the marketing, she had never had the opportunity to talk to one.

Contrary to everything she had been taught about the Negro people, Josephine was quick-witted and funny. Rebecca had never met anyone so clever. Josephine was also the only person in the jail who believed Rebecca had been aware of her actions instead of merely a pawn in someone else's machinations. Rebecca figured that if there was anyone who understood what it was like to be underestimated, it was Josephine.

As the days passed and it became known Rebecca was spending her spare time in the kitchen, the men started to go there as well whenever they had a break. Even some of the boys from across the street at the jail, Castle Thunder, would sneak over on occasion.

Rebecca made them learn Josephine's real name, which was shortened to Josie when a private brought her a posy in an attempt to get an extra serving of cobbler. He got his extra dessert, and the

335

nickname stuck. From then on, Josie got a posy whenever there was cobbler on the menu.

Rebecca had her favorites and gave them warm biscuits instead of cold. As ridiculous as it was, Rebecca sometimes pretended that she was a proper Southern lady entertaining her gentleman callers. It was a fun game to play in her head even if she knew that none of them would be interested in her in that way. She pictured herself in a huge dress floating gracefully into the room to greet her guests—her limp always disappeared in her daydreams. She was charming and always knew what to say. The gentlemen would laugh at her witty remarks and proclaim they had to leave all too soon when the next callers arrived.

In reality, Rebecca was dusted with flour, sweaty, and fumbled for words. She didn't fumble for words all of the time, only when Lieutenant Johnson came in. It was as if the proverbial cat had her tongue. She would stammer and blush. He would smile. She would blush some more, then busy herself getting him another biscuit. When Rebecca found out that he was older and thus could be an appropriate suitor—he had 28 years to her 26—she stammered and blushed even more. It took many embarrassing encounters before she was able to string more than three words together in his presence.

Josie always found something important she had to do, usually on the other side of the kitchen or outside, every time he came in, so Rebecca was left to fend for herself. Rebecca both hated and loved Josie for this. Rebecca knew Lieutenant Johnson was only being nice; however, she added him to her prayers at night, and he was often the last thing she thought about before drifting off to sleep.

Once, when there was a bit of extra jam leftover from a

breakfast the commander had with some important men, Rebecca squirreled it away for her lieutenant. Josie had seen her hide it and gave her a look, but she kept quiet until after he had left.

"Oooh, you sweet on that boy and the feelin' is mutual!"

Rebecca spun to Josie, blushing a deep crimson. "Don't be ridiculous."

"Girl, that boy ate nine of your biscuits, and he ran out of jam on number three. Ain't no man stick around long enough to eat that many biscuits unless he enjoyin' the company."

"That doesn't mean he's sweet on me. How could anybody like me? I'm a cripple."

"You must be as naive as you are crippled. That man comes in here every day, and it is not to see me! Besides, you plenty whole in the places that count." Josie waved her kitchen towel suggestively.

"Oh! You are awful!"

"Nine biscuits!"

"Stop it!"

"Nine!"

Rebecca threw a biscuit at Josie who easily deflected it and returned to her work chuckling and muttering to herself. Rebecca managed to blush further still, this time from pleasure not embarrassment.

41
Let Me Fall on the Sword

Anna picked up the letter from the desk and compared it to the original. She smiled. She had almost perfected the counterfeit of Captain Henry's script. Another week of practice and even he would not be able to differentiate between the two. Carefully she folded the love letter that Henry had written to Kady and tucked it into her bodice. Then she carried a candle and her practice letter to the washbasin. She set the letter alight and dropped it in to burn away the evidence.

Anna watched as the flames licked up the page, hungrily devouring her intended deceit. Henry had insisted Kady return to Richmond, and the general had decided it would be best if they did the same, so he rented a house. Anna spent almost all of her time at Kady's house. She even had her own room. To her relief, the general seemed content with the arrangement. Everything was quite satisfactory, except for the fact that Anna felt useless as of late. Most of her contacts and modes of passing information revolved around the plantation. In Richmond, she was disconnected and had to rely on the connections Kady had made. It was better than nothing, but Anna was itching to do more. Once she had perfected her new forgery talent, she would be able to wreak havoc by sending false messages and reports that even Henry would have to agree were in his script. The idea made her giddy. She poked the burning letter deeper into the basin when Mary burst into the room, half scaring the wits out of Anna.

"Heavens! Have you forgotten how to properly enter a room?"

"Apologies, ma'am, I didn't think you would want me to wait. You have to come quick!"

"What is wrong?"

"I don't rightly know. The captain he come burstin' in, raisin' Cain about being betrayed. He found Miss Kady in the drawing room and now is hollerin' about some letter. I think he may be aimin' to kill her!"

The blood drained from Anna's face, as myriad possibilities of how Kady had betrayed Henry flitted through her mind. Which one, or worse yet which ones, had he heard, and where in God's name had he heard them? Anna headed for the door, and when Mary started to follow, she stopped and turned.

"No! I need you to stay here and make sure that burns completely," she said, pointing at the washbasin. "Once it has, get rid of the ashes and clean the soot."

With a nod of understanding from Mary, Anna picked up her skirts and rushed from the room.

Kady had not seen it coming, so when the flat of Henry's palm connected with her cheek, the shock hit her first. She staggered a few steps from the impact and fell to the floor as the pain exploded across her face. Whoever had spoken to him had been well informed of her actions. Everything he was accusing her of had been accurate, and the proof he now demanded was burning a hole in her bodice. He had burst in so unexpectedly, Kady hardly had time to fold the letter from Jacob, much less hide it in the front of her dress. It wasn't a love letter, as Henry had accused her. Jacob called her his dearest, though, and confirmed that all was in place to move Rebecca out of Richmond as soon as she was released from jail. It was equally as damning.

Henry now paced in front of Kady like an angry lion denied his dinner. Apparently he was giving her a moment to reconsider her refusal to relinquish the letter, before "ripping every piece of clothing" from her body to gain possession of what he desired. She did not think he would hit her again. The look on his face betrayed that he regretted dealing that first blow. But there was a hurt set deeper in his eyes, and she knew that would be fuel enough for him to carry out his threat. Her mind raced trying to come up with something to say or do when her mother came bursting through the door.

"Oh my Lord! Kady!" After a momentary pause of shock at seeing Kady on the floor, Anna made a beeline to her, but Captain Henry stepped in her way.

"Leave her," he growled.

"I most certainly will not! She's bleeding!" It was common knowledge that Anna did not like or approve of the captain as her daughter's husband and she let the contempt show through. She pushed past him and rushed to her daughter's side. Kady had not realized she was bleeding until she heard her mother's words and reached up to discover a trickle of blood coming from the corner of her mouth. She wiped it away with the back of her hand.

"Oh stop, you'll make a mess," Anna chastised as she reached into her bodice to grab a kerchief. She moved so fluidly Kady barely noticed her mother pull out a letter with the kerchief.

"Here, use this." Anna daubed at her lip and Kady reached up to take it from her. Her mother held firm and continued to fuss over her in a most uncharacteristic way. Henry resumed his pacing, never taking his eyes off them. Anna mouthed the word, "Where?"

A wave of relief washed over Kady. Mary must have lingered in the hall long enough to overhear what Thomas wanted before running to tell Anna. Bless that woman. Kady pulled her own kerchief from her sleeve and reached up to her face, pausing for the briefest of moments to brush her hand over where the letter hid.

"Here mother, use mine. I don't want you to ruin yours." Anna plucked the kerchief from Kady's fingers.

"Don't be silly. You embroidered this for your dowry. Or at the least had a servant do it. Mine is old." With that, Anna stuffed the kerchief into Kady's bodice and with it, the letter she had in the palm of her hand.

The whole thing happened so quickly Kady herself would have doubted it had occurred had her mother's letter not shoved Jacob's further down her bodice.

With one last daub at her lip, Anna helped Kady into a chair before turning abruptly to the captain.

"And as for you, sir," she said with venom in her voice, "what makes you think you have the right to burst in here and hit my daughter?"

Kady had never seen her mother worked up like this, and, in all honesty, she was glad she was not on the receiving end. Henry had no such compunction. Her mother's words seemed to stoke the fire in him so his ire rose, obliterating the earlier hurt.

341

"She is my wife, and I will punish her for defyin' my will as I see fit!" At that, Anna wheeled on Kady so fast she even took the captain by surprise.

"What did you do?" Kady caught Anna's intent immediately. Their relationship had been built on such animosity for so many years it was easy to slip back into her old self. A fresh torrent of tears flowed down Kady's face.

"I didn't do anything!"

"She has a letter she refuses to produce." Henry pointed over Anna's shoulder like a child in the schoolyard tattling on a playmate.

"Is that true?" Anna crossed her arms and pursed her lips until Kady reluctantly nodded her head. "Hand it over right now, or I will stand by and watch him take it from you in whatsoever way he sees fit!"

With a satisfied look on his face, Henry stepped up next to Anna, his new ally, and they both stared down expectantly. Kady let her lower lip quiver slightly as she reached up to retrieve the letter. She strove to keep up her look of petulance as a sense of relief filled her. Having no idea what this new letter was, she carefully unfolded it and made a quick perusal of its contents before handing it to her mother, who then passed it on to Henry without a glance. It was Henry's love letter from Christmas. Her mind raced to think of a plausible reason why she would be carrying it around, for one, and for two, why she had been reluctant to produce it to the man that had been its author.

Mercifully, no excuse was necessary. As Henry read the letter, the stress and tension left his rigid posture leaving him utterly deflated. Without glancing at either mother or daughter, Henry shoved the letter into Anna's hands and took his leave. The front door slammed to announce his exit from the house.

Kady flinched with the sound. Instead of feeling relieved, she simply felt as if she had been granted a stay of execution. The love letter had bought her time, not a pardon. Her mother broke the silence.

"Tell me exactly what he said. What does he know?"

"He knows everything! He knows I've been passing information about his missions; he knew about Jacob, he even knew I would have Jacob's letter with me."

"He knew about Jacob?"

"Not by name, Thomas called him my lover."

"Good Lord." Anna closed her eyes and took a deep breath.

"How did he find out all of that? I've been so careful."

"First things first. We need to figure out what we are going to do; then we can attempt to ascertain his source."

"What can we do? He knows everything!"

Anna paced back and forth for a minute thinking. "We need to convince him you have been wrongly accused. Here." Anna shoved the love letter at Kady. Dazed, she took it, then almost dropped it when Mary softly knocked before entering. Apparently, her nerves were frayed a bit more than she had originally thought.

"I did as you asked, ma'am. Oh, my dear Lord, Miss Kady, your face!" Upon seeing her, Mary rushed to her side and gingerly cupped her injured face in her hands. "Lordy, that will be a black eye for sure. I'll fetch a compress." She clucked disapprovingly as she made to leave.

"Thank you, Mary."

Mary looked back at Kady, nodded, then left.

Reaching for her kerchief, Kady realized she had Henry's letter in her lap. "What should I do with this?"

"Keep it in your bodice. That letter is to become a permanent part of your daily dress. You will tell Henry you keep it on you always as a reminder of the man who stole your heart."

"What if he asks why I wouldn't show it to him?"

"I don't know . . ." Anna's voice trailed off as she searched for a reason. The obvious strain etched upon her face accentuated when she rubbed her temples to help her think. "Tell him you were so offended by his accusations you did not want to give him the satisfaction of knowing you keep a token of his love with you at all times."

Kady would never cease to be amazed by her mother. The way she was able to weave a fabrication into the truth so the two were indistinguishable was truly beautiful.

"Let me see Jacob's letter."

Kady fished the letter out of her bodice and handed it to Anna. Anna unfolded it and paced the room reading. She stopped and turned abruptly to Kady.

"Why isn't this letter encoded?"

Kady let out an exasperated sigh. "Sometimes he doesn't encode them. I have lost track of how many times I have told him he has to. He's gotten better about it, he really has, but I still get an occasional letter like that."

"Unbelievable. No wonder Henry knew everything that was in this."

"Actually he didn't. He thought I would have a love letter." The shock began to dissipate. "We can use that. Not all of his information was accurate."

"So he was expecting to find a love letter from . . ."

"My lover, which technically he did."

"Yes, he did! Only the lover was himself, instead of another man. This is good, it means he is now doubting everything he was told."

"Is that enough?"

"No, but if he intercepts this letter—"

"Mother, no! That letter is about Rebecca's escape from Richmond. They will know she is a traitor for sure."

"Kady, we don't have a choice! Besides, everybody already knows she was working with us. She is in jail! That an exit is in place for her will not be surprising to anybody. Besides, Jacob simply says all is set, he does not mention anything about my family's cabin in New York."

"Then how will giving him the letter help us? It will prove he was right; there is a spy!"

"Exactly. We prove to him that his information is correct, with the exception of the identity of the spy. Then this new spy will say Rebecca was being used and was never given any information. Henry will be a hero for uncovering a traitor, Rebecca will be released, and you'll be wiped of suspicion."

"You propose we falsely accuse someone of treason and then ask them to help Rebecca? That will never work!"

"I did not say falsely accuse. We are going to let him catch a spy."

"Where are you going to find a spy willing to hand themselves over to the Confederate army to save me?" Kady was frustrated. She wished her mother would stop talking in riddles. Then Kady froze, an icy chill running down her spine as the pieces fell into place and she realized what her mother intended.

"No! No, you can't!"

"What choice do we have, Kady?"

"I don't know, let him catch me! The letter is to me not you."

"The letter is addressed to 'My Dearest' and is signed 'All my love, J.' This letter could be to anyone and from any number of hundreds of men. It's perfect."

"Mother, no, this is my mess. Let me clean it up." Fresh rivulets of tears had begun cascading down Kady's face. "You can't get caught; you're too good at this. I need you." From the way her mother paused before responding, she knew her words had an effect on her.

"Don't be ridiculous. I haven't been of use for some time." Anna walked over and knelt down in front of Kady. "But you, my darling, are invaluable. I will not let the sacrifice you made by marrying that man go to waste."

"Fine, get caught, then flee Virginia. If you run they will know for sure that you are guilty; it is perfect. You can go to the cabin in New York! We already have transportation worked out. Jacob will simply take you instead of Rebecca."

"Darling, no. If I'm not here to confess, to say that you and Mary had no idea of what I was doing, then they will investigate both of you. Jacob might be able to smuggle you and me with him, but he isn't set up to transport Mary, and I will not leave her behind. As long as I stay, I can protect you both. Mary will be here to help you. You will do fine without me."

"No, I can't." She protested, but her heart wasn't in it. Kady

346

knew she was not going to win this argument. Her mother's mind was decided, and from a purely logical standpoint, Kady knew she was right. As the wife of Captain Henry, she was the best-placed Union spy to gather information on supply routes and, therefore, had to be protected. But Kady did not want to think logically. This was her mother. She had wanted to be close to her mother her entire life, and now that she had finally achieved that, it was all falling apart.

"Kady, it's going to be all right. Even if they find me guilty and are able to come up with even more proof of my activities, they will never hang me. I am a woman; the South would never hang a woman. Worst-case scenario, they imprison me until the end of the war, which you will work to bring about as quickly as possible. Let me do this."

Kady could not bring herself to speak so she nodded her head.

"Now go. This will be a lot easier for you if you don't know any of the details of what is going to happen next."

Kady nodded again and, without looking at her mother, got up to leave the room. Mary entered carrying the compress just in time for Kady to brush past her out the door. Flustered, Mary turned to Anna.

"Missus Anna?"

"Go look after her, please."

With a lingering look at Anna to try to decipher what had happened, Mary left the room as well.

Anna took a deep breath, then crossed the room, sat at the desk, and pulled out pen and paper to hurriedly compose some messages. She had to warn everybody of what was about to happen, and she had no idea how long she had to do it.

347

35-31 45-35-44 41-31
62-65-55-61-31-46-24-51-44
31-51-44-46-31-51-62-36 45-54-51-35-36-24
36-65 44-31
35-51-14 62-65-44-51 61-31-65-36-65-62-65-41

NR and LR compromised
Redirect agents to DR
New code protocol

42
Of Mice and Men

It was well past midnight before Anna heard the front door open and then slam shut as someone stumbled inside. Her heart quickened; it was time. She stood poised, ready to signal Mary with a candle in the window as soon as she could confirm that Henry was home. It did not take long. The butler heard the commotion and came hurrying to aid his master's arrival.

"Leave me. I am fine. I said, I'm fine!"

It was Henry and he certainly did not sound fine. He was clearly drunk. Anna placed the candle. She had worked everything out earlier. Mary would wait, hidden from view, until the signal. Then she would walk around the block so she could approach the house as if she were coming from town. Once to the house, instead of entering through the kitchen, as she would normally do, she would go around to the side parlor and enter through the door on the veranda. If history proved accurate, that is where Henry would go to brood over a nightcap, and that is where he would catch Mary delivering a letter addressed to Anna. If all went well, he would immediately confiscate it from her, read it, and discover the identity of the spy in his midst.

After much negotiating, Anna had finally gotten Mary to agree to play dumb to the traitorous activities going on. Mary was ready to be branded as a spy right alongside her mistress. It was only after Anna reminded her that as a Negro, she could be shot for treason where she stood, no questions asked. Not to mention, if Anna had used her slave, it would throw every person that Mary interacted with under suspicion, too—every merchant, every farmer, and every slave. Mary finally relented and agreed to the story: she had been sent into town to pick up a headache tonic from the doctor, and because of the chill in the night air, Anna had given her a wrap to wear. While in town, a man approached her and asked her to deliver a letter to the owner of the wrap.

It was not a great story, but Anna was hopeful it would hold up. Since Mary was a slave, and a woman, they hoped it would take little to convince the captain that she was both naive and ignorant.

Searching into the darkness, Anna prayed Mary had gotten her signal and was on her way. Taking a deep breath to steady herself, Anna blew out the candle before anybody else saw it, then climbed into bed to wait.

She lay perfectly still, listening. She had not realized it, but she was holding her breath. Over time, she had become accustomed to the emotions and thrill of almost getting caught. The pounding of her heart, the dampness of her palms, the way she was able to sense her surroundings and think so acutely. Even better was the giddy thrill of victory that washed over her when the danger had passed.

This was new, sitting and waiting to be caught. With every moment that passed, she had to fight the mounting urge to flee, the urge to intercept Mary, stop the delivery, and delay the inevitable. She knew she could not, so instead she lay perfectly still and waited.

It did not seem to be in the captain's nature to rant and rave. She had never seen him drunk, though, so anything was possible. Most likely, he would barge into her chamber and confront her. Then, of course, that did not sound like him either. Maybe he would wake Kady and send her in, or worse yet, maybe he was planning on waiting until the morning to confront her. Anna took a deep breath and resigned herself to the possibility she might be in for the longest night of her life. She had begun to contemplate sneaking from her bed and stealing downstairs when the front door slammed shut. Startled, she abandoned all caution and rushed downstairs to the parlor. Once inside, the scene she saw stopped her dead in her tracks. Mary was still standing by the open veranda door with a horrified look on her face. Across the room, Captain Henry lay splayed across a chaise snoring as if he was the very herald of the morning.

"Mary, what happened? Where is the letter?"

"He took it, ma'am."

"How did he take it? He's unconscious!" She knew whatever had happened was not Mary's fault, but she could not help the rising fear and frustration.

"Not the captain. Your husband, Master Bell."

The implications of Mary's words hit Anna like a dose of cold water, and the subsequent dread that filled her made her feel as if she would never be warm again. Anna thought she had run through every possible scenario she might encounter this night, and she had readied herself for all of them—but not this. Not her husband escorting a drunken Henry home. How had they wound up together? Had Henry sought out Andrew, or was it simply happenstance? Above all else, where had Andrew gone and what was he planning to do?

"Mary, tell me what happened. Tell me exactly what happened."

351

As the insistence in Anna's voice grew stronger, Mary began to break down. Anna rushed to her, grabbed her shaking hands, led her to a chair, and sat her down.

"I'm sorry, I'm sorry. It's my fault. I shouldn't have given him the letter. I should have ..."

"Hush now. It's all right, you had no choice. Tell me what he said."

"When I walked in I was holdin' the letter out, like you told me to, and I startled the master as'n he was layin' out the captain over yonder. He asked me what it was I was doin'. Before I could answer, he saw what was in my hand and his eyes got this crazy look to them, and he demanded I give him the letter. I tried to play dumb, but there it was and he had seen it. So he ripped it from my hand and had already started readin' by the time I found my tongue to tell him he had no right to read your letter. He stopped readin' right then and gave me a look that set my insides to crawlin'. I swear, I thought he was gonna kill me. I think he wanted to, because he made to take a step toward me before he turned around and stormed out without another word."

"He didn't say anything else?"

"No. The next thing I know, you was comin' in."

Anna lowered her forehead onto their clasped hands and tried to think. Where would Andrew have gone? After reading the letter, Anna was certain that he would want her dead; but if he had been with Henry then hopefully Henry had told him about the accusation made against Kady from a third party. That meant there was someone out there who could levy the accusation again. So if Andrew killed Anna, then there would be nobody to refute the accusation against Kady, just a cryptic

352

letter. Andrew would not be willing to risk his daughter's life on something so flimsy, which meant that Anna was safe for now. But only if Henry had told Andrew. Frustrated, Anna looked up at Mary.

"Go make some coffee. Strong coffee."

"There ain't no coffee, hasn't been for months."

"Then go get whatever there is that is close to coffee. We need to talk to the captain."

"Oh, you lookin' to talk to a drunk man. My mama had a trick for that."

Anna stood to let Mary hurry out and crossed the room to Henry. She could smell the whiskey on him from several feet away. Bless him, but he did love Kady. He had not taken this news well at all. Anna struggled to get him upright on the sofa, but he was big and heavy, and she had only managed to get him propped sideways by the time she heard Mary reenter.

"Step back now, Miss Anna."

Anna had barely moved out of the way when she felt the cold spray of water rush past her arm. As Henry half bellowed, half sputtered in surprise, Anna turned to see Mary holding an empty pot with a sheepish grin on her face.

"Coffee has to be drunk; a dose of cold water works every time."

Anna stifled a giggle. "Did you have to use so much?"

They both looked down at Henry who had fallen to the floor and was flailing about trying to save himself from drowning. Anna knelt down and after a few tries was able to catch one of his arms, which he jerked back in fear. Her touch had evidently been enough to alert his sodden brain that he was on solid ground, because he calmed.

"You're all right now. All is well." Anna spoke soothingly and gently wiped the hair off his face.

"Where, where am I?" His speech was that of a child woken from a deep sleep.

"At home. You made it home."

"Bed. I want bed."

"Yes, you can go to bed in a moment."

"No, now." He started to get up. Anna easily pushed him back down.

"In a minute." She cupped his cheek with her hand and spoke warmly. "Did you tell General Bell about Kady?"

He mumbled something in return and closed his eyes. Anna patted his cheek, and when that did nothing, she drew her hand back and slapped him. His eyes flew open.

"Thomas, did you tell General Bell about Kady?"

At the use of his first name, he focused his eyes on Anna. "Yes."

"What did he say he would do?" Henry lowered his eyes and looked like he might start crying, so Anna grabbed his face with both hands to force him to look at her. "No, don't cry. Everything is all right. When you told General Bell about Kady, did he say that he would take care of it?"

Henry nodded his head.

"Good, good! Did General Bell say what he was going to do?"

Henry shook his head. "Said it was all lies and he would get to bottom of it."

"Good boy. I am sure he will. Do you want to go to bed now?"

Henry nodded his head. Anna grabbed one of his arms to help support him and turned looking for Mary, needing her help. Kady must have heard the commotion because she was standing inside the doorway with Mary's arm wrapped around her. Both women moved forward to help, and between the three of them they got Henry to his feet. Upon seeing Mary he perked up somewhat, calling her Sally. Mary went along with his confusion and was able to get one of his arms around her shoulder. Kady got his other arm around hers, and the two of them led the shuffling man out of the room.

Anna sat down heavily on the sofa, only to jump back up because it was soaking wet. Pulling the wet cloth of her nightdress away from her body she crossed the room to the fireplace. The embers were barely glowing, but there was still some heat coming from them. She turned to face the room and warm her backside. What had just happened? Henry had clearly told Andrew about the allegation against Kady. Judging by how drink tended to loosen tongues, Anna guessed that Andrew now knew more particulars of Henry's story than she did. Anna was sure that her husband would protect his beloved daughter. Now that he had the letter proving Henry's information to be faulty, Andrew would be able to convince Henry to drop the matter, and then Andrew would take care of the real spy himself. That thought made Anna shudder, so she didn't let herself dwell on it.

The real question was who else had Henry told? If he had told someone else before finding Bell, then things would be trickier. How could she protect Kady now? Anna smiled ruefully and shook her head. She and Andrew had never once agreed on how best to raise Kady, but in this instance, she was positive that their thoughts were one. Andrew would sacrifice Anna to save his daughter. If he wasn't already speaking to the authorities, he would the second he heard Kady's name even whispered in the same sentence as an impropriety.

Mary entered the room. "We got him to bed. Kady's undressin' him." Mary looked like the weight of the world was on her shoulders. "What do we do now?"

Anna took a deep breath and squared her shoulders. "Now, we wait for me to be arrested."

Mary started to say something, but Anna stopped her and continued, "I think our plan still works. Whether Henry turns me in, or Andrew turns me in, the end result is the same. As much as I am sure Andrew would like to kill me where I stand, he needs someone to take the blame to save Kady. Someone told Henry, so as long as that person is free to tell other people, Andrew will keep me alive. So we move forward as planned. You will drop off the advertisement at the newspapers tomorrow morning. Then go to Elizabeth—"

"Who?"

"Sorry, Baker's Daughter, in the mansion on Church Hill. Tell her that I will try to get Rebecca released from prison. I've arranged everything in New York. That scoundrel Jacob was in charge of transportation, so someone will have to find him to get those details."

Mary nodded her head. "I saw eggs in the kitchen, I'll empty two out for the messages. Church Hill first, then the paper. I reckon I can be back before the sun is fully up."

"Perfect. Then you and Kady need to remove yourselves from anything spy related. Get rid of your hollow-heeled shoes and anything else that might incriminate either of you. You must be beyond reproach."

"I know. I got rid of everythin' already."

"Good." Both women were on the verge of tears. "Take care of Kady for me. Take care of both of you. Stay safe."

Mary nodded and the two women hugged. Anna could have stayed in that embrace forever. Mary broke free and held her at arm's length.

"I'll go get them eggs, and you go get them newspaper ads. With any luck, I'll be back before they take you away."

Doctor Must Be Found!
Our Roses have caught a blight and immediate action must be taken before it can spread. Direct all correspondence to 4625 Main Avenue, Room 31, or 1536 W. 24th Street.

43
Goin' Somewhere

Rebecca and Josie had been tripping over each other all morning. The commander had decided at the last minute he wanted to throw a dinner to celebrate his birthday, which of course meant they had been scrambling to find enough food to serve and then to get everything prepared. On top of making her biscuits, Rebecca had also been helping by chopping vegetables. She was slow, but Josie was thankful for any help she could get. Rebecca finished with the carrots and turned her attention back to the oven. She had doubled her recipe and, as such, was running out of space to put the cooling biscuits. She had just pulled a fresh batch from the oven when Lieutenant Johnson walked into the kitchen. Rebecca smiled, relieved to see him instead of flustered, and gestured toward the table.

"Give me a hand, will you? Those should be cool, will you move them aside?"

Johnson leapt to obey her, moving the biscuits with alacrity and claiming one for himself as payment for his service. He took a bite and moaned in appreciation. Rebecca laughed.

"I am going to miss these here biscuits. I swear you bake a little bit of heaven into each one," he told her.

She started to laugh, then stopped short as she registered what he had said. "What do you mean miss my biscuits? Are you goin' somewhere?"

"Well, no. That's why I've come, Miss Rebecca. It seems they've arrested a genuine lady spy." Rebecca froze. "Not that you aren't a genuine spy, or a lady, I didn't mean it like that; but this one was caught with letters and she's confessed to runnin' a whole operation." Johnson smiled at her and hesitantly touched her arm. "She said that you were an informant not a spy, that you provided observations but did nothin' and knew nothin' more. Since that matches what we already know, you are being released. You are free to go, Rebecca."

Rebecca was in shock. Loathe as she was to admit it, she was afraid of leaving. Even if her sister would take her back, she did not want to go back. But she would have to—what other option did she have? Moreover, poor Kady! How had she been caught? Rebecca tried desperately to recall if she had said something, anything, that might have led them to Kady. Johnson gently squeezed her arm and, coming back to the present moment, Rebecca looked up into his face and smiled.

"The boys and I hired you a cab, so's you don't have to walk home. It will take you wherever you want to go." On impulse, Rebecca fell into his arms and hugged him. He squeezed her back, hard, and kissed the top of her head before holding her out at arm's length. "We sure are goin' to miss you."

Rebecca laughed, fighting back tears. "I'm goin' to miss all of you, too."

Rebecca felt as if she had finally found a place where she was welcome, and now she had to leave it—the men and Josie and her lieutenant. A breath caught in her throat and Johnson pulled her back in for a quick hug. Then with his arm around her shoulders, he directed her toward the door.

"I say we leave this mess for someone else. Let's go pack up your things."

Rebecca stopped in her tracks and turned back to Josie. "Oh no! The dinner. I can't leave!"

Josie stopped what she was doing long enough to give Rebecca a look. "Don't you be silly, girl! You think I can't run a kitchen without you? I can handle this fine." Josie crossed the kitchen, pulled Rebecca into a hug, and before breaking away whispered, "You are free, so you go."

Rebecca squeezed her tightly, a tear escaping from one eye. "I am goin' to miss you, Josephine."

Josie let go, and without looking at Rebecca, turned and grabbed a biscuit. "Here, you better take one of these along." She handed it to Rebecca and went back to her cooking. She didn't seem to be able to look Rebecca in the face. "Now you get goin' and let me get back to my cookin'."

Rebecca watched Josie for a moment, who kept her back turned, engrossed in a pot on the stove. Rebecca wanted to say goodbye but could not bring herself to utter the words. She didn't like to think that she may never see this woman again. In the end, Rebecca turned and left without saying another word.

She had few possessions, so it took no time at all to pack her bag. Johnson shouldered it and, offering his elbow to her, led her outside. The other guards on duty were all waiting to say goodbye. She exchanged hugs and kisses with all of them and promised she would write. The men practically lifted her into the carriage, and she was still waving goodbye out the window when it started to roll down the street.

She waved to them all, but she was looking at the lieutenant.

As they turned the corner and she could no longer see the men, she sat back to assess her situation. She had assumed the driver knew her sister's address and that was why no one had asked her for a destination, until she realized that they were heading in the wrong direction. A feeling of dread filled her insides. What if she and the guards had been lied to? What if they had only pretended to release her so they could take her away to some dark and dank prison somewhere, where there would be no kitchen, no Josie, no friendly guards to make her smile and laugh? Her dread was quickly turning into panic. Rebecca frantically tried to get the driver's attention, and finally he heard her and stopped.

"Where are you takin' me? I was told I was released. My sister's house is in the other direction."

The driver laboriously got down from his seat and opened the door, and she noticed suddenly that he only had one leg.

"My name is Jacob; Kady sent me." Rebecca was taken aback. This was the last thing she had expected to hear. "She tried to get a message to you in jail, but you were not allowed any outside correspondence, so Kady moved forward with her plans. She had your things from your sister's house packed up and has arranged for lodging and money for you in New York. However, if you would prefer to return to your sister's I can do that, too. It's up to you."

Rebecca knew immediately what her choice would be. How had Kady arranged this? She was in jail herself!

"How? I was told Kady had been arrested and it was her confession that secured my release."

Jacob frowned for a second, then understood her confusion. "Not Kady, her mother. Anna has been arrested. Oh!" Jacob dug in his pocket and produced a wadded up kerchief that he handed to Rebecca. "Kady gave me this so you would know you can trust me."

Rebecca took the bundle and opened it, discovering her little pewter mouse. Despite the pain she felt for Kady's mother, relief washed through Rebecca, and she laughed clutching the treasure to her chest. Kady had fixed everything. God bless her. Rebecca looked Jacob squarely in the eyes and spoke without hesitation.

"New York. Take me to New York."

Jacob nodded and closed the door to return to his position. Rebecca's whole body trembled as she let out a breath. In the blink of an eye, her entire life had changed. Her head was spinning, and she did not know if it was from the motion of the carriage or the emotions in her heart. Either way, it was an overwhelming feeling.

44
The Road to Redemption

Henry kept playing that night over in his head, as if he were doing penance. Why had he been fool enough to believe that girl? What had Kady ever done that made him so willing to believe her capable of such deceit? His beautiful, innocent Kady—and he had hit her. He had hit her for carrying one of his own love letters close to her heart. Frustrated, Henry pounded his fist onto the pommel of his saddle, causing his horse to snort and pull at her bridle in protest for bearing the brunt of his anger. Henry, repentant all over again, apologized to her in a soothing voice and ran his fingers through her mane until she had settled.

This behavior this served to frustrate Henry even more. Why could he not keep his anger in check? Was he cursed to spend his life apologizing for his actions? After a childhood of watching his father hit his mother, Henry had sworn he would never act in such a way. Then at the first discord, he had struck Kady. If she never forgave him, he could not blame her. He had apologized profusely in the days of utter chaos that followed. Even after her mother was arrested, Kady remained stoic, or maybe she had been in shock. The only person she would speak with was her mother's servant, Mary.

Therefore, when Henry had gotten orders that he was needed in the Dismal, he had requested that General Bell allow Mary to stay by Kady's side and it was arranged. He still hated to leave her. He had no choice, though, and knew his presence was unwanted anyway. This thought twisted his heart. In her hour of darkest turmoil, she did not want him there. Realizing that if he did not find something to distract his mind, he would go mad, Henry pulled his orders out of his pocket and read over them for the hundredth time. With the stalemate at Petersburg continuing to drag on, Lee's men were in need of food. Richmond and the surrounding land could not provide it; however, almost all attempts to move supplies to Lee en masse were thwarted. Without looking conspicuous, Henry's men were to travel to Petersburg by foot as pairs or solo, carrying as much as possible.

Each man was also to carry a small packet addressed to General Lee, himself, containing a single bar of gold. As they were no bigger than half a deck of playing cards, the packet would fit easily among the provisions. The sheer weight of something so small might rouse the suspicion of the men, but Henry had to trust that his men would understand the importance of their job and see the packets into Lee's hands. After the ambush of Henry's men, President Davis had been wary of moving the gold again, or even of letting anyone else know of its existence, including Henry's new company. Therefore, this new courier system was a perfect cover. Henry would not help carry the supplies. As soon as he had seen his last man off, he would load gold into his saddlebags and ride with all speed back to Richmond. His men were to take circuitous routes into and out of Petersburg, thus allowing Henry to drop his gold and make it back to the swamp before they did. This assumed, of course, that everything went according to plan.

He shook his head. When did anything go according to plan?

At least it would get him back to Richmond sooner rather than later, and he would be able to see Kady. Damn. Like clockwork, his mind had returned to her. All of his strategic planning melted away, replaced with self-loathing. He would never forgive himself for what he had done. Perhaps there would still be some way to make amends. Kady, after all, was a much better person than he was, so she might be willing to forgive. For the first time since that night, Henry felt a glimmer of hope. He did not let himself hold on to it—he did not deserve it—but he enjoyed its faint shine all the same.

Coming into view of the camp, Henry could see his men gathered around the fire pit. It was a brisk day and the fire looked inviting. However, eschewing their company, Henry quietly made his way to the den, dismounted, and entered without drawing attention to himself. Moving several crates aside, then squatting to dig in the dirt at the back, Henry unearthed several of the bricks. As quickly as he could, he inserted one piece into each of the packets he had been given back in Richmond and sealed them. Once each packet was sealed, he replaced the dirt and moved the crates back into place.

Henry barely had time to resurface and place the packets into his saddlebags when he heard the approach of footsteps. He looked up to see Tom. Henry liked Tom; he was the only one of his new company he had opened up to. A little runt of a man, Tom's energy more than made up for his lack of stature, and it was hard not to like him.

"I thought I saw your horse over here. Welcome back, Captain! How's Richmond?"

Henry grimaced. "Hectic. Get the men. We have a lot to do, and I want you all ready to leave the swamp as soon as it gets dark."

"Yes, sir." Forgetting Henry's rule about staying quiet, Tom turned back toward the men and putting his little fingers into either side of his mouth emitted a high shrill whistle that had to carry for at least a mile. Henry glared at Tom who looked back sheepishly. "Sorry, Captain."

"Perhaps next time, you can walk over and get them."

"Yes, sir. Sorry, sir." It was clear Tom was indeed sorry. That didn't stop him from smiling at a job well done when all of the men headed toward them in quick order.

Henry relented and smiled too. He had to admit, that whistle was effective. Obnoxious, but effective.

The next several hours were spent loading and unloading the packs in order to fit the most food into each bag. The men were to walk instead of take their horses, hoping that a man on foot was less likely to be robbed than a man with a fully loaded horse. Henry questioned the validity of this theory, but orders were orders. It turned out that more fit into the rucksacks if they mixed the types of foodstuffs according to shape instead of ingredients for an actual meal. He had also neglected to consider the relative size of each of his men. Apparently, no one else had thought of this either, until Tom strapped on his pack, promptly staggered, then fell over backward from the weight.

Instead of becoming angry or humiliated, Tom simply acted as if he had done it on purpose and started pretending as if he was doing the backstroke across a lake. As the men howled with laughter, he wriggled free of the straps and stood on top of the pack as if a great explorer that had scaled a mountain. Henry reprimanded him for squishing the food, and he scampered down. They all set about repacking yet again in an attempt to lighten Tom's pack, while still carrying the same amount of food.

The men were able to repack all but two small bundles that would have to be left behind. Henry reiterated their orders and made each man repeat the exact route he would be taking. Then Henry pulled the packets from his saddlebag and distributed one to each man. Under threat of court martial, no one was to open the packets, except General Lee himself. Not even his chief of staff, Taylor, was to be trusted with them. The levity from earlier had faded and each man nodded his understanding at the task being entrusted to him. With nothing left to say, the men tucked their packets away, hoisted their loads, and made off into the darkness. They had not been able to finish before the sun had gone down, but Henry felt they would still have plenty of time to make it out of the swamp and find cover before daybreak.

As soon as the last man left his sight, Henry grabbed his saddlebags, returned to the den, moved the crates, and dug up more gold. He layered the gold on the bottom, stopping short of filling it completely as he did not want the bag to look overstuffed. Satisfied he had all he could carry on this trip, Henry once more replaced the dirt and moved the crates back into place. He looked around his den. With the exception of a few odds and ends, it was now empty. Then Henry remembered the bundles of food he had left topside. Shouldering his bags, he made his way to the top, only to freeze in the entrance. He could hear something rooting around in the bundles, and cursed himself for carelessly leaving them unattended. Pulling his pistol, he hoped it was something small he could scare away. If it was a bear, he might wind up spending the night in the den. Unless, of course, the bear wanted to stay in the den. Henry said a quick prayer that it wasn't a bear.

Creeping out, he strained to see through the dark to identify what he was up against. There were several smallish humped forms, and Henry did not recognize the silhouettes as any of the wildlife native to the Dismal. Suddenly one of the shapes stood, and Henry sighed in relief. They were Negroes. Standing to his full height, Henry took two paces toward them and cocked his pistol, pointing it at the standing figure. At the sound, all of the figures turned to stone; it was as if they were not even breathing anymore.

"All right. All of you stand up and move away from the food."

Slowly they stood and, at Henry's direction, moved away with their hands up. Upon closer inspection, Henry realized there were six of them. A grizzled old man and woman, a young woman, and three children of whom he could determine neither the age nor the sex. One of the younger ones had started crying, and the young woman clasped the child to her without ever taking her eyes off Henry. They were looking at Henry with immense fear, except for the grizzled old man, who seemed to have contempt burning behind his eyes. Henry addressed him.

"Is this your family?"

The man's eyes did not waver. "Yes, sir."

"Are you trying to make your way North?"

No reply.

"You are runaway slaves, are you not?"

No reply.

"I'll take that as a yes."

Again, no reply.

"You understand it is my duty as an officer of these Confederate States to return you to your master?"

The young woman let out a brief cry, before she was silenced by a look from the man who then turned back to Henry.

"I know that."

Despite this admission, the man stood as erect as before. Henry marveled at his fortitude—to be caught and still have that kind of dignity. This man might be a slave, but no one owned him. Henry looked over at the old woman and was shocked to see her fear had grown into a similar defiance. She knew what her fate was to be, yet she still would not bow her head. Henry knew his duty. He also knew he could not do it. Uncocking his pistol, he lowered the weapon. A moment of confusion flickered across the old man's face. Henry holstered his gun and shifted the weight of the saddlebag on his shoulder.

"You're lost aren't you?"

Warily the man nodded his head. His skin was so dark, the movement was almost imperceptible, save for the whites of his eyes in the darkness.

"Are you trying to make it to one of the Negro camps or out of the swamp completely?"

The man's eyes widened in shock.

Henry chuckled. "I know every inch of the Dismal; so yes, I know about the camps."

The man looked at his family then, making a decision, turned back to Henry. "We lookin' for my son's camp. He escaped a year ago but wouldn't go no further without us."

369

Henry nodded his understanding, and looking over the family once more, noticed for the first time how emaciated they all were. He shifted his gaze down to the bundles of food.

"Take those; I'll show you the way. It might not be the right camp, but I'll take you to a camp." No one moved. They all stared at Henry. "Or don't take them. We're moving out."

They fell on the bundles and had them gathered up before Henry had finished with his horse. Mounting, he steered his way around them, and then looked back over his shoulder.

"This way and be careful. We should be able to make it before daybreak."

45
Blood Is Thicker

Emma walked as quickly as she could toward the courthouse without drawing undo attention. When the scandal of the arrest of General Bell's wife for spying for the Union had reached her, she had been furious and made her way to Richmond. Henry had misunderstood somehow and accused the wrong woman. It was supposed to be Kady under arrest, not her mother. The only way to hurt both Henry and Jacob was by bringing down Kady. Emma was hell-bent on correcting the mistake, even if she had to march into the courtroom and set things straight herself. She had even stolen another skirt for the occasion. It looked atrocious with her men's shirt, but at least she would not be arrested for indecency for wearing pants.

When she finally came within sight of the courthouse, she was astonished to see that there was a small crowd gathered in front and a small cadre of soldiers barring the entrance. She swore under her breath and pressed forward. Apparently, the people of Richmond had nothing better to fill their day, so they were all loitering in order to be the first to hear the news from the trial. Emma eventually made her way to the front and approached the soldiers to gain admittance. They stopped her and gave her a queer once over.

The soldier who seemed to be in charge told her, "The courtroom is closed." Then as an afterthought, "Even if it wasn't, there would be no admittance to the likes of you."

Emma checked her flaring temper. "I have to get inside; I have information the court needs to hear."

The men laughed at her. "What could you possibly know about today's proceedin's? You don't even know how to properly dress yourself. Go home."

"I have information!" Emma's exasperation only seemed to encourage the scorn of the soldiers.

"I'm sure you do. Now run along and tell your dollies." The soldier grabbed her arm and began to escort her away from the door. Emma turned back to see a new officer exiting the building. Emma shouted to him.

"You have the wrong woman! I have proof! I have proof the court needs to see!"

The new officer stopped dead in his tracks and stared at Emma who was now struggling wildly to slow her removal. She was making such a scene the crowd had pushed in to see what the commotion was about. The officer addressed the soldier who was trying to drag her away.

"You there! Bring her back."

The soldier turned, intending to berate whoever was speaking to him, but upon seeing the officer's high rank, immediately obeyed.

Once the soldier and Emma were close enough, the officer snapped at him.

"Tell me soldier, are you in the habit of turning away people who claim to have critical knowledge that could change the outcome of proceedings?"

The soldier looked down at his feet. "Sir, look at the way she's dressed!"

"Look at the way you are dressed!"

The soldier glanced down at his mismatched, filthy uniform.

The officer grabbed Emma by the arm and gestured to the soldier. "Get back to work and try employing some sense hereafter."

The soldier slumped back to his guard duty, while the officer escorted Emma into the courthouse. Unlike the soldier, his grip on her arm did not bite into her flesh. He approached a door off to the side and, glancing both ways to make sure no one was around, opened the door and guided Emma into a small office. Once inside he finally let go of her arm and closed the door behind them.

"Sir, thank you for your assistance. It is urgent that I speak with the court," Emma said.

"I understand, but as you can see, this has caused quite the scandal. So I need to make sure what you have to say is actually relevant before I bring you before the judges. We can't be wasting anyone's time, now can we?"

His condescension was not lost on Emma; however, as he was the one who had gotten her this far, she bit her tongue.

"You have the wrong woman—well, you don't, she is also a spy. But you should be trying Anna Bell *and* Kady Henry. Kady is the one I told Captain Henry about."

His eyebrows shot up. "I see. You did well to come here. You said you have proof of this?"

There was an edge to the officer's voice that Emma did not understand. She did not have time to puzzle it out now, so she dug into her breast pocket and produced her papers.

"Here. These are letters I got from a Union spy about a shipment of gold." She vigorously pointed to the bottoms of two letters. "Look, this is NR and here is LR. LR, or Little Rose is Kady, and NR, or Northern Rose, is her mother. They are details for one of Captain Henry's missions."

The officer took the letters and looked over them carefully. "This is good. What is your proof of the identities of LR and NR?"

"Ja—a Union soldier told me that Northern Rose was Anna Bell. I figured out Little Rose on my own after I saw a letter that was signed 'Kady.' It was the exact same handwriting as this letter signed 'LR.'" Emma pointed to the letter again. "Therefore, LR has to be Kady Henry."

"Do you have that letter with you or hidden away somewhere for safekeeping?"

"Oh no. I put that letter back in the soldier's bag so it wouldn't be missed. I only have these letters and what I've seen with my own two eyes."

The officer was still looking over the papers. "Good, very good. You were right to come."

"Thank you. Now we must hurry and present this to the court."

"There is no need to rush. Now tell me, who else knows about this?"

"Knows about the letters? No one. Well, Captain Henry, myself, and now you."

"I will make sure that these get to the proper authorities."

"No, I have to take them myself. I have to explain, to make sure they get it right this time."

"My girl, there's no need for that. I will be sure to convey all of the details." The officer folded the papers, tucked them into his jacket, then looked at her and smiled. It was a satisfied, unsettling smile.

"Give those back. I need them as evidence." The officer turned to go. "If you don't let me go into that courtroom and give my testimony, I...I will go tell the crowd outside what I know! And if they don't believe me, I'll go to the papers, or I will go camp out on President Davis' doorstep until he will see me and I can tell him!" The officer stopped. "Rest assured," she continued, "I will not stop until Captain Henry is disgraced before the entire Confederacy because of his wife!"

The officer turned back to face her. "And you will not be content with anything else? Think of the poor girl."

"Poor girl? She is a spy for the Union!"

A darkness clouded over the officer's face, and Emma had an uneasy feeling in the pit of her stomach. She suddenly wanted to be anywhere but in this room.

The officer took a step toward her. "I cannot let you spread these lies about Kady."

Emma's uneasy feeling turned into all-out panic as she tried to push past the officer to escape. He grabbed her roughly. She tried to scream but the officer's hands had found her throat, preventing any sound from escaping. Emma fought back against him. It was no use. He was too strong and, after a moment, she started to see black spots. She struck out with her foot, trying to kick him while grasping ineffectively at his hands. Again, no good. He had driven her back against the wall, so she could not get any power on her kicks and her foot caught in her skirt. She tried scratching at his face, struggling so he would lose his

375

grip. Nothing she did helped, and it became harder to struggle, harder to focus her attacks. She was so confused; why would a Confederate officer kill her for delivering news of a Union spy?

The officer exited and closed the door behind him, looking around. To his great relief the corridor was empty. With any luck, the body of the girl would go undiscovered for a day or two. He straightened his jacket, patted the pocket to reassure himself that the papers were still there, and made his way toward the front door. From behind him, he heard hurried footsteps.

"General Bell! General Bell!" Bell turned to see a young lieutenant running toward him. The lieutenant skidded to a stop in front of him and saluted. "General Bell, I was sent to find you. Your wife has been found guilty and is to be put under house arrest. Your attendance is requested to arrange the details."

Bell's face was unreadable as he heard the news. He made a curt nod of acknowledgment and, before the lieutenant could say anything further, made a smart turn and marched toward the exit of the courthouse.

"General Bell?" The lieutenant took a step to follow, but abandoned the effort and stood perplexed as to what to do next.

46
Have Your Cake and Eat It Too

Anna knew next to nothing about how trials were conducted, but she was almost positive that what she had experienced that morning was not the usual way of things. The big room was empty except for a small handful of people in the audience and five officers sitting at a long table. Apparently, there had been such a mob trying to get in to see the proceedings that they had closed down the courthouse to all except those directly related to the case. Anna stood in front of the men alone. As they already had her written confession, all that remained was to answer a few yes or no questions: Yes, she had disclosed all she knew. No, she did not have any other names to reveal. Yes, she repented her actions and begged the mercy of the court. After which, the officers mumbled among themselves and then ordered Anna be removed to the jail.

This time she was not taken to the same comfortable room where she had been kept earlier. Instead, they took her down a dark stairwell and, with apologies, locked her in a proper cell.

The young soldier escorting her tried to reassure her that they had "swept up special" for her and had replaced the ticking on the bed with fresh.

Anna eyed the cot suspiciously; her definition of fresh clearly differed from the soldier's. However, exhaustion got the better of her and she sat down. She thought this must be some sort of special area of the jail as there were only three cells in the room. By closing the wooden door, she was separated from everything. This was not what she had imagined jail to be like. As the other two cells were empty, she had no one to ask if this was abnormal, no one to tell her what to expect next, or what was going to become of her.

She leaned her head against the back wall and tried to take deep breaths. At first, she could not get her mind to settle. It kept bouncing from one thought to the next. She began to recite the Lord's Prayer in her mind and, after several times through, felt her body ease and relax. Her breathing began to slow. Anna was just dozing, when she heard the door open, and her eyes sprang open. At first, nobody entered. Then, hesitantly, Kady stepped over the threshold and Anna's heart went cold. Their ruse had not worked after all and Kady was caught.

Kady looked back over her shoulder and spoke.

"I will only need a few minutes."

It took a moment for Kady's words to register. When they did, Anna felt as if she would die from relief. Kady was visiting. She was all right.

"Kady? What are you doing here?"

She replied, barely above a whisper, "It was Thomas's idea. He said I needed to say goodbye."

"Goodbye?" Anna's heart skipped a beat.

"I would have thought they had told you by now. You were found guilty of treason. They said hanging a woman goes against everything that is Southern, so that punishment is commuted. However, as they do not want to imprison a lady for the long term, and they know Daddy to be a staunch Confederate, you are to be released and put under house arrest on Daddy's plantation—with no visitors allowed."

Anna felt like laughing. She was being sent to the plantation and Kady was safe. This was working out better than she had hoped it would. That plantation had been her prison for years; it could be so again with little discomfiture on her part.

"My darling, this is wonderful news!"

"Is it?" Kady started to make a move toward Anna, then stopped herself.

It was only then that Anna saw how truly worried she was.

"The siege on Petersburg continues, and from everything I hear, Butler, Meade, and Grant all want to make a move on Richmond as well. If Bell Plantation has not become a battlefield already, it is only a matter of time. You will be sitting directly in their way."

Anna moved to the bars, but Kady stayed where she was. "I will be fine."

"What about Daddy? He is horrible to you, even for the smallest of indiscretions. What will he do to you now? I can't be there to protect you, I am not allowed!"

Anna had not let herself think about this, and she did not want it to ruin her relief by doing so now. She was being released from prison and Kady was safe. That was what mattered.

"Darling, it's simple. We will devise some way to whisk me away to the North, and I will finally get to meet this Rebecca of yours. All will be well; this is good news."

Kady smiled but it did not touch her eyes.

Anna guessed at what was actually disturbing Kady. "And you will be fine here without me. You have been fine without me your entire life; a little bit longer won't change anything."

"I don't want to be without you! I finally get to have you in my life and now you are being ripped away. It isn't fair!"

Anna felt as if her heart was tearing down the middle, and it took every effort to keep from crying. "I know it isn't fair, but this war can't last forever. We can be together again, after. We will figure out a way."

She held out her hand to Kady, who cautiously looked back to make sure the door behind her was closed before taking it and squeezing it with all her might.

"Promise me. Promise me that my husband and my father will not trap me here. Promise me we will be together again after this horrible war is over."

"I promise, my darling girl. I promise, even if I have to come back down to Virginia and free you from their clutches myself."

They both laughed at the improbability of that statement ever being a reality; but Anna could see in Kady's eyes that it had comforted her all the same. They stood for a moment, holding hands, saying nothing, when they heard the heavy steps of a soldier coming toward the door.

Kady dropped Anna's hand and leapt back from her a pace.

Anna gripped the bars and hurriedly whispered instructions to Kady.

"My darling daughter, you must throw a fit unlike any you have thrown before."

"What? No, why?"

"You must convince them that I have betrayed you along with

everyone else. Convince them that this was not a heartfelt goodbye."

Kady reached out, grasped her mother's hand around the cold iron bar, shaking her head ever so slightly no.

Anna wrapped her other hand around her daughter's and squeezed.

Kady found her mother's gaze, her lower lip trembling.

Anna whispered, barely audible. "You know you must. I am so proud of you. I love—"

"I hate you!" Kady cut her off, catching her off guard so the words landed like a slap across her face. It took a moment to realize that Kady did not mean those words. She had begun her act. Kady tore her hand away from the bar as the door opened behind her.

"I hate you! I hate you! I hate you! How could you do this?" The tears had begun to stream freely down her face. "How could you do this to Father, and to Thomas? How could you do this to me? I loved you!"

Anna managed to keep her composure until Kady's last line. Anna knew the hurt she saw in Kady's eyes was real. Against her best efforts, tears started to trickle down her face. She wanted to stay strong. She knew if she cried, if she showed her pain, it would be that much harder for Kady. She couldn't help it, she couldn't stop the tears any more than she could stop her heart from breaking as she watched a second soldier rush in upon hearing the commotion to escort her screaming daughter out of the cells. As the door shut behind them, Anna collapsed onto the cot and let the sobs that were fighting to break free rack her body.

By the time they reached the entrance of the jail, the two officers were practically carrying Kady. She was still wailing and had lost track of when the acting had stopped and her real grief had taken over. The new problem was that she did not know how to stop. The only thing propelling her forward in this world was her grief, and once that subsided, she did not know if she would be able to stand, much less put one foot in front of the other.

Standing by the door was her salvation. There was Henry, tall and stoic, with a pained look on his face. She threw herself into his arms and sobs replaced her screams. She felt the tension leave his body, as if he was relieved she had come to him.

He wrapped his arms around her and let her weep into his uniform jacket. He held her tight and made no motion that they needed to go. Instead, he alternated kissing her hair and murmuring to her how sorry he was, and that he would do anything in his power to make her happy again.

Eventually they grew silent and Henry held her with his cheek resting on the top of her head. When her tears dried, he looped his arm around her waist and guided her outside. He had a cab waiting and lifted her into it without hesitation. After a word with the driver, he climbed in after her and took her into his arms once more. The next thing she knew, they were home and he was lifting her out and helping her inside, up the stairs, and into the bedroom. He held her at arm's length looking into her face.

She was numb. All she could do was stand as if a propped-up rag doll. The thought of calling a servant to undress her and then climbing into her cold bed alone made her tears start afresh.

As if he could sense their origin, Henry took the task of undressing her upon himself. He undid the ties and buttons until Kady stood in her shift with a pool of brocade and silk at her feet. Free of her encumbrances, Henry was finally able to lift her fully into his arms, which he did as easily as if she were indeed a doll. He carefully settled her into the bed, before doffing his shoes and outer garments and crawling under the counterpane where he drew her tightly against his body.

Kady gratefully allowed this and lost herself in his muscular chest with his strong arms wrapped around her. She did not sleep, and he did not break her pained silence. He simply held her close and let her grieve as she may.

47

The Piper Demands His Fee

While Anna had not expected her husband to fetch her from jail himself, she had expected him to send someone for her. After all, she was being remanded into his custody. However, much to the consternation of her guards, Bell nor any of his people could be found. They finally hired a cab to take Anna back to the general's house in town, where an armed soldier would remain on duty until Bell could be located. Anna thought this was a splendid idea, as she had no desire to stay another minute in her cell, much less spend the night. In all of the possible scenarios she had run through her head, she had neglected to imagine what would happen if her husband abandoned her. He was a prideful man, and she knew there would be hell to pay when she faced him, but maybe she would not have to face him at all. A flutter of hope sprang up in her chest. Perhaps she would never see him again.

"Let me help you, ma'am." Anna had been so absorbed she hadn't realized the soldier had disembarked and was waiting to hand her down. She grabbed her bag and took his hand. After seeing her safely down, the soldier paid the driver and turned to Anna.

"After you."

Anna watched as the cab drove away. "How will you get back to your barracks?"

"I'm afraid I am here for the night. A few more boys will be along shortly, and we will all be relieved in the mornin'. One of them will bring me a horse."

"How dreadful for you. You have to stand here all by yourself until then." The soldier chuckled and Anna smiled at him. "Come in, I will make you some tea."

"I do thank you, ma'am, but my orders are to stay right here in front of this door to make sure you don't go nowhere and that none of your associates try to spring ya. I reckon I better do that."

"Are you sure?"

"Yes'm. Now git on inside with you, so I can do my job proper. And don't you try nothin' funny before the other boys get here. I'll be watchin'."

Anna laughed and touched his arm. "As you say, soldier."

She took the steps, only pausing when she reached the door. She had not been inside the house the general had rented since the day they had arrived in Richmond. Anna had spent all of her time at Kady's house, and as such wondered if she even had any belongings inside. Upon opening the door, she saw that she need not worry about her things. A slave at Kady's had packed them up and sent them over. They sat piled neatly in the foyer, awaiting the trip to the plantation. Closing the door, she ran her hand along her trunk as an idea formed in her mind. There was one soldier set to guard her and he was at the front door. She listened for a moment and heard no sound. The slaves had already left. She was alone.

She made her way through the house until she found the kitchen in the back, and as she had expected, a back door. A blissfully unguarded back door, but not for long. The thought of never having to face her husband emboldened her. Holding her breath and biting her lower lip, she inched the door open first a crack, then a few inches, then far enough that she could stick her head out and look around. With the exception of a little boy poking a stick into a hole a hundred yards away, the alley was empty. Anna waved at the little boy, who looked up. Deciding that whatever was in the hole was more interesting, he went back to work. Anna dug into her bag until she came up with two silver coins. She waved at the boy again, this time flashing the money. His eyes fixed on the silver, and leaping to his feet, he ran to her. Upon seeing she was a lady, and not a servant, he dropped his eyes, but couldn't help peeking up at the coins. Anna smiled and dropped the coins in her hand so they clinked.

"Can you keep a secret?"

The little boy looked up eagerly. "Oh yes ma'am, yes'm I can."

"Good. I'm going to give you this coin now." The little boy's eyes widened. "And you are going to go find me a carriage. But! You have to bring it to this door here, and do not let anybody in front of the house see you. Can you do that?"

"Yes'm, I get cabs all the time. Yes'm I can do it."

"Perfect. Then when you get back, you can help the driver move my things and I will give you another coin. Do we have a deal?"

"Yes'm! It's a deal!" The little boy nodded enthusiastically and held out his grubby hand for the coin.

Anna paused before giving it to him.

"And no running. You walk as if you do not have a care in the world. Don't draw attention to yourself."

"Yes'm. I blend in mighty good."

Anna placed the coin in his palm and the little boy started to run off, then remembering Anna's admonition, slowed to an exaggerated, nonchalant walk. Anna shook her head. If this worked, she would give that little boy a whole handful of coins. Knowing she had no time to spare, she shut the back door and hurried back to her things. Her mind was racing. She did not have time to stop and think. After a moment of poking around, she ascertained all of her belongings were there. The one thing that was not there was money. Not that she had expected to find any, but she had hoped there had been some squirreled away in her jewelry case. No such luck. She would have to search the house. Hopefully her husband hadn't packed up all of his belongings yet, and she would be able to find enough to pay the driver to take her out of Richmond.

By the time she got her trunk closed and relocked, she heard the sound of hooves and wheels from the alley. She looked toward the front of the house. The silhouette of the guard that she could see through the gauzy curtains hadn't moved. A giddiness started to build in Anna's chest. God bless that boy, he was quick. As if her thoughts had summoned him, he came running into the room excited.

"I gots—"

Anna shushed him, and his loud voice instantly cut off as he slapped his hands over his mouth. Anna spoke to him in an exaggerated whisper. "Did you get the carriage I asked for?" The boy nodded his head, hands still over his mouth. "Good! Now have the driver help you carry my things. Do it very quietly."

The boy nodded again, then carefully removing his hands, asked breathlessly, "Then I get my coin?"

"Then you get your coin. Take this," —she handed him a

387

valise— "and get the driver. All of this needs to be loaded."

The boy took the bag from her and ran toward the back door. Anna let a shiver of excitement run through her body. This was going to work! They had left her an opening and she was going to take it. First things first, she needed to get a note to Kady. Anna started toward the parlor to fetch paper and pen, then stopped herself. No. She could write Kady later. Right now, she needed to get out of this house before the additional guards arrived. Glancing back through the window, she saw her soldier was still unmoved. How horrible it would be to be this close to getting away and be stopped by him. Perhaps she should find some sort of weapon to fend him off should he come in. No. She dismissed that immediately. Anna could do many things, but kill a man simply because he was trying to do his job was not one of them. The boy and the driver had returned and between them awkwardly lifted her trunk. Seeing the driver, Anna's mind returned to her immediate concern. She needed money to pay for her escape!

Knowing her husband only ever kept his money in his room, she hiked up her skirts and ran up the stairs. This of course was a mistake, and she had to pause at the top to regain her breath, her corset poking painfully into her torso as she tried to breathe. Once recovered, she hurriedly started opening doors until she found the general's dressing room. As the shade was almost completely drawn, the room was dim. It occurred to her that in the twenty years she had been married to the man, this was the first time she had ever stepped foot into one of his rooms. A heavy, musky smell assaulted her nose, as her eyes adjusted. She could make out a chest of drawers to her left so she began her search there.

She made quick work of pulling open each of the drawers and rifling through the contents. She was only halfway through when she found exactly what she was looking for: a slender black wallet with crisp Union notes inside. The general might bleed Confederate gray, but even he was too practical to invest much stock in the faltering Confederate dollar. Pressing her find to her chest, she offered up a prayer of thanks and let out a little squeal of delight. With this kind of money, she would be able to go wherever she wanted. However, as she turned to leave, the door to the room drifted closed to reveal the general leaning back in a chair, his hands resting in his lap.

"So you intend to steal from me, too?"

Letting out a strangled cry, Anna froze as the wallet slipped out of her hand and landed on the floor with a muted thud.

"It's not enough you used me and ruined my name. You had to sully my daughter with this, too." He did not yell. In fact, he did not even sound angry. Each word he spoke was cold and calculating, sending chills running up Anna's spine.

"Oh, God, no. Andrew, she had nothing to do with this. She is innocent. I will never speak to her again. I will leave. I promise. I am leaving right now; there is a cab waiting downstairs. She will never see me again. She is your little girl, always will be."

"I guess once you start lyin', it becomes impossible to stop. I have been sittin' here debatin' what to do with you, and you come and make my decision easy."

Before Anna could discern a movement, the general raised his arm and discharged the weapon in his hand. The flash from the muzzle illuminated the room allowing Anna a split second to see that he had been crying, before the little iron ball tore its way through her blouse and corset, shattering a rib and coming to its final resting place in her heart. Catching her off guard, the impact of the shot knocked her against the chest of drawers where she crumpled slowly to the ground.

The general got up, walked over to his wife, and picked up his wallet.

"Woman or no, traitors and thieves deserve to be shot."

48
Shared Grief

Kady did not know how long she had been in bed. She had lost count of the trays of food that had come and gone untouched. When Henry had brought her news of her mother's death, she was not surprised. She had known in her heart that she would never see her mother again after that day in the jail. What was mildly surprising was that her father had pulled the trigger and that it seemed natural. She did not doubt or question the story in the least. She realized that she had expected nothing less.

This begged the question, had she always known her father was capable of such an act? Or had this hideous war brought out the evil that was buried deep within him and shown it to be acceptable in the light of day? She dwelt on this for some time.

Her thoughts eventually turned to her two husbands. They were both seemingly good men. If put in the same circumstances as her father, what action would they take? She found it hard to make that determination. After all, she only knew their actions in a time of war, and how can one truly gauge the measure of a man in a world of atrocities? Although maybe that was the best time to take the measure of man. It is easy to be a good man in good times. It is remarkably harder to be a good man in trying times.

Again, her attention returned to her father. Before the war he had always been brusque, quick to anger, and quicker still to resort to violence when a servant aroused that anger. She had never given this a second thought as a child, taught that Negroes were less than human. Her ignorance shamed her now. Child or no, she should have known better. Inherently she had known better. She willfully ignored the niggling chastisement deep within her soul.

Henry had known better. After waking him from a bad dream one night, she had asked him why he had kept calling out to save Nat. He had told her of his childhood playmate, his Negro half-brother, whom he loved. Even now, he treated their servants with dignity and respect. She had never seen a man treat a servant so well. However, she also suspected that he had killed many people, children included, if the whispers she heard were true. How could one reconcile the two faces into the same man?

What of Jacob? Had she fallen in love with the man or the idea of the war hero? She was not sure. She was afraid it was the latter. After all, what did she know of him? He was a Northern soldier who was injured while acting as a messenger, and after healing, he became a courier for spies. That was all. No wonder her mother had been so furious when she wed him. Her mother. The aching pit in her chest ripped open anew and threatened to engulf her once more. Her mother. Kady forced herself to focus on her mother, to counter the grief with memories. The good and the bad. What was the measure of her mother?

Her mother had hated her, of that she was sure. She had felt it every second of every day as a child. Her mother had seen in her every part of the South she hated, especially her husband and his values. The way her father had always doted on her must have been a thorn in her mother's side all those years, because he never had a kind word for Anna. And Kady had done nothing to win her mother's favor, preferring instead to acquiesce to her father's every wish and live in the constant adoration he showered upon her. Guilt swelled in Kady's throat, threatening to choke her. She had loved the wrong person. Her father was a monster, had always been a monster, yet she had been his little girl through and through. Kady had ignored and belittled her mother as much as her father had.

Could she blame her mother for her hatred? Kady had been only a child, but, then again, her mother was human and as prone to being hurt as anyone else. Having that hurt shoved in her face every day had to have taken a toll. As much as she wanted to deny her forgiveness, Kady could not find it in herself to hold a grudge. She understood, now, the pain that was her mother's life. Kady was no longer that child, so who was she not to forgive? Besides, beyond the hatred, beyond the hurt, her mother had, in fact, inexplicably loved her. She had loved her more than life itself. How many years had Kady wasted loving the wrong person?

Kady squeezed the pillow tighter to her chest as a tear slowly started to make its way down her face. How had she not seen from the beginning that the only outcome to Anna's exposure as a spy would be her death? How had she not seen the only way her father could accept that kind of betrayal was with the death of the perpetrator? How had her mother made the decision so easily? She had to have known that death was the only outcome.

The answer flooded her with a wave of sickness. Her mother had known and made the choice anyway. Kady could no longer hold back the sob that had been fighting to be free for so long. Like a death knell, her cry filled the room, and there was a clatter outside her door. The household had become so entrenched in the mournful silence that the noise scared the servants half to death. Mary came bursting into the room and immediately gathered Kady up in her arms and started stroking her hair. Kady clung to the only person who could possibly understand.

"She knew. She knew she was going to die and she did it anyway." Mary paused for a moment, not contradicting or affirming Kady's statement. "She did it to save me. She sacrificed her life to save mine."

"Of course she did, child."

At Mary's words, Kady felt a new wave of grief wash over her. Mary lifted her face so they were looking eye to eye, and held her gaze so intently, so lovingly, that Kady felt a quiet calm slow her breathing.

"Of course she did. You were her only child. Sittin' back and watchin' harm come to those you love is worse than death."

Then it occurred to Kady, she was not the only one mourning the loss of her mother. Mary had lost her, too. One more loss to add to all of the others. Kady had known the only person her mother had for support for so many years was Mary. It was only now that Kady realized Anna was the only support Mary knew. Kady's heart ached anew; this time for Mary. Sitting up, Kady took Mary's hands in hers and paused—seeing for the first time the rough and aged hands of a woman who had been forced into servitude from the day she was born—then slowly looked up to meet her gaze.

"I'm sorry." That was all she could get out. Her eyes said the rest.

Mary started to say something, then stopped, looked down at their hands, and slowly, imperceptibly, her shoulders began to shake.

It took Kady a moment to realize she was crying, because there was no sound.

Mary pulled her hands away and wrapped her arms around herself, trying to console her own grief.

Kady's heart broke at this woman's loneliness and desolation. Crawling out from below the bedclothes, Kady pulled Mary into her chest and held her tighter than she had ever held anyone before.

Slowly Mary allowed herself the comfort of the embrace and slipped her arms around Kady's waist. They clung to each other, crying out their shared loss.

49
Moment of Truth

Henry stalked around the camp, kicking anything larger than a pebble that dared to cross his path. He had been loath to leave Kady behind yet again, so he dragged his feet, postponing his departure for as long as possible. The hard truth of the matter was that he wasn't doing her any good by being there. Kady remained practically catatonic from the time she had heard of her mother's death, until Henry left. At Henry's orders, a doctor came to look at her, and even the doctor said there was nothing to do. There was simply a want of time for grief to run its course. So Henry left explicit orders with the servants and rode back to the swamp. Several times he took back roads to avoid riding straight through a Union deployment, which delayed his arrival even further. Therefore, it was with a great deal of shock that he found the camp deserted.

It was inconceivable that none of his men were back. Henry's first thought leapt to the gold. Maybe someone had found out about it and doubled back to retrieve the rest. However, a quick reconnaissance into the den proved this theory false. Something else must have happened then. His men had been captured, or killed. Henry didn't know if he could stand losing yet another squad of men. Although the more he thought on it, the less likely it seemed. Every man had headed out in a different direction, toward a different part of Lee's lines. The only place to capture all of them in one fell swoop was when they delivered their packages to Lee himself. Henry doubted the probability of Lee arresting or killing men for delivering packages full of gold. Henry let out a particularly vicious kick at a root and winced at the pain that shot through his big toe. Frustrated, he limped over to a log and sat down to massage his foot. No sooner had he gotten his boot off, then he heard a voice behind him.

"Serves you right. What did that tree ever do to you?" Henry practically fell off the log in his haste to spin around and pull his gun on the intruder. Tom's lighthearted chuckle filled Henry first with relief then annoyance. Henry lowered his weapon. Finally, some answers.

"Where the hell have you been?"

Tom dropped his pack and plopped down on the log next to Henry. "I see you saved some of that spit and vinegar for me, too." Henry cut him a glare, and Tom answered his question, "I stuck around to help those boys dig some trenches. It is the damnedest thing I ever saw. A whole network of trenches, as far as the eye can see. I'd wager those boys are handier with a shovel than they are with a musket by now."

"And your goods?"

"Oh, ho! Was I the man of the hour when I showed up with food! It was like I was the King of England come to pay them a visit." Tom chuckled, but it faded into sorrow. "That food was gone by the time I left, though. Every last crumb. So I handed the packets off to General Lee hisself and hightailed it back here."

"And the others? Have you heard anything of them?"

Abruptly Tom stood up and paced away, distancing himself from Henry, as if his news was best delivered from afar. Henry tensed

397

and held still, waiting. Tom paced a bit more, before stopping and looking straight at Henry.

"Now you have to understand, they're not bad men. They saw an opportunity and couldn't pass it up." Tom paused, expecting a reaction from Henry, but got none. "They sold their goods. They're probably halfway home by now."

Henry hung his head and let out a deep sigh.

Tom continued. "They couldn't help themselves. If you know where to go, you can sell a pound of flour for more than $10, and each of them had at least three pounds. Those boys are nothin' but backcountry pie eaters—that's more money than any of 'em could ever hope to make back home."

Henry nodded his head. He still did not look up. "Why didn't you go along with them?"

Tom kicked the dirt sheepishly. "Heck, what do I need that kinda money for? I ain't got no family to send it home to. 'Sides, somebody had to deliver those special packets to General Lee."

At this, Henry looked up, and encouraged, Tom continued, "The boys all caught up with me after we left camp that night and explained their plan. They knew them packets were important, so they gave 'em to me and sent me on my way." Tom kicked at the dirt again. "They gave me their hardtack, too. They know I have friends on that line. Both lines, actually."

Henry watched as Tom toed the dirt for a while. Henry knew he should be furious. He couldn't quite work up the requisite emotions, though. While those men on the line desperately needed food, he understood why his men deserted. It was obvious to everyone willing to admit it: this war was near the end, which meant his men would return to their homes and back to poverty. True, they would have a roof over their heads again instead of camping out, but there would likely be less food. Henry's men were fed; one of the benefits of moving supplies. As long as you stayed judicious about it, no one noticed when you took a small cut for your own men. No, Henry was not mad. It had been apparent to him for some time which side of the war God supported. This was simply one more piece of evidence.

Henry raised weary eyes up to Tom's face. "So, the long and the short of it is that it's you and me now."

Tom stopped and looked up at Henry, shrugging. "I guess so."

Henry chuckled, startling Tom. "You really stuck around to help dig trenches?"

Tom smiled broadly and held his palms out for inspection. "Even have the blisters to prove it!"

Henry admired the roughened skin and shook his head, smiling at Tom's pride. "Let's heat up some dinner and I'll tell you our new mission. We leave at first light tomorrow."

Their mission was simple, or at least it would have been with all of his men. Now that there were only two, Henry had to rethink things. They were supposed to travel through the swamp down to North Carolina. Once in Carolina, they were to pick up supplies and head back up through the swamp to deliver them to Lee's men. There were not a lot of supplies, but every little bit helped. However, with only two men the amount they could carry made the effort almost laughable. Therefore, Henry had decided they would make a detour to his father's plantation, where they would commandeer a small barge in the name of the Confederacy. They could then float the barge up Goose Creek into the Dismal and carry on to their rendezvous. This plan added precious time to their task, but it could not be helped. So Henry and Tom made their way south.

Henry debated how much to tell Tom about his father. On one hand, he preferred not to speak of him at all. On the other, Tom deserved some kind of warning as to what to expect. In the end, Henry simply said they would not be receiving a cordial welcome when they arrived, and Tom had the good sense not to inquire further.

Instead, Tom talked incessantly about anything and everything: the swamp, the weather, the war, the folks he knew back home. Normally this would have annoyed Henry. On this particular day, he was glad for the distraction, and Tom's easy, lighthearted nature was infectious. Before too long, Henry was able to temporarily forget about his troubles back in Richmond and enjoy their ride through the swamp.

When they stopped for a brief lunch, Tom managed to catch a fox and, after cleaning it, promised barbeque for dinner—or as close as they could come with a fox instead of a hog. Thoughts of a barbeque dinner led to a discussion of barbeque, and before they knew it, they were good-naturedly arguing over the finer points of what constituted proper sauce ingredients. Tom, a South Carolinian, insisted that any good sauce needed a generous dollop of mustard. Henry, a North Carolinian, declared the addition of mustard sacrilegious.

Henry was enjoying himself so much, he didn't notice they were about to exit the swamp onto his father's land until the last moment. He reined his horse in and motioned for Tom to do the same. They both

400

fell quiet, their dispute forgotten. Dismounting, Henry handed his reins to Tom and carefully made his way forward, scouting the landscape. He did not expect to see troops, but you could never be too careful. He was correct; there was not a uniform in sight. For that matter, there was not a breathing soul in sight, which struck Henry as peculiar. There should at least be a hand or two out in the fields, yet they were empty.

Henry hurried back to Tom and mounted his horse, the look on his face telling, because Tom gave him a concerned look.

"Somethin' not right?" Tom asked.

Henry nodded his head and spurred his horse forward. As soon as they reached the fields, he gave the mare her head and let her break into a run. The closer they got to the house, the more ill at ease Henry felt. The fields were overgrown and the quiet had begun to feel eerie. As they slowed to ride into the yard, a smell hit them, and both men clamped their hands over their noses and the horses grew agitated. Henry knew this smell and clenched his teeth as they rode around to the back of the yard to find its source. Upon rounding the corner, the drone of flies announced the location of what looked like a man crumpled on the ground. Henry could not tell from the body itself, but from the whip that lay next to the corpse, he surmised the unfortunate fellow was his father's overseer.

Henry got down, and when Tom went to do the same, Henry gestured for him to remain mounted. Henry pointed to a path that went through the trees.

"That path will lead you down to the creek. Go see if there are any barges left."

Tom nodded. "What happened here? Where is everyone?"

"If I had to guess, I would say there was an uprising."

Tom crossed himself and Henry pointed at the path again.

"Follow that path. If there is a barge, get it ready. If not, scavenge around to see if there is anything worth taking. I am going to see if there's anything left inside."

Tom nodded again. "Yes sir." Then added as an afterthought, "Take care."

Henry smiled, "You too."

Henry braced himself before flinging open the back door. He had expected to be greeted with another stench, and was pleased to discover there wasn't one. He made his way carefully through the house. It had been thoroughly ransacked. It was not until he entered the front parlor that he found signs of inhabitants. There, in the middle of the floor, pinned under a fallen grandfather clock was his father. He recognized the clock as the one his father used to hide the few pieces of precious jewelry in the house. The servants were not to be trusted, so the clock had been made to order, with a hidden drawer at the top. A chuckle bubbled up from Henry's chest. The damn fool had been trying to get to the drawer and knocked the clock over. Another laugh broke free. For the life of him, Henry did not know why he was laughing. His father was prone on the floor, yet he couldn't suppress his mirth. Suddenly the body moved, and startled, Henry quieted.

"Who's there? Who's there?"

The strength of the voice shocked Henry; however, upon moving closer he saw someone had left food and water, probably Sally. No one else would have cared enough or dared to enter, as evidenced by the fact that it was the only room still containing valuables.

Unable to turn his head to see who was there, Henry's father barked, "Who is there, goddammit? Don't stand there slack-jawed, get this thing off me."

Henry shook his head in disbelief. Not only was his father not dead, he did not even appear to be overly hurt, just pinned down by a large clock. Henry stifled a laugh at the absurdity of the entire situation and picked his way around the clock so his father could see him. Henry knelt.

"How much do you have to be hated that your own people leave you to die, instead of lifting up a clock?"

Fury screamed across his father's face, distorting his features as he yelled something unintelligible at Henry.

"Sorry, what was that?" Henry smiled, which incensed his father still further.

"Get me out of here, you worthless son of a bitch!"

Henry mumbled under his breath, "Good to see your temperament hasn't been impaired in any way."

Henry stood and surveyed the broken clock, trying to determine the best way to move it. The easiest way would simply be to shove it to the side. That would likely cause his father further damage and agony, so Henry considered that option for a moment. He discounted it due to the fact that the clock itself might still be salvageable. He needed to find a gentler option. A quick look at the base of the clock revealed that it couldn't stand on its own until repairs had been made. Henry settled on wedging his shoulder under one side in order to lift it enough for his father to pull himself free. His father was not a fan of this plan, as it required him to expend effort during his own rescue. In that case, he told the old man, he could stay pinned. Henry settled himself into an armchair with a glass and a bottle of whiskey, until his father relented.

Henry took off his jacket and gun belt, then set to work. It took three tries before Henry's father was freed and Henry was able to lay the clock on its side. The clock's damage appeared superficial, nothing that couldn't be fixed. Henry gave it a gentle pat before turning to his father. His father was pale and sweating profusely from his efforts, and even without the look of pain on his face, Henry knew immediately that he had grossly underestimated his father's injuries. Henry had assumed his father had simply been pinned. In truth, both of his legs were crushed and the right had begun to bleed freely. The weight of the clock had stanched the blood flow up until now. Ironically, it was the clock itself that had kept his father alive.

Scrambling to action, Henry removed everything from his gun belt and used it as a tourniquet. His father screamed in agony as Henry pulled the belt tight. With the blood flow stopped, Henry helped his father to sit up against the arm chair then examined his legs. The left was clearly broken, but there was no bleeding and the skin outside of the bruising looked healthy. The right leg, below where it had been crushed, had turned a sickly blueish black, the sight of which caused bile to rise in Henry's throat. That leg was beyond saving. With any luck, they would be able to amputate at the knee instead of the hip. Henry pulled the pant leg back into place to hide the grisly sight, then handed his father the bottle of whiskey. He took a restorative gulp, sputtered and coughed, then took another swallow. The color had returned to his face and with it his ill humor.

"I bet you're happy now." Henry stared at his father in disbelief.

404

"Seein' me helpless like this. Standin' over me like some goddamned king, high and mighty, decidin' my fate."

"What is there to decide? I need to get you to a surgeon."

"Why bother? I will never make it that far. Let me die." He drank deeply from the bottle, settling further into his resignation. "You've waited years for me to die."

"No, I haven't." Although the words had come out automatically, Henry realized they were true. While Henry despised his father, he did not wish him dead. Especially not like this, helpless, yet ultimately savable. "A surgeon will have to take that leg, possibly both of them, but he can likely save your life."

"My life?" He scoffed. "What life would that be? Limpin' around like a cripple with some colored woman lookin' after me. Or were you plannin' on being my nursemaid? You're certainly soft enough."

Henry fought down his pique, trying not to rise to his father's bait. "If I have to take care of you, yes, I will do it. Trust me when I say that I do not relish the thought."

"At least we agree on that." He took another swig of whiskey.

Henry watched his father nurse the bottle, and for the first time he did not see the strong plantation master whom all feared—not because of his injuries but because of the look in his eyes.

He was afraid. Afraid of losing his legs, afraid of being dependent on someone, but mostly afraid that he had lost control. In a mere moment, the flick of an instant, his rule had ended. Without the threat of violence and the capacity to carry that violence out, he was nothing and everyone knew it. There was no coming back from that, no recovery that would not wound his pride irreparably. Whatever Negroes Henry would be able to convince to come back and work on the plantation, his father would have to be civil to them.

Henry had never known his father to be civil to anyone. To his surprise, Henry felt sorry for him. His father recognized the look and lashed out at Henry, throwing the now empty bottle.

"Don't you pity me, boy! Don't you dare, you are beneath me! Have always been and will always be. Don't you think that this" —he motioned to his legs— "changes anything. You are your mother's son and there is no escapin' her filthy foreign blood."

"No." The word startled even himself.

"What did you say to me?"

"I said, no. My mother was never beneath you."

His father scoffed.

"Scoff all you want. My mother was a loving, brave woman, and I am proud to have her blood. You are a coward. You hid behind your whips and your threats and made everybody fear you. Now that all of that has been taken away, you are nothing but a sniveling waste of a man spitting insults."

"You are the coward! You had to wait until I was laid low and at your mercy before you could summon up the guts to stand up to me. You have never disobeyed an order in your life, too lily-livered to ever think for yourself."

"That is not true! I never obeyed a single order you gave concerning Nat. You were just too dumb to figure it out." His father turned beet red and struggled for words. Henry continued without waiting for a response. "When you forbade me to play with him, we

406

stayed out of sight in the swamp. When he attacked you and I ran after him? I caught him and then I let him go. And when the Confederate Army tasked me to catch him and return him back to his owner, I did as *he* asked and shot him. He preferred death over being returned to you. Out of mercy I killed him."

His father's face melted into indignant outrage. "You had no right! He was my property!"

"He was your son! He was a bastard, but he was yours, and you would have tortured him to death. I loved my brother even if you didn't!"

"He was a slave!"

"He was a better man than you'll ever be!" Furious, Henry snatched his jacket up from the chair and turned to leave.

"Where are you going, boy? Don't you leave me here!"

Henry turned back to him. "I am going to get a stretcher so I can take you to a surgeon. After that you are at God's mercy, because I won't ever be coming back for you."

"You can't abandon me!" Desperation flooded his voice. "Thomas! Get back here! Get back here!"

Henry ignored his calls. Emerging into the sun, Henry slammed the back door shut and stood breathing raggedly, fighting back the tears in his eyes. He had done everything in his power to help his brother. If it hadn't been for that damn snake, maybe he could have done more. The second they stepped foot back on this God-forsaken plantation, Nat's fate was sealed. There was nothing more that Henry could have done. He took in a deep breath, trying to steady himself, but gagged. If it were possible, he thought that the stench had actually gotten worse.

After finding a surgeon, he and Tom would have to return to dig a grave for the overseer; the body had already been left out for too long. That would put them even further behind.

It would be so easy to pretend that they had never been here and leave his father for dead, or show mercy and shoot him before leaving. However, unlike Nat, that would not be mercy, it would be murder, and Henry was done killing. If there was a God in the heavens, Henry would not be forced to take another life for the rest of his days. He didn't care if this sentiment made him weak. Or did it make him weak? Henry realized that those were his father's words in his head. No matter what he did, his father would always see him as weak. In this instance, his father was wrong. Choosing not to kill came from a place of strength, not weakness. It was then he heard Kady's voice in his head, telling him that he was a good man. Henry clung to the memory of her voice and drew strength from her conviction.

The crack of a gunshot ripped Henry from his thoughts. Instinctively he reached down to draw his gun, only it was not there. He panicked for a moment, before remembering he had taken it off so he could use the belt as a tourniquet. Time slowed as the color drained from his face. His gun was in the parlor, next to his father.

50
Paths Crossed

Tom and Henry stayed long enough to bury Henry's father and the overseer. At Tom's insistence, they also took the time to carve their names into rudimentary wooden crosses that they stuck into the ground at the head of each grave. Despite the sentimentality, Henry was glad they had spent the time. He would not have felt right leaving his father's grave unmarked, especially since he already felt guilty over the whole affair. His father had used his gun. Henry knew how defeated his father had been, and yet he left a gun within reach. It was almost as if Henry had dared his father to do it. Henry had outright stated he would be leaving his father to fend for himself. What other choice did he have? A sudden flare of anger surged in Henry. His father could have faced the difficulty and learned to be a better man! The anger faded as quickly as it had risen. No, there was no way his father would have changed. He would have been an awful old man until the end of his days. His father's way of life was ending and he could not face that. That was not Henry's fault. Despite the logic in this, the guilt remained.

By the time Henry and Tom arrived for their rendezvous, they were almost a week late. Henry did not know if it was because of their delay, or if something else had happened, but no one ever showed up with supplies. He and Tom stayed for three days, only venturing into town at the appointed time of the rendezvous in case the men they were to rendezvous with were also running late. By day three, they decided no one was going to come, and as they were tired of sleeping outside in the cold, they rented a room. Over dinner they decided they would try to sell the barge and then buy whatever supplies they could find for Lee's men.

They found this plan was easier said than done. No one was in the market for a barge. Even if someone had been interested in it, no one had extra food to sell. Discouraged, they bought a few provisions for themselves and trudged back into the swamp. With one horse on each bank of the creek, they hooked the barge to the horses and began to head upstream. They had no use for the barge, but it seemed wasteful to leave it behind.

They traveled for some time in silence, until Henry could hear a faint whistle coming from Tom's direction. Smiling, Henry began to whistle along until Tom broke out in full voice singing a rendition of "Yankee Doodle" that Henry had never heard before.

When Tom had warbled out the last note, Henry stopped and applauded. Tom swept his hat off his head and bowed formally again and again—at first only to Henry, then to other imaginary audience members who were clearly clapping louder than Henry had been.

Still laughing, Henry gathered up his mare's reins and encouraged her to walk again.

Tom, promising his audience an encore at his next performance, planted his hat back on his head and caught up to his horse. Out of breath, Tom walked quietly until Henry broke the silence.

"How is it you are always so happy? Through all of this, you keep your spirits up."

Tom shrugged. "I dunno. I guess I get it from my

grandmother."

Henry kept quiet, waiting for the explanation to continue.

"My mama died when I was little, and my daddy run off, so I lived with my Nana. We didn't have much, so there were nights I would go to bed without anythin' for supper. Not because I had been bad, mind you, because there wasn't nothin' to eat. Well my stomach would get to rumblin', and I would get to cryin', and my Nana would come over and ask me, 'Why's you cryin?' I'd tell 'er, 'I'm hungry,' and she'd laugh and tell me that wasn't nothin' to cry over. Then she would tell me stories about monsters and such, and my belly would provide the sounds. Before I knew it, I would be laughin' right alongside her." Tom stopped, his eyes turning inward in contemplation. "Right before she died, I made her a promise. I promised I would only cry if it were impossible to laugh. I reckon in times like these it makes me look a bit of a fool. A promise is a promise though."

Tom looked down sheepishly and Henry smiled. "You don't look like a fool at all."

A light snow had started to fall by late afternoon, and as they technically did not have anywhere to be, they tied the barge to a tree by the shore and built themselves a makeshift shelter on high ground. Henry got a small fire going, then practically trampled it out in his haste to get away when he turned and saw a water moccasin draped over Tom's legs. The snake was dead of course, but Henry did not realize that until he had thoroughly embarrassed himself.

When Tom stopped laughing long enough to catch his breath, he explained that a man back in town paid him to kill it.

"This here guy got confused with the warm weather last week

411

and come outta hibernation. When it got cold again, he found shelter in a dryin' shed and let it be known that he was the new lodger when the previous owner found him. That old coot was so thrilled that I could take care of his problem for him; he not only paid me, he let me keep the carcass too. I didn't say nothin', because I wanted it to be a surprise, and boy am I glad that I waited!"

"Little? That thing is huge!"

Tom fell to laughing again. Henry glowered at him, then rolled up his sleeve as evidence of why he was perfectly justified in being jumpy around that particular kind of snake.

"Hooey, I bet that hurt!" Tom exclaimed.

Henry laughed despite himself. "You could say that. I'm lucky I didn't lose my arm; the damn snake was as big as that one."

"Luck had nothin' to do with it. If you're gonna get bit, you want the bigger ones. The little ones don't know any better and release all of their poison on the first bite. The big ones give ya jeeeest enough to convince you to leave 'em alone."

"It gave me enough for that all right!"

Tom laughed. "Who healed ya? They did a mighty fine job." By now, Tom had skinned the snake and was skewering pieces onto sticks to hold over the fire.

"My old mammy. She always does the healing on the plantation." Henry frowned. "Well, she did at any rate."

Henry realized that he had no idea where Sally was or if she was okay. He had no idea about any of the servants. Henry stared at the fire and listened to the meat sizzle as he tried to convince himself it did not matter. They were not his concern. He turned to say something to Tom and realized Tom was no longer beside him. Henry was about to call out, when the hair on the back of his neck stood on end. They were being watched. Tom had sensed it and slipped away to investigate. Deciding his best course of action was to stay where he was and act natural, Henry settled himself under the canopy and began to turn the sticks, so the meat would not burn. He also slid his pistol out of his bag.

In the next moment, Henry heard a yell and a thump and, whirling around, saw Tom tackling a Negro to the ground. Two more Negroes were running up to help, so Henry stood, aimed his pistol at the men, and pulled back the hammer. At the sound, all of the men froze, including Tom.

"You all right, Tom?"

Tom struggled to his feet, brushing himself off. "Yeah, no thanks to him."

Tom got in one last kick then stalked over to Henry, while the other two Negroes helped their companion to his feet.

Henry gave Tom a once-over to verify he was indeed okay, before addressing the three men.

"What are you doing out here? Are you runaways?"

No one spoke, or moved.

"I am going to take that as a yes. Are you trying to make your way to the camps by the lake?"

The men looked at each other in shock and Henry smiled. Hadn't he recently had this exact same conversation? Henry motioned with his head upstream.

"If you follow the creek you'll get there before daybreak."

Tom interjected, "But, Captain, they was tryin' to steal our

413

barge! You're goin' to let 'em go?"

"Sounds like a better plan than standing like this all night getting snowed on and letting our dinner burn."

Henry directed this last comment to Tom who cursed and dove toward the fire to save their meat. Seeing that it had been salvaged, Henry redirected his attention to the men.

"Now what did you boys want with my barge?" This time Henry waited for an answer.

Eventually one of the men stepped forward; he had a heavy Caribbean accent.

"I am no slave, I am free man. Dese men me brudders, dey free men. But our families no is free. Slavers come and take dem away, so we leave our country to find dem. We find dem, but de big man of de house he make us work for free or he sell off our children. So we work for free, until we can escape. Our children, dey is small, and some of our women, dey is old. We need de barge to move dem."

While Henry contemplated the man's speech, Tom spoke up. "Why shouldn't we arrest you and turn you over to the army?"

Infuriated, one of the brothers stepped forward but was restrained by the first man. "We is free men!" he yelled.

"And you free men were tryin' to steal the property that had been commandeered for the Confederate government!"

Henry reached out a hand to pull Tom back before things could escalate further. "Tom, we are not going to arrest them." He looked at the men. "We are not going to arrest you. Where are your families now?"

Assured his brother had calmed down, the first man turned back to Henry and said, "Dey down de river a bit. Hidden."

Henry uncocked his pistol and lowered it. "Go get them. The creek is too shallow back that way to carry any weight on the barge, so they'll have to board here."

"You're givin' them the barge?" Tom was indignant.

"No, I'm letting them use the barge. We'll take it back when we reach Lake Drummond." Henry turned back to the men. "Hurry, we'll want to travel by night."

"We will hurry." The brothers headed off, with the exception of the first man who looked directly at Henry and said with deliberate enunciation, "Thank you," before following them.

Henry watched them go before returning his attention to Tom, who was now sitting in front of the fire devouring the snake meat. Henry laughed. "You're eating as if that's the last meal you'll ever get."

"Stick around with you long enough and it might be! First, you give away free rides on the barge; next, you will be serving them my food for their dinner. I aim to have it gone before you can!"

Henry laughed and sat next to Tom who handed him a spit that still had meat on it. Not knowing how much time they had, Henry tore into the meat. To his amazement, water moccasin was actually quite good—even the bits that were a little blackened.

True to their word, the men were back in short order with their families in tow. Henry eyed them, skeptical that they would all fit. Apparently, the man in charge had already had the same thought and had selected a few of the older children to walk along the bank with the men. Tom had finished hooking the horses up to the barge on either side of the creek, while Henry had struck their camp. All that remained was to load the people. Henry had rehearsed a little speech about the necessity to stay quiet, but he saw it would not be needed. No one spoke as they helped the women and children aboard. All communication was done through hand signals. As each person settled in their assigned space, it was as if they turned to stone. Had Henry not been counting each person as they embarked, he would have had no idea how many people were on the barge. The combination of their stillness and dark skin made them blend into the night.

Henry and Tom would each lead a horse, while the Negroes on foot would follow twenty to thirty feet behind. If their group encountered soldiers, Henry would state they were transporting property for safekeeping. Normally he would not have worried about this eventuality, however, with both the Army of the Potomac and the Army of Northern Virginia entrenched at Petersburg, as well as the mayhem that Sherman had caused in the South, there was more foot traffic than normal in the swamp. Most soldiers they had encountered were lost, so Henry was hopeful that if he provided directions, any soldier would be thankful and let them pass unmolested.

Despite the dark, they were able to make good time and did not meet any obstacles until they were nearly to the lake. Several trees had fallen across the waterway. Henry could not tell if they had been felled on purpose to create a bridge, or if nature had simply run its course. Either way it was impossible for them to continue with the barge. As they were already so close to Lake Drummond, Henry announced that they would walk the rest of the way. The Negroes disembarked as quietly as they had boarded; not even the children sleeping in their mothers' arms stirred.

Once he had them all gathered, Henry instructed Tom to stay with the horses, then addressed the group. "Stay here while I scout up ahead."

With everyone hidden, Henry ventured up onto the path to make sure the coast was clear. By now, he had traveled this route over half a dozen times and it had begun to feel like second nature. All was clear here. Henry continued up the path until he could see around the bend. It was clear, so he trotted back to the group.

"All right, follow me and be quick about it. We're going to be exposed, but it can't be helped."

The men scampered up onto the road first and then helped the women and children up the bank. They were all able-bodied and moved relatively quickly, even the adults who were carrying children. One exception was a young boy who was clearly tired and having a hard time keeping up. Henry motioned to one of the men who scooped the boy up and handed him to Henry, who swung the child up onto his back and started down the road.

Despite his reassurances that the road was clear, the group continued their silent vigil. They continued for some time before coming to a hill. As they approached the top, Henry set the boy down and made a hand gesture for them to hang back. He would crest first and appear to be alone. There was still no one in sight. What could be seen was the lake, barely visible in the breaking dawn. With a hurried gesture, Henry signaled the all clear, then scooped up the boy and began to trot down the hill. The Negroes hurried after, the sight of the lake bolstering their spirits.

As they wended their way ever closer, the group began to relax but still did not speak.

Henry told them he would have them at the lake in less than ten minutes. Where they would go from there, Henry did not know. Nor did he care to. He had done his job and gotten them safely through the swamp.

Henry found it eerie how steadfastly quiet the Negroes kept. He was accustomed to the idle chatter of his men. He could not blame them for their silence, though. If he were on the verge of a brand new life of freedom, and that dream could be ripped from his grasp at any second, he would probably do his best to blend into the background as much as possible, too. This silence left their approach unannounced. They rounded a blind corner and found themselves less than fifty feet from a Union soldier who was busily rearranging crates in the back of an open supply wagon.

Henry tried to get his group to reverse their direction, hoping they could disappear before the man noticed. But it was too late. In a moment, both Henry and the officer had guns drawn and leveled at each other.

It was only when the man painstakingly made his way out of the wagon that Henry realized this was the same man who had killed his men. It was old One Leg, and this time Henry was armed and had a clear shot. He would have taken it, too, if it weren't for the little boy on his back who tightened his arms and buried his face in Henry's neck. If Henry fired, One Leg would fire and the boy might wind up dead. True, this man deserved to die and Henry owed that death to his men, but not here. Not in front of this boy and so many others whose lives would be put at risk by his actions.

With great effort, Henry relaxed his trigger finger but kept his aim true. He did not trust this man. A flash of recognition had lit the man's eyes when he saw Henry, yet Henry still had no clue how this man knew him. Thus, as the one-legged man held the upper hand, Henry held his tongue and his position in front of the slaves, waiting for the Union officer to speak first. After what seemed an eternity, the officer gave a smirk and spoke.

"Well now, Captain Henry," the man said, placing emphasis on the name. "You seem to be going the wrong way. Don't you Southern gents generally round up the slaves and take them back to their rightful owners instead of leading them further into the swamp?"

Henry did not speak, and after a moment the officer continued, "In fact, I do believe there are generally some pretty handsome rewards for doing that. Maybe I should take a couple of them off your hands and take them back myself."

One of the women gasped and Henry narrowed his eyes, simultaneously cocking his gun. "And I thought you Northern gents had plenty of supplies without having to steal them."

"Oh ho! Stealing, you say. Oh no, these supplies are mine. I am simply hauling them to sell elsewhere. You would be amazed at how much you Southerners will pay for a pound of salt beef these days."

Before he could stop himself, Henry shook his head in disgust. This man was stealing supplies from his own army to sell to his enemy.

"Oh, you disapprove do you? The great and mighty Captain Henry disapproves. You better shake your head harder, 'cause I've had

419

this business running for quite some time now."

Frustrated, Henry took a deep breath through his nose to calm himself. Who was this man? Henry looked him up and down once more and stared at him hard in the face. He could not place him.

"I'm afraid you have me at a disadvantage. You seem to know me, but I don't know you," Henry confessed.

"Of course you don't, we have never met. I know all about you, though. We have, let us say, a mutual acquaintance."

Henry's mind raced as he tried to think of someone he knew that would also know a one-legged Union officer. Then his thoughts snapped into focus and it was clear. Anna.

"I find it interesting this acquaintance mentioned me to you, but not the other way around," Henry prodded.

The officer gave a laugh, as if this were some sort of joke. "Interesting, but not surprising."

Yes, Anna was the connection. Not that this knowledge helped him in his predicament, but it did put his mind at ease some. Henry did not let on he had figured this out, though.

"As you say."

"I do say."

They both stared at each other until Henry broke the silence.

"It seems to me we have reached an impasse. I don't want to shoot you in front of the boy. Even if you are able to kill me with your first shot, the Negroes will overtake you to ensure their freedom."

The officer cocked an eyebrow, then addressed the Negroes, "I promise you that if this man falls, I will let you go on your way, so long as you let me go on mine."

Henry shifted uneasily. "You really think they will believe that promise?"

"I'm willing to take the chance."

The man fired. Henry staggered back a step or two, then remembering the boy on his back, propelled himself forward and fell into the dirt. There were more shots and he could hear chaos around him. People running and screaming. Someone yanked the boy off his back. He thought he heard laughter, but the sounds around him were distorted. Who was laughing? Henry tried to push himself upright. He only succeeded in moving forward a couple of inches. He felt the ground beneath him growing damp as his blood soaked into the dirt. The warmth was oddly comforting, like climbing into a warm bed and drifting off to sleep.

51
Forced Goodbye

Kady and Mary had been left on their own to grieve Anna's death. A servant would bring food, but after several trays returned to the kitchen with spoiled food from sitting out all day, a change occurred. Things like cheese, cured meats and bread replaced the prepared meals. These also remained largely untouched.

By the time Kady had felt up to dressing and descending the stairs into the main part of the house, she discovered there was a secondary reason for the change. Richmond was in an uproar. With the Union Army closing in, the government was packing up to head south, as were any residents who had the means to do so. Whatever food could be found was packed and loaded on trains for the troops. Not even servants with ready money, prepared to pay exorbitant prices, could procure the necessities to lay a proper table.

Kady was stunned. She had not been holed up in her room for that long, so how had so much changed? She asked the servants if they had any word from Henry. They had not. She asked if there were any letters or correspondence. There were not. Kady ran back upstairs to tell Mary to go check all of their usual drops. Kady was not expecting her to find anything. After Anna had been arrested their entire spy ring had severed contact with the Roses, but Kady wanted to be sure. She then ransacked her jewelry case, pulling out anything of value and tucking those pieces into a wooden box that she wrapped in a shawl.

Returning downstairs, she grabbed two kitchen girls, handed them her wrapped box, and instructed them to bury it along with the good silver and the candlesticks in the backyard under the bushes. She might be a spy for the Union, but this was the house of a Confederate officer. She was not so naive that she thought she would be spared the looting that was sure to take place when the Federal troops started to roll through. The servants scurried away to accomplish their task. Kady set about the house trying to determine what else needed to be buried or hidden. For the most part, the house contained the possessions of the previous occupants, so they held monetary value not sentimental value. She would save the pieces she liked and not worry about the rest.

Kady grabbed a few more things to be hidden, when she came upon her piano. She could feel the grief rise up in her chest and tried to temper it. It was silly. There was no way common looters would try to run off with a piano. However, they might damage it out of spite. The thought of something happening to her beautiful instrument broke her heart. It was her first gift from Henry, and a gift so thoughtful that she had known Henry truly loved her. Moreover, her mother had played this piano. The look on Anna's face when Kady had walked into the room would forever be clear in Kady's mind. She was like a child caught with her hand in the cookie jar, followed by the indignation of having felt guilt when one had not done anything wrong. Kady smiled at the memory.

There was no way she could move the piano. Maybe covering it up would help. Rushing from the room to grab a sheet, Kady ran directly into someone in the hall. From the bulk, she knew she had run into a man and immediately hoped to see Henry. Henry would be able to move the piano, or at the least protect it! Her hopes vanished when she looked up to see her father. The color drained from her face and her emotions began to fight a pitched battle. She did not know if she wanted to cry, scream, run away, or disappear on the spot. Instead, she reached back and slapped him across the face as hard as she could. Tears started to flow down her cheeks, as he stared at her in disbelief. When he did not say anything, she slapped him again, then balled up her fists and struck out at his body screaming at him in a blind rage.

Regaining his wits, Andrew caught her hands to stop the blows and wrangled her into the parlor where he deposited her roughly into a chair. The commotion had attracted the attention of the servants who came running, but stopped short when they saw Andrew. He growled at them to go away. They did, without a glance at Kady who was ineffectually trying to wipe the tears from her eyes. Andrew turned his attention back to his daughter, and pulling a handkerchief from his coat, growled at her, too.

"Pull yourself together, you look hideous."

Shock from her father's words stopped her crying short. She had heard him say harsh things to her mother all the time. This was the first time he had directed any of them at her. She wiped her face and looking up at her scowling father, she saw him as her mother had always seen him, as the servants had always seen him. He was ugly and mean. She wanted to say something, but confronted with this new visage of the man she had adored her entire life, she found herself speechless.

He, however, was not.

"That's better. Get your things together; we are leavin'."

"We're what?"

"We're leavin'. Get your things and don't make me say it again."

Kady cringed and realized he had not even raised his hand.

"You thought I was going to hit you? Well maybe I should. It might get you movin'."

Before Kady could respond, Andrew grabbed her and hauled her out of the chair. With his fingers digging into her upper arm, he escorted her across the room. They were almost to the door before Kady was able to rip her arm free from his grasp.

"No! Why would I go with you?"

"You are my responsibility, and I will take you to safety."

He reached for Kady's arm again. She stepped back, pulling her arm away.

"I am the responsibility of my husband."

"And he is nowhere to be found. Now go get your things."

"No."

"No?"

"No. I'm staying here."

"Don't be rash—"

"I am not being rash, and I am not going anywhere with you. I don't want anything to do with you." She could see the color rising in her father's face and guessed what would come next. "I don't care what you say; I don't even care if you hit me, like you always did Mama. You are a horrible, horrible man. You killed my mother!"

"Is that what this outburst is for? Your mother? I protected you, girl. I've protected you in ways you don't even know about and this is the thanks I get?"

"I don't need your protection!"

425

"The hell you don't! You would be in jail thrice over if it were not for me. That woman and her Negro coerced you into helping them. I had to protect you. I saved you from them before it was too late."

Before she could stop herself, Kady laughed in her father's face. Did he truly believe what he was saying? Had she been able to pull off the naive coquette so thoroughly he believed her to be completely innocent? Or was he simply deluding himself? From the look of desperation in his eyes, she decided on the latter. He wanted her to be innocent so badly, he had convinced himself a lie was the truth. With one word, she could either confirm his beliefs or bring his entire world crashing down. A cold resolve filled Kady's voice.

"Mama didn't coerce me into doing anything. On the contrary, I begged to join her."

"No, don't say that."

"Oh yes, she tried to talk me out of it. Tried to convince me to return to my simple life of being your little pet." She practically spat the last words out at him. "But I knew what I wanted, and didn't you always teach me that I got to have whatever I wanted?"

"Don't you turn this back on me! This is the doing of that duplicitous woman."

"Maybe she would not have needed to be duplicitous if you had shown her an ounce of kindness. If you had let *me* show her kindness. She was miserable and it was all your fault! You used me to make her wretched! You used her own child against her, and you never thought I would realize what you were doing, that I would never see that you are truly craven."

"You shut your mouth, girl. I saved your life!"

426

"She did that! Mama saved my life, not you!"

"Don't be ridiculous; it was her spyin' that put you in danger." He was desperately clinging to his delusion. Kady was through being gentle.

"I am a spy for the Union Army and if I am in danger, I put myself there. I do not want your protection or anything to do with you. Either get out of my house or turn me into the authorities." With that, Kady saw the look of desperation in her father's eyes turn into pure hatred. He slapped her across the face before she even saw it coming.

"You ungrateful bitch. With that woman for a mother, I knew this day would come. Bad stock always shows through in the end."

Despite the red-hot pain across her cheek, Kady did not touch or acknowledge the blow. She would not give him the satisfaction.

"My mother deserved better than you."

"Your mother deserved exactly what she got." Reaching to the small of his back, Bell pulled a pistol and pointed it at his daughter; a manic look flashing across his eyes. "Traitors and thieves deserve to be shot."

Kady took a step back, trying to keep her composure, while raising her hands defensively in front of her. "Are you going to shoot me, like you did her? Carry out the justice you think I deserve?"

"I should"—his resolve seemed to falter—"and that damn Negro."

"Then do it and get it over with."

A look of shock crossed Andrew's face, and the gun wavered in his hand. Kady took full advantage and brushed the gun aside before shoving him back a step.

427

"I said do it! You killed your wife, now kill your daughter. Show everyone what kind of man you are." She shoved him again.

"I will turn you into the authorities! Let them deal with you!"

Sensing she had won, Kady began to shove her father toward the door in earnest.

"Get out of my house!" Kady made some headway with her shoving and eventually her father turned to leave of his own accord. However, still incensed, Kady kept pushing him from behind. He spun, grabbing her arms and pulling her into him, an impotent rage reddening his face.

"You will regret this. You will regret all of this." He tried to say more but could not find the words.

He flung her to the floor and pulled the gun once more. Kady stared him down refusing to give any ground despite her weakened position. He cocked his pistol, and Kady clenched her jaw, keeping her gaze steady. He could not bring himself to pull the trigger, and slowly his hand started to shake. At first only slightly, then more forcefully as if he was fighting against the weapon itself. Then without warning, he deflated, his arm dropping to his side. His rage was completely washed away and replaced with a profound pain. He made a motion as if he was going to say something or move toward her, then thinking better of it, he turned and walked silently out the door.

When Mary returned empty-handed, she found Kady picking herself up from the floor in the front hall, having missed the general by only a few minutes. Mary rushed to help Kady.

"Miss Kady! Are you all right? What in heaven's name happened?"

"I'm fine." Kady was clearly rattled. She realized Mary was still looking at her anxiously. "It's nothing. Daddy was here."

This was explanation enough for Mary. She set about helping Kady to her feet and brushing off her dress, while muttering to herself. "You would think killin' your mother would be enough. Oh no! He has to come back to interfere some more. I swear on your mama's grave, if I ever see that man ag'in I'll spit on 'em. I don't care if'n he sends me to my grave for doin' it."

Kady grabbed Mary's hand, stopping her. If the general came back, it would be to kill Mary, and probably her daughter, too, if he remembered that she had one. She did not think he would return, but if he did, he would have no qualms about shooting them.

Kady was not willing to take that risk. "No, you can't ever see him again! He will kill you."

"I don't care if'n he do." Mary started to turn away from Kady, obviously not aware of the seriousness of the situation. Kady grabbed her.

"I care! He took my mother away. He's not going to take you or your daughter away, too!"

Mary turned and stroked Kady's cheek gently. "All right then. We will keep out of sight should he come 'round ag'in. For you."

"No, that's not good enough. He is vindictive and he is looking for retribution. We need to get you and your daughter out of Richmond. Out of the South completely."

March 29, 1865
Conductor needed for precious cargo.
Stockholder at the Rose Garden with
greenbacks.
LR

25-55-41-16-46 33-53 65-66-32-22
16-15-45-54-63-16-42-15-41 45-21-21-54-21-54
12-15-41 11-41-21-16-52-15-63-34
16-55-41-24-15
34-42-15-16-31-46-15-51-54-21-41 55-42
42-46-21 41-15-34-21
24-55-41-54-21-45 64-52-42-46
24-41-21-21-45-43-55-16-31-34
51-41

52
Missing in Action

It had taken the better part of the day before Kady finally found someone who was willing to take Mary and her daughter via the underground to the North. They couldn't afford passage for all three of them, so Kady stayed behind. The man had required ten times the usual rate for expenses. He said he would get them across the Potomac to Port Tobacco, then they would be on their own. It was not ideal. Kady believed that with the money she had given Mary—everything left of Anna's savings—they should be able to make their way north. Kady kept repeating this to reassure herself everything would work out. She could not afford to think otherwise if she wanted to keep functioning. As it was, she might never see them again, and that pain was bad enough without the thought of them dying. No. That was not going to happen. They were on their way, and all would be well.

In the meantime, Kady had her own problems. She was now positive that her father would return to look for Mary. Kady was not sure how he would react when he discovered Mary had fled. She did not think he was capable of truly hurting her, his beloved daughter, but she also had not thought he was capable of pulling a gun on her. She had been wrong about that. Short of running away herself, the easiest solution was for her to be with Henry.

Earlier in the year, Henry had been reassigned to Commissary General St. John—something about scavengers sticking together.

Apparently, it was a joke the men passed around; Kady did not find it to be particularly funny. She did, however, appreciate that St. John was stationed in Richmond, and therefore she would be able to ask him the whereabouts of her husband.

The commissary general's office was in even greater disarray than the rest of Richmond. They were in the midst of sending out a huge shipment of rations, while also packing up all of their records for the evacuation. Kady spoke to several soldiers, all of whom informed her she would not be able to see the general. Each time she demanded to speak with somebody higher ranking, and each time she was told to wait. Then, when the higher-ranking official would come forward, they sold her the same company line.

The next man to come out was a small wisp of a man, and Kady figured she could probably bowl him over with her skirts alone. The only reason she did not was because the men studiously working behind him would surely stop her if she broke through his line of defense. Therefore, Kady decided to fall back on the trick that had worked her entire life. As the man quietly explained to her why she could not see the general, Kady started to work herself up, until she was in such a state of hysterics the men were scrambling about for something, anything, to calm her. Eventually, hollering over her crying, the wispy man called for somebody to fetch the general.

Kady had to remind herself not to smile, and to slowly ratchet down her theatrics. By the time St. John finally appeared, Kady had calmed herself to the odd gasp and a sniffle. The wispy man explained the circumstances as the general rubbed the back of his neck. Taking her arm, he drew Kady away from the men toward the front door. This startled her, as he was obviously leading her out. She had not come this far only to be escorted out by the man she had come to see. He sensed her unease.

"Never fear, Mrs. Henry. I'm goin' to tell you everythin' I can. However, as I am tryin' to get 80,000 rations mobilized for Danville along with our evacuation, I hope you can appreciate I am a busy man. However, I have an errand down the street, and I see no reason why you can't accompany me."

Kady sighed in relief. "Thank you so much, sir, and I am sorry to have intruded today. I didn't know where else to go."

"That is understandable, ma'am. Now how can I help you?" He extended his elbow to her and she took it as they began to stroll. Kady figured this was probably the first time he had slowed down all day, because it took him some effort to keep his pace relaxed.

"I am trying to find my husband. I haven't heard from him in some time. With all of the commotion in Richmond, I'm worried about what I should do."

He patted her hand. They had apparently reached his destination, because he stopped in front of a door and turned to Kady.

"I am sorry to say, ma'am, that I have no news of your husband. I had expected to hear back from him by now, so he appears to be missin'." He put up a hand to forestall any questions. "That being said, I don't think you should worry. With things the way they are, communication has been ragged at best, and he is likely lyin' low in the swamp until the enemy passes. As for you, I suggest you return to your house. Barricade the door and set your biggest houseboy on watch if it will make you feel better. As long as you are well away from the munitions yards, you should be fine."

Kady started to speak, but he held up his hand to stop her once more. "I am sorry I don't have better news. I must be goin' now. Be well, Mrs. Henry."

"Thank you, sir."

Kady made a shallow curtsy, and the general returned it with a bow before turning on his heel and entering the door in front of them. As soon as the door closed behind him, Kady turned and hurried off. She had not found out what she wanted to know about Henry, but she had found out something even better. There were 80,000 rations on their way to Danville.

53
Credit Where Credit's Due

Jacob cursed his luck. He had managed to shoot Captain Henry and distract the Negroes long enough to get out of the swamp unscathed, only to run into Union troops on his way to Richmond. Of all the roads to be traveling on, that damned officer and his men had to be on the same one he'd chosen. Then they had to stick their noses in his business. Apparently, a man, not in uniform, with a cart full of army supplies looked suspicious. Jacob had already sold a few things obtained from the swamp, but the real money was in Richmond. However, unless he could get free of these imbeciles, there was no chance he would ever make it there. He had considered ambushing the soldiers. With this lot of ninnies it would have been easy. However, the officer accusing Jacob of being a smuggler had disarmed him personally. The officer had even gone so far as to confiscate his horse whip.

Jacob's other option was to bribe one of the men. He could talk the color out of a Negro's skin if he set his mind to it, but again the officer thwarted him. All of the men had been ordered to march outside of casual earshot of Jacob. He had to raise his voice to speak with any of them, and that was no way to form alliances. Besides, unlike their counterparts, these Union boys had been fed recently.

He had at least been able to improve his prospects. Instead of being taken to the nearest provost marshal and handed over, Jacob had been able to convince the officer that he was on a special mission to capture goods from a rebel courier and deliver them personally to Lieutenant General Grant. The officer had been skeptical, but not having any evidence to contradict Jacob's claim, and afraid to defy an order from Grant, the officer offered to serve as escort. The supplies were valuable, after all. Jacob was proud of this little bit of trickery.

What Jacob needed was a plausible explanation for the cash hidden in his knapsack. There was no way he could explain it away; he would be arrested on the spot. There was no way he could explain that away. Only a profiteer would have that kind of cash. Therein lay the problem: what was a plausible story? The truth was out of the question. Then it struck him—the truth was actually perfect. Well, at least, a variation on the truth. He would say he confiscated the supplies in the swamp. His wife, a Southerner who was a Union spy, had sent him in after them. No, better yet, he had gone in because he did not trust anybody else to carry out the task correctly.

He was a genius. This was not only plausible, it would stand up to scrutiny. If anybody questioned his story, he would drop names. He would tell them the Roses were informants of his. Surely, they had heard of the death of the Northern Rose. Claiming he held the allegiance of the Northern and Little Rose would give him instant credibility. All questioning of his story would cease and they would thank him for a job well done. Yes!

No. Shouting out he was a spy to the first person who started questioning him would ruin his credibility. He had to speak to Grant and no one else. Surely, no one else could be trusted with his vital information. True, he did not have any vital information exactly, but he would be able to make something up that sounded good. Jacob smirked.

Much to the chagrin of Grant's staff, Jacob refused to speak with them. Not even Rawlins, the chief of staff, could persuade him to talk. He remained steadfast that what he had to say was for Grant only. After all, you never knew who had a cousin on the other side. This implication rankled Rawlins who wanted to arrest Jacob on the spot. Then Grant himself arrived. Jacob remained stoic while Rawlins explained the cart full of supplies and Jacob's refusal to speak with anyone. Grant chewed on the end of his cigar for a spell, then grunted his assent for a private meeting before brushing past Jacob and entering the cabin he had turned into his headquarters. Rawlins gave Jacob a long cold glare before he grudgingly stepped aside to allow Jacob to follow.

Once inside, Jacob found Grant standing by a table covered with maps. He was pulling at the neck of his shirt and motioned with his other hand for Jacob to sit down. Jacob did so, gratefully, and leaned his crutch against the table. Grant scrutinized him before speaking.

"You have exactly ten seconds to explain yourself before I have you clapped in irons and arrested as a smuggler."

Unfazed, Jacob looked around at the other soldiers in the room and gave Grant an expectant look. Grant bristled, but acquiesced.

"Gentlemen, if you please."

The men looked at Jacob suspiciously, but left without comment. Once the door had closed behind them Jacob leaned in closer to Grant and spoke. "You have heard of the Northern Rose, yes?"

A flicker of recognition flashed in Grant's eyes.

"I thought so," Jacob continued. "Which, of course, means you have also heard of Little Rose, who happens to be my wife."

437

No reaction.

"I received intelligence the rebs were moving supplies through the Dismal Swamp to Lee's men, so I went in to confiscate them."

Grant looked at him for several minutes, his face stony, before replying, "You expect me to believe you are not a smuggler, but instead a part of one of the biggest spy rings in Virginia? Moreover, that you single-handedly took out a rebel supply shipment. Do I look stupid to you?"

Jacob smiled; his gamble had worked. "Of course not, sir. What I said is the God's honest truth. How else would I know the Northern Rose was the codename for Anna Bell who was arrested and later killed by her husband for being a spy? And Little Rose is the codename for Kady Hart, better known by her Confederate name, Kady Henry."

"Go on."

"Both of the Roses are my informants, and upon hearing that Captain Thomas Henry would be personally escorting that wagon of supplies through the Dismal Swamp, well, let's say I couldn't help myself. I had to go in."

"And where is Captain Henry now?"

"As I shot him, I would wager he is some swamp creature's supper by now. Of course, I didn't shoot him until I had learned all about Lee's plans." Jacob grinned hugely; he had just come up with that last bit.

Grant stood, walked to the door, and summoned Rawlins. "Get me Meade, immediately," he said when Rawlins entered.

"Yes, sir."

Grant crossed over to his desk and rummaged around until he

438

came up with a box of cigars. He offered one to Jacob.

"Don't mind if I do. Thank you," Jacob obliged.

Grant snubbed out the cigar he had been chewing on and lit himself a fresh one before leaning against the table. He turned his attention once more to Jacob.

"Once my general gets here, you are going to tell us everything you know about the activities in Richmond and of Lee. I believe you might prove to be useful."

"Yes, sir. That's what I came here for, sir." Jacob drew on his cigar encouraging it to light. He had better come up with something to tell them about the activities in Richmond that sounded believable that they would not be able to disprove until he was long gone. This was going to be fun.

54
Revelations

Things had not gone the way Kady wanted. After the difficulty of getting Mary and her daughter out of Richmond, she knew it would be hard to find a messenger. She, however, had not counted on it being impossible. All of her regular contacts had disappeared without a trace, and her information needed to be passed on immediately. There was no way she could risk leaving a note somewhere. The odds of it being checked in a timely manner was low. Therefore, after a sleepless night, Kady struck out on the road herself. Thankfully, Henry had been able to keep the army from commandeering their mare because she was technically already in the employ of the army. If Henry had to ride hard from the swamp to Richmond and return immediately, he had to have a horse in reserve. Thus, he always had one waiting for him at a nearby stable.

So when a note from the Henry house arrived at the stable, the horse was made ready. Kady had expected questions when it was she who arrived. There were none. They simply changed out the saddle for a sidesaddle and asked if she wanted to take the saddlebags as well—apparently Henry had packed provisions for her and the mare in the event that she would ever have to leave Richmond on short notice.

The forethought and care Henry had shown in these arrangements caused her no little amount of guilt, but she could not let herself dwell on Henry. She was a Union spy. This was her job. Henry was fine; he had to be. Men went missing all the time; it did not mean anything bad had happened to them. He was fine.

Kady accepted the supplies and headed out of Richmond. She had the servants back at the house packing her things and loading them into the coach, so that as soon as she returned, she would be able to leave again immediately. All she had to do was find the Union Army, deliver her message and ride back to Richmond—without getting caught or killed.

The most imminent threat of death was falling off her horse and breaking her neck. She knew how to ride, but she could not remember the last time she actually had. By the time she was out of the city and heading into the countryside, she had lost feeling in her fingers from squeezing the reins so tightly. She tried to loosen her grip. Recognizing this was a futile exercise, she gave up and continued with numb hands.

She had a general idea of where the Union Army was—somewhere south of Richmond yet north of Petersburg. She had no illusions she would find them easily and was praying she would run into a Union soldier and be able to convince him to take her to an officer in charge. It was a long shot and she knew it. If she ran into a Confederate soldier first, she had a story. Her husband was missing and no one was looking for him, so she had come out to look for him herself. She figured she would start crying and make herself seem to be more trouble than she was worth. They would hopefully let her continue on her way. If they insisted on accompanying her, or on taking her to their camp, she would spur her horse, ride hard, and hope she looked hysterical instead of suspicious. However, that would only work if the soldiers were on foot. If they were mounted, she would probably have to go with them. She hoped it would not come to that.

The evening was coming on fast and with it a chilly spring breeze. Kady still had not encountered any soldiers. She was tired, sore, and so despondent she was considering turning herself in as a spy to the first soldier she met if it meant getting off her horse and stretching her stiff body.

That's when she saw the soldiers ahead on the side of the road. There were only a handful of them and they did not have tents. They did have a fire going and bedrolls laid out. Kady encouraged her horse into a trot, eager to reach them faster. As she came even with them, they all stopped talking and eyed her suspiciously. None of them blatantly reached for their weapons, yet Kady saw that they all had them near to hand. Oddly, they had a fire burning, yet they were not preparing any food. The men saw where she was looking and one of them spoke.

"If you are hopin' for some supper, you're out of luck. We haven't had rations in weeks."

It was only after he had mentioned their lack of food that Kady noticed how gaunt all of their faces looked. What clothes they had hung loosely off their frames, and the man who had spoken had rags wrapped around his feet instead of shoes. She couldn't find any insignias that would identify to which army they belonged. From their condition, she was almost positive they were rebels, but not rebels that would pose her any sort of threat if she played her cards right.

"No, I'm not looking for supper. Simply a place to lie down to keep warm and safe for the night. If you gentlemen"—a few of them chuckled at this address, but Kady ignored them—"can provide that, I am willing to provide supper."

This offer more than got their attention and the men sprang to life with newfound energy. The man who had spoken approached her horse with a formal air.

"I do believe that is a satisfactory arrangement. Allow me to help you down, ma'am."

Kady smiled. "I would be most grateful."

The man caught her as she slid off her horse and then he steadied her for a moment until she found her legs under her.

"You don't normally ride, do you?"

"No. Hardly ever, in fact. I didn't know a body could be this sore." Kady stretched and immediately felt self-conscious. She was wearing a riding dress, which of course did not include hoops or a bustle and therefore revealed much more of her figure than she was accustomed to showing in public, especially on a deserted road in the presence of five men whom she did not know. It crossed her mind that if these men decided to steal her horse and belongings there was nothing she could do. She had grabbed a knife from the kitchen before leaving, but the thought of brandishing it in front of five soldiers was laughable. She took a steadying breath and sent up a quick prayer that these were the good Southern boys she assumed them to be, and that they would protect her instead of bringing her harm.

Her prayer sent heavenward, Kady turned to the business at hand and unbuckled a saddlebag. With that firmly in her possession, she turned to the men. She considered giving them a false name but decided there was no harm in revealing her real name. She turned to the man next to her and held out her hand.

"My name is Kady Henry."

The man took her hand and kissed her knuckles gently. "Pleased to meet you, ma'am. My name is George, and this here is Orville, John, Jedidiah, and Samuel." He pointed each man out as he said his name, then turned back to Kady. "I believe you said somethin' about supper?"

Kady smiled, opened her bag, and started to rummage around. "I did indeed. I have some cornmeal, salt pork, beans, and. ..." Disbelief stopped her words. She didn't know where Henry had procured it, or why he had left it for her, but she finished, with a huge grin, "And some coffee." At her mention of the coffee one of the men actually moaned in pleasure. "I do believe there is a decent supper in here."

George smiled hugely and took the bag from Kady's outstretched hands. "Decent? That's the best meal we've had in months!"

The men whooped in delight and their giddiness made Kady laugh. Orville sidled up to Kady and offered her his arm to escort her to the fire, while John took care of her horse, and the rest began preparing the food. Orville leaned in conspiratorially. "Now, that is real coffee you have in that bag, right? Not the swill they've been pawnin' off on us."

"It is real coffee, as far as I know," Kady replied.

Orville whooped again and did a little dance. Then he dropped her arm and grabbing the blanket that John had unbuckled from her horse, he smoothed it out for her in front of the fire. "My lady, the best seat in the house." He dropped into a low bow.

"I thank you, sir."

Kady sat down and arranged her skirts, smiling, caught up in the men's merriment. Orville stood from his bow and went over to see what he could do to help with the preparations, although the other men had it well in hand. Coffee was brewing, beans and pork were heating, and the first corn dodgers were being rolled. The new atmosphere in their little camp could not have been more different from when she had first ridden up. Once the food was ready, George, the self-proclaimed chief cook and bottle washer, divided it out into six even portions. However, Kady insisted she was not overly hungry, so he redistributed some of her portion. In truth, she was ravenous, but these men were literally starving. They needed as much food as they could get.

They presented Kady with her meal first, then fell into silence as each man became absorbed in his supper. Orville started with his coffee, a look of pure ecstasy at the taste. Kady could tell the men were trying their hardest not to inhale every last morsel. They were forcing themselves to eat slowly in order to stretch the meal out, to savor every bite as their hollow stomachs filled. When the meal was over, they all sat in a happy, companionable quiet, accentuated by the occasional burp, followed by chastisements and apologies. Kady assured them that she was not offended in the least and was glad they had enjoyed their meal.

Eventually she got them to talk about their unit. Specifically, why it had been so long since they had eaten. Apparently, the entire Army of Northern Virginia was starving. Although it was never stated outright, Kady got the distinct impression that these men were deserters. She did not ask though, and they did not ask why she, an obvious lady, was traveling across the war-torn countryside on her own. It was almost as if there had been an unspoken agreement that there would be no direct inquiries. Kady decided to tell them why she was out traveling anyway, or at least tell them the lie she had come up with to get the information she needed. She told them her husband was missing, and she had heard a rumor that he had been captured by the Union. Therefore, she was looking for the Union Army so she could inquire as to whether they had him or not. When she finished speaking, Kady waited in silence, her body taut with tension.

Orville whistled lowly. "Whooee! You must really love that man. I don't think my wife would come lookin' for me if I were lost. Unless of course there was a reward for finding me!"

The men laughed at this. Kady joined them, agreeing that, yes, she did love her husband. When she mentioned his name, the men got excited. They had heard of him. He was known as the "swamp captain" among the infantry. Through the laughter, Kady could tell there was a good deal of respect for him. Henry and his men had delivered ammunition and other goods to their unit on more than one occasion. Once their initial excitement of meeting the swamp captain's wife had died down, they began to talk in earnest. None of them had known he was missing, much less where he might be. However, they were a wealth of information as to where they thought Kady should go the following day.

After much argument and drawing of rudimentary maps in the dirt, they decided Kady would have the most luck, and least danger, in trying to intercept Sheridan's troops. She had heard of the man before. He was a general, or possibly a major general, and would be as good as anybody to deliver her intelligence.

The men were still dubious as to the wisdom of her riding into any military camp, much less a Union camp. However, since she had fed them supper, they would help her as much as possible, fool's errand or not.

Once Kady was confident she understood where she was to go, the maps were rubbed out and the men set to telling stories and smoking. Kady listened for a while. When she realized that she was falling asleep sitting up, she excused herself and retired to her bedroll. Someone had been kind enough to lay it out for her. The ground was hard and the blanket threadbare, but to Kady it felt as if she were relaxing into her feather bed back at home. She sighed contentedly and fell directly to sleep.

The next morning she awoke to the smell of fresh corn dodgers and coffee on the fire. The men had wisely held back some of the provisions from the night before. The rest of the camp had been packed up, and she saw someone had re-saddled her horse. As they were obviously getting ready to leave, she rose quickly because she did not want to delay them. The breakfast was finished hurriedly, and once they ascertained that Kady knew the route, they helped her onto her horse. Kady thought she had been sore the night before. She was wrong. Now the pain was excruciating. The thought of riding for another day made her want to cry. She waved goodbye to the men, gritted her teeth, and headed down the road.

The farther she traveled, the more people she came across. Most were civilians heading to safer locales. Other than looking at her as if she were crazy for going toward the armies instead of away from them, these people did not pay her any mind. She also ran into a handful of

447

soldiers here and there. Each time she asked if they had seen her husband, and each time they answered no and kept moving. Kady began to suspect some of them were not even listening to the name she was saying. She was obviously not the first woman to ride out looking for a lost loved one. Even though Kady was not actually looking for Henry, it was disheartening every time she saw the look of disinterest on the soldiers' faces.

It occurred to her that if she did find Henry, she would likely abandon her mission. Not only to stay with him, but also because the thought of denying starving men their rations made her feel guilty. That is, after all, exactly what she would be doing if she found Sheridan—men like George and Orville would stay hungry. She did not like that thought. She rationalized that cutting the rebels off from their supplies would hasten the end of the war, and then they could all go home. However, the look of pure bliss when those men started eating the night before would not leave her mind.

Kady forced herself to remember why she was doing any of this in the first place. Yes, it had started out as a lark, but it was so much more than that now. Her mother had abhorred slavery and lost her life for this cause. For her mother, Kady had to continue to find and pass information to the North that would help end this war. That is why she was doing this—to end the bloodshed and the killing and the hurt. Only then could the country start to heal. She would complete her mission.

As it turned out, she did not have to make the choice. None of the Confederate soldiers she passed had any information about Henry for her. By late afternoon, the men she saw in the distance were better dressed, and she could smell food cooking. She had to be approaching a

Union camp.

To their credit, the men from the night before had told her true. She had found Major General Sheridan's camp, and to her amazement, it took little convincing to get an escort to his quarters. When she told the officer outside of Sheridan's tent that she had information from Little Rose, she was shocked to realize the man recognized the name. He scurried inside at once. A line of men immediately made their way out of the tent and Kady was escorted in.

The man sitting on the cot rose and asked if Kady had eaten. Before she could answer, he ordered food be brought in for her by the junior officer. Once the officer had left to fetch the food, Sheridan kissed Kady's hand warmly.

"Do I have the honor of speaking to Little Rose herself?"

"Yes, you do." Kady replied, bewildered. How did this man know her? She had barely heard of him!

"On behalf of Lieutenant General Grant, President Lincoln, and the rest of the United States, I would like to thank you for your service and offer condolences for your mother. From all I have heard, she was an exceptionally brave woman."

Kady's head started to spin. "How do you know about my mother?"

Seeing the confusion and shock on her face, Sheridan motioned for Kady to sit before he replied, "We've known for quite some time that a mother and daughter, under the monikers Northern and Little Rose, were working to move information out of Virginia. It was only recently we learned the full scope of it when we got a firsthand report from your husband."

449

Kady's mind jumped to Henry, and panic started to well in her chest, until she realized he had to be talking about Jacob.

"Lieutenant Hart gave us the full rundown of his operation and told us how helpful you and your mother have been to him," the general continued.

At these words, a spark of outrage replaced Kady's shock. "Helpful to him?"

"Yes, he said your assistance has been absolutely invaluable to his efforts."

"His efforts?" The spark was growing into a flame of outrage.

"From the sounds of it, it's quite big. I do not think any of us realized how vital Lieutenant Hart has been for the Union Army. He will probably receive a commendation. He has more than earned it."

"He hasn't earned anything." The bile rising in her throat caused her words to come out half under her breath. This caught Sheridan's attention.

"Pardon? What was that?"

Kady wanted to scream that Jacob was a louse, that her mother and Mary had been correct, he was a scoundrel. He had done next to nothing! His efforts? The effort belonged to her mother and then her. Jacob was a piece, a small piece, of the puzzle. Nothing more than a glorified messenger and he had taken credit for everything! Kady struggled to keep her emotions in check. She knew it would be pointless to try to contradict what this man thought he knew. After all, she was a woman and she had no proof. Why would anyone believe her? Kady took a deep breath, then looked into Sheridan's eyes.

"I said I have information for you." He looked puzzled, certain

450

that was not what she had said a moment earlier. She ignored his look and continued. "There is to be a train leaving Richmond toward Danville. It has 80,000 rations on it for Lee's troops. I don't know the exact departure date, in fact it may have already left. If you can stop that train from getting through, Lee's army will remain crippled with hunger."

Sheridan stood up straight and took a step back. "Are you sure? That's not what Lieutenant Hart said."

"Positive." There was an edge to her voice that Sheridan did not seem to notice. "I heard about the rations from General St. John's own lips in Richmond."

"Extraordinary. I have to get this news to General Grant. We need to mobilize." He started to leave, then turned back to Kady. "If you'll excuse me. Please stay and have some food. Take my tent for the night. Thank you. Thank you, Mrs. Hart."

With that, Sheridan disappeared into the approaching night, leaving Kady to speak to the silence.

"It's Henry. Mrs. Henry."

55
Square

Henry fought his way to wakefulness. His body was content to stay asleep, but his mind was a whir. Where was he? What had happened? Then he remembered a wagon, the one-legged man, and being shot. Instinctively he reached up to his shoulder where the bullet had hit him to confirm that his recollection was correct. He grunted with pain. Yes. He had been shot. He remembered that correctly. Where was he? Despite the pain, Henry attempted to sit up, but he was restrained and pushed back by a firm hand. This startled him, as he thought he was alone. Turning his head, he realized his eyes were a bit bleary and all he could see was a dark blur, now sitting on the edge of his bed. He reached up to scrub his eyes, ignoring the pain in his shoulder.

"You're awake for three seconds and already you movin' that arm all about. You 'bout to undo all the good healin' I've done."

Henry smiled. He would recognize that voice anywhere. "Sally." His voice cracked from disuse and he was immediately aware of the dry state of his mouth.

Sally grabbed a glass of water from the table and carefully held it while Henry drank.

"Of course it is. Who else got the patience to nurse you?" Her tone was annoyed, but the warmth behind it betrayed her relief.

Henry chuckled and fell into their old banter. "No one, Miss

Sally. Only you."

"That's right. Lucky for you they found me, and lucky for me that ball in your shoulder went almost all the way through. I's able to get it out easy."

"So you're an expert on gunshot wounds now, are you?"

"That's not the first one I seen this war; let's leave it at that." The humor fell away from her face. She tried to hide it, busying herself by putting the cup back on the table. "Let's get you sittin' up and see if you can hold down some broth."

With Sally's help, Henry got up to a sitting position with a minimum of pain. "How long have I been here?" he asked.

"A good while now." She brushed the hair out of his eyes and cupped his cheek in her hand. "We thought we was gonna lose you for a time there. I never seen someone with so little blood in their body. You was white as a ghost." She patted his cheek. "I'll get you some broth and send that fool man a yours in with it. He been under my feet since y'all got here. 'Bout ready to smack him on the nose and send him outside like the yappy little spaniel he is."

"Thank you, Sally."

Henry squeezed her hand, then watched her go. He rubbed his head in an attempt to clear his thoughts. He must be in one of the slave camps by Lake Drummond—either that, or he was having an incredibly vivid dream. He discounted his latter thought. Of course Sally and his father's other servants had fled into the swamp and made their way to the camps. Where else would they have gone? Moreover, they had not been far from the lake when he had been shot. Henry did not think the camp inhabitants would have ventured out to investigate a gunshot, so

Tom must have found him somehow. The thought of Tom made his mind jump to other people under his charge. Oh God, Kady! She must be worried sick. Even if she sought out information, no one knew where he was or what had become of him. They had been running several days behind. What a mess. Henry's head started to throb.

Tom entered balancing an overflowing bowl of broth. He let out a hiss of air every time some of the liquid sloshed over the side. Finally, he made it to the bedside and placed the bowl next to the bed.

"I think that woman is tryin' to get me to burn my hands off, fillin' that bowl so full." He wiped his brow in an exaggerated manner. "I'd let that cool a bit unless you want to add a burnt mouth to your list of wounds."

"It's good to see you, Tom."

"You too, Cap'n. Glad we didn't lose you." Tom looked down and shuffled his feet.

"Sally tells me you've been a nuisance."

Tom's head shot up. "A nuisance? When was I nuisance? When I was haulin' all of that water for her? Or gatherin' wood for her fire? Maybe it was when I caught those fish for her? I may have stuck close by out of concern for you, but I earned my keep!" Tom puffed himself up to his full height, indignant at the slight, which made Henry chuckle.

"I'm sure you did, Tom. Thank you."

"Thank you for what? You're my cap'n, I was just doin' my duty."

"No, thank you for getting me here. I know that couldn't have been easy."

Tom looked at him confused for a moment, then realized the

454

misunderstanding. "Oh, no. I didn't bring you here. Sally already had you all bandaged up by the time I got here."

"Then how did I—"

"It was them Negroes. Apparently, that blue belly didn't stick around long after he shot you. He left all of them whole as the day they were born. When they were sure they were safe, they come out from their hiding places to see if you were alive. One of the women wrapped up your shoulder real good and the men picked you up between them. Some of these here camp Negroes heard the shot and went to see what the hullabaloo was about. One of them recognized you, so they carried ya back here. They sent a group of boys to fetch me and the barge."

"The Negroes saved me?"

"Yeah, who else?"

"I had thought it was you."

"Nope. From where I was, I didn't hear a thing. By the time I would have come to investigate, you woulda been dead. You were almost dead as it was."

"Well then, I'll have to thank them."

"Oh, I already thanked 'em, but I can go get 'em for ya all the same. Well, one of them at least. The Negro from the camp that recognized you, he's an older feller. He's still around. The rest headed out around the lake to find their kinfolk."

Henry smiled at Tom. "Yes, please get him for me."

Tom beamed and stooped to pick up the now cooled broth. "Right away." He passed the broth to Henry. "You better drink that before old fussy britches comes in here and smacks me for keepin' food from her patient."

Tom left the tent and Henry sipped some of the broth. The wetness alone was heavenly for his parched mouth and throat, and the residual heat was calming. He sipped it slowly, feeling the warmth trickle through him. Despite how long he had slept, he was still tired. Even the bowl of broth felt heavy. He rested the bowl on his lap, leaned his head back, and closed his eyes. He had been in this position for a minute or two when he heard Tom reenter, and Henry reluctantly opened his eyes.

"Sorry, Cap'n, we didn't mean to disturb you. Go on back to sleep."

"No, it's all right. Come in, I'm awake."

Tom moved to the side and allowed the second man to enter. Henry recognized the defiant old man from the swamp immediately—the one who refused to be cowed even at the threat of being returned to slavery.

"It seems I owe you my thanks, and quite possibly my life as well," Henry acknowledged. "Thank you."

The man nodded before speaking. "No thank-you needed. I owed you my life, the life of my family. I saved your life, guided those with you. Now we are square."

Though the man said it as a statement, Henry could see the question in his eyes. Did Henry consider them square?

"Yes, we are square."

The man nodded again. "Good," he replied, then left.

Tom watched him go then turned back to Henry.

"That one ain't much of a talker is he?"

Henry chuckled. "No, apparently not." Henry looked down at the broth in his lap and swirled it. He could feel the tiredness creeping back over him, weighing down his eyelids. Seeing this, Tom took the bowl away.

"You get some more sleep."

"Yes, that is a good idea." Henry nestled back into his pillow, wincing when he put too much pressure on his shoulder. Right as Tom was leaving, Henry remembered something and called out, "Tom, find out from Sally when I'll be able to ride. We need to get back to Richmond."

"Yes, sir."

56
New Ventures

Jacob was bitter. First, the army confiscated all of the supplies he had worked so hard to steal, then by the time he finally made it to Richmond, the damn war was over. Of all the rotten luck! Not that it mattered. His plans to raid the commissary for whatever the rebels had left behind had proved fruitless. There had already been so much looting and destruction in the city that everything of value was long gone. Jacob also discovered that Kady was nowhere to be found. Seeing a candle lit in an upstairs window, he thought he was home free. When he knocked on the door, the dour-faced Negro that answered said no one was home. He doubted this and stood watch for two days. A candle appeared every night, yet he never saw her. What was it with that girl and candles?

Resigned, Jacob retired to the only place he felt at home—the nearest tavern. Settling in at a table in the corner, he nursed an ale and his bruised ego. The war was over and he had nothing to show for it. Nothing! Any real money he had made had been pissed away gambling or on whores. The golden goose he had landed was gone; and judging by the way she had run away from him to go to her precious Captain Henry, it was clear whom she preferred. Although with Henry dead now, he might have a shot. He had to find her first, though.

He swirled the ale in front of him, staring into the amber liquid for inspiration. All it did was make him hungry. With some effort, Jacob levered himself up from his chair and made his way to the bar. Instead of the buxom barmaid coming to greet him, her pock-faced father approached. Just his luck.

"Food. Whatever you've got."

The man stared at him blankly, then walked away without saying a word. Jacob hoped that meant he understood and was heartened when the man slipped into the back to the kitchen. Jacob did not return to his table right away. He stuck around to see if he could attract the attention of the girl. Instead, two men sitting next to him got *his* attention.

During the war, Jacob had perfected the art of eavesdropping on conversations and he put his skills to work. The men were drunk, which made things markedly easier. Apparently, they had procured a rather large stock of whiskey and were planning to drive south selling it at exorbitant prices to the grieving and disheartened rebels. Jacob knew he liked these fellows. He could think of one major flaw in their plan, though: Jacob didn't have a role in it. Their glasses were almost empty, so Jacob called over the barmaid.

"A round for me and my friends if you will be so kind," he instructed.

At first, the two men looked at him suspiciously. But when they got their ale and saw Jacob pay for it, they decided he was indeed one of their friends.

Jacob smiled at them and prepared for his first assault.

"I apologize for interrupting you gentleman. I couldn't help but overhear you are planning on heading south."

The larger of the two men answered, "Why, yes, we are. Tomorrow mornin', in fact."

"Well, good luck to you." He raised a mock toast to them and drank, slightly shaking his head and waiting for them to take the bait.

"Now what do you mean by that?" The man was on the verge of being cross.

"What I said? No offense intended. It's only, you are going to need some luck if you plan to haul merchandise right now without an armed escort."

The smaller man spoke up. "An armed escort? Why would we need that? The war's over or haven't you heard? Lee surrendered."

"Not quite over. Lee may have surrendered, but that does not mean that everybody has given up fighting. You are gonna run into places with no authorities to keep the unscrupulous types at bay. Things are all in upheaval. So good luck to ya."

The small man's eyes narrowed and the two men fell into a hushed conversation. Jacob smiled inside. He had them. Now he just had to act like he didn't have a care in the world while they riled themselves up. Jacob finished his ale and ordered another one. He had just taken his first sip when the large man broke the silence. "I suppose you know where we can get one of these armed escorts?"

Jacob pretended like he hadn't heard. "Pardon?"

The large man moved closer to Jacob and repeated himself. "Do you know where we can get one of these armed escorts?"

"Oh no, I was only making a suggestion. I mean, I used to do it during the war, but as you pointed out, the war is over."

The small man practically leapt out of his seat. "Not quite over, you said so yourself! So you can do it for us!"

"Now, now, I wasn't trying to involve myself in you gentlemen's business; I was simply makin' conversation."

"That may be so, but Junior's right," the large man said. "We need an escort, and if you can do it, well then, we need to hire you. I mean you can do it, can't you? You being a cripple and all."

Jacob laughed good naturedly and patted his leg, "This actually makes my job easier. They don't expect a man with one leg to be able to take care of himself, so I can pull the wool over their eyes before they can say, 'Whoooee.'"

Both of the men smiled hugely and conferred quickly with each other. The big man, whom Jacob guessed to be the father of the pair, turned back to Jacob and spoke. "We would like to hire you on, mister. Now we can't pay you up front, but we will give you a fair share of our profits."

"Oh, I would never expect any payment up front. Payment comes after, for a job well done."

Both men beamed and Jacob saw the pock-faced man coming out from the back with a plate of food.

"Gentlemen, are you hungry? Sir, two more plates, please!"

The pock-faced man gave an incredulous look, set the plate on the bar, and returned to the back.

"Why don't we move on back to my table where we can eat and talk over this grand venture that we are about to embark upon? Junior, why don't you take this first plate?"

The smaller man, who had been eyeing the food hungrily, did not have to be told twice. He grabbed the plate and headed back to the table Jacob had indicated.

Jacob slapped the larger man on the back.

"After you, sir."

It took two more plates of food and many more rounds of ale before he had all the details of the plan. They had hidden their wagon for safekeeping. For good measure, they had propped a broken wheel up against the front. From a distance, it looked broken down.

Unbeknownst to the men, Jacob had stopped drinking long before they staggered off to their beds. Therefore, instead of falling face first into his pillow like the other two men, Jacob made his way to the outskirts of town. The wagon was exactly where they said it would be, with the horse still hitched. Jacob patted the horse's rump consolingly. Those two galoots were gettin' what they deserved. Leaving a horse hitched to the wagon all night was just plain cruel. Good thing he had come along.

With some effort, Jacob hauled himself up into the driver's seat. He looked into the back at the gorgeous barrels of whiskey like they were better than pure gold. Turning back to the front, he clucked softly to the horse. The horse moved slowly at first, then once up on the road, it fell into a gentle trot. They had been planning to head south, so Jacob would go north. He smiled; maybe post war would not be so bad after all.

57
Home

Rebecca sat down on her porch and took a deep breath of the crisp spring air. She still could not believe this was her home now. Without ever leaving Richmond, Kady had been able to set Rebecca up in a cottage to call her own. The girl was a marvel and Rebecca still said a little prayer for her every time Kady entered her thoughts. Rebecca had received letters and a hearty welcome from several members connected to Kady's spy ring, but she had not heard from Kady herself until last week. The message had been short and vague. Even so, seeing her precise penmanship again had warmed Rebecca's heart. All she knew for certain was to expect two guests in the next week or two whom Kady had implored that Rebecca welcome warmly. This could have gone unsaid. Rebecca knew she would cherish anyone Kady sent her way.

Thus, the waiting game had begun. Unlike with the candles, this waiting made her impatient. She would try to sit and write to distract her mind. An hour later, she would still be staring at a blank piece of paper. She had cleaned the cottage from top to bottom. Twice. She had set up and rearranged the second bedroom so many times she had lost count. She knew there were to be two guests; however, she did not know whether to expect two women, a man and a woman, or two men. This last possibility made her blush and she discounted it immediately. Kady would never ask her to play host to two men. On the other hand, a married couple was another matter, and could be possible. Eventually,

Rebecca decided to expect two women, because that option caused her the least amount of stress. If she was wrong, she would deal with it when her guests arrived.

The only thing that seemed to make time move again was when Rebecca sat down to write to Lieutenant Johnson. Shortly after she had arrived in New York she wrote him but couldn't work up the courage to actually send the letter. It made her feel like she still had a connection with him simply by writing his name. Shortly before Kady's letter arrived, she had worked up the courage to actually post one of the letters. She had rewritten the letter numerous times until she could think of no other way to make it better. She had little hope it would reach him and, even if it did, less hope that he would reply. Therefore, when she answered a knock on her door to discover a courier with a weathered letter from the lieutenant, Rebecca was speechless. His handwriting was clumsy and his spelling atrocious, but his charm came through in every word. His letter became her most prized possession, except for her pewter mouse, of course. She would always hold that closest to her heart.

After hearing of Lee's surrender, she feared that her lieutenant would no longer be at the prison. Surely now that the war was over, they would release the prisoners of war. If there were no prisoners, then there would be no need for guards and Lieutenant Johnson might have been reassigned. If he had, Rebecca had no idea where to send her reply. She sent it to the prison despite her doubts, this time with a great hope that her message would find its way to him eventually. She rocked in her rocking chair and sent up yet another prayer that all would be well.

It occurred to Rebecca that she needed to check on her stew. If her guests were to arrive today, it would not do to serve them burnt supper. Even so, she could not muster up the energy to leave her peaceful porch. She also had fresh biscuits and butter, which would make up for a little burnt stew. She smiled, imagining her sister's reaction to such nonchalance, such impropriety. It gave her a girlish delight to be so openly flouting what her sister stood for. It also reminded her of her loss. She missed Rachel. For all of her faults and harsh words, Rachel would always be her sister. Rebecca forced herself to stop reminiscing before her mind moved on to her brother-in-law and her nieces and nephews. She knew if she thought about them she would find herself in tears, and that certainly would not do. She might be content to serve guests burnt stew, but she would do it dry-eyed. At least Rachel would approve of that.

Then Rebecca saw someone coming down the path. She froze. This had to be them, as there were clearly two people. Excited, Rebecca hurried inside to warm the biscuits and put some water on to boil. If they had been traveling all day, they would need something hot to drink. For good measure, she stirred the stew and then checked the bedroom one final time.

By the time Rebecca had finished fluffing the pillows again, she heard a quiet knock on the door. Taking a deep breath, she forced herself to walk at a calm pace instead of rush like an excited child. When she opened the door, she saw a woman and a young girl, both with dusky complexions. Rebecca realized that this whole time she had assumed Kady was sending white people, so it took her a minute to adjust her expectations. The woman on the porch spoke first.

"Are you Miss Rebecca? We are lookin' for a Miss Rebecca."

465

"I am. Were you sent by Kady?"

The woman's face noticeably relaxed. "Yes, we were. I was afraid you wouldn't get her message before we got here."

"Oh, I definitely got it. I have been waitin' for you. Please, come inside. Did you have any trouble findin' your way?"

The woman and her daughter stayed fixed outside. "We only have a little bit of money. Hardly anythin' left from what Miss Kady gave us. It is yours and we will work. We won't be no burden, but we won't be no slaves neither."

Rebecca saw the fear and strength in the woman's eyes for the first time, and before she could stop herself, Rebecca flung her arms around the woman and hugged her. The woman stood stiff under her arms, not sure what to do. Rebecca let her go and awkwardly looked at the floor.

"I'm sorry. I just realized you must be Mary. Kady spoke of you with such love and kindness. You are Mary, right? You were Kady's mother's servant?"

"Yes. I took care of Miss Anna since the day she arrived in Virginia." A slight catch to her voice belied her underlying emotions.

Resisting the urge to hug her again, Rebecca held out her gnarled hand to shake. "It's a pleasure to meet you, Mary. As you can see," Rebecca nodded at her hand, "I could definitely use some help in keepin' up our new home."

Mary gently took her hand and from the added glisten in her eyes, Rebecca was confident she had understood Rebecca's use of the word "our." Rebecca could feel her own eyes starting to tear up so she turned her attention to the girl.

"What is your name?"

The girl looked at her mother, and when Mary nodded yes, she answered, "Margaret. Everyone calls me Maggie."

"It's nice to meet you, Maggie. Come in, both of you! I have fresh biscuits and stew and that water should be hot by now." Rebecca took a step back and motioned toward the second bedroom. "Your bedroom is right over there."

Maggie looked up at the two women. "We get an entire room *in* the house?"

Rebecca laughed. "Yes, from now on you always get a room in the house. Go put your things in there while your mother and I get some tea started."

Despite having walked for most of the day, Maggie ran as fast as she could into the bedroom, carrying their meager possessions. Mary followed her in more slowly and stood almost in shock as Rebecca closed the front door and made her way over to the fire. She started tea brewing and put a plate of biscuits on the table before she noticed Mary still standing by the door. She crossed to Mary and reached out gently to touch her arm.

"It's all right. You've made it. You are safe." Then as an afterthought she added, "You're free."

At Rebecca's final words, Mary's resolve broke and she started crying. Rebecca folded her in her arms once more, and this time Mary hugged her back.

"Welcome home."

58
Demons to Be Faced

A shiver ran up Henry's spine that had nothing to do with the brisk night air. His shoulder ached, and he should have rested his horse hours ago, yet he could not bring himself to stop.

The war was over.

He sent Tom and any interested Negroes back to his father's plantation to set things right. He was on his way home to Kady. The prospect both thrilled and terrified him. Death he could face; he held no fear of death anymore. It was living that scared him—living with the things he had done and with the man he had become. Not just the things he had done as a soldier, the things he had done to Kady. Her mother was dead, and it was because of him. He knew the damage he had caused was irreparable, a stretch of barren wasteland that could neither be crossed nor eliminated. Kady was the one person in the world he truly cared for, and the one person in the world he had truly failed.

Henry decided he had two choices: he could be a tyrant and demand respect from his wife and those in his employ, even though his actions had far from earned it. Kady would bear him a son and he would teach that son how to be a man. He would beat the lessons into him if need be. He would be despised by all those around him, yet so feared no one would dare to openly defy him. In short, he could be his father. Or, he could start over and earn their respect. He was not exactly sure what that course looked like, having never seen an adequate example. He imagined it ought to start with him begging Kady's forgiveness on bended knee. He would have thought the idea of begging anybody for anything, much less his wife, would sicken him. Yet he found the thought oddly comforting, a penance and reprisal for his crimes. In fact, the more he thought about it the better he felt, and he urged his horse onward despite the hour.

Perhaps that forgiveness could begin tonight. Secretly, Henry harbored a hope that arriving exhausted and wounded in the middle of the night might catch Kady off guard and allow him a few precious seconds of the carefree girl before the hardened resentment properly awoke. Perhaps her concern over his injury, and relief that he was alive would provide him with a few moments more. And perhaps in those moments, if he fell to his knees and begged, she would grant him clemency, even if only for the night. The odds were not in his favor, but he had hope.

The widespread destruction throughout Richmond dashed some of his hope. and Henry felt anxiety rising in his chest as he traveled through the city. If something had happened to Kady, he didn't know what he would do with himself. He needed *her* almost as much as he needed her forgiveness. However, as he rounded the corner and saw his house at the end of the lane, his heart skipped a beat. Not only was it unmolested, a solitary candle burned as if a beacon through the night from their bedroom window. He had not thought anybody would be expecting him. After all, not even his commanders had heard from him in over a month. Nevertheless, Kady must have guessed, with the war over, he would be returning soon because there before his eyes was a candle burning to light his way home. He spurred his horse into a gallop for the last hundred yards of their journey. Maybe he had underestimated Kady's love for him. Maybe she was hoping to start anew like him. The distance between his arms and her warm, soft body was not closing fast enough, yet his horse could go no faster.

Finally, painfully, he reached the house. The clopping of his horse's hooves on the cobblestones had broken through the night with enough urgency to pull a servant from his bed to investigate. He arrived in time to catch the reins that Henry threw toward him before racing into the house. Not caring about propriety, Henry threw the front door open, bounded to the stairs, and took them two at a time. His exhaustion all but forgotten, he rushed down the long hallway to their bedroom. All around him, he could hear the scurrying of servants leaving their beds to see who would so boldly dare to storm into the house at such a late hour. He knew he should announce himself, or wait for someone to see him so he could allay their fears. However, their discomfiture was far from the forefront of his thoughts.

Without altering his stride, Henry reached the double doors of their bedroom, threw them open, and braced himself for the affection that was surely forthcoming. It took him a moment to realize that nothing had happened, nor was anything going to happen. He was standing inside the doorway of a cold, empty room. Henry scanned the room to be sure, and each time his eyes found their final resting spot on the bed, pristine, without a pillow out of place. Tearing his eyes away, he found himself drawn to the window where the candle burned its false hope, and there, sitting right to the side of it, was a letter.

Mechanically, Henry made his way over picked up the letter, and sat stiffly in a hard-wooden chair. He opened the envelope, taking care not to rip it, and pulled out the folded letter. A bitter taste of dread filled his mouth as he set the envelope down and unfolded the paper. It was in Kady's elegant script.

April 10, 1865

Dearest Thomas,

As you have surely ascertained, I have left. I gave instructions that a candle was to burn through the nights until you returned because no man should come home to a dark house. I pray my instructions were followed. I am certain some would think this to be sentimental and foolish, as I do not know when you will be returning, or if you are even still alive. However, I cannot bring myself to believe this war has taken you. It has taken so much, but I cannot believe it has taken you.

Though I know what I am about to say will hurt you, I feel it must be said. You are a good man, and you deserve to know the truth. When you accused me of being a Union spy, you were correct. Both my mother and I stole secrets from the South and gave them to the North. Your missions failed because I told the Union when and where they would be occurring.

471

Your men died because I relayed information about your plan with the gold. Their deaths pain me more than I can put into words. Please know I never intended for anyone to lose their lives; that plan was changed without my knowledge. That doesn't make it any less excusable. I could never ask you to forgive my betrayal, which is why I have left.

If it is any consolation, I do regret the pain I have caused you. Despite the circumstances, I did grow to love you dearly. In any other time, in any other place, I do believe we could have been very happy together. However, we live in this time, in this place, and we must face the demons of our realities. You have played the villain, and played your part well. However, I do not believe you are a villain; you have too good a heart. No, I see you as a hero, a reluctant hero perhaps, but a hero nevertheless. My dearest wish is that you are able to choose a new path in this new time, where you can play the part that was meant for you.

Love,
Kady

With the weight of a nation's bloody war wearing hard on his bones, Henry let his arm fall limply as the letter slipped from his grasp to the floor. With heavy, lidded eyes he looked up at the candle in the window, then out beyond into the darkness. He was at once blinded because he could now see. Henry licked his fingers and snuffed out the light.

59

Epilogue

Kady gathered her skirts in her hand and stepped down out of the coach. She did not know what city she was in; she had not been paying attention. All she knew was she wanted a room somewhere for the night before continuing her journey the next day. Her driver approached, dragging her trunk behind him, and informed her, "We can keep the horses at this stable, but the inn's full up. There's another down yonder. I s'pose you'll be wantin' to check there."

Kady's face fell. "Yes, let's check there."

She had not considered the possibility that she would not be able to find a room. She would deal with that eventuality if it came to that. She led the way down the sidewalk with the man noisily dragging her trunk behind her. She entered the new establishment to discover a kind-looking older gentleman sitting behind the desk. Upon seeing her, he stood up.

"Well, good evenin', ma'am. To what do I owe this pleasure?"

Kady smiled at the man. "I am hoping you have a room available for the night."

As Kady finished speaking, the driver burst into the room, practically falling over the threshold. Once inside, he made a production of straightening the trunk, plopping himself down on top of it, and pulling out a handkerchief to wipe his brow. Both Kady and the innkeeper watched him with amusement through to the end of his act and then turned their attention back to the matter at hand.

"Well, I don't have nothin' near fittin' enough for a lady like you," the innkeeper said apologetically.

"Nothing fancy is needed. All I require is a bed and a basin with some water to wash my face. Nothing more."

"Well, in that case, I have a little closet of a room upstairs on the third floor. It's not much to look at, but it's warm and clean."

At the mention of the third floor, the driver groaned.

"It sounds perfect," Kady replied and glanced over a the driver. She turned back to the innkeeper. "However, do you have somewhere nearby where I may store my trunk for the night? I don't see the need in carrying that heavy thing farther than necessary."

"Of course, of course." The innkeeper gestured to the driver, "You can put that back in the office."

The man got up and, giving Kady and the innkeeper an appreciative nod, dragged the trunk back into the office.

"Well, all right, then. Follow me and I will show you to your room. You kin settle up when you leave."

"Thank you." With a sigh of relief, Kady followed the man up the stairs.

"What's the name, so's I can put you in the book?"

Kady paused, made her decision, then spoke. "Kady Henry."

"Well, Mrs. Henry…."

Kady interrupted him. "Miss."

The innkeeper stopped, startled.

"It's Miss Henry. My husband was lost in the war."

"Well, I am sorry to hear that, Miss Henry."

Kady nodded a thank-you and the man continued up the stairs in silence. She did not know why she had corrected him. If she was planning to keep the name Henry, then technically the innkeeper had been correct. If she wanted to return to "Miss," then she should revert to her maiden name. Yet that thought put a sour taste in her mouth. No, she would never return to the name Bell. Perhaps she was harboring a hope that Henry would be able to forgive her, and by keeping his name she would make it easier for him to find her. However, she knew that, realistically, she needed to acclimate herself to the thought that she was as good as a widow now. That must be it. Regardless, the whole thing was silly. She was never going to see this innkeeper again, so what did it matter? They reached the third floor and the innkeeper opened the door to the room, gesturing for her to enter.

"Thank you for the room. I will be leaving first thing in the morning."

He nodded, but stood awkwardly staring at his feet as if trying to come up with something comforting to say. "I suppose the South will get their revenge sometime. For all them that died, you know?"

Kady looked at him kindly and before closing her door said to him softly, "Only survivors seek revenge. Those about to be lost to the void fear only for the love they will never feel again. We would do well to remember that."

Cipher Keys by Date

September 8, 1863	536241	641253
November 1, 1863	356241	165234
April 28 – May 22, 1864	245361	435126
*June 8, 1864	124653	265413
June 28 – July 25, 1864	235146	546213
September 26 – October 16, 1864	642531	413526
October 28 – December 12, 1864	253416	524361
January 12 – February 4, 1865	315426	153264
March 29, 1865	462531	153624

*King Arthur's Polybius Square

Polybius Square used by Anna and Kady's spy ring

R	N	B	H	T	X
V	1	U	8	4	W
E	M	3	J	5	G
L	A	9	0	I	D
K	7	2	Z	6	S
P	O	Y	C	F	Q

Polybius Square used by King Arthur's northern spy ring

	1	7	D	4	K	W	I
	2	Y	0	V	P	2	S
	4	R	J	E	9	Z	C
	6	3	N	A	H	T	5
	5	G	X	1	M	B	6
	3	O	8	Q	U	F	L
		2	6	5	4	1	3

Acknowledgements

Looking back over the journey this book has taken, I am truly humbled by the sheer number of people who were willing to take time out of their day to read my work and give me feedback. A thank-you buried at the back of the book seems paltry recompense for the wealth of insight you all have provided. Please know how grateful I am for all of you, and know that there is a piece of each of you in this book.

Adina, I have no words. What would I have done without you? Your willingness to read draft after draft, and your courage to straight up point out the things that didn't work were invaluable. Emma is the character she is today because of you. Thank you.

To my book club ladies – Christa, Emily, Karah, Lisa and Stacey – you made receiving criticism fun. If I ever figure out how you did that, I'm going to write a book and make millions. There will of course be a pantry, and Jethro will narrate. I love you all, thank you!

Thank you to my readers who tackled the entire manuscript and shared your thoughts - Aila, Ben, Brad, Janet, Jodie, Lauren, Mary Kay, Melanie, Melissa, Rich, Sara and Tara. Some of you had a few notes, and some of you had many more than a few. I'm sure I owe some of you new red pens. Regardless of quantity, each of you provided at least one 'Aha!' moment that helped me fix something. Thank you!

Then there are those that jumped in to read bits and pieces as I struggled with sections. I can't imagine it was easy listening to me roughly describe what was going on, then ask for an opinion on a paragraph, a page or a chapter. Annie, Dina, Earl, Jayme, Jen, Jolene, LeVanna and Patrick, you all jumped in with gusto and helped out where and how you could. Thank you so much for that! And a special shout out to Jen for double checking all of my ciphers.

Last, but certainly not least, a huge thank you to my editors - Susan, Deb and Sonja! I gave you so much to wade through, and your thoroughness and discernment was so much appreciated. And I apologize for the grammatical errors in this. I proofed it by myself so it would be a surprise.

All my love,
Kat

CPSIA information can be obtained
at www.ICGtesting.com
Printed in the USA
LVHW040824010419
612519LV00007B/53